The School Inspector Calls!

A Little Village School Novel

GERVASE PHINN

The School Inspector Calls!

HODDER

First published in Great Britain in 2013 by Hodder & Stoughton
An Hachette UK company

First published in paperback in 2014

2

A CIP catalogue record for this title is available from the British Library

ISBN 978 1 444 70607 9

Printed and bound by Clays Ltd, St Ives plc

Hodder & Stoughton policy is to use papers that are natural, renewable
and recyclable products and made from wood grown in sustainable forests.
The logging and manufacturing processes are expected to conform to the
environmental regulations of the country of origin.

Hodder & Stoughton Ltd
338 Euston Road
London NW1 3BH

www.hodder.co.uk

For my daughter,
Elizabeth Anne Mary Phinn

Gervase Phinn is a teacher, freelance lecturer, author, poet, educational consultant and visiting professor of education. For fourteen years he taught in a range of schools, then acted as General Adviser for Language Development in Rotherham before moving on to North Yorkshire, where he spent ten years as a school inspector - time that has provided much source material for his books.

Gervase is a Doctor of Letters of the University of Leicester and the University of Hull and Doctor of the University of Sheffield Hallam. He is also a Fellow of the Royal Society of Arts and a Fellow of York St John's University and Leeds Trinity University.

He lives with his family near Doncaster.

www.gervase-phinn.com.

I

Elisabeth Devine, head teacher of Barton-in-the Dale village school, stared down at the letters on her desk and sighed. She had expected the first piece of correspondence from the Education Office but now, as she read the contents, she felt her chest tighten with apprehension. She looked out of the classroom window at the vast panorama of fields criss-crossed by silvered limestone walls which swept upwards to a belt of dark green woodland, the distant purple peaks and an empty azure sky. She dropped her eyes, read again the contents of the letter and sighed.

She had been invited to a meeting with Ms Tricklebank, the Director of Education, to discuss the forthcoming amalgamation of Barton-in-the-Dale village school with the neighbouring primary school at Urebank. The Education Committee, in an effort to save money, had decided to close some small schools in the county and amalgamate less successful ones and those which were losing pupils. The number of children at Urebank had decreased and it had been decided that the school would become part of a consortium with Barton-in-the-Dale.

The 'one-to-one consultation', the letter informed Elisabeth, would be for Ms Tricklebank to outline plans for the amalgamation which would take place the following term and it would give Elisabeth the opportunity of 'talking things through' with the Director. Then a series of meetings involving the staff of the two schools which would soon be combined would be arranged. Elisabeth welcomed the opportunity of meeting the Director to discuss the arrangements but did not look forward to the meetings with Mr Richardson, the head-master (as he liked to style himself) at Urebank, and his staff which would follow. She knew, however, that as the newly appointed head teacher of the integrated schools, this was one very large nettle she would have to grasp – and pretty firmly too.

Elisabeth's appointment had not been without its difficul-ties. She had been in competition for the post of head teacher with Robin Richardson, a self-important and condescending man who had been offered the post as her deputy, which he had grudgingly accepted. It would be a real challenge, thought Elisabeth, to get the teachers of both schools to work as a team and an even greater challenge to get the man who had been in competition for the head teacher's post, and who felt angry and embittered, to accept the situation and work *with* her rather than against her.

The second letter did nothing to lighten her mood. It was from Mr Steel, Her Majesty's Inspector of Schools, informing her of an intended visit some time later that term. He said he would inform her of the date in due course.

A head appeared around the classroom door, a face as large and round as a full moon.

'Is it all right if I come in, miss?' asked the pupil cheerfully. She was a plump girl with bright ginger hair tied in bunches at the sides by two large bows. Smiling widely, she displayed an impressive set of shiny silver braces clamped on her teeth.

'Yes, of course, Chardonnay,' said Elisabeth, her face brightening at seeing one of her most good-humoured and enthusiastic pupils. 'My goodness, you're here bright and early at the start of term.'

'To tell the truth I'm right glad to get back to school, miss,' replied the girl. She scowled and wrinkled her nose as if an unpleasant smell had wafted her way. 'I just had to get out of the house. There's been nothing but moaning and groaning and shouting and squabbling all the holidays. My dad's as grumpy as a bear with a sore bum. He's been in a right rotten mood since his van got nicked with all his tools in. And my gran's been as bad, complaining after being taken to hospital when she fell over line dancing and broke her ankle. My dad said it was her own fault because she'd had too many lager and limes. My mam said they were both doing her head in and she had enough trouble of her own, having had a right old ding-dong with the manager at work. Now that our Bianca with the baby has gone to live in Clayton with her boyfriend I've had no one to speak to.'

Elisabeth shook her head and laughed. 'Quite a time, by all accounts,' she said.

'Did you have a nice Easter, miss?' asked the girl.

'I did, thank you, but like you I'm glad to get back to school. There are a lot of things to do this term.'

The girl grinned. 'You're getting married soon, aren't you, miss?' she announced.

Elisabeth smiled. 'I am, yes.'

'He's dead nice is Dr Stirling, isn't he, miss?'

'I think so.'

'It's right romantic,' said the girl, sighing heavily. 'Just like in the book what I'm reading. It's called *Sweet Dreams Are Made of This* and there's this right dishy doctor and—'

Elisabeth changed the subject. 'How are your sister and baby by the way?'

Chardonnay's sister Bianca had given birth unexpectedly on Christmas Day. The girl, sixteen and barely out of school and fearful of how her parents would react, had managed to keep her condition a secret. She had taken to wearing a large shapeless coat, baggy jumpers and smocks and putting off the inevitable. Little Brandon had arrived, kicking and screaming lustily, delivered on the floor of the living room by Mrs Lloyd, a retired midwife who had been dragged from her festive dinner. Bianca, pleased at leaving home and all the recriminations and complaints, now lived with Clarence, her partner, and their child in a council flat in Clayton.

'They're doing right well, miss,' the girl told her. 'Bianca's still got her part-time job at the Rumbling Tum café in the village and her boyfriend is working at the bread factory in Clayton. He's on the Farmhouse Crusties at the moment but he hopes to be promoted to the slicers next month.'

'I'm really pleased to hear that things have worked out for them,' said Elisabeth. 'I guess Clarence's Uncle Fred is missing him on the farm?'

'He is, miss. He wants him to go back but our Bianca won't have it. She said Clarence was taken advantage of and his uncle's a mean-minded old bugg . . . so-and-so.'

Of course Bianca was quite right. Mr Massey, Clarence's uncle, was a tight-fisted, grasping and curmudgeonly old man and not well liked in the village.

'Well, I'd better put the kettle on in the staff-room miss,' said the girl. 'The teachers will want a cup of tea when they arrive.'

Chardonnay and her friend Chantelle had volunteered to be tea monitors the previous term, and they took the job seriously. They were charged with washing the cups and saucers in the staff-room, emptying the teapot and putting on the kettle for the teachers' morning and afternoon tea. The health and safety regulations precluded them from actually brewing the tea, something which the girls thought to be 'just plain daft', accustomed as they were to doing it all the time at home.

'By the way, miss,' said the girl, 'we need a new rubber what-do-you-call-it on the teapot.'

Elisabeth looked at her quizzically.

'You know, miss, that rubber nozzle thing what goes on the

end of the spout to stop the tea from dribbling. I was empty-ing the tea-leaves down the lavvy this morning and it come off and got flushed away.'

'We'll get another,' Elisabeth told her. 'I don't think, however, that it's a very good idea to get rid of the tea-leaves down the lavatory bowl. You remember what trouble we had last term when the toilets got blocked.'

'We've always done it, miss,' replied the girl. 'Anyway, I couldn't get it out before it got flushed away.'

'I see.'

'I've always managed to get it out in the past,' the girl told Elisabeth casually, 'and put it back on the spout, but this time I wasn't able to fish it out.'

Elisabeth stiffened and her mouth curled with revulsion. Perhaps, she thought to herself, the teachers should make their own tea in future.

Mrs Scrimshaw, the school secretary, sat behind the desk in her office, her unfashionable horn-rimmed spectacles dangling on a cord around her neck. She stared wide-eyed and anxious at the screen and keyboard before her.

During the Easter holidays, when she had called into school to deal with the mail, she had discovered to her consternation two large cardboard boxes in her office. She knew what they contained, for the head teacher had forewarned her. The new computer and printer had arrived. Reluctantly she had unpacked the contents and gazed in bewilderment at the assortment of wires, plugs and discs.

The caretaker had arrived at the office to see what she was up to. Mr Gribbon was a tall, gaunt man with a hard beak of a nose and the glassy protuberant eyes of a large fish. He spent a great deal of his time regaling anyone willing to listen about the excessive amount of work he was expected to do and how he was a martyr to his bad back.

'Computer, eh,' he remarked, jangling his keys. He perched on the corner of the desk.

'Yes,' replied the secretary irritably, 'a computer.'

'I didn't know you were *au fait* with computers, Mrs Scrimshaw,' he remarked.

'I'm not!' she snapped.

'Well, what are you doing with a computer then?' asked the caretaker.

'Mrs Devine's got it into her head that I should use it instead of my electric typewriter.' She picked up a long black wire and held it as she might a venomous snake, her face screwed up in distaste. 'I've no idea where this goes,' she said.

'Well, there'll be a socket for it somewhere,' said the caretaker.

'Mr Gribbon,' retorted the school secretary, scowling, 'I am not entirely unaware of the strikingly obvious. Of course there'll be a socket. The machine is full of sockets and there are all these wires and plugs. I shall never get the hang of it. I'm supposed to be going on a course at the Teachers' Centre when school starts next week, to learn how to use it, and I'm dreading it. I'll feel such a fool with all those clever people who will know what to do. I don't know why I can't just use my typewriter.'

'We have to move with the times, Mrs Scrimshaw,' the care-taker told her unhelpfully.

'Is that so? And since when have you moved with the times?' she asked crossly, thrusting the tangle of wires back in the box. 'You're still using that old sweeping brush and you've been wearing that threadbare overall for as long as I can recall. You're not exactly *au fait*, as you put it, with things modern.'

The caretaker made to speak but Mrs Scrimshaw hadn't finished.

'And as for moving with the times, in my view if the wheel isn't broken, it doesn't need fixing. I was perfectly happy with my typewriter and I have had no complaints.'

'The thing is, Mrs Scrimshaw,' said the caretaker, who should have had the common sense to let things lie, 'everybody's into word-processing these days. I mean, from what Mrs Pugh was telling me, the secretary down at Urebank School is very clued-up on the computer.' Mrs Pugh was the part-time cleaner who spent two days at Barton-in-the-Dale and the remainder of the week at the neighbouring school of Urebank. 'Mrs Pugh,' continued Mr Gribbon, jangling his keys, 'says the secretary down there rattles the letters off in no time.'

'Does she really. Well, bully for her,' said the secretary.

'Mrs Pugh was telling me that the secretary down at Urebank—'

'Mr Gribbon!' interrupted Mrs Scrimshaw. 'I am not interested in what Mrs Pugh has to say, or anyone else for that matter. Now, did you want something?'

'I just popped in to say hello and to see if you wanted anything.'

'What I want is for this wretched machine to work,' she replied. 'You can make yourself useful and see if you can find out where all these wires go.'

'Oh no!' snorted the caretaker, sliding off the desk. 'Not my province. Anyway, I've got things to do. My floors need buffing.'

'Then I suggest you get on with buffing them,' she told him tersely.

The caretaker departed, leaving the school secretary staring in dismay at the computer.

The following Monday morning, on the first day of the summer term, Mrs Scrimshaw sat staring at the machine on her desk. She had tried to get the computer to work but to no avail, and wondered just how she was going to cope.

A small boy entered the office. He was a rosy-cheeked child of about eight or nine, with bright brown eyes and hair cut in the short-back-and-sides style and with a neat parting. He could have been a schoolboy of the 1950s, dressed as he was in short grey trousers, a crisp white shirt and striped tie, a hand-knitted grey pullover, long grey stockings and sensible shoes.

'Hello, Mrs Scrimshaw,' he said cheerfully.

'Oh, hello, Oscar,' she replied glumly. 'You're here nice and early.'

'I was keen to get back to school,' he told her brightly. 'To be honest I've been pretty bored over the holidays. At a loose end, as my mother would say. I think she's quite glad that I'm back at school.'

Yes, I can well believe that, thought the school secretary. The boy could be annoying at times.

Oscar's eyes lit up when he caught sight of the machine. 'Wow!' he cried. 'A computer.'

'Yes,' she replied, weariness in her voice.

'It's a really top-notch one,' said the boy excitedly as he ran his fingers across the machine.

'Really?' the school secretary said, with little enthusiasm.

'I have a computer,' Oscar continued. 'I got it last Christmas, but it's not as hi-tech as yours. Pretty basic actually. I'm hoping my parents will upgrade it for my next birthday.'

Mrs Scrimshaw lifted her head sharply, like a dog picking up a scent.

'You know how this thing works then, do you, Oscar?' she asked.

'Oh yes.'

'And you know where all these wires go?'

'Actually they are called leads,' the boy told her, 'and each fits into a socket. All the sockets are different so it's impossible to put a lead in the wrong one. It's quite simple really. Would you like me to show you?'

'Thank you, Oscar,' said Mrs Scrimshaw. 'I would.'

She watched fascinated as the boy plugged in one lead after another and brought the computer to life.

'It's easy when you know how,' he explained, his small fingers tapping away on the keys. 'Shall I show you how to get on to the word-processor so you can write your letters?'

'If you could,' said the secretary, leaning over him.

When Mrs Devine put her head around the office door a moment later, she found the school secretary and Oscar scrutinising the text on the screen in earnest discussion.

'Hello, Mrs Devine,' said the boy. 'Mrs Scrimshaw is just showing me how her new computer works.'

At the staff meeting that morning before the start of school, Elisabeth welcomed her colleagues back and mentioned the proposed visit of the HMI and the forthcoming meetings with the teachers of Urebank which would take place later that term.

Mrs Robertshaw, the teacher of the lower juniors, was a large, red-faced woman with a broad, friendly face and steel grey hair twisted up untidily on her head. She was dressed in a brightly coloured floral dress and shapeless lavender cardigan and sported a string of hefty glass beads. She folded her arms, narrowed her eyes and, with her face creased into a frown, said tartly, 'Well, all I will say is that I cannot see that we will be able to work with the teachers at Urebank. I'm sorry to be so negative, Elisabeth, but it has to be said. As you know, I went to look around the school when I was minded to apply for a post there. I've been in this business long enough to smell a happy school, and Urebank is not a happy school. The older children looked subdued and bored and the infants were disorganised and over-excited. Mind you, the teacher of the infants was at least friendly, which is more than can be said for the po-faced teacher of the upper juniors, the deputy head, who looked as if he'd been dug up. They should have closed the school when they had the chance.'

'Surely it's not that bad, Elsie,' volunteered Miss Brakespeare, the deputy head teacher, who was wearing a stylish navy-blue suit and lemon blouse. She was aware that her colleague was prone to exaggeration.

'Oh, but it is, Miriam,' continued Mrs Robertshaw. She turned to Elisabeth. 'You may use all your charm, diplomacy and powers of persuasion but you've as much chance of getting them to work with you as getting the Pope to visit a lap-dancing club. The head teacher at Urebank, that dreadful Mr Richardson, is a cold, disagreeable, humourless, ill-tempered and pompous individual who will do everything to undermine what you attempt to do.'

'Really, Elsie,' said Miss Brakespeare, with a wry smile, 'why don't you tell us what you really think about the man.'

Miss Wilson, teacher of the infants, could not help but chuckle. She was a slim young woman with short raven-black hair, a pale, delicately boned face and great blue eyes.

'You can laugh, Rebecca,' said Mrs Robertshaw, 'but you'll not be laughing when you have to work with him. He has the personality of a lump of petrified wood.'

'The deputy head teacher by the sound of it doesn't sound a whole lot better,' remarked Miss Wilson.

'A pea out of the same pod, is Mr Jolly,' Mrs Robertshaw told her, 'and that's a paradox if ever there was one. He's about as jolly as a funeral bell. I think he is of the belief that he is doing the children a favour just by turning up for school. I mean, you've met him, haven't you, Miriam?' she asked the deputy head teacher. 'It was that time when you went with our pupils to the poetry competition and his nose was put out of joint when one of our children won first prize and one of his was disqualified for copying out somebody else's poem?'

'Well, yes,' agreed the deputy head teacher, 'he wasn't the most agreeable person I have to admit.'

'Well, at least the infant teacher sounds nice enough,' said Miss Wilson.

'She's all right, I suppose, but a bit wishy-washy, as is the teacher of the lower juniors. They've probably become disillusioned and who can blame them, having to work for Mr Richardson and his sidekick.'

Elisabeth, who had been quiet but acutely attentive during this tirade, with her hands clasped on her lap, at last spoke.

'Well, we have little choice in the matter,' she said. 'The amalgamation is to take place, so we will have to work with them come what may.'

'I'd be the first to put a bomb behind the teachers at Urebank,' remarked Mrs Robertshaw.

The staff-room became silent as the teachers contemplated what had been said and what lay ahead of them.

'I guess there will be difficulties,' said Elisabeth, 'but we have to make it work for the good of the children. I am, of course, looking for your full support.'

'That goes without question,' said Miss Brakespeare.

'Hear, hear,' chorused the others.

'Now, to more pleasant things,' said Elisabeth. 'We need to be thinking about the end-of-year school production. Any ideas?'

'What about *Oliver!*' said Miss Brakespeare. 'It's such a lovely heart-warming story and with some very catchy melodies.'

'They put on *Oliver!* at one of the schools where I was a supply teacher,' said Mrs Robertshaw, 'and it was a disaster. They had a nasty-tempered bull terrier called Butch for Bill Sikes's dog. Ugly beast it was, with teeth like tank traps and a fat round face. It attacked the Artful Dodger and then disgraced itself on stage by lifting its leg—'

'I don't think we need to go down that road, Elsie,' interrupted Elisabeth, smiling.

'What about an adaptation of one of Oscar Wilde's stories?' suggested Mrs Robertshaw. 'We've been reading them in class and the children have really liked them. Perhaps an adaptation of *The Selfish Giant* or *The Happy Prince*?'

'It's certainly worth considering,' replied Elisabeth, 'but they are rather sad stories. I was thinking of something a bit more cheerful. It needs to be a production that has a strong storyline, which involves a lot of children, has some memorable tunes, bright costumes and with some humour and maybe a little sadness.'

'What about *The Wizard of Oz*?' suggested Miss Wilson.

'Of course,' said Elisabeth.

'Excellent idea,' trilled Miss Brakespeare.

'An inspired suggestion,' agreed Mrs Robertshaw. 'I know just the children to take the leads.'

'Well, we all seem agreed,' said Elisabeth. 'So *The Wizard of Oz* it is. We'll send for the play version straight away.'

'And we will start auditions at the drama club as soon as it arrives,' added Mrs Robertshaw.

There was a sharp knock at the door and the caretaker entered.

'Yes, Mr Gribbon?' said Elisabeth.

He held up between finger and thumb the rubber spout from the teapot. 'You will never guess, Mrs Devine, where I found this?' he asked, grimacing.

At morning break Elisabeth called into the school office to find Mrs Scrimshaw tapping away happily on the keyboard of her new machine.

'You seem to have got to grips with the computer,' she said. 'I'm very impressed.'

'Actually, Mrs Devine,' replied Mrs Scrimshaw, looking up, 'it's relatively easy once you know how.' She was feeling quite smug.

'It's a wonder you managed to get all those wires in the right sockets.'

'Actually they are called leads,' the secretary told her, sharing her new-found knowledge, 'and each fits into a socket. All the sockets are different, so it's impossible to put a lead in the wrong one. It's quite simple really.'

'I hope young Oscar wasn't being too much of nuisance. He's a very inquisitive child and sometimes can be a bit meddlesome.'

'No,' replied the school secretary, 'he was just interested. He likes to know what's going on in the school, does Oscar.' The boy in question had given Mrs Scrimshaw a crash course that morning and offered to continue with the lesson after school, during the time he waited for his mother to collect him.

'I really didn't expect you to be using the computer until you had been on the course this Friday,' disclosed the head teacher. 'I imagined that you would still want to use your typewriter until you were *au fait* with the new machine.'

Mrs Scrimshaw gave a little smile at hearing the use of the phrase '*au fait*'. 'Oh no, Mrs Devine,' she said. 'I thought I'd make a start. In my book the sooner one becomes conversant with the new technology the better.'

'I am very pleased you feel that way. I have to admit that when I first broached the matter of you using a computer, I did have an inkling that you were not all that keen on parting with your typewriter.'

'One has to move with the times, Mrs Devine,' the school secretary told her.

'Actually,' said Elisabeth, 'I called in to say that I'm expecting a couple of parents – a Mr and Mrs Banks. They are coming in to see me after school this coming Thursday. If you could put that in your diary. When they arrive, could you show them down to my classroom, please? They want their son to start here. Evidently things haven't worked out for Robin at his last school.'

'Robin Banks!' exclaimed Mrs Scrimshaw. 'The child's called Robin Banks?'

'Yes,' replied the head teacher.

'Well, how ridiculous. Fancy inflicting a name like Robin Banks on a child.'

'I am afraid that sometimes parents do not think things through when they come to naming their children,' Elisabeth told her.

'I'm sure some do it deliberately,' remarked the school secretary, sniffing. 'I remember we've had at the school a Sunny Day and a Sandi Beech, Hazel Nutt and Daisy Chain, twins called Armani and Chanel, and one poor child was burdened with Terry Bull.' She paused and shook her head. 'And once we had a girl named Jenny Taylor.'

'Jenny Taylor?' repeated Elisabeth, looking puzzled.

'I shan't explain, Mrs Devine,' said the secretary. 'I shall leave you in blissful ignorance.'

Mr Gribbon, having alerted the head teacher to the fact that 'some of the kids have started putting foreign bodies down the toilets again', strode off to his small store-room near the boiler, his keys jangling in his overall pocket. There he found Mrs Pugh, the part-time cleaner, awaiting him with a mug of steaming tea in her hand.

'I've just made a pot, Mr Gribbon,' she said chirpily.

The caretaker's face brightened. 'Oh, hello, Mrs Pugh. All done, have we?'

'All done, Mr Gribbon,' she repeated, handing him a mug. 'Shelves dusted, tables wiped down, toilets cleaned, carpets swept and the floors buffed just as you like them. You can see your face in the floors.'

'I was going to buff the floors myself,' he told her.

'Well, I've saved you the trouble. Everything's tidy, as my sainted Welsh grandmother would say.'

'She'd not be saying that if she could see the classrooms at the end of the day after the kids have been let loose,' complained the caretaker. He exhaled noisily through his teeth. 'And the teachers are just as bad. It'll look as if a bomb's been dropped on the place.'

'Well, it keeps us in a job, Mr Gribbon,' she said cheerfully.

'Aye, I suppose so,' he grumbled, looking down at his tea. Then after a thoughtful pause he looked up. 'I can't tell you what a godsend you've been, Mrs Pugh, since you started here.' He took a gulp of his tea and flopped into his old armchair.

'That's very kind of you to say so, Mrs Gribbon,' replied the part-time cleaner. She gave a small, self-satisfied smile and patted her purple-tinted perm.

'Oh yes, you've lifted a heavy weight from off of my shoulders and no mistake since you started here,' he said.

'Well, I'm surprised you managed for so long without any help,' she sympathised.

The caretaker nodded in agreement. 'I'm not a one to complain, Mrs Pugh, but it has been hard, what with having to do all this rubbing and scouring, polishing and cleaning single-handed.'

'What with your bad back and all and the heavy lifting,' she added, with genuine concern in her voice.

The caretaker put in a martyred expression. 'Yes, I sometimes wondered myself how I ever managed. The last head teacher, Miss Sowerbutts, was a tartar and the present one is not much better, always wanting something or other doing. I was never off of my feet.' He stretched out his legs and took another gulp of tea.

'Taken for granted, Mr Gribbon,' observed the part-time cleaner.

'You're not wrong there, Mrs Pugh.'

'Well, you've got me to help now,' she said.

The caretaker leaned back and rested his head on the back of the chair. 'I have indeed, Mrs Pugh, and as I've said, you've been a godsend.'

'I just wish the caretaker down at Urebank was as appreciative as you, Mr Gribbon,' she said. 'Face on him like a wet weekend in Port Talbot and always finding fault with something or other. And the head teacher, well, don't get me started on him.'

'Taken for granted, Mrs Pugh,' observed the caretaker.

'You're not wrong there, Mr Gribbon.'

'They don't know how lucky they are, Mrs Pugh,' said the caretaker. 'I wish I could have you full-time.'

'Beg pardon, Mr Gribbon?'

The caretaker's face flushed. 'W . . . w . . . what I meant was that I wish you could work here all the time instead of me having to share you with Urebank.'

Mrs Pugh smiled. 'Well, next term when this amalgamation takes place there's every likelihood you will have me working with you full-time.' She patted her purple hair again. 'You'll probably get sick of the sight of me,' she added coyly.

'Never!' protested the caretaker.

'Tea all right?' she asked.

'Champion. Just the way I likes it.'

'My sainted Welsh grandmother, God rest her soul, always liked her tea strong,' the part-time cleaner told him. '"Strong enough to stand a spoon up in it," as she was wont to say.'

'I remember if I left a spoon standing up in a cup of tea,' said the caretaker, smiling at the memory, 'my grandmother used to say that that was how Nelson lost his eye.'

'You are a card, Mr Gribbon, and no mistake,' said the part-time cleaner, chuckling.

'Well, you make a lovely brew, Mrs Pugh,' said the caretaker. 'I bet you're a good cook as well.'

'As a matter of fact I have been told so,' replied Mrs Pugh. 'My coffee and walnut cake is the talk of the Townswomen's Guild, and at school in cookery Miss Reece said my spotted dick was the best she had ever tasted.'

'My wife doesn't cook,' said the caretaker gloomily.

'Sadly, I don't get much opportunity to cook cakes and puddings these days,' continued the part-time cleaner. 'My husband is a boiled beef and carrots man. He hasn't got a sweet tooth in his body. He likes his savouries, does Owen.'

They were quiet for a while.

'Kids will be arriving soon,' observed Mr Gribbon, breathing out loudly. 'By the way, I took that rubber spout you found down the toilet to Mrs Devine. I told her she needs to speak to the kids about putting foreign objects down the toilets and nip it in the bud before they all start doing it. Last term this little tyke called Oscar—'

'I met him this morning,' interrupted Mrs Pugh. 'He has far too much to say for himself, that young man. Only started to tell me that there was still dust on some of the books, just after I'd given the school library a good going-over.'

'He's a pain in the neck, is that lad,' barked the caretaker. 'Last term he started putting ping-pong balls down the toilet.'

'Ping-pong balls!' exclaimed the part-time cleaner.

'Said the boys could aim at them and stop them dribbling on the floor.'

'I've never heard the like,' said Mrs Pugh.

'And it started a craze,' continued the caretaker. 'Soon the other kids started putting things down and the pipes got blocked with tennis balls.'

'Tennis balls!'

'And I had water and I don't know what else all over my parquet floor.'

'Dear me.'

'It took some buffing, I can tell you.'

'I bet it did.'

'I don't know what gets into kids these days,' sighed the caretaker, blowing out his cheeks.

'They have it too easy,' declared Mrs Pugh. 'Owen and I never had children.'

'Nor us,' said the caretaker, 'but if we'd had children they wouldn't have turned out like that Oscar, I tell you that for nothing.'

There was a sharp knock of the door. Outside stood the boy in question.

'Ah, there you are, Mr Gribbon,' said the boy cheerily. 'I've been looking all over the school for you. I think you should know that there's a rather unpleasant smell in the boys' toilets and there's a dripping tap.'

2

After school had finished for the day on Friday, Elisabeth met Mr and Mrs Banks. They hovered indecisively in the doorway before entering the classroom. The husband was a large man with a wide square face which gave the impression of having been left out all night in the wind and rain. The skin was the colour and texture of an over-ripe russet apple. He had a thick neck and heavy shoulders like a bull. Tufts of sandy-coloured hair stuck out from his head at rebellious angles. His wife, in contrast, was a tall, thin, intense-looking woman with a face as pale as a lily and dominated by heavy black-rimmed glasses. Her iron grey hair was parted savagely down the middle and stretched around her head in a thick plait.

'Thank you for seeing us, Mrs Devine,' said the woman timidly. She sat on the very edge of the chair, her body held stiffly upright and her thin fingers locked together on her lap. Elisabeth perceived something dark and troubling in her eyes.

'Aye, thank you for seeing us,' echoed the man, leaning forward and resting his fat hands on the desk. His fingernails were ridged and dirty.

'It's a pleasure,' said Elisabeth, smiling. 'I should explain that I teach all the week so that the only time visitors can see me is at breaks and lunchtimes or before and after school – so I'm grateful you could come in now. I believe you are thinking of sending your son here to Barton?'

'Well, yes,' replied Mrs Banks.

'If you'll 'ave 'im,' grunted her husband.

'How old is Robin?' asked Elisabeth.

'He's nine going on ten,' the woman told her.

'An only child?'

'Yes, we've just the one.'

'Perhaps before we have a chat about things, you may like to have a walk around the school.'

The parents looked at each other.

'Well, yes,' said the woman, 'but we would like to tell you about Robin before we do.' She glanced again at her husband. 'It's just that . . .' The sentence remained unfinished.

'We've bin telled this is a right good school,' Mr Banks said unsmilingly.

'I should like to think so,' Elisabeth replied.

'The woman in the village store said it was the best in the area,' said Mrs Banks, 'and that you – how can I put it – that you know how to deal with children who are a bit, how shall I say, a bit different.'

'T''lad's different all right,' muttered her husband.

'All children are different, Mr Banks,' replied Elisabeth. 'Every child is unique. Each has his or her talents and his or her special needs. I'm sorry, that must sound rather patronising. It's just that I believe that no children are alike and therefore every child should be treated as an individual.'

'What t'wife means, Missis Devine, is we've been told you can deal wi' kids what are difficult,' said the man. He shifted uncomfortably in the chair. ''E's not an easy lad. 'E needs firm 'andlin'. 'E can be a bloody nightmare at times. Last week—'

The woman rested a restraining hand on his arm and stared at him balefully. 'Frank, please,' she said. She turned to Elisabeth. 'We've been told, Mrs Devine, that you're very good at dealing with children who have problems like our son's. They just couldn't cope with Robin at his last school and the headmaster, Mr Richardson—'

'He was at Urebank?' interrupted Elisabeth.

''E was, yes,' said Mr Banks, cutting in, 'an' Mester Richardson said 'e needed special 'elp because 'e was unmanageable. Bit the deputy head teacher he did.'

'I think Robin was picked on,' said his wife. 'He came home once with bruises—'

'Oh, don't give me that, Rita!' exclaimed her husband. 'You're allus mekkin' excuses for 'im. Let's be clear, t'lad's a real 'andful. Mester Richardson said 'e'd be better off in one o' them schools what deals with kids like 'im, some kind of behavioural unit or other.'

'Robin was expelled,' said Mrs Banks dolefully.

'Was he?' said Elisabeth quietly.

'An' I agree wi' Mester Richardson, t'lad should be put in one of these units but t'wife's not keen,' he said. 'It were t'same at t'school before wi' moved 'im to Urebank. They couldn't deal with 'im eether. Spittin' and swearin' 'e was and I don't know what. T'thing is, Missis Devine, t'lad just won't behave 'imself. I just don't know what's up wi' 'im.'

'He never used to be like this,' said Mrs Banks. 'He was such a lovely baby. I had him late in life, you see, and thought him a little miracle when he was born. When he was small people used to stop me in the street and—'

'We don't know why 'e behaves as 'e does,' her husband butted in impatiently. ''E's rude and unruly.'

'I see,' said Elisabeth. 'And did Mr Richardson say what he thought was Robin's problem?'

'Some sort of mental disorder,' said the woman. She bit her lip so she wouldn't cry.

Her husband glanced at the floor and shook his head. 'Mental disorder my foot,' he mumbled.

'He said Robin's got what he called some sort of attention deficit,' she continued. 'That he can't concentrate and is disobedient and noisy. Mr Richardson said that he needed to be in a special school for badly behaved youngsters and put on some sort of medication. He said there was a residential school in Marfleet.' She looked desperately at Elisabeth. There were tears in her eyes. 'I don't want Robin to go away to a special school.'

''E just needs to behave hissen,' said the husband dogmatically. 'I don't think t'lad's got any mental disorder; 'e's just disobedient and wants 'is own way. I'm afraid 'e got away with murder before I married 'is mother and she still spoils 'im.'

'No, Frank I never, I—' started the woman.

'Oh yes you do, Rita,' interrupted her husband dismissively. 'And it's left to me to try and drum some discipline into t'lad.'

'So Robin is your stepson then, Mr Banks?' asked Elisabeth.

'Aye, 'e is,' replied the man. 'And it's not easy bringin' up someone else's kid, not easy at all.'

'My first husband was killed in a mining accident,' Mrs Banks told her. 'His death hit Robin very hard. When I married Frank, Robin didn't take it too well. They've never got on. Maybe that's the reason . . .' Her voice tailed off.

'I've done mi best for 'im,' said Mr Banks, 'but 'e took agin me from t'start.'

'Trying to come to terms with such a change in his life, particularly the death of his father, might account to some extent for Robin's behaviour,' said Elisabeth, 'but I have known children who initially don't accept a step-parent but get on well with them after a while.'

'Aye, well, 'e's not one of them,' grumbled the man.

'Tell me more about this problem you think your son has got,' said Elisabeth gently.

'He's so moody and bad-tempered and can be very naughty,' said Mrs Banks. 'When Frank's out at work or away from home—'

'I'm a plasterer and 'ave to go weer t'work teks me,' her husband butted in again.

'I might tell Robin to do something,' continued Mrs Banks, 'and he answers me back. I just don't know what gets into him.' Her face was decorated with misery.

'Won't do as 'e's told,' added the husband. ''E mooches about t'ouse' wi' this sulky face on 'im an' if I ask 'im to do summat or tell 'im off, 'e gets in a real paddy. Starts swearing an' shouting and sayin' I'm not 'is proper dad and I can't order 'im about. When I 'ave a go at 'im 'e answers me back and when I smack 'im, it meks it worse.'

'Smacking isn't the answer,' replied Elisabeth. Her voice was solicitous and kindly.

'We really don't know what to do, Mrs Devine,' said Mrs Banks. 'We really don't. I'm at my wits' end. It's making me ill.'

'What help have you received from the various support agencies?' asked Elisabeth.

'Support agencies?' she repeated. 'I don't know what you mean.'

'Well, has Robin been referred to an educational psychologist for example, has he received counselling, have the Welfare Service and the Child and Adult Mental Health Service been consulted?'

'None of those,' said Mrs Banks.

'And in the previous schools, were there policies in place and approaches adopted to deal with challenging children like Robin?'

'No.'

'So your son has received no professional help at all?' asked Elisabeth.

'No, not as far as I know,' said Mrs Banks quietly.

'Goodness knows I've tried mi best wi' 'im, Mrs Devine,' said her husband, 'but 'e won't behave hissen. As I've said, it's a big job tekkin on somebody else's kid. Now I've told mi wife that this school, if you'll 'ave 'im, will be 'is last chance. If 'e dun't behave 'issen 'ere and settle down and frame 'issen then 'e'll be goin' to one o' these special schools.'

'We need help, Mrs Devine,' said Mrs Banks, biting her bottom lip.

'I can assure you that if you decide to send Robin to Barton he will receive the very best attention, that he will get specialist help and that we will work with both of you to help him control his temper and for him to do well in his work.'

'You mean he can come here?' asked Mrs Banks. Her lip began to tremble and her eyes filled with tears.

Elisabeth reached across the desk and patted the woman's hand. 'Of course he can,' she said. 'He can start next Monday. Now let's have a look around the school.'

Thoughts swirled around in Elisabeth's head as she lay in bed on Friday night. A blustery wind tugged at the window frames and a light rain pattered on the glass. It was always the same after the first week of a new term. She would drift into a threadbare sleep only to wake up in the dead of night and go over and over in her mind the events of the last few days. She had much to think about that night. Words and images buzzed around in her head until she was too exhausted to think any more and at last fell asleep.

At dawn the stillness of the night was disturbed by the striking of the long-case clock in the hall and by the chorus of early birds. As she lay there Elisabeth thought of Mr and Mrs Banks; such a sad, anxious, confused woman tied to an obdurate, bad-tempered husband, both at a loss to know how to deal with a difficult and demanding son. The words of the boy's mother came back to her: 'He was such a lovely baby. I thought him a little miracle.' Elisabeth thought *her* child had been such a lovely baby too, a little miracle. She recalled the nurse placing the new-born baby boy in her arms. 'Such a perfect child,' she had said. And John was a perfect child, with his large dark eyes, pale unblemished skin, small fingers and nails like tiny pink sea shells. How he smiled and gurgled. Simon, the proud father, had held his son high in the air and predicted he would be the handsomest, cleverest, best-behaved child in his school and become an eminent doctor, a celebrated lawyer or a famous politician.

By the time John had become a toddler it had become evident to Elisabeth that things were not right. He was not like other children: active and sociable, affectionate and curious. He didn't like to be cuddled and avoided eye contact; he didn't speak and became obsessed with routine. Changes made him anxious and he would spend hours carefully arranging and rearranging his coloured bricks, oblivious of the world around him.

Simon at first refused to believe that his son had any sort of special need. He just could not accept that there was anything wrong, and felt his wife was just another fussy mother. Elisabeth finally persuaded him to come with her to a specialist in childhood disorders. John was examined and assessed, and they were informed that their son had a severe form of autism and would never lead a normal life if that meant going to a mainstream school, playing sports, passing exams, getting married and having children.

Elisabeth pictured the two parents who had been to see her that day: the inordinately thin, prematurely aged woman who had sat stiffly upright on the end of the chair and her tetchy husband, who interestingly never referred to his stepson by name. She recalled the dark troubled eyes of the woman.

Cracks had appeared in Elisabeth's marriage. There were arguments and days of simmering silences. Then Simon walked out of her life and that of his son. She heard he had remarried, to a young and up-and-coming colleague in the accountancy firm where he was a senior partner. Elisabeth had learnt subsequently that the marriage had not worked out and after a bitter divorce Simon had left the firm.

When John was eleven, Elisabeth, by now a highly regarded
head teacher of a successful primary school in the city, looked
for a special school for her son, one dedicated to the care and
education of the autistic child. Forest View Residential School
was considered to be the best of its kind in the north, and
Elisabeth secured a place for John. When the position of head
teacher arose at a small village primary school a stone's throw
from Forest View, Elisabeth applied and was appointed to
Barton-in-the Dale. She bought a cottage in the village, threw
herself into her work and turned a moribund school destined
for closure into a thriving establishment. After a strenuous
campaign the school was reprieved, but things had barely
settled down before the Education Department at County
Hall decided that Barton-in-the-Dale village school should be
amalgamated with its neighbour. Elisabeth had been in
competition with the headmaster at Urebank, Mr Richardson,
for the newly created post of head teacher of the merged
schools, and she had been appointed head teacher designate.
Her adversary had grudgingly accepted the post as her deputy.
Now wide awake, Elisabeth thought of the problems she
would have to face.

She got up to make herself a cup of tea. In the kitchen she
looked out over the shadowy garden. There was a watery
moon in the pale dawn sky. A gusty wind bent the treetops.
How she loved her home. She would be sad to leave it when,
after the wedding, she would move into Clumber Lodge,
Michael's old, square, grey stone villa with its huge bay
windows and greasy grey slate roof.

When she had first bought Wisteria Cottage it had been
near-derelict. Standing alone at the end of a track of beaten
mud overgrown with nettles, it was a small pale stone building
with a sagging roof, peeling paint and a neglected garden.
Inside, the cottage was musty and cheerless with its thick,
faded curtains, threadbare carpet, rotting window frames and

a naked light bulb dangling from a yellowing electric flex, but Elisabeth had immediately seen its potential. She knew at first sight that she had to have it and would transform this old, former estate cottage into her dream home.

Elisabeth thought it strange how things had turned out. She could never have foreseen how her life would change so dramatically. So much had happened in the relatively short time she had lived in Barton, and not just at the school. She had anticipated that she would make new friends, for she was an affable and gregarious person by nature, and she expected that she would now be able to see her son regularly at Forest View, but she could never have predicted the greatest change which would come about in her life – that she would meet Michael Stirling, the man she was to marry. Who would have believed barely a year ago, when she had first met him, that she would one day fall in love with this man?

The following Monday morning, before the start of school, Elisabeth found Mrs Robertshaw putting the finishing touches to a display in her classroom. She was humming happily to herself as she stapled the last of the children's work to the wall.

'This looks very impressive,' said Elisabeth, entering the classroom

'Thank you,' replied the teacher turning, her face brightening at the praise. 'We've been reading "The Highwayman" by Alfred Noyes. I love this poem. All the rhythms and rhymes, all the colours and images, and it's such a wonderful narrative. I have to admit I get quite tearful at the end when the landlord's daughter is killed.' She babbled on. 'The children have been writing descriptions based upon it. Oscar's, as one might expect, is excellent – very vivid and detailed – and little Roisin's—'

'I'm sorry to interrupt, Elsie,' said Elisabeth, 'but I do need to talk to you about a new pupil who is to start this afternoon and who will be in your class. Could we just sit down for a moment?'

Elisabeth then explained about Robin, the boy whom the teacher might find rather difficult to handle.

'Well,' said Mrs Robertshaw, having listened with a weak smile on her face, 'of course, I'll do my best with the boy but I haven't had a whole lot of experience of dealing with problematic children before, so it won't be easy. I remember at one school where I was doing some supply teaching this boy was completely out of control and—'

'Let's not judge the child until we've met him,' Elisabeth cut in. 'I think sometimes people tend to put labels on children rather too soon. From what his parents have told me I think he is a little boy with a few issues, but I believe with firmness, patience and encouragement we can help him. After all, we managed with Malcolm Stubbins, didn't we? You will recall he was a real handful and he's very little trouble now.'

'You're probably right,' agreed Mrs Robertshaw, nodding dully. Elisabeth could see in the teacher's face that her colleague was unconvinced.

Elisabeth changed the subject. 'So have you decided on the parts for the *The Wizard of Oz* yet?'

Mrs Robertshaw, keen to start producing the school play, had visited the local library the previous week and found a copy of the book. She had decided that she would adapt it herself for the stage rather than use the commercially written version.

'Very nearly,' she replied. 'I thought of casting Roisin as Dorothy. She just looks the part, small and innocent, and I can see her in a gingham dress with that lovely red hair in plaits, but then I heard her sing. I expected to hear this sweet little voice but when she sang "Over the Rainbow" at the auditions on Friday she sounded like a bat stapled to a door.'

'Surely not.'

'You should hear her.'

'Of course you know who has the finest voice in the school,' said Elisabeth.

'That's my dilemma. Chardonnay brought tears to my eyes when she sang at the Christmas concert, but she just doesn't look the part. I don't mean to be unkind, but she's such a dumpy child and of course there's her accent.'

'I think you should give her the chance,' said Elisabeth. 'We don't need to have another Judy Garland on stage and I'm sure she could handle an American accent. She's quite a mimic.'

'I'll think about it,' said Mrs Robertshaw.

'What about the other parts?' asked Elisabeth.

'Well, Danny Stainthorpe is a natural for the scarecrow, Eddie Lake will make a splendid tin man and I thought of Malcolm Stubbins for the lion. I was surprised that Malcolm turned up for the auditions but he read the part really well. He does a very convincing growl.'

And who would have thought a few months ago, Elisabeth thought to herself, that such a difficult and uncooperative boy could turn out so well. Perhaps the new boy might do the same.

'Darren Holgate will be the narrator,' continued the teacher, 'and, of course, all the infants can play the Munchkins, the bees and the winged monkeys.'

'I have an idea who you have thought of for the part of the Wizard,' said Elisabeth.

'Well, it has to be Oscar,' said Mrs Robertshaw.

'And the witches?'

'I thought at first of Chantelle for the Wicked Witch of the East and Chardonnay for the Wicked Witch of the West.'

'Why not switch the parts you first had in mind – Chardonnay as Dorothy and Roisin as the Wicked Witch of the West?'

'But Roisin doesn't look a bit like a witch, she's more like an elf or a fairy, and Chardonnay, as I've said, doesn't look the part of Dorothy.'

'It's worth considering,' said Elisabeth.

'I'm not sure,' replied Mrs Robertshaw.

'Why not get them to read through the parts and sing a few numbers and then you can finally decide?'

The following day Elisabeth found the opportunity of speaking to Chardonnay. The girl, who had been relieved as tea monitor, had now been given the responsibility of looking after the plants. She took the job seriously and toured the school at lunchtime with her watering can. Elisabeth discovered her in the school entrance, tending to a large shrub.

'Hello, Chardonnay,' said Elisabeth.

'Oh hello, miss,' replied the girl. 'I think this plant wants pruning. It's growing too big for its pot.'

'I've been speaking to Mrs Robertshaw about you taking the part of Dorothy in the school play. She tells me you are not sure if you want to audition for it.'

'I don't, miss,' replied the girl.

'I think you would make a wonderful Dorothy,' Elisabeth told her.

Chardonnay stopped what she was doing and put down the watering can.

'I'd like to do it, miss,' she admitted, 'I really would, but I don't think I'm right for it.'

'Why do you say that?' asked Elisabeth.

'Well, look at me, miss,' sniffed the girl.

'I'm looking,' said Elisabeth, 'and what am I supposed to see?'

'Miss, I'm fat and I know I'm not good-looking like some of the other girls in our class, and I don't talk proper. And what about these braces on my teeth?' She rubbed her eyes. 'I'm frightened that when I'm up on stage in front of all them people, they'll laugh at me.'

Elisabeth put her arm around the girl's shoulder.

'Everyone who is on that stage will be a bit frightened. They will have butterflies in their stomachs and feel nervous and worried but once they open their mouths it will disappear. You know, we all get afraid at times and it's always best to face it. You have to believe in yourself and have the courage to do that, Chardonnay. And you can do it, I'm certain of that.'

'Everyone will laugh at me, miss,' said the girl sadly. 'I just know they will.'

'Nobody will laugh at you, I promise,' said Elisabeth. 'When you start to sing they will be in the palm of your hand, and as for being fat and not very good-looking, you really are being silly. You're a pretty young woman and with your talent you will delight those who listen to you.'

'I know miss, but—'

'When I was your age,' Elisabeth cut in, 'I was a bit on the plump side too, I had braces on *my* teeth, freckles on my cheeks and frizzy hair the colour of straw and I was very conscious of my appearance.'

'You were?'

'I most certainly was, but as I grew older my figure changed, I got rid of the braces, and had a new hair style which suited me. I've kept the freckles because I think they look quite attractive. Now I want you to put out of your mind the idea that you are not right for the part and I want you to audition for it. Mrs Robertshaw and I wouldn't ask you if we thought you couldn't do it.'

'Yes, miss,' sniffed the girl and then added, 'but I haven't got freckles.'

Mrs Banks sat very straight in a small chair in Elisabeth's classroom, her face as bloodless as a bone dug up from a dusty pit. She twisted the wedding ring on her bony finger nervously. Elisabeth had asked her to bring her son into school at lunchtime for him to start that afternoon. Seated next to her was Robin, a small twig of a boy with shiny chestnut brown hair cropped as close as a doormat, a pale freckled face and a small upturned nose. He studied Elisabeth with large watchful eyes as bright as polished green glass, as if she were an object of mild curiosity.

'So, Robin,' said the head teacher cheerfully, 'are you looking forward to starting at a new school?' The boy did not meet her eyes and shrugged.

'I believe you didn't get on very well at your last one?' she continued.

He tossed his head and shuffled in his chair. 'No, I didn't,' he said with a sniff.

'And why was that?'

The boy raised his little chin defiantly and stared at her. His expression was unreadable. He shrugged again.

Elisabeth thought for a moment. What did she see in those bright green eyes? Anger? Resentment? Insolence? Certainly. But there was also the unmistakable flash of distress. Perhaps beneath the child's apparent sharpness and bluster there was a sad and lonely little boy who couldn't understand himself why he behaved so wilfully.

'Now Robin, when you speak to me,' continued Elisabeth calmly, 'I would like you to call me "miss".' There was a gentle reproof in her voice.

'Why?' he asked. He gave her a level stare.

'Because that is how it is in this school. All the children here call their teachers "miss".'

The boy hunched his shoulders and folded his arms across his chest. 'Whatever,' he replied, and then added 'miss' with obvious emphasis.

Elisabeth had handled difficult children in the past but she could see that this child would be a real challenge. The boy's mother, who had until now remained perfectly still and in miserable silence with the strain showing on her pale face, stroked her son's hair as if he were a tame creature. He pushed her hand away roughly and scowled. 'Don't do that!' he snapped.

'Now Robin,' said Elisabeth coolly, resisting the temptation to reprimand the child for speaking so rudely to his mother.

'I'm called Robbie!' he interrupted. There was the same look of defiance on his face. 'I don't like Robin. It's a stupid name. I'm not a bird.' Elisabeth saw real anger in the boy's eyes.

'Thank you for telling me, Robbie,' she replied good-naturedly. 'I was going to tell you that we have lots of really interesting things going on in the school. We have a foot-ball team, a choir, a drama group and an art class at lunchtimes. This term we are starting a chess club and a book group. We also have visits out of school to interesting places. I am sure there will be something which will appeal to you.'

The boy made it clear by the way he leaned back in his chair and stared up at the ceiling that he didn't appear at all interested.

'We have a very happy school here where children behave themselves and work hard.' Elisabeth's voice had taken on a serious edge. 'I expect you to behave yourself and work hard too and then we will get along.'

The boy lowered his head and narrowed his eyes and there was a trace of a smile on his lips.

'I'll take you along to Mrs Robertshaw's classroom now,' Elisabeth told him. 'She is the teacher of the lower juniors. Would you like to say goodbye to your mother?'

'Bye,' said the boy wearily and, stretching like someone who had just got out of bed, he rose from his chair.

'Goodbye, love,' said Mrs Banks, getting to her feet and pecking his cheek, 'and do try and be a good boy, won't you.'

At the end of the day Elisabeth called into Mrs Robertshaw's classroom to find out how the new boy had got on.

'Well?' she asked warily.

The teacher breathed out noisily. She looked tired and flustered. 'Well indeed,' she replied.

'Oh dear,' said Elisabeth. 'Shall we sit down and you can tell me the worst.'

'Where shall I start?' sighed the teacher. 'I would have expected a new pupil to be rather shy and nervous on his first day at school.' She shook her head. 'Not this young man. He stood at the front, legs apart like a gunslinger, and stared at the class as if challenging someone to provoke him. Then he slumped in a chair and spent the first part of the lesson scowling. I explained to him what we had been doing, reading the poem "The Highwayman", and I suggested he might like to read it. He shook his head. Then I asked him to write something about himself so I could learn what he was interested in.'

'And did he?' asked Elisabeth.

'What do you think?' asked Mrs Robertshaw. 'He sat there twisting a rubber band around his fingers and staring out of the window. I asked him to get on with his work and he told me it was boring. I've seen the dull glare of a defiant child before, Elisabeth, and I know that this boy is trouble with a capital T. At afternoon break Oscar approached him. You're aware how nosey the boy can be. Oscar has to know about everything that's going on. He asked this Robin—'

'Actually he likes to be called Robbie,' Elisabeth told her.

Mrs Robertshaw pulled a face. 'Does he really? Anyway, Oscar, true to form, starts to quiz the new boy. Where did he live? What was his last school? Did he like reading? That sort of thing. This Robbie listened to him with a jaded expression on his face and then he said, "Bugger off, four eyes!" I told him such language was not acceptable in my classroom and to apologise to Oscar, but he just shrugged and then started fiddling with the rubber band again. I'm afraid I don't think I can handle him, Elisabeth, I really don't. I've been teaching for over twenty-five years and dealt with some difficult children in my time but this one takes the biscuit. I think this young man is just plain bad.'

'I don't believe that any child is just plain bad, Elsie,' Elisabeth replied. 'I consider that a child needs our care and compassion when he deserves it the least. Every child matters, however demanding he might be.'

'I'm sorry, Elisabeth,' retorted Mrs Robertshaw, 'such conviction is all very well but one has to think of the other children in the class. Their education is important as well. A child like this – disruptive and disobedient – can have a dire effect on their learning. He can upset the whole classroom. What he needs is to be at a school where they know how to handle children like him.'

'I see,' replied the head teacher. 'Well, that may be a final option. I shall give some thought to how we might proceed. I think in the first instance I shall have a word with Mrs Goldstein, the educational psychologist. She more than anyone will know how we should go about dealing with Robbie.'

'Well, I wish her luck,' said Mrs Robertshaw. 'She'll certainly need it.'

'Look, Elsie,' said Elisabeth, 'let Robbie stay in your class for a few more days and see how he gets on. If there's no improvement in his behaviour, then I think the best thing to do would be to move him into the upper juniors with me.'

3

Later that day Dr Stirling received a visitor at Clumber Lodge. It was a chilly April evening and Elisabeth needed to talk things through with him. She was shown into the sitting-room by the housekeeper.

'I've lit a fire,' said Mrs O'Connor. 'It's so nippy for this time of year, so it is, cold enough for two pair of shoelaces, as my grandmother would say. I'll tell Dr Stirling you're here.'

Elisabeth sat on the sofa warming herself by the crackling log fire.

'Hard week?' asked Michael, coming to sit next to her and putting an arm around her. His fiancée rested her head on his shoulder and closed her eyes.

'You could say that,' she replied, giving a weak smile.

'Join the club. I've had a week and a half at the surgery. I've had haemorrhoids, a strangulated hernia, varicose veins, wax in the ears, ulcerated leg, gallstones and an ectopic pregnancy.'

'You should see a doctor,' Elisabeth replied, yawning. 'You sound in a bad way.'

Michael smiled and kissed her cheek.

'I've had a letter from the Director of Education,' she told him, 'asking me to go and see her about the amalgamation – not something I am looking forward to. The thought of working with Robin Richardson is not something I welcome.'

'Now come on, Elisabeth, you thrive on a challenge,' said Michael. 'You'll have the poor man twisted around your little finger in no time. He'll be putty in your hands.'

'Chance would be a fine thing,' she said yawning again.

'The boys have told me you have a new addition,' he said.

The boys in question were James, Michael's eleven-year-old son, and Danny, who was being fostered at Clumber Lodge.

'I'm sorry,' Elisabeth said, her voice slurry with tiredness. 'What did you say?'

'The boys, they said you have a new pupil and from what they've told me he sounds a bit of a handful.'

Elisabeth laughed. 'That's something of an understatement. He is a very mixed-up young man.'

'A good dose of old-fashioned Mrs Devine's discipline will soon sort him out.'

'I wish it were as simple as that.' She sat up. 'I know you are not a one for all these labels people put on children, these disorders and syndromes, but—'

'But I have been proved wrong,' he said, finishing her sentence.

He *had* indeed been proved wrong. When Elisabeth had first started at the village school she had come to see Dr Michael Stirling about his son James. She was worried about this diffident little pupil, a sad and solemn-faced child who seemed to dwell in his own lonely, silent world. At school he only talked to his best friend, Danny Stainthorpe, and when spoken to by any adult would lower his head shyly and not reply. Elisabeth had been a teacher long enough to know that boys aged ten are usually lively, noisy creatures. James was very different. She was of the opinion, as she told the boy's father, that young James might have a condition called selective mutism, where a person speaks only to a few chosen others. The disorder, she had gone on to say, if untreated, could get worse until the person stopped talking altogether. Dr Stirling had dismissed her suggestion out of hand and explained that his son was still grieving for his mother, who had been killed in a riding accident two years before. There was nothing wrong with him.

'Mrs Devine,' he had told her sharply, 'James has no condition or problem. He is just a quiet, under-confident little boy. I weary of hearing and reading about all these so-called children's disorders and syndromes. James will soon grow out of it.'

Following this heated exchange, Dr Stirling decided a small preparatory school would be better suited to cater for his son's needs. James, desperately unhappy at the prospect of starting at a new school and being separated from his only friend, ran away from home. He was later discovered late at night in Elisabeth's cottage garden, cold and frightened. Dr Stirling admitted he had been wrong and agreed to Elisabeth's request for her to seek help for James, who returned to the village school.

With sensitive support and encouragement, James began to come out of his shell. His father started to fall for this strong-minded, caring and dedicated head teacher who had made such a difference in his son's life. Elisabeth, too, found that the more she got to know Michael Stirling, the more she was attracted to the man who she had initially thought disagreeable and pig-headed. Beneath the brusque exterior she discovered a caring and thoughtful man, a man with whom she fell in love and who, before the school broke up for the Easter holidays, asked her to marry him.

'So what is this new pupil like?' asked Michael now.

'He's rude and disobedient,' Elisabeth told him, 'an angry and confused young man. His parents just do not understand why he is like this or how to deal with him. It's a sorry situation. The head teacher at his last school thought he had ADHD, you know, when a child cannot concentrate, is hyperactive and misbehaves and—'

Michael smiled. 'I *have* heard of it, Elisabeth,' he interrupted.

'I'm sorry. Of course you have.'

'Children with that condition are usually put on some kind of medication,' Michael told her. 'Ritalin seems to calm them down. Maybe you should get his parents to refer him to a specialist if he's as difficult as you say, and have something prescribed.'

'But I don't think the child has ADHD,' Elisabeth replied. 'It's a term that these days seems to be used as the standard reason for the badly behaved child. Anyway, I don't put much weight on what Mr Richardson says.'

'He was at Urebank then?'

'Yes, and from what I gather he had a pretty rough time there.'

'Well, I suppose when the educational psychologist gets a chance to look at the lad you'll find out what the problem is.'

'The boy is certainly not overactive,' Elisabeth told him. 'In fact quite the opposite, and he is very attentive. When I speak to him he sits there quite calmly, looking at me as if I were some rare specimen in a museum case. In class, from what his teacher tells me, he doesn't apply himself to his work and can be very rude.'

'Perhaps he's just your classic naughty boy,' said Michael. 'Some children are biddable and good-natured and others misbehave. Isn't it something that can be put down to character? We had a fair few rogues when I was at school. One lad in our class was never out of trouble and spent more times in the headmaster's office than in the classroom, getting six of the best across his bottom for what he got up to. Of course, this boy you're talking about seems to have more of a problem.

Maybe his behaviour is more likely the result of the way he has been brought up.'

'Yes, you may be right,' Elisabeth replied. 'I'm afraid that is often the case. The boy's mother seems nice enough, caring and concerned, perhaps a little indulgent, but I didn't take to the boy's stepfather at all. He was a very forceful and domineering character who hadn't a good word to say about the boy.'

'So what are you going to do?' Michael asked.

'I've spoken to Mrs Goldstein, the educational psychologist,' she told him. 'She's recommended that the boy is assessed by a consultant paediatrician and neurologist – something which should have happened at his last school. Then we can take it from there.'

Elisabeth arrived at Forest View Residential School for the usual Saturday morning visit. She found her son sitting at his favourite table by the window, staring intently at a set of large coloured cards which showed pictures of everyday objects: a kettle and cutlery, cups and plates, hats and coats. The boy tapped the table top rhythmically and then began to sort the cards according to shape and size. His forehead was furrowed with concentration. She sat next to him and watched him for a moment. He was such a good-looking eleven-year-old, she thought, with his large dark eyes, long lashes and curly blond hair. Elisabeth took his hand in hers and pressed it gently. He glanced around and smiled and then returned to arranging the cards.

Elisabeth kissed his cheek gently. He didn't react. 'It's such a lovely sunny day, I thought we might go for a bit of a walk,' she said. 'I know you like the rain so you can splash in the puddles, but it would be a shame to stay indoors today.'

John continued to arrange the cards.

Elisabeth talked for some time, telling her son about the

start of the new term, the teachers at her school, the play they were to perform and her anxiety over the amalgamation. The boy never looked up from the cards. His face was expressionless. Elisabeth wondered just how much John understood of what she was saying, but each week she would go through the same routine of talking to him. Perhaps, she thought, it was having no benefit for her son but, even if it didn't, she found speaking out loud to him therapeutic for her. It's quite a change, she thought, to be able to talk to someone and not be interrupted or disagreed with. Until she had met Michael her son had been the only person with whom she could be really honest and share all her hopes and fears and feelings.

'Hello, Mrs Devine.' John's teacher, a young man with a wide smile and china blue eyes, came to join her. 'Have you come to take this young man off my hands for an hour?'

'Oh hello, Mr Campsmount,' she replied. 'Yes, I thought we would go for a walk and get some fresh air.'

'If you can drag him away from those cards,' he said grinning. 'He's fascinated with them.'

'So what has he been like this week?' she asked.

'He's doing really well,' the teacher replied. 'As you can see, he's taken to those picture cards and likes arranging and rearranging them. When we have put the actual objects in front of him he's started to make the connection with some of the pictures, which is terrific. I'll show you later. I think there's a greater level of understanding lately.'

'That's good to hear,' said Elisabeth.

'I think John is making slow but significant progress,' he said, sounding like a teacher on parents' consultation evening. 'As you know, he's certainly content and settled, but like many of the autistic children here he still seems to be happy in his own world. He's always been a quiet, gentle-natured lad, no trouble at all and a pleasure to teach. Some of the children do have outbursts, but apart from that one time last term John's been fine.'

Elisabeth thought for a moment of the unhappy, angry little boy who had just started at her school. Robbie was quite the opposite. However was she to deal with that temperamental and unpredictable child?

'You know, the more I read about autism and work with these children,' Mr Campsmount was saying, 'the more intrigued I become. It's such a complex and confusing condition.' It was clear to him Elisabeth wasn't listening. She was looking pensively out of the classroom window. 'Mrs Devine?'

'I'm sorry,' said Elisabeth, emerging from her thoughts, 'I was thinking of a child who has just started at my school. He has some special needs but rather different ones from John's.'

'We all have some sort of special need, Mrs Devine,' said the young teacher. He shook his head. 'Sorry, I must sound like one of my tutors at college.'

Elisabeth smiled. 'You like your job, don't you, Mr Campsmount?' she asked.

'I love it,' he replied, his eyes shining with enthusiasm. 'I've always wanted to teach. It's the best job in the world. Good teachers change lives. I would never teach any other kind of children but those with special needs. They are special in more ways than one.'

'And the teachers are rather special too,' added Elisabeth.

'We try our best,' said the teacher.

'Thank you for all you are doing for John,' she said. There was a slight tremble in her voice. She could feel tears springing up behind his eyes. 'He's so happy here.'

The young man coughed self-consciously. 'You know that this son of yours caused me quite a bit of embarrassment lately,' he said cheerfully.

Elisabeth reached into her handbag for a handkerchief and then blew her nose. 'Really?' she sniffed.

'I took John out for a walk to the local park last week. As you know, he loves water and I thought we'd go down by the lake. It was a bit wet and windy – the sort of weather he loves. I was holding his hand as usual, because he does tend to run off if I don't. Anyway, he suddenly starts jumping in the puddles with me in tow. We both got soaking wet. It was like a scene from that film where the man splashes in the puddles and starts singing in the rain. You can imagine the strange looks we were getting from people out walking their dogs. I think John would have leapt in the lake if I had let him.'

They both began to laugh.

John stopped staring at the cards at the sound of their laughter and began laughing too.

'I think he understands a whole lot more than we credit him for,' said the teacher.

On her way out Elisabeth turned in the corridor and came face-to-face with a frightening-looking character. He was a short, heavily built individual with a bullet-shaped bald head and a neck as thick as a pit bull terrier's. On the curiously flat face were a crooked misshapen nose and a vicious-looking scar above one eyebrow. The large ears looked red and swollen. The man reminded Elisabeth of Magwitch, in the novel *Great Expectations* by Charles Dickens, the escaped convict who terrifies the young Pip in the churchyard.

'Mrs Devine,' he said in a deep, resonant Welsh voice.

'Yes,' replied Elisabeth tentatively.

'I'm Owen Pugh,' he said.

'Do I know you, Mr Pugh?' asked Elisabeth.

'No, but you know my wife Bronwyn,' he replied. 'She's a cleaner at your school.'

'Oh yes, of course, Mrs Pugh.'

The man held out a hand as big as a spade. Elisabeth shook

it. 'I'm pleased to meet you, Mrs Devine,' he said. 'I've heard a lot about you.'

'Good things, I hope.'

'Oh yes, all good,' he told her, smiling and showing a set of tombstone teeth. 'I wanted to have a word with you before you left. Bronwyn is very happy working at Barton-in-the-Dale.'

'I'm pleased to hear it,' said Elisabeth.

'Oh yes, very contented she is. She's hoping that when this amalgamation takes place she'll be able to work at your school permanent like. You see, she's not that happy at Urebank. She's not treated right, see. The headmaster's a funny bugger and the staff never speak to her. Caretaker down there doesn't appreciate what she does. She's not allowed in the staff-room at Urebank except to clean it. She has to have her coffee in a classroom when she has a break. She says it's different down at Barton. She's appreciated and made to feel like a member of staff.'

'Well, she is a member of staff, Mr Pugh,' Elisabeth told him. 'Everyone at Barton, whether they are teachers, secretaries, caretakers or cleaners is a member of staff.'

'That's what my Bronwyn says. If you speak to Mr Gibbon—'

'It's Gribbon actually,' Elisabeth told him.

'Well, if you speak to him I think you'll find that he is very satisfied with her work.'

'He has already told me so,' said Elisabeth.

'Well, is it possible for her to work at Barton full-time when this amalgamation takes place?'

'It's not really up to me,' Elisabeth answered. 'That will be in the hands of those at the Education Department who deal with the appointment of school cleaners, but I shall certainly put in a good word for your wife.'

'Thank you very much, Mrs Devine,' he said. 'By the way,

your son is a grand young man. I sometimes take some of the boys down to the Miners' Welfare Club. Your John likes to come with me. He's become quite a favourite with the lads down there.'

'He comes with you to the Miners'Welfare?' said Elisabeth, unable to disguise the surprise in her voice.

'Oh, he doesn't drink,' the man told her. 'Just a lemonade. He's no trouble at all. I hope you don't mind him coming with me.'

'Not at all, Mr Pugh,' replied Elisabeth, thinking there were quite a few things she did not know about her son.

Elisabeth called in to see the head teacher of Forest View before heading off home. Mr Williams greeted her with his usual warmth.

'Good morning, Elisabeth,' he said genially as he ushered her into his office and to a chair by his desk. 'Mr Campsmount had a word with me about John just before you arrived. I guess he told you how very pleased we are with how he's getting on.'

'Yes, he did,' she replied. 'Mr Campsmount is an excellent teacher, isn't he?'

'He is,' agreed Mr Williams. 'Very enthusiastic and committed. I only hope I can keep him. Teachers of his calibre tend to get promoted quickly. I should be very sorry to lose him. Mind you, I don't think he's ready to move yet. He's not been in the job long.'

'I also had a word with Mr Pugh,' said Elisabeth.

'Oh, you've met Owen, have you? He's quite a character, isn't he? He's a very valuable member of our staff here,' Mr Williams told her.

'What exactly is his role?' she asked.

'He's a classroom assistant.'

'Really?'

'That's right. Some of our students do have outbursts from

time to time and can be violent and need restraining. If their routine is interrupted or something makes them feel uncomfortable or distressed, it might be quite trivial, they can flare up. It doesn't happen often, but when it does they can hurt themselves and others too. We have quite a few big strapping lads here so we need someone like Owen to hold them for a moment until they calm down. He's become very skilled at it.'

The head teacher leaned back in his chair. 'Owen worked down the mines for many years before moving up north with his wife. I got to know him when he joined the male voice choir. He's a wonderful bass. You should hear him sing solo. His "Myfanwy" brings tears to your eyes, it does.'

'He looks as if he's been in the wars,' remarked Elisabeth.

'Rugby,' Mr Williams told her. 'He played number three prop forward in a valley side back in Wales. Five foot ten of muscle. I'm afraid in that position you have to expect a few clashed heads, cut lips and split eyebrows. I believe he was known as "the no-neck monster". I guess he was quite fearless and fearsome on the pitch. He told me once he was up before the disciplinary committee for punching a player from the opposing side when they were in the scrum. This player played dirty and sank his teeth into Owen's injured ear. I should imagine it was a vicious upper cut and the recipient was carried off on a stretcher. I wouldn't like to fall out with Owen Pugh.'

'Is this supposed to reassure me?' asked Elisabeth, chuckling.

'Oh, Owen is a good-hearted sort,' Mr Williams told her. 'He does have a bit of a short fuse but with our students he's as gentle as a lamb.'

'I'm very glad to hear it,' said Elisabeth.

'On one occasion he was accompanying the teachers and some of the pupils to the Wildlife Park near Ruston,' Mr Williams said, smiling widely. 'A group of lads were making fun and laughing at our students, mimicking the sounds they made and pulling faces. Owen went over to have a quiet word and persuaded them to desist. It took quite an effort for the biggest of the lads to get out of the litter bin where he had been deposited.'

The following Tuesday morning Robbie arrived at Elisabeth's classroom with a cut lip and a bruised cheek. He stood boldly at the front next to the teacher's desk with his hands thrust deeply in his pockets and his small shoulders hunched. His face was as hard as flint. The children in the upper juniors regarded him suspiciously.

'That teacher I was with when I started here,' he told Elisabeth sullenly.

'Her name is Mrs Robertshaw,' she told him.

'Yeah, her, well she's told me I have to move into your class.'

'That's right.'

'Why?'

'Because we feel it would be better if you stayed with me for the time being.'

'Why?'

'Because Mrs Robertshaw and I think it would be for the best.'

'Why?'

Elisabeth was aware that her pupils were watching her, intently interested to see how she would react to this odd, ill-mannered little boy. She turned to face them. 'For the first part of the morning we have silent reading,' she told them in a serious tone of voice, 'and silent reading means just that: the classroom is silent, noiseless. I do not want to hear a sound.' She turned to the boy. 'I would like to have a word with you outside please, Robbie,' she told him. Her voice was almost a whisper.

In the corridor Robbie stared up at her, his sharp, foxy face devoid of any expression.

'Robbie,' she said calmly, 'do try and be a bit better-mannered. You make it very difficult for yourself and for others by being rude. I would appreciate it if you didn't reply in that tone of voice and I would like you to call me "miss" when you speak to me.'

The boy shrugged.

'So would you like to tell me how you came by a cut lip and the bruise on your face?' she asked.

'It's nothing,' he replied in an offhand tone and then added, 'miss'.

'Clearly something has happened,' Elisabeth said, resting a hand on the boy's arm. 'Now come along, Robbie.' He looked at her hand for a moment and then pulled his arm away. 'You don't get a cut lip and a bruised face by doing nothing.'

'I can't remember,' he told her.

'Did this happen at home?' she asked.

Robbie looked startled. 'No.'

'Who did this to you?' she asked. 'Have you been in a fight?'

The boy shrugged again. He remained stubbornly silent.

'You have a cut lip and a bruised face and you cannot remember how it happened?'

'No . . . miss.'

'You don't want to tell me, do you?'

'I told you, I can't remember,' he repeated. His small mouth was puckered.

'All right, Robbie,' said Elisabeth. 'At morning break I would like you to remain in the classroom and I want you to have a little think about it. Someone has done this to you and I need to know who it was.' She touched his arm again. 'I am here to help you.'

The boy regarded her impassively but made no reply. He maintained his proud, stony silence.

That morning Robbie, sitting apart from the other children, found a book which seemed to interest him and sat quietly.

Elisabeth, watching the sad little figure, wondered just what was going through the boy's mind. She had found his truculent attitude and reticence exasperating but the child was clearly very unhappy and in some distress. She would have to remain calm and patient.

At break time, when the other children had left the room, Elisabeth approached Robbie. He looked up from his book.

'So, has your memory returned then, Robbie?' she asked softly.

The boy shook his head.

'You know,' she said, 'I can't help you unless you tell me what happened.'

The boy mumbled something deliberately too low for Elisabeth to hear.

'What did you say?' she asked sharply.

'Who said I wanted any help?' he replied angrily. His eyes flashed. 'I don't want any help.'

'I'll ask you again, did this happen at home?'

The boy's mouth remained a tight thin line.

'Robbie,' said Elisabeth. 'Did someone do this to you at home?'

'No!' he replied. 'How many more times do I have to tell you?'

Elisabeth decided not to pursue the matter for the moment but would discuss the situation with Mrs Goldstein when she called into school later that afternoon. For the rest of the morning the boy sat in moody silence.

At the end of the school day as she tidied up the classroom Elisabeth noticed one of her pupils hovering outside in the corridor. He was a large-boned individual with tightly curled hair and prominent front teeth. Eventually he entered the room and approached the teacher's desk.

'Did you want to see me, Malcolm?' asked Elisabeth.

The boy shuffled his feet and looked down sheepishly. 'I thought you'd want to see *me*, miss,' he mumbled.

'And why would I want to see you?' she asked.

'About what happened yesterday after school, miss,' he replied, looking up.

'I'm afraid you've lost me.'

'That new kid. Didn't he tell you what happened?'

'About what?' asked Elisabeth.

'How he came by his split lip,' replied the boy.

'No,' replied Elisabeth. 'Robbie didn't say a word. He wouldn't tell me, but I guess you can.'

'I smacked him one, miss,' admitted the boy.

'Oh dear,' sighed Elisabeth, her face clouding.

'He was asking for it, miss!' cried Malcolm. 'He really was.'

'You know how I feel about violence!' Elisabeth said sternly and raising her voice. 'I will not have it in this school.'

The boy looked down mulishly at his feet again.

'I am very disappointed in you, young man. Last term you made really good progress, you got on with your work, you stayed out of trouble and there was no fighting or bullying.'

'I know, miss, but—' started the boy.

'Let me finish!' snapped Elisabeth. 'As I explained to your mother when she urged me to have you back here at Barton after you were expelled from Urebank, I will not tolerate bad behaviour, and I said that if you stepped out of line you would find yourself asked to leave.'

'I know, miss,' sniffed the boy. His bottom lip began to tremble and his eyes filled with tears.

'For goodness sake, Malcolm, Robbie is half your size and he's new to the school. You know how unhappy you were as the new boy at Urebank being picked on by the other pupils. You of all people know how upsetting it can be starting at a new school.'

The boy began to cry in earnest and rubbed his eyes with

his fists. 'I don't want to leave, miss. Don't send me to another school.'

'Why did you hit Robbie?'

'He was asking for it, miss,' explained Malcolm. 'You can ask anybody. He's round the bend, that kid. He's got a screw loose, he really has.'

'So what made you hit him?' asked Elisabeth.

The boy wiped his nose on the back of his hand. 'After school yesterday he started calling people names for no reason.'

'Sticks and stones, Malcolm,' interrupted Elisabeth.

'I know, but he wound me up. You asked me to look after any new pupils, keep an eye on them like, to make sure they weren't picked on like what I was when I was at Urebank.'

'I did, and you were doing a good job, Malcolm,' Elisabeth told him. 'Up until now, that is.'

'Anyway, miss, I tried to be friendly like and he told me to "Bugger off!" and when Chardonnay said he shouldn't swear he called her a fat cow and when I told him to watch it he started on me and called me a rabbit-faced twat and then—'

'I don't need to hear all that he said, thank you Malcolm,' cut in Elisabeth. 'I've got the idea.'

'Anyway, I told him to shut up or he'd get a good hiding but he just stared at me and kept on. Then he kicked me.' Malcolm bent down and rolled up his trouser leg to show the bruise on his shin. 'So I slapped him.'

'You could have really hurt him,' said Elisabeth, 'a boy of your size and strength.'

'I know, miss,' Malcolm replied. 'I'm sorry.'

'Hitting someone is not the answer. Violence never solves a problem, and I will not have children hitting others in this school. Do you understand, Malcolm?'

'Yes, miss,' said the boy miserably.

'Well, off you go,' Elisabeth told him. 'I shall have to think about what to do with you.'

The boy stood in front of the teacher's desk as if rooted to the spot.

'Was there something else, Malcolm?' asked Elisabeth.

'Yes, miss,' he replied.

'Well?'

'Miss, can I still play in the football team next Saturday?' he pleaded.

4

The appointment with the Director of Education to discuss the forthcoming amalgamation of the two schools had been arranged for five o'clock so, on the sound of the bell signalling the end of school, Elisabeth set off for the city to make sure she was not late for the important meeting.

County Hall was a huge, grey stone mansion of an edifice, built to last. It stood proud, like many a Yorkshire town hall, sturdy and imposing and dominating the centre of Clayton, and was equalled only by the great pale stone cathedral. Built in the late nineteenth century when Clayton flourished as an important mill town, County Hall, with its impressive pillars and decorative porticos, exuded wealth and self-importance. It stood in stark contrast to the crumbling concrete civic buildings of the sixties which disfigured some neighbouring towns. Surrounding County Hall were formal gardens with carefully tended lawns, box hedges, symmetrical herbaceous borders and neat gravelled footpaths.

Elisabeth arrived in good time, so she thought she would get a breath of fresh air and after a short walk along the gravel paths sat down on a bench overlooking the gardens. A young man with a shaven head and an assortment of silver rings and studs in his ears, sporting a brightly coloured tattooed snake which twisted around his neck, approached. He was pushing a barrow-load of hedge clippings.

'Champion day,' he said.

'It is,' agreed Elisabeth. 'It's a lovely time of year. The gardens look magnificent, by the way.'

The youth coloured a little and stopped in front of her. 'Well, I does mi best.'

'It's a pleasant job, I guess, working outdoors?'

The young man laughed. 'Aye, it is. Beats bein' inside.'

'I wish I could get my lawn to look like that,' she said, pointing to the dark green expanse of grass cut as close as velvet.

'It needs feedin' and careful nursin' to gerrit like that,' the youth told her. 'Prevention's better than a cure, tha knaas. Yer lawn needs to be fed at t'right time wi' right fungicides otherwise tha'll get red thread and moss. An' when tha cuts it, mek sure your mower cuts it to t'right length.'

'I see,' said Elisabeth. 'My garden is plagued with rabbits. They seem to eat every plant I've put in.'

'Well, now,' said the youth, parking the wheelbarrow, 'yer can get what's called rabbit-resistant plants – red hot pokers, sunflowers, tulips, Michaelmas daisies, violets, snapdragons. There's 'undreds of 'em.'

'I ought to take notes,' said Elisabeth, laughing. 'You're a mine of information.'

'I do know a bit about plants,' said the young man. 'Mi granddad 'ad an allotment an' I 'elped 'im at weekends.'

'Well, if I need any more advice, I shall know where to come.'

''Appen I'll not be 'ere much longer,' he said.

'Why is that?' asked Elisabeth.

He thought for a moment. 'I'm on community service, yer see. Got into a spot a bother. I reckon I struck lucky being given this job. I could 'ave been pickin' up litter and sweepin' roads wi' all mi mates laughin' at me. I'd like to do this fulltime but it's only temporary. They're not likely to tek me on permanent what wi' me havin' a record an' that.'

'You never know,' said Elisabeth. 'You're making a really good job of the gardens. I am sure they're very impressed with what you are doing.'

'Are you one of the councillors then?' asked the youth.

'No, no. I'm here for a meeting,' she told him.

'I were just thinkin' like, that if you was, then you could put a good word in for me.'

'I wish I could,' Elisabeth replied.

'No sweat,' he said. 'It's been nice talkin' to you.'

The youth raised the wheelbarrow and got on with his work.

The interior of County Hall was like a deserted museum, silent and cool, with seemingly endless echoing oak-panelled corridors, high ornate ceilings, marble figures and busts, long leather-covered benches and highly polished doors. Covering the walls were huge framed portraits in oils of former councillors, mayors, aldermen, leaders of the Council, high sheriffs, lord lieutenants, Members of Parliament and other dignitaries, all of whom stared down self-importantly from their gilded frames. It was a gloomy and intimidating place.

Elisabeth was shown into Ms Tricklebank's office.

'The Director of Education will be with you shortly, Mrs Devine,' said the secretary. 'Could I get you a cup of tea?'

'No thank you,' replied Elisabeth. She was feeling rather nervous.

The room was large and impressive. A huge solid mahogany desk inlaid with an olive-green rectangle of leather dominated the centre. Tall glass-fronted bookcases lined one wall, and framed pictures and prints drawn and painted by the county's children and students were displayed on the other. Opposite the bookcases a huge window gave an uninterrupted view over Clayton, busy and bustling with afternoon traffic. Elisabeth stared out of the window, thoughts about what she would say, questions she would like to ask and projects she hoped to get support in implementing running through her head.

She was soon joined by the Director of Education. Ms Tricklebank was a dumpy, rosy-faced woman with grey appraising eyes. She had seemed to Elisabeth on first meeting her the previous term to be rather stern and forbidding, a person of strong views but few words. Ms Tricklebank had proved, however, to be a perceptive and highly competent woman for whom Elisabeth had a great deal of respect. She had visited both Barton and Urebank schools as the senior education officer before her promotion and had sat on the interview panel for the head teacher's position for the new school, so she was fully aware of the potential problems which might arise. The situation would need all her tact and diplomacy.

'Good afternoon, Mrs Devine,' Ms Tricklebank said in a brisk business-like manner. 'Thank you for coming.' Rather than sitting behind her desk as her predecessor had been in the habit of doing, she pulled up a chair to sit next to Elisabeth and shook her hand. 'I know how busy things must be in school at the start of term, but I felt it was important to see you early on and get things sorted.' She glanced at a delicate watercolour painting of a stone barn and a millpond which had pride of place on a wall. 'The work of one of your pupils, I think,' she said.

'Yes,' replied Elisabeth. 'Ernest has quite a flair for art. He came second in the County Art Competition last year with that painting.'

'It's very good,' said the Director of Education. 'And I believe you have quite a few gifted children at Barton. I had a very complimentary letter from the Methodist minister in the village saying that one of your pupils has a fine singing voice and is a regular participant at his services.'

'That would be Chardonnay,' said Elisabeth. 'She has a talent.'

'And you also have a future chess champion?'

'Oscar. Yes, he's quite a character.'

Ms Tricklebank rested her hands in her lap. 'I think you too have quite a talent, Mrs Devine – for bringing out the very best in children.'

'I don't know about that,' replied Elisabeth, rather embarrassed by the compliment.

'Every child should reach his or her potential,' continued the Director of Education, 'and the good teacher discovers a talent which can often lie dormant.'

'I agree.'

'And how is your son getting on at Forest View?'

This woman had certainly done her homework, thought Elisabeth.

'Very well,' she replied. 'It is an outstanding school and John's very happy there. I was so relieved when the Education Committee reprieved Forest View. I believe it was in line for closure.'

'It was,' said the Director of Education simply. Ms Tricklebank had fought a long and hard battle behind the scenes with her predecessor and with the councillors who had been intent on making cuts in the education budget.

'The reason I wanted to teach in Barton,' Elisabeth told her, 'was so I could be near my son.'

'Yes, I was aware of that,' said the Director of Education. 'It's good to hear you are well-satisfied with the school. I have a great deal of time for Mr Williams. He is one of the world's enthusiasts.'

'He is,' agreed Elisabeth.

'So, let's talk about the amalgamation. It's going to be an interesting time for you and your staff.'

Elisabeth smiled. 'Yes indeed, very interesting,' she replied.

'I do not underestimate the difficulties you might encounter,' continued the Director of Education, 'but I have every confidence that you will rise to the challenge.'

'I hope so,' replied Elisabeth.

'Of course you will. There is no one in the county better suited to take on this job.'

'I have to say I am rather anxious about working with Mr Richardson,' admitted Elisabeth. 'He's obviously very disappointed that he didn't get the head teacher's position and relations with him in the past have not been very good.' When the Director of Education didn't reply, Elisabeth continued. 'And I don't think he's very happy about having to work with me.'

Ms Tricklebank knew that this was an understatement. The man in question was angry and bitter. He had requested a meeting with her the day following the interview for the headship. He had been 'greatly aggrieved', as he termed it, and 'astounded' that he, 'a very experienced and well-respected head teacher who has worked in the county my entire teaching career', had not been offered the post of head teacher in the new consortium. The Director of Education had explained to him that it was the governors' decision to whom the post should be offered. She was there merely to advise. She could have told him that his interview had been mediocre, his answers sketchy and his manner condescending. She could have told him that the governors' decision to appoint Mrs Devine had been unanimous and she had agreed fully with it. She could have told him that when she spent a day at Urebank she had been less than impressed with his leadership and management, and could have referred to the school inspector's report, which judged the school to be in need of improvement in several important areas. But she judiciously resisted doing so, thinking it would serve little purpose to add fuel to the flames.

It had come as a great blow to him, Mr Richardson had continued. However, he hoped that when a suitable position next arose for a head teacher in another school in the county, he could be redeployed there. Ms Tricklebank had been blunt and told him that again it would be for the governors to decide who would be offered such a post. He could of course apply but there was no guarantee that he would be successful. Mr Richardson had left the meeting feeling he had been treated shabbily. No, the Director of Education thought, Mrs Devine would have a difficult time ahead of her.

'I should imagine,' said Elisabeth now, 'that Mr Richardson will be looking for another position?'

'Perhaps,' replied Ms Tricklebank non-committally. On this occasion she decided to be circumspect. 'Now, I have asked Mr Nettles, one of the education officers, to join us. I believe you know him. He was the representative of the local author-ity on the governing body at Barton, wasn't he?'

'He was,' replied Elisabeth, recalling how evasive and inef-fectual the man had been. Each time she had telephoned his office at County Hall for some advice or clarification, she had been informed by his snappish clerical assistant that he was 'tied up'. Mrs Scrimshaw, on being told this for the umpteenth time, remarked derisively that 'they want to tie him up permanently'. She had gone on to declare that he was 'about as much use as a chocolate fireguard'. When the school secretary had heard that he had been moved from organising school transport to managing the school meals' service, she predicted, rightly as it turned out, that he would 'make a pig's ear of that'.

'I have asked Mr Nettles to be involved in the amalgama-tion and ensure that things run smoothly. He will liaise between us and be on call for any problems which might arise.' Elisabeth gave her colleague a weak smile which wasn't lost on the Director of Education.

'I shall, of course, keep a close eye on things myself,' reas-sured Ms Tricklebank. She could have told Elisabeth that she was less than happy with Mr Nettles's performance. He was a man with an inflated idea of his own capacities and blessed with the ability to appear to be very busy whilst actually avoiding much of the work for which he was responsible. In his present position of organising the school meals he had proved heavy-handed and inept. Perhaps, she thought, he might be more successful in this new role.

Elisabeth felt inclined to object to Mr Nettles's involvement but did not wish to be negative at so early a stage, so she merely replied, 'I see.'

There was a tap at the door.

'Enter!' shouted the Director of Education.

Mr Nettles appeared, smiling inanely.

The Venerable Archdeacon Atticus wandered amongst the tombstones in the churchyard, his long white hands clasped behind his back and an expression of melancholy on his thin-boned face. Despite the brightness of the morning and the joyful twittering of the birds in the trees, he was in a sombre mood, for he had much on his mind. Had it been at all wise of him to accept the bishop's request that he should become the Archdeacon of Clayton, he mused. There was so much to do, so many problems he was expected to sort out, so many difficult people with whom he had to deal. A gentle-natured, contemplative and easy-going man, he had been perfectly happy as a country priest with a small but dedicated flock and a relatively quiet, stress-free life. Perhaps his wife had been right when she told him he would be 'like a fish out of water' as the Archdeacon.

'You will have to deal with all the tiresome administration, petty arguments and disputes about one thing and another,' Marcia, his wife, had declared when he had broached the matter of his preferment with her. She had recalled how the pressures and tensions of being an archdeacon had taken their toll on her poor father. 'He had to implement all these unpalatable diocesan policies,' she had lamented, 'sort out the buildings, inspect the churches and deal with all the problems the bishop pushed his way. It was most stressful for him.'

Yet it had been his wife who had for many years complained about her husband's lack of ambition and how he had been 'passed over' for advancement within the Church, remaining a mere country parson while others less deserving had climbed the ecclesiastical ladder, leaving him on the bottom rung. It was only when she had secured a place at St John's College to train as a teacher, with her teaching practice conveniently arranged to be at the village school, that she had changed her mind and was quite content to stay at the rectory.

The Archdeacon continued to amble about the churchyard glancing at the headstones, some dangerously tilted, others broken, many clothed in thick ivy. He stared for a moment at the dead flowers arranged in jam jars and the garish plastic bouquets. His disposition hardly improved as he came across the pale and heavily weathered sandstone tablet on which a large skull had been carved. He particularly disliked this deeply disheartening memorial. As he read, not for the first time, the ornate lettering inscribed below the skull, he sighed heavily and considered his own mortality.

> Traveller behold as ye pass by,
> As you are now, so once was I.
> As I am now, so shall ye be.
> So be prepared to follow me.
>
> Josiah Titus Sowerbutts
> Born 1805
> Died 1889

He moved on to the newest addition to the churchyard, the grave of Albert Fish. It was a rather elaborate white marble gravestone with a somewhat overly sentimental inscription:

> If love could build a stairway,
> And tears could build a lane,
> I'd walk right up to heaven's gates
> And take you home again.

He could not imagine Marcia selecting such a verse for his memorial stone when his time came. Under the yew tree the Archdeacon came upon a carefully tended grave with a small, shiny black granite headstone. 'Les Stainthorpe, dearly loved grandfather,' it said simply. The cleric smiled ruefully. That is the sort of dedication I would want, he thought, something simple and unpretentious.

The Archdeacon rarely visited the churchyard these days. Since his elevation from a country parson to the Archdeacon, with his office in the nearby cathedral city of Clayton, he had delegated many of his parochial duties to his new young curate, the Reverend Dr Ashley Underwood, a young woman who had proved to be invaluable. Not only was she highly intelligent, dedicated and personable, she had willingly taken on many of the household tasks previously undertaken by Mrs Atticus. His new curate had proved to be an excellent cook. It had to be said that the Archdeacon's wife could not be considered imaginative, gastronomically speaking. Indeed her offerings at the table were frequently quite unpalatable. He still recalled his night of virulent stomach-ache after tackling one of her rubbery rissoles. With the arrival of Ashley, the Archdeacon had enjoyed sumptuous fare.

His mouth watered at the memory of the previous night's splendid dinner of grilled scallops with tomato and garlic, followed by breadcrumbed escalope of veal with lemon and a crisp Caesar salad, and a golden syrup sponge with thick custard to finish. He wondered what lay in store for him that night. Perhaps she might cook his favourite: rump of lamb in a tomato and basil sauce with mango cheesecake to follow. He cheered up at the thought.

His reverie was interrupted when a ruddy-complexioned figure in a greasy cap and dressed in soiled blue overalls shouted from the lych-gate.

'Now then, your reverence, can I have a word?'

The Archdeacon turned. 'Ah, Mr Massey. The very man. I am pleased to see you at long last.' As the farmer approached he continued, 'I guess you have come about the tomb.'

'The tomb?'

'Well, the remains of it at least,' said the Archdeacon, indicating a mound of rubble in the centre of the churchyard. 'You will recall after you cut down the large dead branch of the oak tree and it demolished the tomb—'

'Course I recall!' cried the farmer. 'I nearly broke my bloody neck – pardon my French – in doing it. I was hospitalised.'

'Yes, yes, your accident was most unfortunate,' said the cleric impatiently. 'Now you did agree, if I am not mistaken, to return to clear away the wreckage. That was some time ago.'

The tomb in question, which now lay in ruins, had once dwarfed every other memorial in the churchyard. The great white marble monstrosity had been erected by one of the Archdeacon's nineteenth-century predecessors, the notorious Dean Joseph Steerum-Slack. Mrs Atticus, who hated the ostentatious mausoleum and was quite delighted to see its demise, was very keen that the remains be removed.

'Oh yes,' said Mr Massey now, 'I do recall saying I would clear the debris away.' He rubbed the stubble on his chin and sucked his teeth. 'But you see the thing is, vicar, I'm on my own now, what with my dozy nephew up and leaving me to set up with that Bianca lass in Clayton. I did ask our Clarence to do it. Course, I'd do it myself, but my foot's not been right since I got it stuck in the sugar beet cutter and I'm still receiving treatment from the fall from the tree when I cut down that dead branch.'

The Archdeacon sighed irritably. 'Be that as it may, Mr Massey, you did assure me you would expedite the removal of the remains of the tomb so that we are able to make the churchyard look less like a building site. So, when can I expect you to deal with the matter?'

'I'll get on to it, vicar,' replied the farmer. 'Don't you worry. Now, it wasn't the tomb what I was wanting to talk to you about. It's more of a personal matter.'

'I see. Well, perhaps you might feel more comfortable in the rectory,' the Archdeacon told him.

'No, no, it's nothing like that,' replied Mr Massey. 'I was wondering who owns that bit of track what leads down the side of St Christopher's to my field.'

'It belongs to the Church,' the Archdeacon told him.

'I thought so. It's not a public right of way then?'

'No, it's part of the rectory land.'

Mr Massey rubbed his chin and looked thoughtful. 'I see,' he murmured.

'Now you don't need to concern yourself about that, Mr Massey,' the Archdeacon told him. 'I am aware that you take your cows down that track to graze on your field. I have no intention of preventing you from doing so in future. I can assure you of that.'

'No, it's not that, vicar. It's just that I'm minded to buy it off of you.'

'And why would you want to do that, Mr Massey?'

'Well, between you, me and the gatepost, I've applied for outline planning permission to have three houses built on yon field but I need access. That track of yours leads straight to where the houses would be, so I'd like to buy that bit of land. Take it off of your hands so to speak. I mean it's not going nowhere bar my field, and nobody uses it any more except for me, and it's full of weeds and bushes. I'll make you a fair offer.'

'It is not my track, Mr Massey,' explained the Archdeacon. 'I do not own it. As I have said, it belongs to the Church.'

'That's as may be, vicar,' replied the farmer, 'but sometimes bits of unused land and run-down churches are sold off, aren't they?'

'Well—' began the Archdeacon.

'Now if you were to sell that track to me,' said the farmer, 'you'd get a bit of money and you could repair your church roof and tart up the rectory.'

'Indeed there have been some occasions when Church land and property have been disposed of,' he was told, 'but only in exceptional circumstances.'

'Well, this is exceptional, isn't it?'

'Hardly.'

'People have to live somewhere, vicar,' persevered the farmer, 'and there's a shortage of properties in the village. It seems to me it's a bit mean-minded to stop the building of a few houses so people can have a roof over their heads.'

This was rather ripe coming from the most tight-fisted and least charitable person in the village, thought the Archdeacon. The man had never consciously done good for anybody.

'I'm sorry, Mr Massey,' said the clergyman, shaking his head, 'I am afraid I cannot be of any help. I am not against the building of houses in the village *per se*, but I must reiterate that the land is not for sale.'

'Not for sale?'

'That is what I said.'

'Well, in that case I shall have to take it to a higher authority then and see what he has to say,' said the farmer.

'Mr Massey,' the Archdeacon told him firmly. 'It would be

fruitless to pursue the matter, and I will say again, the land is not for sale.'

'Who is the person who deals with things like this?' asked the farmer. 'I shall go and see him.'

'The clergyman who deals with such matters,' he was told, 'is the Archdeacon of Clayton.'

'And who's that?'

'You are speaking to him.'

'You!' exclaimed the farmer.

'Indeed, and, although I can recommend the transfer of ownership of a particular Church building or a piece of land, it is, at the end of the day, not in my gift to dispose of it. The Church Commissioners manage the Church of England's estates and I am certain they would not be predisposed to sell the track.'

'Well, I'm not letting it lie, vicar,' the farmer protested. 'I shall take it to the Pope in Rome if I have to.'

As Mr Massey stomped off huffing and shaking his head angrily, Mrs Atticus emerged from the rectory. She was carrying a parcel. 'I'm just popping down to the post office, Charles,' she said, inclining her head for a kiss. 'I am sending in my final dissertation today.'

'Congratulations, my dear,' said the Archdeacon, pecking her cheek and saying a silent prayer of thanks that the thesis his wife had spent hours writing was finally completed. Perhaps now, he thought, I can have my study back.

'Was that Mr Massey I just saw?' his wife asked, staring at the departing figure who was shambling off down the road.

'It was, my dear,' he replied.

'Has he finally decided to remove the remains of that eyesore?' she asked.

'Sadly no,' she was told. 'He came to see if he could purchase the strip of land beside the church. He wishes to have some houses built on his field and needs access.'

Mrs Atticus made a noise like a snort. 'I hope you told him—' she began.

The Archdeacon raised a hand as if about to bless a congregation, 'I told him there was no question of selling the land.'

'I should think so. And you might have a word with him about those cows that he takes down that track. They are extremely smelly and make a great deal of noise.'

'Yes, my dear. I will have a word with him,' replied her husband, breathing out noisily.

'And when will he stir himself to remove the remains of the tomb?' asked Mrs Atticus.

'I think after our recent conversation I fear this is the last we will see of Mr Massey.'

'This is most unacceptable, Charles, it really is,' she said with something of her usual sharpness. 'You will just have to get someone else to do it.'

Life was quite difficult enough, thought the Archdeacon, without Marcia adding another problem to his already long list, but, as in most discussions with his wife, he felt it prudent to agree. 'Yes of course, my dear,' he replied.

'And you will get on to it immediately?'

'I will,' agreed her husband.

'When it is cleared away, I intend to plant a tree,' she told him, 'possibly a robinia. It has the most wonderful golden leaves and will look very elegant in summer.'

'Perhaps if you do we might place a small plaque at the base,' suggested the Archdeacon, 'in memory of Dean Steerum-Slack. After all, it was his tomb that once occupied that spot.'

'I really don't think that is at all necessary, Charles,' she replied.

The Archdeacon sighed theatrically. He could think of no reply to make to this and none seemed to be expected.

'By the way, Ashley has left a note for you in your study,' said his wife. 'The other hospital chaplain, Father Daly, is on some sort of religious retreat, so she is covering for him this evening. I shall be making dinner and now I have finished writing my thesis I intend to take on my share of the cooking.'

The Archdeacon gave the thin, forced smile which he reserved for dealing with difficult parishioners. 'Splendid,' he said disingenuously.

'It's braised tripe tonight,' she told him.

5

Mrs Sloughthwaite, proprietor of the Barton-in-the-Dale village store and post office, leaned over the counter of her shop and rested her great bay window of a bust on the top. She was a larger-than-life character, a round, red-faced woman with a fleshy nose, pouchy cheeks and big inquisitive eyes. Her two customers that afternoon, a tall, gaunt woman with a pale, melancholy, beaked face and a dumpy, smiling individual with tightly permed hair the colour of copper-beech leaves, were listening to the latest snippet of gossip. Mrs Sloughthwaite was adept at gleaning tittle-tattle from those who patronised her shop. Initially she drew them out with a little tactful questioning, and should this prove unproductive she would then adopt a persistent inquisitorial approach. The information thus extracted was then circulated throughout the village. She knew everything that there was to know in Barton-in-the-Dale.

Mrs Atticus had been into the village store that morning to post her parcel and had mentioned to Mrs Sloughthwaite the plans Mr Massey had for selling one of his fields for the building of houses. The shopkeeper was relaying the juicy bit of news with great relish.

'And she told me he tried to buy that strip of land by the side of the church which leads to his field.'

'Whatever does he want that for?' asked Mrs Pocock, the thin-faced woman with the tragic expression. 'I thought you said he was selling, not buying.'

'Because he needs a means of access,' explained Mrs Sloughthwaite. 'It's no use building houses if you can't get to them. Anyway, Mrs Atticus told me her husband sent him away with a flea in his ear. There's no way that track will be sold, she said.'

'Well, I'm glad about that,' said Mrs Pocock, sniffing self-righteously. 'We don't want any more houses in the village. There are too many in-comers as it is.'

'People do have to live somewhere,' remarked Mrs O'Connor, the customer with the crimped red hair.

'But not in Barton,' said Mrs Pocock firmly.

'Mrs Atticus was sending this parcel by registered postage so it must have been something important,' revealed Mrs Sloughthwaite in a confidential tone of voice. 'It was addressed to St John's College in Clayton, so I guess it was some sort of work she's been doing. She's nearly finished training to be a teacher, you know. It's beyond my apprehension why at her time of life she wants to take that on, and what with the behaviour of youngsters these days, I certainly wouldn't want to do it.'

'No,' agreed Mrs Pocock, 'young people don't know they're born these days. Kids get away with murder, they do. It was a sad day when they got rid of the cane in schools. My husband was always bending over the headmaster's desk.'

'He was what!' exclaimed the shopkeeper.

'Bending over the desk to get six of the best,' explained Mrs Pocock, 'and it never did him any harm.'

It didn't do him any good either, mused Mrs Sloughthwaite, thinking of the lazy great lump of a man her customer was married to. He hadn't done a day's work in his life and spent most of his time in the pub playing darts or at the betting office. And as for their Ernest, that sullen-faced surly boy of theirs – like father like son. Feckless. Mrs Pocock wants to put her own house in order before she starts commenting on the behaviour of others, reflected the shopkeeper. She rested a dimpled elbow on the counter, and as if smiling at some private joke, kept her thoughts to herself.

'And from what my Ernest told me,' Mrs Pocock told them, 'they've got a right little delinquent started at the school.'

'Oh,' said Mrs Sloughthwaite, standing up and leaning further over the counter. This was interesting.

'Yes, a real little troublemaker by all accounts,' continued the customer. 'From what my Ernest told me, the lad's rude to the teachers he is, won't do his work and then he starts calling the other children names and the language he uses is unrepeat-able. Told that odd little boy with the coloured glasses to "Bugger off!" Would you credit it? He's not been long at the school and he's making his presence felt. He sits at the back of the classroom doing as little as possible, with a face that would turn milk sour.'

'Mrs Devine will soon sort him out,' said Mrs O'Connor. 'Sure she'll know how to deal with the likes of this child, so she will.'

'You're right there,' agreed the shopkeeper. 'She fettled that Malcolm Stubbins. He was a real tearaway until she took him in hand.'

'Well, he's in trouble again,' divulged Mrs Pocock with a small note of triumph in her voice.

'Is he?' asked the shopkeeper.

'Only went and smacked him one.'

'Who?'

'The new boy,' Mrs Pocock told her. 'He called Malcolm some name or other about him looking like a rabbit—'

'Well, it has to be said that the lad is very unfortunate-look-ing,' said the shopkeeper. 'I mean he could eat a tomato through a tennis racket with those teeth of his.'

'My Uncle Brendan had very prominent front teeth, so he

did,' observed Mrs O'Connor thoughtfully. 'They reckon it was because he played the tin whistle from an early age.'

'Excuse me!' cried Mrs Pocock, peeved at being interrupted. 'I haven't finished telling you what happened. As I was saying, he called the Stubbins lad a name and ended up with a split lip and a lump on his head the size of a pullet egg. My Ernest reckons Mrs Devine will expel the both of them and a good thing too. She comes down heavy on fighting.'

Mrs Sloughthwaite, wearying with this conversation and Mrs Pocock's strident voice, turned to Mrs O'Connor wishing to move on to more interesting material. 'And speaking of Mrs Devine,' she said, deftly changing the subject so she could begin her interrogation of the doctor's housekeeper, 'has she named the day yet, Mrs O'Connor?'

'Oh, she's not likely to discuss her wedding plans with me,' replied her customer, being deliberately evasive. She knew Mrs Sloughthwaite's tactics of old and only told her what she wanted her to hear.

'Hasn't Dr Stirling said anything then?'

'No, he's not a one for talking is the good doctor.'

'Well, you must have a bit of inside knowledge,' persisted the shopkeeper.

'All I know is that they intend to get wed some time later this year, so they do.'

'And will they have a church wedding, do you think?'

'I wouldn't think so,' Mrs Pocock butted in. 'I mean, she's a divorcee. I should think they'll probably have a blessing and I bet they hope that new young curate does it. I mean Reverend Atticus is a nice enough man but he could put a glass eye to sleep the way he goes on.'

'There must be something in the water,' observed Mrs Sloughthwaite, giving up on the cross-examination of the doctor's housekeeper. 'First Mrs Devine's getting married and then Miss Brakespeare, and now I hear that Joyce Fish's other granddaughter is to be wed.'

'Well, she'll get wed in the chapel,' declared Mrs Pocock.

'The other granddaughter's was at St Christopher's.'

'I mean Miss Brakespeare,' said Mrs Pocock. 'It will be in the chapel, what with her marrying the organist there and him being a Primitive Methodist as well. And there'll be no wine flowing at their wedding, you can be sure of that.'

'And what a turn-up for the book that was,' remarked Mrs Sloughthwaite. 'Fancy George Tomlinson marrying a little dumpy woman like Miss Brakespeare and his wife barely cold in the grave.'

The door opened and the subject of their conversation entered.

'Good morning,' said Miss Brakespeare cheerfully. 'Lovely day, isn't it?'

That afternoon Elisabeth was tidying up her garden with young Danny Stainthorpe. The boy was in his element out in the open, clipping the hedge and pruning the bushes, digging and planting. After a difficult few months for the boy, things had worked out well for him and he was now happy and settled.

Elisabeth had met Danny prior to her taking up the position of head teacher. With a view to moving into the village, she had been viewing a potential property and came upon Wisteria Cottage. As she stood on the tussocky lawn at the back gazing out at the view of open countryside, she knew this was where she wished to live.

A small boy with large low-set ears and the bright brown eyes of a fox had climbed over the gate in the paddock to speak to her. He was a country lad and Yorkshire through-and-through. Elisabeth had immediately taken to this friendly and confident young man of ten or eleven. She discovered that he lived with his grandfather in a caravan parked in the neighbouring field. His father had disappeared before he was born and his mother had been killed when he was a baby. He had been raised by his grandfather, and the boy and the old man had been inseparable. Soon after Elisabeth had started at the school the boy's grandfather had become ill, and after a brief spell in hospital he had died, leaving Danny alone and grief-stricken. Danny had become confused and anxious, not knowing what would become of him, and the once lively and sociable boy became withdrawn and miserable. However, things had turned out for the best when he had been fostered by Dr Stirling, who was now in the process of adopting the boy and rearing him along with his own son. Danny was now back to his old self, chatty and cheerful.

'I've been thinkin', miss,' said the boy, leaning on his spade and scratching a mop of dusty blond hair. 'When tha gets wed to Dr Stirling, what will I call ya?'

'What about Elisabeth?' she replied.

'Tha wouldn't mind?'

'Of course not.'

'I don't know abaat that,' said the boy uncertainly. 'I think I'd feel a bit awkward like, callin' ya Elisabeth.'

'And why is that?'

'I can't be doin' it,' said Danny, shaking his head. 'I really can't call ya Elisabeth, you bein' t'head teacher at t'school an' all. What would all t'other kids say if I was to walk down t'corridor and say "Mornin', Elisabeth"?'

She laughed. 'You'd call me Mrs Stirling or miss when you are in school like all the other children, but at home you would call me Elisabeth.'

'I don't know,' said the boy, sucking his bottom lip.

'Well, you can't keep on calling me miss, now can you, Danny? Not at home anyway. You have a think about it.'

The boy reflected for a moment. 'I could call ya mum,' he said shyly.

'If you like,' replied Elisabeth.

The boy's face broke into a great beaming smile. 'I don't know what it's like to 'ave a dad an' a mum. I never knew eether of 'em. It's funny 'ow things turn out, in't it?'

He continued with his digging in the borders. After a while he looked up. 'Mrs Devine?'

'Yes, Danny?'

'I'm reight 'appy. I din't think I would be again after mi granddad died but as 'e'd say, every dark cloud 'as a silver linin'.'

'Your granddad was a very wise man, Danny,' said Elisabeth.

'He was,' agreed the boy thoughtfully, leaning on his spade again.

'Would you do me a favour?' asked Elisabeth.

'Course, miss,' replied the boy.

'You know the new boy?'

Danny breathed out noisily and shook his head. 'Robbie? 'E's a reight un, in't 'e?'

'I think he has a few problems,' said Elisabeth.

'Tha can say that ageean. 'E just dunt care what 'e sez or what 'e does,' Danny told her. 'We've all on us tried to be nice to 'im but 'e dunt want owt to do wi' anybody. An' 'e sez nasty things to people. I mean 'e brought it on 'issen when Malcolm Stubbins 'it 'im. 'E were askin' for it miss.'

'Yes, I understand Malcolm was provoked,' said Elisabeth, 'but that is no reason to use violence.'

'Are ya goin' to expel Malcolm, miss?' asked the boy.

'No, I'm not going to expel him but he's had a stern warning. You remember, Danny, when your grandfather died?'

'Aye, I do.'

'And how unhappy you were and didn't want to talk to anybody and you lost interest in your school work and went quiet?'

He nodded.

'And you were very sad and confused?'

'I wasn't really miself, miss.'

'Well, I think something's made Robbie sad and confused and that's why he behaves as he does.'

'But I din't carry on like that, miss,' said Danny.

'People react in different ways. Now you get on with everybody, Danny. You're a very popular boy, perhaps the most popular in the school.'

'I don't know about that, miss,' said the boy, colouring up.

'I think you are. Anyway, I wonder if you can make a real effort to be friendly to Robbie. Could you do that?'

The boy sucked in his bottom lip. 'I reckon I can,' he replied.

'Thank you,' said Elisabeth.

'Hey up!' came a booming voice from the track by the cottage.

'Oh dear. I wonder what Mr Massey wants?' said Elisabeth. Like most in the village she didn't much care for this pennypinching old grouse.

Mr Massey had put on his one suit, a shiny ill-fitting garment he had bought from a charity shop, and wore a knitted tie that had seen better days. He had scrubbed his hands and face and run a comb through his mane of thick ill-cut hair. 'Now then, Mrs Devine,' the farmer shouted in rare good humour as he stood at the gate.

'Mr Massey,' said Elisabeth.

'Lovely day,' he said. 'Birds are a-singing, flowers are a-blooming, sun is a-shining.' He breathed in deeply and exhaled. 'Makes you glad to be alive, doesn't it?'

'Indeed it does,' she agreed.

'I see you've got young Danny helping you,' remarked Mr Massey.

'I have,' Elisabeth said, walking towards him, 'and a great help he is too.'

'Aye, he's a good lad. Hey up, Danny!' he shouted.

'Hello, Mr Massey,' replied the boy, waving.

'How's that ferret of yours?'

'Champion.'

Mr Massey turned his attention back to Elisabeth. 'I've just passed your Chairman of Governors marching down the high street with his nose in the air like Field Marshal Horatio Kitchener himself. Didn't pass the time of day.'

Elisabeth did not wish to discuss Major Neville-Gravitas with such a mischief-maker as Fred Massey, knowing that anything she might say would be broadcast around the village in no time at all. 'I must say you look very smart. Are you going somewhere special?'

'Just coming to see you, Mrs Devine,' he replied.

'To see me?'

'That's right.'

'About what?'

'Could I have a quiet word?' he said under his breath. 'It's sort of confidential.'

'Danny, you finish off here,' said Elisabeth turning to the boy, 'and then you can get off home. I should imagine that Mrs O'Connor will have your tea on the table.'

When the boy had gone she looked at her visitor, intrigued as to why he should want to see her. 'Now then, Mr Massey, what can I do for you?'

'It's about yon track of yours.'

'Oh dear,' she sighed. 'Not the track again.'

When Elisabeth had moved into her cottage she had crossed swords with Mr Massey when she had asked him to stop using the track to take his cows to the field beyond. When Elisabeth had referred him to her deeds and threatened him with legal action for trespass, the indignant farmer had stopped using the track and now took his cows down the one to the side of the church.

'I thought I made myself perfectly clear, Mr Massey,'

Elisabeth told him. 'You cannot bring your cows down there. They were noisy and made a dreadful mess and—'

'Hang on! Hang on a minute, Mrs Devine, and hear me out!' exclaimed the farmer. 'I'm not wanting to bring my beasts back. Vicar lets me use his track down by St Christopher's and that suits me fine.'

'So then what do you wish to speak to me about?' asked Elisabeth.

'It's in a bit of a state, that track of yours,' remarked Mr Massey, rubbing his bristly chin. 'Full of ruts and potholes and it gets very muddy.'

'Yes, I realise that,' Elisabeth told him, rather irritated, 'and I intend to have it resurfaced now that we have better weather. However, I can't see why the state of my track is any concern of yours.'

'Well, I can be of help, Mrs Devine,' he told her.

'Oh yes,' she answered, eyeing him suspiciously. It was entirely out of character for Fred Massey to be of help to anyone unless there was money in it. 'And how may you be of help?'

'I'm prepared to buy that track off of you,' he said, 'and I will pay well over the market value for it.'

'Ah, I see now, Mr Massey,' said Elisabeth. 'I don't suppose this has got anything to do with your plans to have houses built on your field?'

Elisabeth had been informed by Mrs Atticus of Fred Massey's scheme.

He gave a sly smile. 'Well, I have been thinking about it,' he told her. 'You've probably gathered that I need access, Mrs Devine, and yours is the only way into my field bar the one by the church and the vicar says that's not for sale.'

'So I believe.'

'How about it then? Are you willing to sell?'

'I really don't think so, Mr Massey,' said Elisabeth. 'I value my privacy and my peace and quiet. A busy access road down the side of my cottage—'

'There are only plans for three houses,' he interrupted.

'And I use the track to park my car off the road.'

'I could have a little private lay-by built for you. Three houses aren't going to make a lot of difference. They won't spoil your view because you own the paddock at the back of your cottage and you wouldn't see them, and anyway you'll happen not be living here much longer, will you? When you're married to Dr Stirling I reckon you'll be moving into Clumber Lodge.'

'Maybe, Mr Massey, but that is my business, and now if you will excuse me—'

'People have to live somewhere, Mrs Devine,' persisted the farmer, repeating what he had said to the Archdeacon, 'and there's a shortage of properties in the village. It seems to me it's a bit mean-minded to stop the building of a few houses so people can have a roof over their heads.'

'All right, Mr Massey, I'll think about it,' said Elisabeth, keen to get rid of him, 'but I am only saying I'll think about it. I'm not promising anything.'

'Then I shall bid you good day, Mrs Devine,' said the farmer, and ambled off whistling to himself. He turned when he reached the end of the track. 'When might I be hearing from you?' he shouted.

'Goodbye, Mr Massey,' said Elisabeth.

The following Monday morning, before the start of school, Elisabeth had an appointment with Esther Goldstein. The educational psychologist was a small woman with grey thoughtful eyes and a reassuring smile. Her face was framed in an untidy mass of brown hair. Elisabeth got on well with her, for Mrs Goldstein was good-natured, unaffected and easy to talk to and had been of great help supporting her when she had consulted her about some of the pupils.

'I think any child with a name like Robin Banks,' said Mrs Goldstein good-humouredly, 'might experience a few problems at school. However, young people are pretty resilient, and most children who are a bit different in some way take it in their stride. In my time I've come across children called Hadrian Wall and Justin Finnerty, and in one Catholic school I came across a delightful young man called Innocent, named after a string of famous popes. They all seemed to cope remarkably well. After all, as Shakespeare said, "What's in a name?"'

'But I should imagine a teenager called Innocent would be a target for a fair bit of teasing,' remarked Elisabeth.

'He was, but it wasn't so much his first name that caused the boy's problem. It was when it was coupled with his surname – Bystander.'

'No!' exclaimed Elisabeth. 'Innocent Bystander?'

'Oh yes. In my job I have come to realise that parents give their children the most unusual names. So many children these days are named after pop stars, footballers and television personalities – Ozzy and Iggy and Peaches and Poppet. It's the cult of the celebrity. And some parents give little thought to the fact that their children, when they arrive at school, have to cope with such bizarre names. Anyway, let's talk about Robbie.'

'I have to admit he's causing me a few sleepless nights,' Elisabeth confided. 'I have come across some difficult children in my time but none was like Robbie. As I've told you, he's such an angry, hostile little boy and I really need some help on how I should handle him.'

'Well, you are quite right,' Mrs Goldstein told her, 'it certainly doesn't sound as if the boy has ADHD to me. In my experience children with that condition tend to fidget and sometimes can't sit still and they walk around the classroom.

They often shout out, challenge their teachers and have outbursts.'

'Well, Robbie's not like that.'

'He clearly appears to have some form of emotional and behavioural disorder,' said the psychologist, 'but I'll be able to give you a better diagnosis once I have seen him. Is there somewhere in the school where it is quiet and we won't be disturbed?'

'Use the staff-room,' Elisabeth told her. 'There will be no one there until morning break.'

Later that morning Robbie stood before Mrs Goldstein in the staff-room with his hands thrust into his pockets. He gave her a level stare. 'I was told to come here,' he said in a surly tone of voice.

'Hello, Robbie,' said the psychologist cheerfully. 'Would you like to sit down?'

The boy slumped into a chair.

'Do you know why Mrs Devine has asked me to have a word with you?'

'No,' he replied.

'I think you do.'

'Then why are you asking? Are you a mind-reader or something?'

This was one bright, astute little boy, thought the psychologist. 'No, I'm not a mind- reader,' said Mrs Goldstein calmly.

'Who are you then?'

'I'm an educational psychologist. I help children or young people who are experiencing a few difficulties in school.'

'A shrink?'

'No, not a shrink. Someone who can help you with problems you may be having.'

'And what makes you think I have a problem?' asked the boy, staring at her fixedly.

'Mrs Devine has told me that you are not settling in here very well and that you seem unhappy and get angry quite often.'

'Not settling in?'

'That's right.'

The boy sighed and stretched back in the chair. 'Is that all?' he asked.

'You lose your temper quite often, don't you, Robbie?'

'Doesn't everybody lose their temper sometimes?' asked the boy. He stretched further back in the chair and looked up at the ceiling.

Mrs Goldstein was tempted to tell him to sit up straight, but she resisted. 'Yes, they do,' she agreed, 'but most of us control that temper and we don't go around upsetting people and saying unpleasant things to them.'

The boy shrugged. His face was completely blank. The psychologist couldn't tell whether he was taking in what she was saying.

'You seem an unhappy boy,' continued Mrs Goldstein. 'Am I right?'

He shrugged again.

'Can you tell me what makes you unhappy?'

'No.'

'Can you tell me what you're feeling?' she asked.

He looked at her blankly and narrowed his bright green eyes. 'And what makes you think I want to talk to a complete stranger about my feelings?'

'I'm trying to help you, Robbie,' she said. 'You are not making it very easy for me.'

'Can I go now?' the boy asked, sitting up in his chair.

'I would like to help you, Robbie, help you settle in here and be happy. Why don't you tell me what it is that's upsetting you?'

'I'd like to go,' said the boy.

Mrs Goldstein thought it best not to pursue this exchange any further for the moment. 'All right, Robbie, you can go,' she told him, 'but you might want to write down what makes you annoyed and upset if you would rather do that than talk to me.'

'I won't.'

'I would like you to think about what I have said and I would like to see you again.'

'Whatever,' said the boy, getting up from the chair.

Robbie was subdued but his usual distant, uncooperative self in the classroom later that morning. The children, wary of his outbursts, wanted nothing to do with him and gave him a wide berth. Elisabeth decided not to respond on the few occasions when he was offhand or belligerent. She had asked him at break time to go out and get some fresh air but he shook his head and sat with a sullen expression on his face, flicking through a book, before telling her he didn't feel like it. He spent little time on his work during the morning but Elisabeth decided to pay no attention to this. She thought it best not to confront the boy until she had spoken to Mrs Goldstein and taken her advice on how to handle him.

At lunchtime, as she wandered around the school, she found Oscar and Roisin in the small school library, chattering away.

'Hello, you two,' she said cheerfully.

Oscar peered through his glasses. Roisin smiled. 'Hello, Mrs Devine,' they replied in unison.

'We've been talking about family histories,' the girl told her.

'There was a most interesting programme on the television last night,' said Oscar. 'I was telling Roisin about it. We've been looking for some books which might tell us how to trace people's ancestors but we've only found this biology book, which isn't much help.'

'I think you would have to go to the public library to find books on genealogy,' Elisabeth told him.

'Actually it's quite a fascinating subject,' continued Oscar. 'I should love to find out where I come from and how things are passed down from generation to generation.'

'This sounds very interesting,' said Elisabeth.

'You see, Roisin being Irish is probably of Celtic descent,' said the boy. 'I'm more likely to be Anglo-Saxon or maybe Viking. Vikings had red hair, you see.'

'Well, I wish you luck, Oscar,' said Elisabeth.

'The thing is though, Mrs Devine,' he said frowning, 'I think this biology book might have got things wrong.'

'Really?'

'You see it says here that people with blue eyes—'

'Could you just excuse me a minute,' said Elisabeth, catching sight of a group of children gathered in the middle of the playground squabbling. She headed quickly for the outside door, where she was greeted by Chardonnay.

'You had better come quick, miss,' said the girl. 'That new boy's at it again calling people names.'

'Why do you deliberately go out of your way to annoy people, Robbie?' Elisabeth asked the boy after she had taken him into her classroom and sat him down in front of her desk. 'It is really not at all acceptable to call other children names.'

He stared down at his hands. She could feel the tension gathering behind the silence.

'I shall have a word with Ernest Pocock later and see what he has to say, but from what the other children have told me you told him his paintings, which are hanging in the corridor, were rubbish.'

'I didn't,' started the boy. 'I said they were crap.'

Elisabeth sighed and tried to be calm and forbearing with the boy, but was now losing patience with him. 'I suggest you keep your opinions to yourself. I really don't know what to do with you, Robbie. You lose your temper at the slightest thing, you argue with other people, you don't do as you are told and deliberately annoy the other children. What is it that makes you so angry?'

The boy folded his arms tightly across his chest and didn't answer.

'Well, you can stay in the classroom for the rest of lunch-time,' she told him, 'and think about what I've said.'

'Suits me,' replied the boy under his breath.

Elisabeth was in the playground the following lunchtime.

Oscar wandered over, a large book tucked underneath his arm.

'Hello, Oscar,' said Elisabeth brightly. 'And how are you?'

'Oh, I'm tip-top, Mrs Devine,' he replied.

'That's good to hear.'

'You're looking a bit peaky if I may say so,' the boy remarked.

Elisabeth laughed. 'I'm fine, Oscar,' she said. The boy had an extensive repertoire of old-fashioned sayings which always amazed and amused her.

Oscar shook his head. 'That new boy is a bit of an unknown quantity, isn't he?' He sounded as if he was from a bygone age.

'Well, Robbie's new and not settled in yet,' she told him. 'He's still finding his feet.'

'He's very cheeky and bad-tempered,' observed Oscar. 'And can be very unpleasant. When I tried to be friendly he told me to—'

'Yes, I did hear, Oscar,' Elisabeth interrupted.

'And he told Ernest Pocock—'

'I heard about that too.'

'Perhaps he is in need of some counselling,' continued the boy. 'My mother is a fully qualified counsellor, you know. She runs courses on anger management. I'm sure she could give you some help. Shall I ask her to call in and see you?'

'That won't be necessary, thank you, Oscar. Things are in hand.' She quickly changed the subject. 'Now, I gather you are the Wizard of Oz in the school production?'

'It's only a small part,' said the boy. 'I only come in at the end.'

'Every part is important, Oscar,' said Elisabeth. 'We can't all take the lead.'

'Oh, I'm not complaining, Mrs Devine,' said the boy. 'I have quite enough on my plate at the moment and if I had been given a bigger part I would have found it hard to attend all the rehearsals.'

'So what are the important things that are on your plate?' asked Elisabeth. 'Are they still dinosaurs and fossils?'

'Actually, they are not referred to as dinosaurs by the palae-ontologists,' the boy replied primly. 'The correct scientific name is prehistoric lizards, but that's by-the-by. As I mentioned, I am trying to research where we all come from and how things are passed down from generation to generation, what we inherit from our ancestors. As you suggested, I got this book on genealogy from the local library.' He held up the heavy tome. 'I'm afraid it's not much help.'

Elisabeth looked at the title of the book – *Genealogical Research, Volume 2* by Dr Kenelm R. Walker B.Sc., M.Sc., Ph.D., D.Sc., FRSA – and raised an eyebrow.

'It's a big book, isn't it?' she asked. 'It looks rather advanced. Perhaps you ought to look for something a bit easier.'

'It is a bit heavy going, I have to admit,' Oscar told her, 'but I'm sticking with it.'

'And what have you discovered so far?' asked Elisabeth.

'I've found out that everybody has a genetic code which is inherited from their parents. Parents with black skin have a child with black skin and those with white skin have a child with white skin, which is pretty obvious really. People from China and Japan have an epicanthic eye fold – that means slanting eyes. Now the interesting thing is that on a rare occasion, the child is a throwback. This is where he inherits something from a distant ancestor's genetic make-up.' He opened the book and read: 'The reappearance of a characteristic in an organism after several generations of absence, usually caused by the chance recombination of genes, is known as a throwback. It is known as atavism.'

'It sounds very complicated to me, Oscar,' said Elisabeth.

'The thing is, Mrs Devine,' said the boy. 'I think I might be one of those.'

'One of what?' she asked.

'A throwback.'

'And what makes you think that?'

'Well, the thing is, parents who both have blue eyes always have children who have blue eyes too. It said so in the biology book I was reading yesterday.'

'And?'

'My parents both have blue eyes but my eyes are brown.' He removed his glasses, the better to illustrate his point. 'You see. Now, how do you account for that unless I'm a throwback?'

'I . . .'

'It's probably because in the distant past one of my ancestors had brown eyes, don't you think?'

Elisabeth knew enough about genetics to know that this explanation was highly unlikely and that she was entering dangerous waters. The most probable reason was that the boy was not the biological son of one or both of his parents.

'And another thing,' the boy told her. 'Both my parents have dark hair and mine is ginger.'

'All very mysterious, Oscar,' replied Elisabeth evasively.

'It's interesting, isn't it, Mrs Devine?' said Oscar cheerfully.

'It is,' replied Elisabeth, wondering if perhaps she ought to have a word with Oscar's mother.

After school Mrs Goldstein called.

'How's Robbie been today?' she asked Elisabeth as they sat in the staff-room.

The other teachers had gone home, but not before complaining to Elisabeth that Robbie's behaviour was having a detrimental effect on the children in their classes and asking that something be done about him.

'Unfortunately he's been his usual difficult self,' the psychologist was told. Elisabeth then explained what had happened the day before, when he had started calling the other children names. 'How did you find Robbie when you spoke to him today?' she asked. Mrs Goldstein had seen Robbie again and found him as rude and uncooperative as ever.

'Very much the same,' replied the psychologist. 'He certainly has a problem, and I think this pattern of hostile behaviour is very typical of children with what we now have identified as Oppositional Defiant Disorder. These children often get angry and resentful for no apparent reason, they have temper tantrums, argue with adults, actively defy or refuse to comply with adults' requests and deliberately annoy people and blame others for their mistakes or misbehaviour.'

'Well, that sounds like Robbie,' said Elisabeth. 'So what causes him to be like this?'

Mrs Goldstein smiled. 'I wish I could tell you. There are so many factors. It is difficult to say why a person has a psychotic disorder. Maybe it is something innate, a predisposition to act like this, maybe his home life contributes to the way he behaves as he does.'

'I don't think his relationship with his stepfather is very good,' Elisabeth informed her. 'I have only met him the once but he appears to be a very controlling sort of person and hasn't a good word to say about the boy.'

'I will need to speak to the parents,' said the psychologist.

'What I fail to understand,' said Elisabeth, 'is that Robbie has got to nine years of age without anything being done. Why wasn't this disorder identified before? I gather from his record he's been moved from one school to another. What did his teachers at the other schools do to help him?'

'I did contact the head teachers of Robbie's previous schools and the message was always the same – when he did attend, which was infrequently, they couldn't handle him. Rather than contact me as you have done and attempt to do something about his behaviour, they excluded or expelled him. As you say, he's moved from one school to another. You know he didn't last long at Urebank.'

'And do you think Robbie has always been like this?' asked Elisabeth.

'I couldn't say,' replied Mrs Goldstein, 'but when he was at Clayton Primary School he caused quite a deal of trouble, so I heard. On one occasion he sat in the audience when the children in his class performed the Nativity play. His teacher thought it would be a bit too risky to give him a part. When Mary and Joseph arrived at the inn looking for a room he evidently shouted out to the innkeeper, "Tell them to clear off! There's no room!" Then he disrupted the rest of the play by making animal noises. At another time, when his teacher refused to let him leave the room to go to the toilet, he threatened to use the corner of the classroom. The final straw was when he bit the deputy head teacher at Urebank. There was a whole catalogue of troublesome behaviour.'

Elisabeth shook her head. 'So what do we do?' she asked.

'There are special schools for children like Robbie,' the psychologist told her. 'It might be best if he went to a place where his needs are better catered for than here in mainstream school, and where the teachers are trained to deal with children like him.'

'I think if we ask him to leave I will feel a failure, Esther,' Elisabeth told her. 'I believe all children, however damaged or ill-favoured, deserve the best we can do for them. And not much has been done for Robbie from what I can gather. He's such a sad, angry boy, I really would like to try and help him. For the moment I would like him to remain at Barton.'

'I see. Well, it will be an uphill battle.'

'And if he were to stay, how could we best help him?'

'We could try various strategies but I have to be honest, Elisabeth, one child like this can have a negative effect on the other children in the school. He can disrupt lessons, not do as he is told, contradict his teachers, and you will have to spend a disproportionate amount of your time dealing with him. Are you sure you want to take this on?'

'Yes, I'm sure.'

'Then I think we should talk to his parents and see what they think, and then perhaps we can all have a meeting to decide what to do for the best.'

Mr Gribbon appeared at the door of the classroom. Elisabeth beckoned for him to come in.

'Mrs Devine,' he said, his face like thunder, 'I've just had occasion to tell that new boy off for walking over my newly polished floor and I can't repeat the mouthful he gave me.'

Elisabeth looked at Mrs Goldstein and they both sighed.

6

The following lunchtime Elisabeth and Mrs Goldstein met Robbie's mother.

'I'm sorry that my husband can't be here,' explained Mrs Banks. 'He's away working in Barnsley all this week.' She looked tired and sounded flustered.

'Perhaps we might meet him the next time,' said the psychologist. 'It is important that you both hear and understand what I have to say and know how best we can deal with Robbie's problem.'

The woman clasped her hands together fretfully on her lap. Her expression was pinched and desperately unhappy. 'I'll have a word with him,' she said quietly.

'So how has your son been at home since he started here at Barton?' asked Mrs Goldstein.

'Oh, very much the same, I'm afraid,' said Mrs Banks sadly. 'He's been his usual self – difficult, moody and bad-tempered. I really don't know what gets into him. He's not interested in anything and spends most of the time in his room. I have tried to talk to him but . . .' The sentence petered out feebly.

Mrs Goldstein nodded sympathetically. 'I have seen Robbie,' she said.

'And how was he?' asked Mrs Banks hesitantly.

'To be honest, I felt he was testing me. He wasn't very forthcoming.'

'He can be like that,' she agreed.

'Having discussed things with Mrs Devine and from my

own observation, I am of the opinion that your son does have a special need,' said Mrs Goldstein, 'a type of Oppositional Defiant Disorder. Children with this sort of condition for some reason demonstrate quite extreme disruptive behaviour, particularly towards authority figures like parents and teachers. They don't respond to instructions or like taking orders and actively refuse to do as they are told. They can lose their tempers easily, are rude and become annoyed and sometimes aggressive.'

Mrs Banks looked up searchingly. 'That's exactly how Robbie is,' she said miserably. Tears formed in the corners of her eyes. 'I'm at my wits' end how to deal with him, I really am.'

'I have come across quite a few children with this kind of condition,' continued the psychologist, 'and I want to reassure you that it's not that unusual in some young people and it can be treated with what we call behavioural therapy, getting the young person to manage his anger. I want you to know first and foremost that we are going to help Robbie and you to deal with it. How would you feel if we asked a paediatrician and a neurologist to see Robbie?'

'I'm not sure Frank would agree to it,' said Mrs Banks. 'He thinks I've been too soft and easy-going and let Robbie get away with things.'

'It must be hard for you both,' said Elisabeth sympathetically.

'But why is he like this?' asked Mrs Banks. She sounded desperate. 'Other boys his age don't carry on like this. Tell me, am I to blame?' There was some force behind the question. 'I must have failed him in some way.' She looked down at her hands and began twisting the ring on her finger. 'I sometimes think that it's the way me and Frank have brought him up that has been the cause of Robbie's behaviour.'

'It's not clear what causes a boy like Robbie to behave as he does, Mrs Banks,' the psychologist told her. 'It could be something biological, part of his make-up, his temperament, some neurological imbalance, but it can be affected by the way parents treat him. If a parent is confrontational and forceful, or constantly makes critical comments, tells him he's a disappointment, it makes matters worse.'

'My husband's not the most patient of men,' admitted Mrs Banks. It was clear that the words of the psychologist had touched a raw nerve. She lowered her eyes as if ashamed. 'He does try his best with Robbie, but he loses his temper and sometimes smacks him.'

'That's not the answer,' said Mrs Goldstein.

'It's just that Robbie says such hurtful things and gets into such a state.'

'I understand how difficult this can be for you and your husband,' continued the psychologist. 'Dealing with a child like this can be frustrating and physically and mentally exhausting, but I am confident that with help Robbie's behaviour will improve. Will you have a word with your husband about Robbie seeing a paediatrician and a neurologist?'

'I will,' said Mrs Banks, her eyes filling with tears again. 'You're the first person who's understood what I feel like, the first person who's really explained things. In his other schools they either suspended Robbie or expelled him. The teachers said they just couldn't deal with a boy like that.'

'That's often the way some schools deal with the situation,' said Mrs Goldstein, 'and I can understand that reaction from the teachers when faced with a child who disrupts lessons and whose presence is a threat to the welfare and education of the other children.'

'But in this school,' added Elisabeth, 'we are going to make an effort to help Robbie.'

'I've heard that some children who behave like this can be given tablets to control their temper,' said Mrs Banks.

'Yes, there is medication that could help,' replied Mrs

Goldstein, 'but I would not recommend it at this stage. I suggest that a behavioural approach using tried and tested techniques is the best course of action. This means helping Robbie acknowledge that he has a problem, giving him some confidence to believe in his own ability, setting some achievable goals and encouraging and rewarding positive behaviour when we see it. It will be challenging for you and your husband and for Mrs Devine, but I think initially we should try this approach.'

'I'll try,' said Mrs Banks, 'but my husband might need some convincing. He believes in what he calls good old-fashioned discipline, the sort he had when he was a boy. He says that he got a good hiding when he was a lad and answered his father back and it did him no harm.'

'But this clearly hasn't worked with Robbie, has it?' said Mrs Goldstein.

'No, it hasn't,' agreed Mrs Banks. 'If anything it's made matters worse.'

'We have to make Robbie feel positive about himself,' said the psychologist. 'Part of his behaviour could be put down to the fact that he has a poor self-image, and underneath that angry, badly behaved little boy is a child who has little confidence and a low self-esteem. Some would say that this approach is all fashionable nonsense and airy-fairy and that he just needs firmer discipline, but I have been in this job long enough to know that an overly strict and uncompromising approach doesn't work with this kind of boy. It will just make him more indignant and rebellious. There will be things Robbie does which are not acceptable and this needs to be pointed out to him but in a clear and calm way, without shouting and you getting angry. And a whole lot of patience, tolerance and perseverance is required.'

'We'll try,' said Mrs Banks. 'It will not be easy but we will try.'

Elisabeth found the boy in question sitting in the classroom looking blankly out of the window. His hands were wedged underneath his thighs and he was gently rocking backwards and forwards. She sat next to him. 'Hello, Robbie,' she said with deliberate cheerfulness.

He looked up but didn't reply. His small face was set like a mask.

'I've just been having a word with your mother. She called in to see how you are getting on.'

'I know. I saw her,' he replied truculently.

'And how do you think you're getting on?' asked Elisabeth.

The boy shrugged and stared out of the window again.

'There are lots of activities going on this week at lunchtimes you know – a chess club, reading group, the school choir, drama class, a football practice. Is there something which interests you?'

'No.'

'If you try going to one of the clubs you might enjoy it.'

Robbie turned to face her and looked at her angrily. 'I don't want to join no bloody club!' he snapped. His eyes were like arrow slits.

'Please don't swear,' said Elisabeth levelly. 'It's not clever.'

'Who said it was clever?' he retorted and turned his face away.

'Did you manage to finish the work I set for you?' she asked, resisting the temptation to have a confrontation.

'No,' he replied, continuing to stare ahead of him.

'Why was that?'

'Because I didn't feel like it,' he replied.

'Oh, Robbie,' sighed Elisabeth.

The boy turned and fixed her with a cool stare. 'You think by being nice to me that you'll get me to do as you say. You're like all adults, telling me what to do all the time, but I won't. I don't like it here, I don't like the other kids and I don't like you. Now can you leave me alone?'

Elisabeth could quite see what a thoroughly unpleasant little boy he appeared to those who met him. It was going to be an uphill battle with him, she thought, and she would need all her patience to keep calm in the face of such naked hostility. She rose from the chair and left the room.

'So how are things?' asked Mrs Robertshaw, poking her head around the classroom door. It was the end of the school day and Elisabeth was sitting with a stack of papers before her on the desk.

'Just a bit tired,' she replied.

'You're overdoing it.'

Elisabeth gave a weak smile. 'There's a part in *Hamlet*, where one of the characters – I think it's the king – says that "when sorrows come, they come not single spies, but in battalions". Substitute "troubles" for "sorrows" and you have the gist of what I'm feeling at the moment.'

'Sorrows!' exclaimed Mrs Robertshaw, coming into the room. 'Troubles?' She sat down. 'You had better tell me about them.'

'This meeting next week with the staff of Urebank about the amalgamation is preying on my mind.'

'Well,' said her colleague, pulling a face, 'none of us is looking forward to that. It's about as welcome as a sack of soiled nappies, as my husband would say.'

'It will be the first time that I have actually met Mr Richardson, and from what I know of him and what I gather about the staff they are likely to be pretty hostile.'

'Yes, I was talking to Mrs Pugh this morning and she hasn't a good word to say about most of them down at Urebank. She reckons the infant teacher and the woman who takes the lower juniors aren't that bad, though. Still, if anyone can make this amalgamation work it's you.'

'Then there's Robbie,' said Elisabeth, not really listening.

Mrs Robertshaw heaved a sigh. 'Oh yes, how is he?'

'Very much the same. I really don't know what to do for the best, Elsie. Part of me says I should persevere with the boy and another part says he would be better off in a school for children with behavioural problems.'

'Well, my view, for what it is worth, is that he does need to be in a special school. Now I have dealt with some challenging children in my time but that young man takes the biscuit. He's a very messed-up child. You have to think of the other children, and you should not have to spend all your time dealing with one rude and badly behaved child. The other children's education will suffer, and if they see him speaking to teachers as he does then they will start to copy and discipline in the school will go downhill.'

'That's what Michael thinks too,' Elisabeth told her.

'And he's a doctor, so you should listen to him.'

'It's just that I don't want to give up on the boy. I think his parents have. His stepfather, anyway. I don't want to do that.'

'You are not superwoman, Elisabeth,' said Mrs Robertshaw sharply. 'You cannot expect to be successful with every single child you come across. Sadly, there are some children who are unteachable and resistant to any help you may want to give them. I might be speaking out of turn but you have to face that. You have to accept that with the likes of Robbie Banks there is nothing more you can do.'

Elisabeth thought for a moment. 'Perhaps you're right,' she murmured. 'And then there's Oscar.'

'He's as happy as Larry,' replied Mrs Robertshaw. 'Whatever do you think is wrong with him?'

Elisabeth related the conversation she had had with the boy.

'Oh dear, now this is worrying,' said her colleague. 'As you know, mine is a science degree so I do know a little about genetics and I'll tell you this, there is no way that a child with brown eyes is the offspring of two parents who have blue eyes. It's a biological impossibility.'

'That's what I thought,' said Elisabeth. 'So he may be adopted?' she asked.

'Or the man his mother is married to is not his biological father.'

'Perhaps I need to speak to Oscar's mother.'

Mrs Robertshaw shook her head. 'I wouldn't go down that road if I were you. You'll open a whole can of worms. I would leave well alone.'

'Elsie, Oscar is the most intelligent and widely read child I have ever met. He is sure to discover the truth given time.'

'Well, if he does, that's not our concern,' said Mrs Robertshaw dismissively. 'If his parents have decided not to tell him . . . well, that is their choice.' She rested her hand on Elisabeth's. 'You take too much on, that's your trouble. You'll wear yourself out.'

Elisabeth gave a weak smile. 'So how are the rehearsals going?'

'Very well indeed,' said Mrs Robertshaw, becoming animated. 'The children have really taken to the play. I must admit I was a bit hesitant at first. I thought the story was just a fanciful children's tale, a bit too young for ten- and eleven-year-olds to perform, but actually it's very cleverly written and full of wisdom and common sense. Of course I've had to adapt it and change some things. In the book Dorothy has silver slippers but I thought I'd have red shoes, like in the film version. I'm undecided about Dorothy's dog Toto. I was wondering if Lady Wadsworth would lend us her Border Terrier.'

'I thought you were against having an animal on stage,' said Elisabeth. 'I remember you mentioning a production of *Oliver!* where the dog attacked the Artful Dodger and stole the show?'

'It's just that I think it would be a risk worth taking,' said her colleague. 'It would look rather silly Dorothy carrying a toy dog around. Lady Wadsworth's dog seems a placid enough animal and I could see how it gets on at rehearsals.'

'That's a good idea. I gather you've enlisted Ernest Pocock to paint the set.'

'Under Mrs Atticus's supervision,' said the teacher. 'He's become a bit of a prima donna, has Ernest, since he was runner-up in the County Art Competition. He walks around with a paintbrush in his hand holding forth about colour and perspective.'

'And how is Chardonnay getting on?'

'You were quite right to suggest her for the part. We knew she had a fine singing voice but she's got real acting ability as well. As you know, at first she was very reticent about taking on the part and she still needs a lot of reassurance.'

'She got the silly idea in her head that people would laugh at her,' said Elisabeth.

'Well, she's still rather tentative and lacks a bit of confidence but I'm sure she'll be fine. She told me that you had a word with her.'

'I did,' said Elisabeth. 'I told her no one would laugh at her, to believe in herself. I said we are all afraid at times but we have to face it and have some courage.' As soon as she said that she thought of the forthcoming meeting at Urebank.

Mrs Robertshaw laughed

'What's tickling you?' asked Elisabeth.

'So says the Wizard of Oz to the cowardly lion,' said her colleague. '"All you need is to have faith in yourself," he says, "and to confront what you fear the most." He could have been talking to Chardonnay.'

Or to me, thought Elisabeth.

Fred Massey emerged out of the Blacksmith's Arms at lunch-time a little worse for drink. He steadied himself on the door frame and peered down the street, blinking and trying to focus on a dark shape that was heading his way. The shape, he noticed as it approached him, was dressed in a dull pleated tweed skirt, thick brown stockings and substantial brogues and was wearing a silly knitted hat like a tea cosy. The apparition was striding towards him carrying, like a weapon, a large umbrella with a spike on the end. Mr Massey squinted and then recognised the figure.

'Oh hell,' he said to himself, 'it's bloody Boadicea.'

'A word, Mr Massey, if you please!' shouted Miss Sowerbutts, approaching him. The former head teacher of the village school had a menacing look on her face.

'Ah, Miss Sowerbutts,' he slurred, attempting to stand upright to greet her. 'What a pleasure to see you.' He gave a small bow. 'I hope you are keeping well and fully recovered from your haccident. You are looking in fine fettle if I might say so. I hope you've had no more trouble with your moles.'

Miss Sowerbutts sniffed the air like a hound picking up a scent, and then she wrinkled her nose as she detected the strong smell of alcohol. 'You can dispense with the blandishments, Mr Massey. I have a bone to pick with you. Oh, and for your information the moles have been dealt with, but no thanks to your silly nephew and his bottles of bleach. I ought to send you a bill for ruining my lawn.'

'Is there something else I can do for you, then?' he asked, attempting to keep some measure of perpendicularity. He looked at the pinched face with his pale, watery eyes.

'You would be the very last person in the word I would call upon if I *did* require some work doing,' she told him severely. 'You are inept, Mr Massey, ineffectual and inefficient.'

'There's a lot of long words there, Miss Sowerbutts,' he remarked, grunting. 'What it is to be academical.'

'I have just come from the rectory,' she told him, 'and was very pleased to hear that there is no possibility of you buying that track which borders the church. It had come to my ears that you are applying for planning permission to build houses at the back of my cottage and that you tried to buy the track leading to your field.'

'Yes,' replied the farmer, 'but the Reverend Hatticus wouldn't sell it me.' He swayed and hiccupped.

'I should think not! So that has put paid to your little plans,' she said smugly.

Mr Massey smiled, winked and then tapped his nose. 'Not necesscessarily,' he slurred. With a little more persuasion, he thought Mrs Devine was sure to sell the track. Of course he wouldn't be divulging this to the woman who stood before him looking daggers.

'Let me make myself perfectly clear,' warned Miss Sowerbutts angrily and brandishing her brolly, 'there is no possibility of you building houses at the back of my cottage so you can get that idea out of that inebriated head of yours.'

'People have to live somewhere, Miss Sowerbutts,' the farmer told her. He hiccupped. 'I'm just putting a roof over their heads.'

She pointed the brolly like a bayonet. 'Not in my back yard you're not!' she exclaimed.

'Feisty woman,' the farmer mumbled to himself as his nemesis marched off.

After sleeping off his over-indulgence at the Blacksmith's Arms, Fred's first port of call was to the Rumbling Tum café on the high street, where Bianca, his nephew's partner, was a waitress. He needed to speak to her. Clarence, Fred Massey's put-upon and long-suffering nephew, had 'got that dopey lass Bianca pregnant', as he had told the locals in the Blacksmith's Arms, and they had set up home in a council flat in Clayton. 'After all I've done for the lad,' Fred had moaned over his pint, 'then he up and buggers off leaving me in the lurch.' No one who heard him showed any sympathy, for all in the village knew how the old man had taken advantage of Clarence, working him all hours and paying him next to nothing.

Fred was now finding it difficult to carry on with his odd-job business and run his farm without his nephew's help. He was a tight-fisted, bad-tempered old man was Fred Massey, and was not inclined to pay a fair wage, hence he could not get anyone to work for him. His plan was to persuade Clarence to return, but he needed to sound out the boy's partner first. But he didn't want to sound too eager.

Fred positioned himself on a small table by the window and looked nonchalantly across the high street. He gave a great smile as Bianca approached. She was a large, healthy-looking girl with large, watery blue eyes and prominent front teeth.

'Hello, Bianca,' he said with uncharacteristic good humour.

'Hello, Mr Massey,' replied the girl. 'What can I get you?'

'You're looking well, Bianca my dear,' he said. 'And how's that little baby of yours? Tyrone is it?'

'Brandon,' said the girl, 'and he's doing really well, thank you.'

'I'm glad to hear it. And how are you keeping?'

'I'm fine.' She knew exactly what his little game was, having heard how he was struggling now Clarence no longer worked for him. 'So, what can I get you?'

'And that nephew of mine? How is he getting on?'

'He's getting on fine as well,' she replied. This was not what Fred wanted to hear, but he kept the smile fixed on his face.

'So you are both settled in Clayton then?' he asked.

'Very settled, thank you.'

The truth was that they were not settled. Their council flat was dark and damp and smelly and the neighbours were loud and unfriendly. Clarence hated his job at the bread factory and longed to be outdoors again, and Bianca found travelling back and forth from Clayton every day tiring and dispiriting. Added to this, her mother was finding it increasingly wearing having to look after the baby all day.

'So Clarence likes his job at the bread factory then?' asked Fred.

Bianca was not going to let him know how unhappy Clarence was and give the old man the satisfaction of saying, 'I told you so.'

'He loves it,' she lied. 'He's on course for being a foreman next year.'

'Is he really? Well, well, well. I suppose it's a bit noisy and cramped in that little council flat of yours?'

'Oh no, it's lovely,' said Bianca. 'It's really cosy and we have lovely views and nice neighbours. Now, I'd better take your order or I'll get into trouble.'

'I'll have a pot of tea,' said Fred. 'I like it strong, with plenty of sugar.'

When Bianca had returned with the tea, Fred rubbed his chin. 'So Clarence doesn't miss working on the farm then?' he asked.

'Oh no, he's very happy where he is,' replied the girl.

'So he's not keen on coming back?'

'I don't think so, Mr Massey. I suppose he might be persuaded if the money was right and there was somewhere nice where we could live – maybe in one of those small cottages you own, done up of course, and it would have to be rent free. And Clarence can't be working all hours like in the past now he's a family man.'

'Hang on, Bianca!' spluttered Fred. 'I'm not made of brass.'

'From what I hear, Mr Massey, you are,' retorted the girl. 'I heard you're selling one of the fields for building. I should think you'll get a tidy sum for that.'

She's not as daft as she looks, thought the old man, pouring his tea.

'Well, I'll tell Clarence that you were asking after him,' said Bianca, leaving Fred to simmer.

After school Danny headed for home via the mill dam. There was nothing in the world he liked better than being out in the countryside and the great sense of freedom he felt. He ran down the track in the wood which led to the derelict mill, the ground carpeted by dead leaves springy under his feet. The wood was full of clumps of wild flowers and there was the smell of garlic in the air. A grey squirrel ran up the trunk of an ancient tree and then peered at him between the fresh green leaves. High above in a vast and dove-grey sky, the rooks screeched and circled. A brace of rabbits, cropping the grass at the edge of a path ahead of him, scuttled off into the under-growth as he drew near them. Eventually he arrived at the mill dam. The huge waterwheel, rotten and rusted, was silent and the grey stone building a crumbling roofless ruin. Beneath, the water was black and thick as oil.

Danny saw a small hunched figure sitting on the dead trunk of a tree. He was throwing stones into the still water.

'Hello,' said Danny, approaching.

The boy looked round but didn't reply. Then he continued to throw stones into the water.

'It's Robbie, in't it?' asked Danny.

'What's it to you?' replied the boy.

Danny sat next to him. 'I offen cum down 'ere,' he said breathing in noisily. 'Some people think it's a bit spooky but I likes it. Mi granddad told me that years ago a man goin' 'ome drunk from t'Blacksmith's Arms fell in t'millpond and were sucked under and drowned. Some neets 'e comes back moanin' and groanin' and chokin' an' spitting mucky watter. Course, I don't believe it mi sen.'

The boy didn't answer.

'There's a kingfisher down 'ere and a kestrel and sometimes

you'll see a fox,' Danny told him. He reached into his pocket and produced a little sandy-coloured, pointed-faced creature with small bright black eyes. He held the animal under its chest at the front, his thumb under one leg towards the ferret's spine, and using the other hand he gently stroked the creature down the full length of its body.

Robbie looked round. 'What's that?' he asked.

'This is Ferdy, mi ferret.'

'Does it bite?'

'Only when 'e's frightened or when 'e gets angry. Otherwise 'e's dead gentle. You've got to know how to handle 'im, ya see.' He stroked the animal gently. 'Does tha want to 'old 'im?'

'No.'

'Not many people do,' said Danny. 'I suppose it's because 'e's a bit scary like.'

'I'm not scared of it!' Robbie snapped. 'I just don't want to hold it, that's all.'

'Suit thissen.'

'It's a funny pet to have,' said Robbie, eyeing the creature suspiciously.

'No it's not!' replied Danny. 'Yer ferret meks a gradely pet. 'E don't bark, 'e's clean as a whistle, 'e's dead affectionate an' is a reight mischievous little beggar.'

'It stinks,' said the boy.

'Well, I suppose you stink to Ferdy. Anyroad, 'e only smells a bit when 'e's scared or when 'e comes into t'breeding season and needs to attract a mate. 'E's not just a pet, 'e's a working creature. I used to tek 'im ferretin' for rabbits when I lived wi' my granddad. We'd peg a little string net ovver t'rabbit warren 'oles an' let one of 'is jills down.'

'What's jills?' the boy asked.

''Is ferret. A jill's a female ferret. 'E kept 'er half fed to mek 'er keen, tha sees. If she were underfed, she'd 'ave etten t'rabbit and wunt cum up out o' t'ole. If 'e overfed 'er she wunt gu down at all. 'E used to let 'er down t'hole an' she chased t'rabbits out into t'net. Then mi granddad'd brek their necks. 'E were reight good at that. Just a sharp chop. Course afore yer started you 'ad to block up all t'oles' 'cept for one, otherwise t'rabbits'd escape. I've not been ferretin' since mi granddad died. I can't bring missen to kill t'rabbit when it pops its furry 'ead out o' t'hole.' Danny sighed. 'I used to mek a tidy bit o' brass sellin' rabbits to t'butcher.'

'I'm not allowed a pet,' said Robbie, his mouth a thin line. 'I had a rabbit but he made me get rid of it.'

'Who did?'

'My stepfather.'

'I once took Ferdy to school and he bit Malcolm Stubbins on 'is finger,' Danny told him. Robbie gave a slight smile. 'Mind you, 'e deserved it.'

'What did he do?'

''E grabbed mi bag and ran off wi' it. 'E thowt there was some spice inside.'

'What's spice?'

'Sweets. Anyroad, when 'e put 'is 'and in mi bag 'e gorra reight shock. Ferdy bit him. Ferrets 'ave really sharp teeth, ya see, and they 'ang on an all. 'Ey look!' said Danny, suddenly pointing skywards, 'does tha see 'im, yon kestrel? After a fat wood pigeon I bet. Can ya see 'ow 'e 'ovvers theer, waitin' an' watching an' ready to swoop down?' Danny stood up and shielded his eyes. 'There 'e goes, look. See 'im pounce.'

'Where do you live?' asked Robbie.

'Clumber Lodge, wi' Dr Stirling,' Danny told him as he popped the ferret in his jacket pocket.

'Why don't you live with your mum and dad?'

'Cos I 'aven't got none. I never knew mi dad an' mi mum were killed. I were brought up by mi granddad but, as I telled thee, 'e died. Then I went to live wi' Dr Stirling. 'E's fostering me and then 'e's goin' to adopt me.'

'I wish I could be adopted,' said Robbie.

'Tha dun't mean that,' said Danny.

'I do,' said the boy vehemently. 'I hate it at home.'

'Why?'

'Because I do.'

'I berrer go,' said Danny, 'else they'll be worried. I'll see you at school tomorra.'

'You might do,' replied Robbie, picking up a stone which he threw into the water.

As he ran off down the track, Danny thought what a strange boy Robbie was, not like any other nine-year-old. Then he remembered one of his grandfather's favourite expressions, 'There's nowt as queer as folk', and he smiled to himself.

7

'*Bonsoir, monsieur et madame. Enchanté de vous revoir.*' The owner of Le Bon Viveur greeted Elisabeth and Michael in the entrance to his plush restaurant. He smiled and displayed a set of perfectly even and impressively white teeth, then took Elisabeth's hand in his and kissed it lightly before shaking Michael's hand. The Frenchman was a lean olive-skinned individual with glossy boot-black hair scraped back on his scalp and large blue-grey eyes. He smelled of expensive cologne.

'*Bonsoir,*' replied Elisabeth.

'Good evening,' said Michael, resisting the opportunity to try out his French and thankful that the man had not tried to kiss him. 'We have a reservation for eight o'clock.'

'*Ah, oui,* Dr Stirling. Your table is ready. Monsieur, Madame, if would care to follow me.'

They were shown to a corner table covered in a stiff white cloth and set out with plain but expensive china plates, starched napkins and heavy cutlery. In the centre was a tall white candle in a slender silver vase.

The owner lit the candle with a gold lighter which he produced from his immaculate dinner jacket and resting a hand on Elisabeth's arm displayed his flawless teeth.

'*Ah! Que vous êtes très belle ce soir,*' he told her.

'*Je vous remercie, monsieur,*' she replied.

When the owner departed to get the aperitif, Michael leaned across the table frowning. 'He was flirting with you,' he said crossly. 'What did he say?'

'Just that it was a lovely evening.'

'I bet he did!'

'Dr Stirling,' said Elisabeth playfully, 'you're not jealous by any chance?'

He didn't appear to be listening. 'And I'll tell you this,' he declared, 'his teeth have been capped and whitened, his hair is out of a jar, he's wearing contact lenses and he smells like a Parisian brothel.'

'And when, might I ask, have you frequented a Parisian brothel?' she asked, laughing.

'You know what I mean,' he grunted.

Elisabeth smiled. 'You know, you are funny at times, Michael.'

'I didn't like the way he was all over you,' he said.

'It will be pistols at dawn any minute.'

'At least with me you get what you see,' grumbled Michael.

Elisabeth reached across the table and took his hand in hers. 'And what I see I love,' she told him.

'Do you?' He looked like one of the infants, wide-eyed and expectant.

'Of course I do.'

He smiled. 'I thought you could do with taking out of yourself,' he said. 'A romantic meal in an exclusive French restaurant might just make you forget about school for once.'

'I'm afraid when we get married you will have to get used to it, Michael,' she replied. 'I never ever forget about school. That meeting with the Director of Education is preying on my mind and then I have to think of how I might deal with that particularly troublesome boy who has just started and I—'

Michael rested his hand on her arm. 'Please, Elisabeth! No school tonight,' he said, 'otherwise I shall describe some of the more unpleasant complaints of the patients I have seen today

– suppurating ulcers, erupting boils, abscesses and pustules, rashes and—'

'All right, all right!' she interrupted, putting her hands over her ears. 'No school, no ailments.'

The owner returned with the drinks, the menu and the wine list. He flashed his teeth at Elisabeth.

'Thank you,' said Michael sharply, snatching the enormous leather-bound folders from the Frenchman's hand.

'Now perhaps you would like me to take you through what is on the menu this evening?' said the owner.

'No need,' said Michael abruptly, 'We can manage, thank you. As you can tell, my fiancée speaks French.'

The man departed with a Gallic shrug.

'I remember the last time we came here,' said Elisabeth, looking around the sparkling, stylish restaurant to see if a certain diner was there, 'that insufferable Councillor Smout came over.'

'I recall him pontificating when he was on the governing body at Barton,' said Michael, 'and he voted to close the school.'

'I thought we'd agreed not to talk about the school,' said Elisabeth.

'Oh yes, sorry.'

'Danny was helping me with the garden this week,' she said. 'He asked me what he should call me when I become your wife. I said I thought he should call me Elisabeth – out of school anyway. He was keen to call me mum. What do you think?'

'Well, he can't go calling you Mrs Stirling or miss, can he?' said Michael. 'I've not talked to James yet about what he might call you when we are married, but I guess he will want to call you Elisabeth rather than mum. As you know, he was very close to his mother and—'

'You don't need to explain, Michael,' interrupted Elisabeth, 'I quite understand.'

'He's so excited about the wedding,' Michael told her.

'Is he?'

'Of course he is.'

'He's not said an awful lot to me,' said Elisabeth. 'You don't think deep down he resents you getting married again?'

'Not at all.'

'Are you sure?'

'Positive.'

'We ought to talk about the wedding,' said Elisabeth. 'We haven't discussed it yet.'

'I'd like something quiet,' said Michael, 'maybe a blessing at St Christopher's with just a few guests and the reception in a nice hotel.'

'I'd like a huge white wedding,' teased Elisabeth, 'with lots of bridesmaids and Danny and James as pageboys. I think they'd look nice in velvet breeches and buckled shoes.'

'Well, if that's what you want, but I'm not sure about the boys coming as pages.'

'I am joking, Michael. Something small and discreet will be fine, but I would like a church wedding if possible.'

Michael reached into his pocket and produced a small red velvet-covered box. He passed it over the table. 'I think you know what this is,' he said.

'Oh, Michael,' she whispered.

Elisabeth opened the box to find a ring. In a circle of diamonds was a huge emerald which glittered in the candlelight.

'Wow,' she gasped. 'I don't know what to say.'

'As you are aware, I'm not that good with words, Elisabeth,' Michael began, 'but I want to tell you that I love you very much and you have made me the happiest man in the—'

'Well, hello.'

Michael stopped mid-sentence.

'I do hope I'm not intruding or anything,' said Major Neville-Gravitas.

Mr Nettles was a tubby man with thick blond hair sticking up from his head like tufts of dry grass and small steel-rimmed spectacles perched on the end of his nose. His chinless face was pasty and drawn. He had convened a meeting of the new head teacher and staff of the soon-to-be amalgamated schools, to take place in the Small Committee Room at County Hall. It was felt by the Director of Education that it would be politic for the teachers from each of the two schools to meet initially on neutral territory. Ms Tricklebank knew that the meeting was likely to be contentious, given the rivalry of the two schools and the mutual antagonism which existed between the two head teachers, and had intended to chair the meeting herself, but something rather more important had arisen. She gave the education officer clear instructions on what should be discussed and how to handle the meeting.

'Now, as you are aware, this is the first meeting of the staff of the new school and if not handled well – with tact and sensitivity – it could prove difficult. Mrs Devine is a strong-minded woman who holds robust views. Mr Richardson can be a prickly customer and he does tend to have a lot to say for himself. Stick closely to the agenda.' She paused. 'There is an agenda, I assume?'

'Oh yes, I've prepared the list of items which you asked me to.'

'Keep the meeting short and focused,' continued Ms Tricklebank, 'and take notes of what is said. By the end of the session there needs to be a clear plan of action and the arrangements made for further meetings. Is that clear?'

'Crystal, Ms Tricklebank,' he replied.

'And I would like a full report on my desk tomorrow morning.'

'Of course.'

Mr Nettles returned to his office, sat at his desk and leaned back in his chair, rehearsing what he would say. This new liaison role was likely to be very demanding. He felt his stomach churn with nervousness.

Downstairs in the reception area of County Hall, Elisabeth and her teaching colleagues sat on a hard wooden bench just as anxiously.

'I'm not looking forward to this one little bit,' observed Mrs Robertshaw. She shuffled on her seat and scowled.

'I'm sure it will not be that bad,' replied Elisabeth, trying to sound confident and dispel her own uneasiness.

'Huh!' huffed her colleague. 'You haven't met Mr Richardson yet,' she continued in a cold scornful tone. 'He's a pompous, arrogant, self-opinionated man. I should know. As you are aware, I visited the school when a teaching post was advertised there and I thought of applying. I was heartily glad to get out of the place and not have to listen to him prattling on about how wonderful his school was. "I don't really think you are suitable for this post," he told me after a good half hour's interrogation. It was the only time I agreed with him and promptly left. I wouldn't touch the place with a ten-foot bargepole if he was in charge.'

Elisabeth didn't reply, but she shared a similar opinion of the man who would now be the deputy head in the new set-up and with whom she would have to work closely.

'I wonder what the infant department is like,' said Miss Wilson apprehensively, breaking the silence which had ensued. 'I suppose if the juniors are based at Barton and the infants at Urebank I shall have to work down there. The infant teacher sounds friendly enough from what you've said, Elsie.'

'Well, I only met her briefly when we did a whistle-stop tour of the school,' replied Mrs Robertshaw. 'She seemed amiable enough, if rather insipid. I never had the chance to speak to her very much because I was closeted with Mr Richardson in his office and subjected to the third degree.'

A smiling receptionist appeared and asked the three women to follow her into the Small Committee Room. They were shown into a spacious high-ceilinged room in the centre of which was an immense polished mahogany table surrounded by twelve balloon-backed chairs. If this was the Small Committee Room, Elisabeth thought, the Large Committee Room must be vast. On one wall hung a full-length portrait of Queen Victoria; on another was a large wooden panel listing, in elaborate gold lettering, the names of soldiers from the county who had died in the two world wars.

Mr Nettles rose from the chair at the head of the table and smiled uneasily. 'Ah, good afternoon, Mrs Devine. It's good of you and your staff to come along to the meeting.'

'Good afternoon, Mr Nettles,' replied Elisabeth. 'May I introduce you to Mrs Robertshaw and Miss Wilson, two of the teachers at Barton. Miss Brakespeare will not be joining us. You know she retires at the end of this term and so felt her presence was not necessary.'

Mr Nettles shook the teachers' hands. His palms were clammy. 'Do take a seat. I must say, Mrs Devine, I am so pleased that we decided to keep the village school open.'

No thanks to you, she thought, recalling how unhelpful the man had been when there had been the threat of closure.

'Yes, we were very pleased too,' she replied.

'The teachers from Urebank will be with us presently,' he told her. 'I'm afraid parking at County Hall is difficult at the best of times, but particularly problematic when the various committees meet. This afternoon the full Education Committee is in session to discuss further cuts in the budget. Ms Tricklebank is required to be there and sends her apologies.'

'We managed to find a space,' Elisabeth told him, 'and—'
She stopped mid-sentence when the door opened and a dour,
exceptionally thin and sallow-complexioned man with a thick
crop of greying hair entered, accompanied by a group of
teachers.

'Ah, and here is Mr Richardson and his staff,' announced
Mr Nettles with forced cheerfulness.

'We are late,' said the man crossly, 'because we could not
find a parking place. I have been driving around for ten
minutes and eventually had to park on the road.'

'Yes, I was explaining to Mrs Devine that it is tricky at this
time,' said the education officer. He had the smile of a martyr
about to be burnt at the stake.

Mr Richardson gave Elisabeth a cursory glance before
sitting and turning his attention back to Mr Nettles. His
colleagues sat next to him. They stared mutely and looked
decidedly ill-at-ease. There was an uncomfortable silence.

'Is Ms Tricklebank not joining us?' he asked sententiously.

'No, I'm afraid not,' replied Mr Nettles. 'I was just telling
Mrs Devine that the Director of Education has to attend an
extraordinary meeting of the Education Committee concern-
ing the further cuts in the education budget. She sends her
apologies.'

'So you are to conduct this meeting, I take it?' enquired Mr
Richardson.

'I am.'

The education officer sat at the head of the table, crossed
his legs casually and flicked through his notes, attempting to
give the appearance of being entirely at ease. Inwardly he felt
as nervous and anxious as a patient waiting to hear the results
of some medical test. His stomach was doing kangaroo jumps.

'Well, now that we are all here,' he said, 'I should like to take
you through the process and some of the procedures for the
amalgamation next term.'

'Might some introductions be in order?' suggested Elisabeth.

'Yes, yes, of course,' replied Mr Nettles. 'Perhaps you might like to start, Mrs Devine?'

'Yes, of course. I'm Elisabeth Devine,' she said, staring across the table at the unsmiling faces which gazed back at her. 'As you are probably aware, I am, at present, the head teacher at Barton-in-the-Dale village school.' The education officer was expecting her to say more and looked at her expectantly. 'Miss Brakespeare, the deputy head teacher at Barton, is not with us this afternoon,' she continued. 'Since she will be retiring at the end of this term she felt that it would be inappropriate for her to attend.' She thought it would be diplomatic to say nothing more for the moment.

'I'm Elsie Robertshaw, teacher of the lower juniors,' said her colleague confidently and looking straight at Mr Richardson.

'I'm Rebecca Wilson,' said the infant teacher meekly. 'I teach in the early years.'

Mr Nettles looked across the table. 'And from Urebank?'

'Mr Richardson, headmaster,' he said in a hollow tone of voice. His mouth then turned down into a grimace and he looked blankly in front of him but not before adding with some bitterness, 'For the moment that is.'

On his right a bony individual with lank hair and a dull reddish face spoke through his nose in a monotonous drawl. 'I'm Donald Jolly, deputy headmaster at Urebank. I teach the upper juniors.'

'Maureen Hawthorn,' said the woman sitting next to him and giving a small smile. 'I'm the lower juniors' teacher.'

'And I'm Margaret Ryan, teacher of the little ones,' added her colleague.

Both women, of indeterminate age, were remarkably similar in appearance. They were broad and with short steel grey hair and wide, friendly faces. Both were dressed in brightly coloured floral dresses and cardigans and wore beads and matching earrings, and both had large imitation leather handbags on their knees.

'Right,' said Mr Nettles rubbing his hands. He glanced down at his notes. 'The first item on the agenda—' he started.

'And are we to have a copy of the agenda?' asked Mr Richardson.

Mr Nettles took a deep breath. This was going to be a strained and arduous meeting, he thought. It had barely started and he could sense the antipathy. 'Yes, it would have been an idea to have copies for you all but I have been somewhat tied up today with various pressing matters. I'm sorry about that, I was intending—'

'Perhaps we might start,' suggested Mr Richardson, glancing at his wristwatch. 'Some of us do have other things to do this afternoon.'

'Yes, of course,' replied the education officer. 'Well, as I said, the first item on the agenda is to frame an SDP.'

'A what?' asked Mr Richardson.

'A school development plan. It sets out a timetable for the amalgamation and the issues, objectives and the targets we need to address.' He looked at Elisabeth. 'I think this was mentioned to you, Mrs Devine, by the Director of Education?'

'Yes,' replied Elisabeth.

'And she asked you to take a lead on it, did she not?'

'That's right. Perhaps initially Mr Richardson and myself might sit down and discuss this and work out a framework together.'

'Mrs Devine,' said Mr Richardson, acknowledging her for the first time, 'since you are the head teacher of the soon-to-be amalgamated schools I think it fitting that you write this SDP yourself.'

'Of course,' said Elisabeth pleasantly, 'I should be pleased to do so. I just thought you might like to be involved.'

'Not really,' he replied indifferently. He exchanged a small complicit smile with Mr Jolly.

There was an awkward silence. Mrs Robertshaw cast Miss Wilson a sideways glance.

'That's settled, then,' said Mr Nettles, sounding pleased. 'The next item is the staffing. Now I have worked out a suggested structure which I would like you to look at.'

'Do we have a copy?' asked Mr Richardson in a cold scornful tone.

'I'm afraid not.'

'Of course, you've been tied up all day,' he said, as if smiling at some private joke. 'So how are we supposed to look at it when we haven't a copy?' he added in a chilly tone of voice.

'What I should have said is that I shall outline what is suggested,' answered the education officer lamely. 'I will circulate a copy to everyone after the meeting.'

Mr Richardson gave a weary sigh.

Mr Nettles glanced down at his notes and took a breath. 'Ms Tricklebank has shared with me her views,' he continued, 'and, as you are aware, it has been decided that most of the junior-aged children – the nine-to-eleven-year-olds – will be based at Barton-in-the-Dale and the remainder, the younger children that is, at Urebank.'

'And who might I ask has decided this?' Mr Richardson asked coldly. He leaned forward over the table.

'Mr Preston, the former Director of Education, with the agreement of the Education Committee and the councillors in both wards,' he was told. 'Looking at the demography of the two villages, there were found to be more new houses and apartments in Urebank and more families with young children than there are in Barton, which tends to have more of an ageing population. Should we base the infants at Urebank the youngest children would not have to travel quite a distance to school. It was thought that it was far better for the older children to travel.'

'I see,' muttered Mr Richardson with an air of chilly detachment. 'So this is not, as you said, a suggested outline and therefore presumably up for discussion, it is the definitive plan?'

'Well, yes,' replied the education officer feebly.

'Could we make a start, please?' requested Mrs Robertshaw wearily. 'Otherwise we will be here all night.'

'So,' said Mr Nettles, taking a breath, 'with regard to the staffing structure in the new school, I am suggesting . . . I am . . . well, it has been decided that Mrs Devine, Mrs Robertshaw, Mr Jolly and Miss Brakespeare's replacement will be based with the juniors at Barton and—'

'Oh, I'm not at all happy with that,' Mr Jolly interrupted in a high querulous voice. Mrs Robertshaw rolled her eyes skywards. 'I should much prefer to stay where I am at Urebank.'

'And teach the infants?' asked Mrs Robertshaw. She had met the man on her visit to Urebank and found him as odious as the headmaster there.

'I beg your pardon?' he whined.

'I asked if you are wishing to teach the youngest children?' she asked.

'No, I am a junior school teacher,' he replied curtly. 'I have no experience with infants.'

'Well, if you wish to continue to teach the juniors,' Mrs Robertshaw explained, 'you will have to be based at Barton. If you stay at Urebank you will have to teach the infants.'

'Thank you, Mrs . . . er . . .' Mr Richardson interjected.

'Robertshaw,' she replied. She knew full well that he was aware of her name. 'I visited Urebank once, you might recall.'

'My colleague,' said Mr Richardson, ignoring her and addressing Mr Nettles, 'has just pointed out that he has had no experience with young children.'

'Then if he wishes to remain as a junior school teacher he will have to be based at Barton, won't he?' persisted Mrs

Robertshaw with a wry smile. There was a note of challenge in her voice.

'Mrs Robertshaw,' said Mr Richardson, glaring at her and raising his voice, 'with respect, I can't see what this has got to do with you.' His face was hard as flint.

Mrs Robertshaw was about to respond in kind when Elisabeth nudged her elbow. 'One moment, Elsie,' she said quietly. She had considered it expedient to remain silent until this point but now felt she should try to placate the situation, which was fast deteriorating into a disagreeable exchange.

'I am sure Mr Jolly's concerns can be discussed at a later date,' she said calmly. 'I would not wish any member of the teaching staff to be unhappy where he or she is located.'

'Could we then continue?' Mr Nettles entreated, desperate to get the meeting over and done with. A red nervous rash had appeared on his neck and he could feel the perspiration on his face and his suit sticking to his body. 'I will be happy to take any comments all in good time.' He carried on rapidly. 'On the Urebank site will be Mr Richardson, Mrs Hawthorn, Mrs Ryan and Miss Wilson.'

'I'm very happy to be staying where I am,' trilled Mrs Hawthorn, clearly pleased.

'Yes, so am I,' agreed her colleague, nodding like one of the toy dogs one sometimes sees on the back shelf of a car.

'Well, I do not wish to move,' complained Mr Jolly petulantly under his breath.

'Perhaps at this juncture I might be allowed to make a comment?' said Mr Richardson pompously.

'I don't know how you kept so composed with that rude and disagreeable man,' remarked Mrs Robertshaw angrily as she descended the stairs at County Hall with Elisabeth and Rebecca. Her high heels clacked noisily on the marble. 'I felt like reaching across the table and giving him a good smack around the chops. And that miserable deputy of his was just as repugnant. He looks as if he's been dug up. It was clear that they would object to everything that was suggested. They are going to do their level best to be difficult and oppose everything you are trying to achieve. And don't expect any help from that feeble Mr Nettles. He's about as much use as an ashtray on a motorbike. I just don't know how you stayed so calm.'

'In my experience, Elsie,' replied Elisabeth, 'to remain calm in such circumstances is the best way forward. Over the years I have learnt that when dealing with antagonistic people of the ilk of Mr Richardson, the best course of action is to remain unruffled and adopt the simple technique of keeping one's own counsel until the right moment. The first meeting was not the right moment. There is a maxim my father was fond of using, which was that in a conflict one should "trust in God and keep your powder dry". In other words, keep your head, be prepared and save your resources until they are needed. I would not wish the teachers at Urebank to go away thinking I am dictatorial and unreason-able. Actually the infant teacher and her colleague were quite amiable. Didn't you think so, Rebecca?'

'I don't think I can work at Urebank,' Miss Wilson said despondently. Her eyes began to fill with tears. 'I'm so happy at Barton. I can't see myself settling there at all. I don't know anybody and I am certain that I won't get on with Mr Richardson.'

'Well, let's sleep on it, shall we?' Elisabeth told her, feeling as depressed as her colleagues. 'We'll talk about it tomorrow. It's been a long hard day.'

As Elisabeth drove out through the great iron gates of County Hall there was a sudden growl of thunder and a snap of lightning. Then the rain began to fall in earnest. Great drops drummed on the car roof and water snaked down the windows. As she turned into the road she saw a comical sight. Mr Richardson and Mr Jolly were standing soaking wet and staring at a car which had been clamped. Elisabeth could not resist a small smile of satisfaction.

When Elisabeth arrived at Clumber Lodge later that day it was still raining.

Mrs O'Connor answered the door. 'Hello, Mrs Devine,' she said. 'Come along in out of the wet. I had an idea there was a plomp of rain coming.'

'Thank you, Mrs O'Connor,' replied Elisabeth. 'I've never known such weather at this time of year.'

'Here, let me take your coat,' said the housekeeper. She shook her head. 'It's like being back in Ireland. The rain there is like shoemakers' knives. Mind you, as my owld Grandmother Mullarkey used to say: "An hour's steady rain would do more good in a week now than a week's rain would do in a month later on."'

'She was quite a one for the sayings, wasn't she, your Grandma Mullarkey?' replied Elisabeth smiling.

'She was indeed. "I don't mind about the weather so long as it's dry," she used to say, God rest her soul. I remember when we went to view her in her coffin. Bridie Burke, who lived next door, looked at my dear dead sainted Grandma Mullarkey laying there and remarked that she'd never looked better.'

'Well, the gardens can do with a bit of rain,' replied Elisabeth, trying to suppress her laughter.

'It's more like a deluge,' said Mrs O'Connor. 'I remember when we last had rainfall like this it poured down for a fortnight, so it did. The stream burst its banks, the millpond filled up, gardens were swept away, fields became swamps and the road became a river. They had to evacuate a lot of the houses. I do hope your cottage doesn't flood. I have an idea it did when Mrs Pickles lived there.'

The smile left Elisabeth's face. After the nerve-racking meeting she had just had, she was not in the mood for anything else depressing. 'Let's hope not,' she replied quietly.

'Go through into the sitting-room, Mrs Devine,' the house-keeper told her. 'You sit yourself down and I'll make a nice strong cup of tea, strong enough to trot a mouse across it, as my Grandma Mullarkey used to say. '

'Is Dr Stirling not in?'

'He's still at the surgery, so he is, but he shouldn't be long.' Mrs O'Connor departed to put on the kettle.

Elisabeth sat by the window and stared out. The weather matched her mood. A ragged grey curtain of cloud hung from an iron grey sky and a fierce wind drove the rain at a sharp slant against the windowpane. She was tired and depressed. Getting the motley group of teachers she had met that day to work together was not going to be an easy task. Her eyes flitted sideways. When she had first visited Clumber Lodge there had been several photographs in silver frames arranged on a small, walnut occasional table. One showed Dr Stirling with his arm around his wife, a striking-looking woman; another was a more formal portrait of the same woman posing before a horse. There was now just a small lamp and a potted plant on the table.

'The kettle's on,' the housekeeper said when she returned to the room. 'Would you like to stay for a bite to eat, Mrs Devine?'

'No thank you,' replied Elisabeth.

'Sure there's plenty.'

'It's kind of you but I do have quite a lot to do this evening. Mrs O'Connor, where are the photographs which were on the small table?'

'Dr Stirling thought it best to move them.' She spoke in a whisper, as if there had been a death. 'He's put them in James's room.'

'Why?'

'I should imagine he thought that since you're to be married soon and moving in here it would be more considerate to move them.'

'Considerate?' repeated Elisabeth. 'In what way?'

'That it would be more tactful not to have photographs of his dearly departed wife about the place.'

'Did he think it would upset me?' asked Elisabeth.

'To be sure I wouldn't know, Mrs Devine.'

'I've no problem with having his wife's photographs on show,' said Elisabeth.

'Well, I suggest you take that up with Dr Stirling,' replied Mrs O'Connor. 'Sure and isn't that the front door now?'

'Oh, hello,' said Michael, coming into the room. His hair and face were wet. 'Terrible weather, isn't it?'

'I'm just about to make Mrs Devine a cup of tea, Dr Stirling,' the housekeeper informed him. 'I'm sure you could enjoy one. The upstairs has been cleaned, ironing done and the boys have been fed and watered. Your dinner's in the oven.'

'Thank you, Mrs O'Connor,' replied Michael cheerfully. 'Whatever would I do without you?'

'Get away with your blarney,' she said, chuckling and shuffling for the door. 'Now I'll just make the tea and then I'll be on my way.'

'Let me do that, Mrs O'Connor,' said Elisabeth.

'It's no trouble at all, Mrs Devine.'

'No, really, I can do it.'

'I always make the doctor's tea when he gets in from the surgery.' She sounded rather put out.

'I think I can manage to make a pot of tea,' Elisabeth told her. 'You get off home.'

Mrs O'Connor looked at Michael.

'You heard the lady,' he said good-humouredly. 'Off you go.'

'Oh well, if you're sure,' said the housekeeper. She looked rather peeved. 'I'll leave you to it then.'

'Thank you, Mrs O'Connor,' Michael said, as she waddled through the door. 'Goodnight.'

'I'm sorry if I've called at a bad time,' Elisabeth began.

'No, no, not at all,' he replied. 'You know you're always welcome. I was going to give you a ring and see if you wanted to go out somewhere for the evening.'

'Michael, why have you moved the photographs of your wife?' she asked.

He went to the sideboard and splashed a couple of inches of whisky into a glass.

'Would you like one?'

'No thank you. Why did you remove the photographs?' she asked again.

'We will be starting married life soon,' he told her. 'I just thought that when we do, you may not be too happy about seeing pictures of my first wife in such a conspicuous position.'

'Not at all,' Elisabeth replied rather sharply. 'She was such a part of your life and you loved her very much. The last thing I want is for her to be forgotten.'

'She will not be forgotten,' he replied equally as sharply. 'I just thought—'

'Well, you might have asked me.'

'All right, all right,' sighed Michael. 'I'll put the photographs back if it makes you feel better.'

'Didn't James mind you moving his mother's pictures?' she asked.

'No.'

'Did you ask him?'

'Gracious me, Elisabeth, this is like a cross-examination.' He sounded irritated. 'I will put the photographs back. Now could we change the subject?' He finished the whisky in one gulp.

Elisabeth got up. 'I'll make the tea,' she said.

'So what sort of day have you had?' Michael asked Elisabeth

later when she handed him a cup of tea and sat next to him on the sofa.

'Dire,' she replied.

'Oh dear, as bad as that?' He put his arm around her.

'The meeting at County Hall could not have been worse,' she told him. 'Mr Richardson seems determined to thwart anything which is suggested. I really don't think it will be possible to work with him. He's so negative.'

'Well, I suppose the man's still smarting at not getting the job. I'm sure you will be able to win him around.'

'I very much doubt it.'

'There is one simple solution to all the problems you are encountering,' he said.

'Which is?'

'You give up the job.'

'What!'

'When we are married you can be a lady of leisure,' he said. 'You won't need to work.'

'Can you imagine me as a lady of leisure?' she asked crossly.

'Well, perhaps that's the wrong thing to say. You could get involved in village activities, maybe do some charity work, take on a bit of supply teaching, you could even get a position lecturing at the college in Clayton. There are lots of things to occupy a woman of talent like you.'

'I know I complain about things, Michael,' Elisabeth told him, 'but I really love my job and I do not want to give it up. I feel I make a real difference in the lives of the children, just as you make a difference in the lives of your patients. Teaching is the most rewarding job in the world.'

Michael kissed her cheek. 'Shall we talk about something other than school?' he asked. 'It seems it is the only topic of conversation these days.'

'I'm sorry, but there are things that are weighing on my mind,' she told him.

'Look, darling, I appreciate that,' said Michael gently. 'These are worrying times for you, but try not to bring your work home with you all the time. I put all the medical problems to the back of my mind when I leave the surgery. It's the way I have learnt to cope.'

'It's rather different for me.'

'Is it?'

'Of course it is.'

'All right, but can we drop school this one evening? We could talk about the wedding.'

'It's not a good time, Michael,' Elisabeth told him. 'It really isn't. I've so much on my mind at the moment. Anyway, I had better be off. I've got this development plan to work on tonight.'

'So you're not staying for dinner?'

'Not tonight,' she said, getting up. She bent and pecked him on the cheek.

'I love you, you know,' he said.

'Yes, I love you too,' she replied. There were tears in her eyes.

8

Miss Hilda Sowerbutts, former head teacher of Barton-in-the-Dale Primary School, sat stiffly at the small, reproduction mahogany desk in her sitting-room, the telephone receiver grasped in her thin white hand. She narrowed her eyes in that characteristic way she had when she was angry.

'This invoice,' she barked at the person on the other end of the line, 'is quite preposterous!' Around her on the desk were strewn various bills which she had been studying. 'I most certainly have not used all this amount of gas.' The person to whom she was speaking attempted to interrupt but to no avail, for Miss Sowerbutts was now well into her stride. 'Let me finish!' she snapped. 'This exorbitant demand is far in excess of the previous statement with which it has been compared, and more than if I had put the heating on full blast for the entire quarter. I live in a small two-bedroomed cottage, not a stately home, and I do not possess a furnace.' There was a feeble attempt by the person at the other end of the line to get a word in. 'I have not finished. I am extremely economical in my use of heating and during the last quarter was in hospital, when the central heating was turned off and the gas fire not used.'

She failed to reveal that her stay in hospital had been but a few days. She continued angrily, 'So as a consequence I have used the minimum amount of energy in the three-month period.' The woman at the Gas Board finally managed to interject in an attempt to explain but again without success for she was interrupted mid-sentence. 'Well, the reading was incorrect, that is all I will say. The man who read the meter must have very bad eyesight or he is an incompetent. No, I do not intend to give you a meter reading myself. Now, I insist that you look into this as a matter of urgency and while I am on the telephone I have noticed that the heat given out by my gas fire has significantly diminished of late, and another thing, I had to wait an inordinate amount of time to get through to you and was subjected to ten minutes of inane piped music.' With this final salvo Miss Sowerbutts thumped down the receiver.

After pouring herself her second, large, extra dry sherry of the day, she settled down in an easy chair by the window and looked out over her neat little garden, the smooth green lawn, carefully trimmed hedges and tidy borders she so carefully tended. Beyond was an uninterrupted vista, across fields sheltered by silvered drystone walls to open countryside and rolling hills beyond. At least that dreadful Mr Massey would not be spoiling her view with his wretched housing estate. She bristled with suppressed anger as she recalled the disagreeable exchange she'd had with him.

There was a ring on the doorbell.

'For goodness' sake,' she said to herself. 'You can't have a minute's peace and quiet.' She placed the glass behind a photograph of her Siamese cat, which had pride of place on a small bamboo table.

On the doorstep stood Miss Brakespeare, her former colleague at the school. In contrast to Miss Sowerbutts, who wore a prim white blouse and shapeless skirt the colour of mud, her visitor was elegantly dressed in a lightweight mauve dress and stylish pink cardigan. Her hair had been newly tinted and permed and she wore light lavender lipstick. A great transformation had taken place in the deputy head teacher since the retirement of Miss Sowerbutts. This mousy little woman with the round face and the staring eyes, who invariably dressed in an ill-fitting cotton suit, dark stockings and sandals, had appeared dowdy and dull. Her hair had been scraped back in a style which was a good twenty years out of date and there was not a trace of any make-up. But with the appointment of the new head teacher there had been a quite dramatic change in Miss Brakespeare, and not just in her appearance. Unlike her predecessor, Elisabeth had listened to the deputy head teacher, sought her views, involved her in decision-making and supported her in her teaching, and the woman had blossomed.

'Good morning, Hilda,' said Miss Brakespeare cheerily. 'It's such a beautiful day, I thought I'd call in on my way into town to see how you are. English springs are often quite cold, aren't they, so it's nice to see the sun shining.'

'You had better come in,' said Miss Sowerbutts flatly. 'As you know, I suffer from hay fever and keep the doors and windows closed at this time of year. The pollen count is dreadful today.'

Her visitor was shown into the stuffy sitting-room but not before she had slipped off her shoes and left them in the hall. Curled up on one of the easy chairs was a lazy-looking Siamese cat with large pointed ears on the sides of its triangular head. It observed her with almond-shaped eyes. At the sight of her it leapt from the chair, darted towards her and, meowing loudly, began to rub its sleek body against the visitor's leg. Miss Sowerbutts scooped up the animal and deposited it in the hall before closing the sitting-room door.

'I really don't know what's got into Tabitha recently,' she said irritably. 'She never used to be like this. Since she had that period at Clumber Lodge when I was in hospital, she's been quite unmanageable. That housekeeper of Dr Stirling's no doubt fed her on the most unsuitable food.'

'It was very good of the doctor to look after the cat for you,' ventured Miss Brakespeare, thinking how ungrateful her former colleague sounded.

'Be that as it may,' replied Miss Sowerbutts, 'I did stress that Tabitha is a pedigree Lilac Point Siamese and was not to be fed anything but fish and chicken.'

Miss Brakespeare sighed inwardly and changed the subject. 'It's such a pity you can't enjoy this lovely weather, what with your hay fever and all,' she said in a brisk birdlike manner. 'I hope it's like this for when George and I get married.'

The newly transformed Miss Brakespeare had before Easter attracted the attention of a widower who played the organ at the Methodist chapel, and after a short courtship she had consented to be his wife when she retired in July. When she had been told the news, Miss Sowerbutts was more than a little surprised to learn that a man could find this dumpy, twittering, middle-aged woman attractive and that at her age Miss Brakespeare should still find men of some interest.

'I've just had a most disagreeable telephone conversation with a young woman at the Gas Board,' Miss Sowerbutts told her, ignoring the reference to the wedding. 'Some silly slip of a girl just out of school, no doubt, and of no help whatsoever.'

'Oh dear,' sighed her visitor.

Of course it was typical of Miss Sowerbutts not to enquire about her wedding, thought Miss Brakespeare. She was so tied up with her own affairs that she took no interest in the activities or interests of other people and never asked about them. Miss Brakespeare would have been delighted to have outlined her plans for her forthcoming wedding to George and talked about the bungalow with the sea view which they had bought in Scarborough. She glanced surreptitiously at her watch and decided not to prolong this visit.

Miss Sowerbutts was still complaining about her gas bill. 'I've received this outrageous demand for heating which I do not intend to pay.'

'My bill has seen a big rise too,' replied Miss Brakespeare, 'but it was to be expected. After all, it was a particularly cold few months after Christmas, wasn't it, and they did say prices would have to go up in the New Year. And of course when you were at the school full-time and out of your house you would not have had the heating on very much.'

'Thank you for pointing that out to me, Miriam,' said Miss Sowerbutts testily and with obvious sarcasm in her voice. 'That explains why my bill is so high. You ought to work for the Gas Board.' She gestured to a chair. 'You had better sit down.'

Miss Brakespeare opened her mouth to say something in response but, thinking better of it, closed it again. There was an awkward silence.

'I should imagine you'll be glad to finish at the school,' said Miss Sowerbutts. 'All these wretched changes and interference from supposed experts and the pushy parents and badly behaved children. I was certainly glad to finish.'

Not really true, thought Miss Brakespeare. The former head teacher of the village school had been given her marching orders following the dire school inspection. She would have been quite content to stay on at Barton had she not been pressured by the governors and the local education authority to take early retirement. She bitterly resented the way she had been treated, and disliked her successor and all her modern methods.

'Well, I thought it was about time I retired,' said Miss Brakespeare. 'I really didn't want all the upheaval, what with the forthcoming amalgamation next term. I was offered very good terms and George was very keen—'

'I really don't know how you cope with the children these days,' interrupted Miss Sowerbutts, not really listening.

Miss Brakespeare wondered if there was no limit to her former colleague's self-absorption. 'Some children can be a bit of handful at times, I have to admit,' she said. 'Fortunately

I don't teach the most difficult ones. Mrs Devine has those in her class.'

'Does she indeed?'

'Actually we've just got a very difficult boy who has just started. A real little devil, he is. The psychologist is of the opinion he has ODD.'

'He has what?' snapped Miss Sowerbutts.

'Oppositional Defiant Disorder,' explained Miss Brakespeare.

'Oh, for goodness sake!' exclaimed Miss Sowerbutts. 'What will they think of next? Why, oh why do these supposed educational experts always have to give children who are lazy and disobedient some fancy label and excuse their misbehaviour? They are just plain naughty. They want a good dose of old-fashioned discipline, that's all. It was a sad day when they stopped teachers using the strap.'

Miss Brakespeare wished she had never raised a topic which was guaranteed to inflame her former colleague. She quickly changed the subject.

'So how are you keeping?' she enquired, trying to sound cheerful.

'As well as can be expected,' came the po-faced reply.

'And your head?'

'My head?'

'Is it better? I mean you had a dreadful bump when you fell down the stairs.'Miss Sowerbutts, in negotiating the narrow and steep stairs in her cottage with a tray of morning coffee, had not seen her cat stretched out on the top step. She had tripped and fallen headlong, banging her head and breaking her arm in the process. She had spent three very unpleasant days in hospital, where she grumbled about everything from the treatment to the food.

'My head is outwardly fine,' Miss Sowerbutts revealed, looking accusingly at the door behind which the cat, which had been responsible for her accident, had been deposited, 'although I have suffered some throbbing headaches since the accident. It sometimes feels as if there's a hammer inside my head banging away. And I should point out, Miriam, that it wasn't a bump, as you term it, it was a very nasty concussion. I could have fractured my skull.' Her voice sounded peevish and condescending in tone.

'Your garden looks very nice,' her former colleague remarked, attempting to move on to a more cheery topic of conversation. 'I wish mine was as neat and tidy. I've been so busy lately, what with looking after mother, preparing for the new term and arranging the wedding. I just haven't had time to even cut the lawn. The grass is so thick and tufty and full of weeds and—'

'Well, my lawn has just about recovered from the damage caused by that useless Mr Massey and that foolish nephew of his,' cut in Miss Sowerbutts. 'Fancy trying to get rid of moles by pouring bottles of bleach down their runs. It succeeded in killing the grass but not the moles, which if anything seemed to thrive.'

Miss Brakespeare was tempted to say that she quite liked those shy furry little creatures, but she resisted. 'It was very good of young Danny Stainthorpe to sort it out for you,' she commented, 'setting those traps and disposing of the bodies.'

'Yes, it was,' Miss Sowerbutts replied grudgingly.

There was another uncomfortable silence, during which Miss Brakespeare wondered why she still made the effort to keep in contact with such an ill-tempered and splenetic woman. It was sad she had become so bitter. Miss Sowerbutts had not always been like that. Latterly, and particularly after the school inspector had been highly critical of her management and leadership, describing it as 'lacklustre', she had become so tetchy and disagreeable. It had been an ordeal working with her for those last few years, having to listen to her carping and complaining in that penetrating voice of hers. Nothing was ever right for Miss Sowerbutts; everyone except her seemed to be at fault. What a joyless existence she must lead, this dried-up woman.

'I told that Mr Massey and that scatter-brained nephew of his,' continued Miss Sowerbutts, 'that it would be the last time they would be employed to do any work for me.'

'Speaking of Mr Massey,' said Miss Brakespeare, 'I heard in the village store that he intends to sell off some of his land for housing.'

'Really?' Miss Sowerbutts replied, feigning ignorance.

'If he gets planning permission, that is,' continued her former colleague. 'The houses will be built on the field beyond the church and at the back of your cottage.'

Miss Sowerbutts gave a short barking laugh. 'Oh no, they won't,' she remarked smugly. 'I have spoken to the Reverend Atticus and he assured me that the track by the church is not for sale, so without access to the field there will be no houses built.'

'Yes, I heard the Archdeacon had refused to sell him that track but I gather that Mr Massey is now exploring another possibility,' said Miss Brakespeare, smiling slightly in a secretive way.

Miss Sowerbutts shot up straight as if she had been poked with a cattle prod.

'Another possibility?' she exclaimed.

'That's what Mrs Sloughthwaite told me when I was in the village store,' Miss Brakespeare said weakly. 'Mr Massey has been to see Mrs Devine to buy that strip of land which leads to his field down the side of her cottage.'

Miss Sowerbutts's eyes narrowed dramatically for the second time that morning and her lips became a hard thin line. 'Well, I will tell you this, Miriam, there is not the slightest possibility of that dreadful man building houses at the back of

my cottage and spoiling my view. Not the slightest possibility,'
she repeated with emphasis.

Miss Brakespeare managed to summon up a sympathetic
murmur. 'No, I suppose there isn't,' she said under her breath.

Miss Sowerbutts rarely visited the village store and post office,
for she disliked the large nosy woman behind the counter. She
tended to do her weekly shopping at the supermarket in
Clayton and use the post office in Urebank. That afternoon,
however, she had several important letters to send. She had
spent the previous evening writing a series of strongly worded
outpourings to the editor of the *Clayton and District Gazette*;
to the Principal of St John's College of Education, the former
teacher training establishment where she had studied; to Ms
Tricklebank, the newly appointed Director of Education and
to the Chairman of the Education Committee. Her correspondence expressed her deep concern at the way education
was going. She bemoaned the decline in standards, the lack of
discipline in schools, the poor behaviour of children, all these
trendy new methods and modern approaches and the fashionable fads and fancy initiatives which were being introduced.
Of particular concern, she stated, were the ridiculous labels
that so-called experts and educational psychologists gave to
children who misbehaved. 'What children need,' she wrote, 'is
to be taught by traditional, tried-and-tested methods and
receive good, old-fashioned discipline.'

When she entered the village store Miss Sowerbutts found
the shopkeeper leaning over the counter as was her wont, in
conversation with the Archdeacon.

'I think I might just settle with the beans, thank you, Mrs
Sloughthwaite,' the cleric was saying.

'What about a nice slice of boiled ham,' suggested the shopkeeper, 'or a pork pie?'

'Thank you, no,' he replied, 'the beans will be fine.'

The Archdeacon turned his good-natured face to the customer who had just entered and adopted the benevolent countenance he had perfected over the years for those whom he encountered and found trying. And Miss Sowerbutts he found particularly trying.

'Good afternoon, Miss Sowerbutts,' he said in a deliberately jaunty tone.

'Good afternoon,' she replied tersely.

'And how are you?' he asked.

She raised an eyebrow. 'As well as can be expected after falling down a flight of stairs, breaking an arm in two places and ending up comatose with concussion.'

The Archdeacon wished he had not asked. He closed his eyes and inhaled deeply.

Miss Sowerbutts turned her face in the direction of Mrs Sloughthwaite, who stared back at her impassively.

'I take it the post office is open,' she said flatly.

'It is,' replied the shopkeeper without a smile. She disliked this customer, with her curled lip, hooded brow and heavy judgemental eyes. At the sight of her, Mrs Sloughthwaite would recall her mother's comment, when she was a child and pulled a grumpy face, that 'One day the wind will change, my girl, and your face will stay like that.' Miss Sowerbutts rarely visited the village store and when she did she purchased very little and spent all her time complaining.

'I have some very important letters to send,' said the customer. 'Special delivery.'

'Well, if you wait until I've seen to the Reverend Atticus,' the shopkeeper told her in an offhand manner, 'I'll deal with *you* when I've served *him*.'

'Oh please,' said the Archdeacon holding up a hand, 'I am in no hurry. Do serve Miss Sowerbutts.'

Mrs Sloughthwaite made no effort to stir herself and the two women glared at each other like angry cats.

Sensing the animosity, the Archdeacon, who hated any sort of confrontation or unpleasantness, continued in a light-hearted voice. 'I have been left to my own devices making my own tea this afternoon,' he explained. 'I think I can just about manage baked beans. My wife is attending a final lecture at the college and my curate, who usually provides the repast, is on duty at the hospital. Perhaps you came across the Reverend Underwood when you were in the Royal Infirmary, Miss Sowerbutts?'

'No, I didn't,' she replied curtly. 'And to be frank, I had no need of a chaplain. I was just glad to get out of the place.'

Mrs Sloughthwaite thought she would be glad if this particular customer got out of this place. She moved unhurriedly behind the post office counter.

'You wanted something posting,' she said.

Miss Sowerbutts pushed the letters across the counter and proffered a crisp ten pound note, then she directed her attention back to the Archdeacon, who stood clutching his tin of beans.

'I was pleased to hear that the track at the side of the church is not for sale,' she said.

'It is not in my bailiwick,' replied the cleric.

'In your what?' said Miss Sowerbutts.

'I am not in any position to authorise its sale,' explained the Archdeacon.

'Well, I am gratified to hear it,' she said primly. 'Thankfully, you have put a stop to Mr Massey's hare-brained plan to build houses on the field behind my cottage.'

'I can hardly claim credit for that,' replied the Archdeacon. 'The sale of Church property is in the hands of the Church Commissioners, although, in this case, I would have been consulted.'

'Whatever,' said Miss Sowerbutts smugly, 'it has put paid to his little scheme.'

'I should imagine so,' agreed the clergyman.

'Oh, I don't know about that,' said Mrs Sloughthwaite, passing the proof of postage and change across the counter before resuming her position back in the shop. 'I gather from Mrs Pocock that he's exploring other possibilities.'

'You mean the track down the side of Wisteria Cottage?' said Miss Sowerbutts. 'Yes, I've heard some such rumour but I can't see it happening. I'm sure Mrs Devine would not wish her peace to be disturbed by all the noise and the traffic.'

'I heard from Mrs Pocock, whose husband drinks with Fred Massey in the Blacksmith's Arms, that he's approached Mrs Devine and offered to buy the track for a good sum.'

'I don't think Mrs Devine will agree to that,' said the Archdeacon, shaking his head emphatically.

'Oh, I don't know about that, Reverend,' said the shop-keeper, enjoying the discomfort she could clearly see on Miss Sowerbutts's face. 'I gather she is seriously considering it. The houses won't spoil her view,' she added pointedly, 'and in any case she'll no doubt be selling Wisteria Cottage after she gets married and moves into Clumber Lodge, so it's no skin off her nose.'

Miss Sowerbutts jolted upright as if an electric shock was passing through her body. She snatched up the receipts and the coins and hurried from the shop.

'I reckon Mrs Devine is in line for a visit,' observed Mrs Sloughthwaite, with a self-satisfied smile on her round face.

Mr Steel, HMI, a tall, cadaverous man with sunken cheeks and greyish skin, arrived at the school promptly at one o'clock. Attired in a black suit, white shirt and dark tie and wearing shiny black shoes which creaked when he moved, he resembled an undertaker. His voice had the deep and solemn tones appropriate to a funeral. His appearance and his voice, however, belied a warm and friendly manner.

The inspector explained to Elisabeth that he wished to spend the first part of the afternoon with the infants and the remainder with the lower juniors, listening to the children read, looking through their exercise books and asking them a few questions about their work. He also intended to test them on their number work and spellings before he left.

Elisabeth felt confident that he would find everything in order, for on his last visit, earlier in the year, Mr Steel had been impressed with what he had seen. After spending a day in the school he had explained to her that he saw no need for a full school inspection but would make what he called a 'dipstick visit' the following term.

The children in the infants were engaged on a number of activities: practising their reading, copy-writing, acting in the Home Corner, building models, painting, and playing with sand and water when the unusual-looking visitor entered the classroom.

'Good morning, Miss Wilson. Good morning, children,' said the inspector.

'Good morning, Mr Steel. Good morning, everybody,' chorused the children.

'Some of you may remember Mr Steel,' Miss Wilson told the children. 'He is the school inspector who called in to see us last term and was really interested to see what we were doing. This afternoon he would like to find out how you are all getting on.'

Mr Steel could not fail to be pleased with what he saw. The classroom was neat and tidy and the children's work was well-displayed. A large bright alphabet and key words for children to learn decorated a wall, and an attractive reading corner contained a range of colourful picture and reading books and simple dictionaries. The children were busily occupied in a calm atmosphere.

A small, rosy-faced girl was diligently filling a plastic bucket with dry sand. The inspector watched as she upended the bucket. The contents spilled out.

'What you need to do,' he told her, 'is to add some water to the sand and that will hold it together.'

'Don't want to,' replied the child sulkily.

'Adding a little water makes the sand stick, you see,' said Mr Steel.

'Don't want to,' repeated the child.

'Let me show you,' he said.

The inspector took the bucket from the child and scooped up a handful of dry sand and filled it to the top. Then, ladling up some liquid in a small cup from a large tray containing water, he poured it into the bucket, mixed the contents and patted it down. The small girl watched him, screwing up her nose as if there was an unpleasant smell in the room. Upending the bucket and tapping the bottom, he produced a perfect sandcastle. 'You see,' he said smiling. 'I used to make sandcastles like this one when I took my children to the beach. Now, you have a go.'

'Don't want to!' said the child emphatically and raising her voice. 'How many more times do I have to tell you?'

'What seems to be the problem, Rosie?' asked Miss Wilson, approaching.

'Miss, the defector wants me to make a sandcastle like his,' the girl told the teacher. 'I've told him I don't want to.'

'I was endeavouring to explain,' Mr Steel told the teacher, 'that if she adds a little water to the sand, her sandcastle won't collapse. I don't know why she's so insistent not to do so.'

'Is there a reason why you don't want to, Rosie?' asked the teacher gently.

'Yes miss,' replied the child. 'It's because Jamie's weed in the water tray, that's why.'

In Mrs Robertshaw's classroom the school inspector found Roisin poring over a book.

'May I look?' he asked.

'Sure,' she replied.

'Ah, Oscar Wilde,' said Mr Steel, glancing at the cover.

'He was Irish,' the child told him.

'Yes, I know.'

'My father says that all the best writers are Irish. They are great storytellers.'

'So I believe.'

'Our teacher has been reading us some of Oscar Wilde's stories. This is my very favourite. It's called *The Happy Prince*.'

'It's quite a sad story,' said the school inspector.

'Sure it is,' agreed Roisin.

'Would you read me a little?' asked Mr Steel.

The girl read in a clear and confident voice, pausing on occasion as if considering what was in the story. 'It makes me want to cry,' she said thoughtfully.

'You're a very fine reader,' said Mr Steel.

In his many visits to primary schools the inspector could not recall when he had heard such an accomplished and confident reader.

'Could you read me some?' asked the child.

'It would be my pleasure,' replied the inspector, and as he lifted the text from the page the other children stopped what they were doing to listen.

When he had finished Roisin gave a disarming smile. 'You're a very fine reader too,' she told him.

Mr Steel had remained for some time after school, discussing his findings. Elisabeth was pleased to hear that he had been well-satisfied with what he had observed, but it had been a busy and tiring day and she was keen to get back to the cottage for a hot bath and an early night. When the inspector had gone she walked around the silent school as was her habit at the end of the day, turned off a few lights, closed doors and picked up the odd piece of litter which the cleaner had missed before making tracks herself.

Her heart sank when she saw the stiff-backed, stern-faced woman awaiting her. Miss Hilda Sowerbutts, dressed in her thick, pleated tweed skirt, crisp white blouse buttoned up to her thin neck, heavy tan brogues and that silly knitted hat like a tea cosy perched on top of her head, stood like a sentinel at the gate of the school.

Elisabeth took a deep breath and prepared herself for the confrontation which would inevitably follow.

'Mrs Devine,' said Miss Sowerbutts. 'Might I have a word?'

'Yes, of course, Miss Sowerbutts,' replied Elisabeth. 'Would you care to come into the school?'

'Thank you, no. What I have to say will be short and to the point.' A shadow of displeasure crossed her face. When Elisabeth did not reply, she gave a small cough and continued.

'I should like to speak to you about Mr Massey,' she said, 'and his fanciful idea of building houses on the field to the rear in my cottage.'

'And how does that concern me?' asked Elisabeth.

'It has been brought to my attention that you have been approached by Mr Massey to sell the track down the side of your cottage in order that he can gain access to the field. Is this the case?'

'I think this is my business,' said Elisabeth, 'and not anyone else's.'

Miss Sowerbutts gave a hostile stare. 'Mrs Devine, it is most certainly my business, since if these houses were to be built they would ruin the view I have from my cottage. I have lived there all my life and have an uninterrupted outlook. I do not intend to have it spoilt.'

'I am sure that the planning department will take that into

account before granting Mr Massey permission to build,'
Elisabeth told her.

'If you decide not to sell the track,' Miss Sowerbutts
persisted, 'there would be no possibility of houses being built
there because there would be no access. So I ask you again,
has Mr Massey approached you to sell the land and if so what
have you told him?'

'And I will repeat what I said earlier,' replied Elisabeth,
becoming irritated by the woman's fierce interrogation, 'that it
is my business.'

'I see,' said Miss Sowerbutts. She pressed her thin lips
together and narrowed her eyes in that characteristic way of
hers. 'I take it from that evasive answer that Mr Massey has
indeed been in touch with an offer to buy the land. That being
the case, I hope you refused to entertain such an idea. My
family have been in Barton-in-the-Dale for many generations,
and those of us native to the village do not take kindly to those
who have recently moved here trying to change its very nature.'

'I am not trying to change anything, Miss Sowerbutts,' said
Elisabeth calmly. 'From what I gather it is Mr Massey, whose
forebears have lived in the village as long as yours, who is
doing that. I suggest you take the matter up with him.'

'May I have your assurance,' continued Miss Sowerbutts,
undeterred, 'that you will not be selling the track to Mr
Massey?'

'I really do not wish to discuss my business with anyone,'
said Elisabeth, resisting the temptation of adding 'much less
with you'. 'So if that is all, Miss Sowerbutts, I will wish you
good afternoon.'

Elisabeth walked away, leaving the stiff-backed figure glowering at the gate.

9

Limebeck House was not a large residence by stately home standards but was a beautifully proportioned Georgian building of extraordinary charm and beauty. Built in grey ashlar limestone with many large rectangular windows, it stood out square and bright and solid in its vast parkland. A flight of well-worn steps led to the great black door, which was flanked by elegant stone pillars. The house had been built in 1760 by Sir William Wadsworth, who had lucrative estates in the West Indies and who had made his fortune in tobacco and sugar production. He commissioned Joseph Charlesworth, a local architect, to design a residence in keeping with his status and position. His wastrel son Tristram, the black sheep of the family, who spent most of his time travelling around Europe gambling and womanising, and who drank himself into an early grave, had lost most of the family wealth. Prosperity returned with the judicious marriage of his son, Robert, the first Viscount Wadsworth (who reputedly purchased the title) to Leonie Ricketts, daughter of an American stockbroker, who brought with her considerable wealth which enabled him to make extensive additions to the building. Lord Robert had great influence in the area and the family was involved in politics and the church, and even controlled admissions to the hospitals and workhouses. Like many large estates after the First World War, Limebeck declined and deteriorated further when the third Viscount was killed falling from his horse in the Clayton Hunt. His only surviving child, his daughter Lady

Helen Wadsworth, was the present incumbent of Limebeck House.

Over the years Limebeck House had fallen into a perilous state of disrepair and there had not been the money for renovation. Most of the rooms, with their peeling wallpaper and threadbare carpets, were cold, damp and draughty; the roof leaked, the stonework had begun to crumble and the lodge and outbuildings had become derelict. It seemed inevitable that Limebeck House would have to be sold. Then, by a remarkable stroke of luck, Lady Wadsworth's fortunes changed. Two rare seventeenth-century Italian sculptures, brought back from his Grand European Tour by the prodigal Tristram, had been discovered hidden away and at auction fetched a considerable amount of money. Limebeck House was saved and was now about to have a complete overhaul.

That morning Lady Wadsworth sat behind a small gilt desk with tasselled drawers in the library. She rang a small brass bell on her desk and a moment later the butler arrived.

'You rang, your ladyship,' he said languidly.

'I did, Watson,' she replied. 'I have had a request from Mrs Devine at the village school. She would like to bring three classes of children to see the grounds. It is part of a local history project which they are undertaking.'

The butler rolled his eyes. 'I assume you said that this would be all right?' he asked.

'Of course,' she replied. 'I think it's a very good thing for children to learn something about the history of where they live, and particularly about the Wadsworths, who have been so influential in the life of the people hereabouts.'

'In view of the proposed restoration work which is impending, perhaps this is not the most propitious time to have a group of children wandering around the premises,' he remarked.

'They will not be wandering around the premises,' retorted

Lady Wadsworth. She rarely agreed with her butler. 'The children won't be coming into the house itself but will view the exterior and see the grounds. I know that the parkland and gardens are not in a very good state at the moment, but they will give them an idea of what Limebeck House looked like in its heyday.'

'As you wish, your ladyship,' said the butler. 'So when can we expect the hordes to arrive?'

'Really, Watson,' sighed Lady Wadsworth, 'it is a few children, not an invasion of the Vikings. They will be here next Friday, accompanied by their teachers. I would like you to be on hand and could you ask Mr O'Malley to also make himself available? I shall ask him to give the children a bit of a tour of the estate. Oh, and Watson, do take the hang-dog expression off your face.'

'I shall endeavour to do so, your ladyship,' replied the butler with a face which could freeze soup in pans. 'Is that all?'

'No, there is something else,' she replied. 'I have invited the new curate up for coffee next Thursday. She appears a very personable young woman and seems to be making an effort to get to know people in the village. Of course, I am not in favour of woman priests or, I have to admit, the abandonment of the King James Bible in favour of the Good News version, or the *Ancient and Modern Hymnal* in favour of happy-clappy, sing-along tunes.'

'One has to move with the times, your ladyship,' Watson observed. 'We don't live in the Dark Ages any more. From what I gather, the attendance at St Christopher's has increased dramatically since the arrival of the new curate.'

'I do not recall requesting your observations on theological matters, Watson. I was merely expressing my thoughts out loud. However, it is true the church is much fuller but that I don't doubt is due to the fact that one does not have to endure another of the Archdeacon's interminable sermons. Charles

Atticus is a dear man but my goodness his homilies are head-and-shoulders above those to whom he speaks.'

'As you say, your ladyship,' replied the butler. 'Will that be all?'

'Do make sure there is a selection of biscuits available for when the Reverend Underwood calls, but do not purchase them under any circumstances from the village store. Mrs Sloughthwaite has been trying to offload those dreadful chocolate confections for some months now.'

'Anything else, your ladyship?'

'I can't think of anything for the moment,' she replied, 'but if I do I shall ring for you.'

'Of course you will,' he murmured wearily as he headed for the door.

'A most excellent repast, Ashley,' said the Archdeacon, breathing out noisily and patting his stomach.

Mr Atticus, his wife and the new curate had just finished a rack of lamb, the second course of a sumptuous meal.

'Yes indeed,' agreed his wife, placing her knife and fork carefully together before dabbing the corners of her mouth with a napkin. 'Quite, quite delicious. One wonders how you have the time, Ashley, to prepare and cook such a meal with all the other tasks my husband has saddled you with.'

'I wouldn't describe the delegation of some of my clerical duties to my curate as saddling her with tasks, my dear,' answered the Archdeacon, somewhat piqued.

'I really don't feel saddled at all,' replied Ashley. 'I have welcomed the opportunity of taking on the work. I was worried before coming to St Christopher's that like some of the curates in the diocese, the vicar here would always be interfering. Charles has let me get on with the work of the parish without hindrance.'

'Thankfully it was the same for me when I was on teaching

practice at the village school,' said Mrs Atticus. 'Mrs Devine was very supportive without meddling in what I was doing.'

'Perhaps there may be an opening for you in the newly amalgamated school?' suggested her husband.

'Possibly,' she said.

The Archdeacon said a silent prayer that she would secure a full-time post once she was qualified. Prior to her training, rather late in life, to be a teacher at the college in Clayton, his wife had been unhappy and become tedious in her complaints. These days, although she could still be prickly and outspoken, she seemed altogether better-tempered and content.

'I was hoping to have a word about the leaking roof at St Christopher's,' said Ashley.

'Ah, the leaking roof,' repeated the Archdeacon. 'I'm afraid it requires a whole lot of remedial work and lead is so very expensive.'

'Well, now you hold the purse strings as the Archdeacon of the diocese, Charles,' said Mrs Atticus, 'you can get it fixed.'

'No, my dear,' said her husband, 'it is not quite as simple as that. I cannot be seen to favour my own parish. I must appear to be impartial. There are many other churches in need of urgent repair. St Jude's in Ruston, for example, needs a new—'

'Charles,' persisted his wife, cutting him off in mid-sentence, 'what is the point of having the authority to decide on repairs and not using it to the advantage of your own church? When my father was an archdeacon—'

Her husband looked heavenwards and sighed.

'It's all very well you pulling a face,' said his wife tetchily, 'and making a noise like some exhausted beast, but when my father was an archdeacon—'

'Actually, Marcia,' interrupted the curate, 'I do see Charles's point of view. He has to be seen to be scrupulous and fair. The reason why I raised the matter of the leaking roof is not to ask for money from the diocese but to suggest that I might organise some fund-raising activities.'

'Now that is something of which I am very much in favour,' said the Archdeacon.

'I thought of holding some events in the church, such as concerts.'

'Ah,' said the Archdeacon, sounding less sympathetic, 'what sort of concerts have you in mind? Not pop concerts, I trust.'

'Musical evenings, recitals, poetry readings, literary presentations, celebrity lectures, that sort of thing,' replied Ashley.

'This sounds an excellent notion,' said the Archdeacon. 'We could ask the bishop to speak.'

'Well, if you do, you can guarantee only a small audience,' remarked Mrs Atticus. 'I imagine few people would give up an evening in front of the television to come and hear Bishop Bill spouting on about his missionary work in Africa.'

'We could perhaps start with an organ recital,' said Ashley.

'I'm afraid Mrs Fish, who accompanies the hymn-singing, is not up to a recital,' said Mrs Atticus. 'It takes her enough time to hit the right notes and she never keeps pace with the singing. And of course she is incapable of using the pedals. She is also prone to falling asleep at the organ.'

'I thought I might ask Mr Tomlinson,' Ashley told her. 'He plays the organ at the Methodist Chapel. I have heard he is very good.'

'I am not sure that Mrs Fish would take kindly to another organist playing at St Christopher's,' said the Archdeacon.

'Oh, Charles, really,' said Mrs Atticus. 'I am sure Ashley can speak to her tactfully.'

'Well, perhaps you are right,' said her husband. 'Maybe if we had a recital, we could prevail upon Lady Wadsworth to open proceedings.'

'Actually, I've been invited to have coffee with Lady Wadsworth at Limebeck House next Thursday,' Ashley told him. 'She spoke to me after the Morning Service and said there was a matter she wishes to discuss with me. I could mention the idea when I see her. She seems a very agreeable woman.'

'She is, but I wouldn't like to get on the wrong side of her,' Mrs Atticus remarked. 'She is quite a forceful and influential person in these parts, is Lady Wadsworth.'

The Archdeacon coughed. 'Actually,' he said, 'I have an idea what she wishes to speak to you about, Ashley. She had a word with me after Evensong regarding the various changes you have made at St Christopher's. I gather she is not greatly in favour of them. I guess she might want to tackle you on the matter.'

'Really?' said the curate.

'She tells me,' continued the Archdeacon, 'that you have introduced some modern hymns into the Morning Service.'

'They appeal so much more to the present-day church-goers than do the old-style tunes,' she told him. 'Modern Christian music can be inspiring and uplifting, often more meaningful to younger generations than traditional church music, and furthermore it attracts more worshippers.'

'Indeed, that may be so,' responded the Archdeacon, look-ing somewhat ill-at-ease, 'but the time-honoured hymns have a greater appeal to the older members of the congregation.'

'You can be assured I shall not abandon the established hymns,' said Ashley. 'I just thought it would be good to intro-duce some modern tunes.' She paused. 'I take it Lady Wadsworth is not happy with this?'

'Not really.'

'Well, she should attend the services you take then, Charles,' said Mrs Atticus, 'Evensong or the Communion Service. Everyone else seems very happy with what Ashley has intro-duced and I for one am all for a few innovations at St Christopher's.'

'And Mrs Fish, the organist?' asked Mr Atticus, ignoring his wife's intervention. 'How is she taking to the modern hymns?'

'She took a bit more convincing,' Ashley replied, 'but once she saw how much the choir enjoyed singing the contemporary hymns she's been converted.'

'Well, it will certainly go down well with Bishop Bill,' said Mrs Atticus somewhat disparagingly. 'The confirmation service at which he presided at the cathedral was like a revivalist meeting, all that loud singing and clapping and hand-waving.'

'And I see you prefer the modern version rather than the King James Bible?' continued the Archdeacon.

'Again I think it relates better to people in this day and age.'

'But do you not feel that the language of the King James Bible is so much more—'

'Please, Charles,' interrupted his wife, 'must we always have a theological discussion at the dinner table?'

'Maybe not, my dear,' said her husband. He did not wish to argue with his wife, for he knew from experience that it would be unprofitable to do so. 'Perhaps, Ashley, we might discuss it at a more apposite time,' he said.

'And you are still enjoying life here in the village, Ashley?' asked the Archdeacon's wife.

'Oh yes,' replied the curate, 'I am very happy here.'

'It's not too quiet and uneventful for an Oxford scholar such as yourself?' asked Mrs Atticus.

'No, not at all. The village is a delightful place.'

'Delightful is not a word I would use,' remarked Mrs Atticus, raising an eyebrow. 'Insular would be more appropriate, as I recall mentioning to you when you first came here. The village is a hotbed of tittle-tattle and if you wish to have a private life, Barton-in-the-Dale is not somewhere one would choose to reside.'

'And *I* recall saying, my dear,' interposed the Archdeacon, 'that you were being a trifle hard on the village. The people here are a simple, unpretentious sort, the very salt of the earth and generous to a fault.'

'And what, pray, about Miss Sowerbutts and Mr Massey?' asked his wife. 'Then there's Mrs Pocock and that good-for-nothing husband of hers. They are hardly generous to a fault and as for being the salt of the earth—'

'My dear Marcia,' interrupted her husband, raising a hand, 'might we talk about something else?' He smiled at the curate. 'Tell me, Ashley, how are things going at the hospital? It was very good of you to volunteer to be assistant chaplain there. I hope you are not taking too much on.'

'It's one of the most rewarding parts of my work,' she replied. 'The other chaplain, Father Daly, is a dear old priest. We get on very well.'

'And you have to travel by bus into Clayton every time you visit the Royal Infirmary?' asked Mrs Atticus, shaking her head. 'It is not something I would wish to do. You ought to use the car.'

'Oh, I don't mind the bus.'

'And using a bicycle to visit the parishioners,' continued the Archdeacon's wife. 'Can you imagine me on a bicycle, Charles?'

'No, I most certainly cannot, my dear,' replied her husband.

'You want to be careful, Ashley,' warned Mrs Atticus. 'It may be tolerable to ride a bicycle around the village in summer but the winters here are fierce. I really think you should use Charles's car.'

'And tell me, Ashley, how are the nuptials progressing?' asked the Archdeacon quickly, keen to change the subject. Although usually of a kindly disposition, the Archdeacon was not inclined to share his recently purchased car with his curate. He would need it to undertake his many duties in the diocese.

'Which do you mean?' she asked. 'I have several weddings planned. Mrs Fish's second granddaughter is to get married in June, then young Clarence and Bianca follow in late July, and shortly before that Dr Stirling and Mrs Devine are tying the knot.'

'Dr Stirling and Mrs Devine?' said the Archdeacon, startled. 'I assume rather than a wedding they are to have a blessing?'

'No,' replied Ashley, 'they want to be married in church.'

'In church?'

'Yes, at St Christopher's.'

'I have to say I am not altogether happy about that, Ashley,' said the Archdeacon, looking vexed. 'Mrs Devine is a divorced woman.'

'That's not her fault!' exclaimed Mrs Atticus, hurriedly coming to Elisabeth's defence. 'Her husband, like so many feckless men these days, had an affair and ran off with one of his colleagues at work. A woman half his age, I may add. Mrs Devine was the innocent party, left with a disabled son and not a sight of the father.'

'That is all very well, my dear,' replied the Archdeacon, 'but the fact remains she is a divorcee. I feel very well-disposed towards her, but the Church of England teaches that marriage is for life. Remarriage is allowed if the person's former spouse is dead but the matter becomes more complicated if one or both of the former spouses are still living.'

'Well, I can't follow that logic,' retorted his wife, 'bearing in mind that the very founder of the Church of England divorced a couple of his wives – those who didn't have their heads chopped off – so presumably this made the same thing possible for his subjects.'

'It is not a question of logic,' explained her husband. 'It is a matter of doctrine. Just because remarriage is legally allowed, that does not mean couples have an automatic right to remarry in church. Jesus was quite unequivocal about the matter when he said in Mark's gospel, "What God has united, man must not divide." Even if a couple separates legally, they are still joined together spiritually. In Matthew, chapter 19, verses 4 to 6, Jesus says that, "He who made man from the beginning, made them male and female." And he said, "For this cause shall a man leave father and mother, and shall cleave to his wife, and they two shall be in one flesh. Therefore now they are not two, but one flesh. What therefore God hath joined together, let no man put asunder."'

Mrs Atticus sighed. 'Charles,' she said, 'you are not in your pulpit now. Your habit of quoting scripture is quite irritating and—'

'Perhaps if I might come in here?' said Ashley hesitantly. She turned to the Archdeacon, who sat stern-faced and with a furrowed brow. 'You will allow, Charles, that the Church of England also recognises that some marriages sadly do fail, and, if this should happen, it seeks to be compassionate and understanding to those involved.'

'Well, of course, Ashley,' he replied, 'that goes without question.'

'And do you not accept that the Church recognises that, in exceptional circumstances, a divorced person may marry again in church during the lifetime of a former spouse, something which actually was agreed overwhelmingly at the General Synod? Does not the final decision rest with the clergy member who is to perform the marriage?'

'There you are, Charles,' said the Archdeacon's wife rather smugly, 'it's all been explained to you. Now what's for dessert?'

'It'll be a summer wedding then,' said Mrs Sloughthwaite to her two most regular customers.

'And who told you that?' asked Mrs Pocock. She was

standing, arms folded tightly over her chest, before the counter in the village store with Mrs O'Connor.

'I asked Mrs Devine when she called in for her order yesterday,' replied the shopkeeper. She turned accusingly to Mrs O'Connor. 'Did you know they were getting married in the summer?'

'Yes I did, as a matter of fact,' replied the customer, looking uncomfortable.

'I thought you said it was to be in the autumn.'

'Sure, they've brought it forward.'

'You never said.'

'Dr Stirling told me in confidence, so he did.' Mrs O'Connor had learnt to be very circumspect when talking to the shopkeeper about certain matters, knowing that whatever she divulged in the store would be around the village like wildfire.

'It can't be all that confidential if Mrs Devine told me,' said Mrs Sloughthwaite. 'And I suppose you know where they are getting married?'

'Well, yes, I do,' replied Mrs O'Connor.

'And I suppose that was told to you in confidence as well, was it?'

'I didn't like to say,' replied Mrs O'Connor.

'It's like getting blood out of a stone with you, Bridget O'Connor,' said Mrs Sloughthwaite. 'Talk about being tight-lipped.'

'So where is she getting married?' asked Mrs Pocock.

'At St Christopher's,' the shopkeeper told her, resting her bosom on the counter and feeling rather pleased with herself at being privy to the information. She prided herself that there was nothing she could not find out – one way or the other.

'In the church!' exclaimed Mrs Pocock. 'Can she do that what with her being a divorcee?'

'That's what she told me. It'll be a church wedding,' she

said. 'Evidently it's going to be a quiet affair. She didn't say where the honeymoon would be.'

'Don't look at me,' said Mrs O'Connor. 'I don't know where they'll be going. I did mention the wedding to Dr Stirling only last night and he was very unforthcoming.'

'Well, he's not a one for conversation,' remarked Mrs Pocock. 'When I saw him about my varicose veins he didn't say above two words.'

'Perhaps he's got a lot on his mind,' said the shopkeeper.

'Or having second thoughts,' added Mrs Pocock.

'Oh no,' said Mrs Sloughthwaite, 'he's asphyxiated with Mrs Devine.'

'I mean it's a big thing getting married again,' observed Mrs Pocock. 'I know I wouldn't bother if anything happened to Mr Pocock. Once is enough for me.'

10

One afternoon after school Danny decided to go down to the woods. His best friend James, with whom he usually walked home, had a piano lesson and had been collected by his father to be taken to his teacher in Clayton. Danny loved the woods; he loved the beauty of the trees which changed colour with the seasons, the wild flowers, rocky banks and the rusty red beck. This was his unspoilt world. He loved to wander the twisting hidden paths with the sun on his face in summer, soft rain in his hair in autumn and snow crunching under his feet in winter. He liked to build hiding places and hidden dens, climb trees, hunt, fish, pick flowers, watch birds and set traps. He was a country lad through-and-through. Sometimes in summer he would sit under a tree in the cool green shade watching the drifting clouds in an azure sky and listening to the chattering sparrows and the distant fitful cry of the curlew. Then, high above, he might see a circling buzzard, its great wings outstretched, soaring alone. He loved the sights, the sounds, the smells and the subtle impressions of Nature.

As Danny headed for the mill dam down the narrow path, dark beneath a canopy of spreading branches thick with leaves, he sensed that he was being followed. The wood was silent save for the sporadic snap of a twig underfoot or the rustle of a bush. He paused to listen and waited, hiding behind the thick trunk of a huge oak tree. Then he heard the footsteps coming closer and he caught sight of his pursuer. He stepped out and confronted him.

'What are tha following me for?' Danny asked.

'I wasn't,' replied Robbie self-consciously.

'Aye, tha was, I heard ya.'

'It's a free country,' Robbie said suddenly, sounding indignant. 'I can go where I want. You don't own the woods. I don't have to have your permission.'

'All reight, all reight!' cried Danny laughing, 'tha dun't need to get t'mug on. Tha can come wi' me if tha wants. I'm goin' down t'mill dam. There's a pair o' kingfishers theer an' some fox cubs. I'll show you if tha likes. Tha dun't need to skulk abaat.'

'I wasn't skulking about and I don't want to come with you.' His eyes were hard and challenging.

'Tha can suit thissen,' said Danny, walking off.

Robbie kept his distance a few yards behind but continued to follow.

After a while Danny turned to face him, rested his hands on his hips and shook his head. 'Tha's a reight funny onion thee, an' no mistake.'

'I'm a what?' asked the boy.

'That's what mi granddad used to say abaat people what 'e couldn't mek out.'

'Well, it's a bloody daft thing to say, calling somebody a vegetable.'

''E sed a lot o' things did mi granddad but I reckon most o' t'time what 'e sed med a lot o' sense. 'E also sed that them what swears 'aven't got t'intelligence to use proper words.'

'I don't care what your granddad said,' replied Robbie.

'No,' Danny told him walking away, 'I reckon tha dun't.'

Robbie continued to follow.

Danny stopped in his tracks and turned around. 'Are ya comin' wi' me or not? Tha's like mi shadow.'

At the mill dam they sat on the dead tree trunk. The sun

shone on the black water, making patterns that hid what lay beneath.

'I love it down 'ere,' said Danny, sighing. 'This wood is full o' secrets. You think ya know it but ya don't, you'll allus be a stranger.'

They sat there without speaking, looking out across the oily water.

'What is it wi' you an' grown-ups?' asked Danny after a while.

'Adults make me sick,' Robbie told him, 'saying what you should do and what you should say and always getting at you. Then they promise one thing and do another. They're always right and you're always wrong. They never let you be yourself. World would be a better place without them, for they decide how to run everything and they make a bloody rotten job of it.'

'Well, I suppose somebody's got to run things,' said Danny thoughtfully. 'I mean, kids can't do it, can they?'

'They'd make a better job.'

'Well, when tha's grown up, tha might change yer mind,' Danny told him. 'I'm 'appy as I am an' I'm not that keen on growin' up.' He smiled. 'Mi granddad used to say, "I don't let owld age get me down cos it's too hard to get back up."'

'Why do adults always think they know the answers?' asked Robbie.

'Well, I reckon cos most o' time they do.'

'Not the ones I know.'

'Well, tha's met wrong uns then,' said Danny. 'Mi granddad didn't know all t'answers an' 'e wasn't allus right. 'Ee let me be missen and didn't decide how to run everythin'. We used to talk things through. If 'e med a mistake, then 'e'd say so an' 'e never raised 'is 'and to me.'

'You were lucky,' said Robbie. "I hate my stepdad. Nothing I ever do is right for him. It never has been. He's always shouting and saying I'm useless and a waste of space and I'll never make anything of myself and I'll end up in prison. He thinks by shouting and hitting me that I'll do as I'm told but it's only made me hate him more. I'm not frightened of being hit. I don't care if it hurts any more. You're lucky not to have to live with someone like him.'

'Not all adults are like that,' said Danny. 'Missis Devine's all reight. I din't like t'one who were 'ead teacher at t'school afore 'er – Miss Sowerbutts. She were dead strict an' never smiled an' was allus telling kids off. She were like one o' t'grown-ups you were on abaat. Mi granddad used to call 'er Miss Sowerpuss. 'E said 'e felt sorry for people like that – miserable and unhappy – and reckoned summat in 'er past made 'er like she was. Missis Devine's not like that.'

'You're always going on about your granddad,' said Robbie.

'Aye, 'appen I do.' Danny breathed in. 'I miss 'im. 'E were mi best friend as well as mi granddad. I could tell 'im owt, talk about owt. We had some gret times together.'

'I wish my stepdad was dead,' said Robbie.

'Tha dun't mean that.'

Robbie looked at him and his eyes glistened with tears. 'I do. My mum and me were all right until he came to live with us, throwing his weight about, always having his own way.'

'What about your mam?'

'She lets him do as he wants and say what he wants. She never stands up to him. And if he hits me I just take it. I never let him see me cry and that he hurts me and that makes him even madder.'

Danny took a deep breath and exhaled noisily. 'Blimey,' he said, thinking of another of his grandfather's expressions: 'Hard as a hammered nail.'

They sat in silence for a moment. 'Look!' Danny cried pointing to the sky. 'See 'im? The buzzard. Beautiful, in't 'e?'

Robbie looked up. 'I wish I was as free as that bird,' he said sadly.

'The Reverend Dr Underwood,' announced Watson, showing Ashley into the library at Limebeck House.

The lady of the manor rose from a huge plum-red, uphol- stered armchair and smiled warmly. At her feet a small bristly haired terrier gave a rumble like a distant train and displayed a set of teeth. 'My dear,' said Lady Wadsworth, extending a hand, 'do come in. Ignore Gordon, he's all bark and no bite.'

The butler coughed theatrically.

'Well, sometimes he does bite but only when he gets excited. I am so pleased to see you, Reverend Underwood. It's very good of you to call.'

'It's a pleasure,' replied her visitor, looking around the room with its imposing carved marble fireplace, bearing the Wadsworth coat-of-arms, the heavy burgundy velvet drapes and the huge patterned Persian silk carpet. Her eyes were drawn to a wall lined in highly polished mahogany shelving and crammed with leather-bound books.

'Do sit down,' said Lady Wadsworth, indicating a French gilt chair carved in an ornate style. 'Watson, you may bring us some coffee now, please.'

The butler nodded and departed.

'What a wonderful room,' remarked Ashley. 'And so many books.'

'I like the library,' her ladyship told her, resuming her seat. 'It's so much cosier than the drawing-room. I'll give you a little tour of the building later if you are interested.'

'I would like that very much,' replied Ashley. 'It's such a beautiful house and with such a delightful aspect.'

'My family have lived here for several hundred years,' Lady Wadsworth informed her. 'Of course in its heyday there were many servants. We even had a mole catcher and a man to wind all the clocks. There were grand balls and house parties, banquets and shoots, and it played host to some very distinguished visitors. Sadly over the years, as with many stately homes, it has declined, but as my grandfather always maintained' – she gestured to the huge portrait in oils of the second Viscount Wadsworth, who stared self-importantly from the canvas, attired in his scarlet robes – 'when one door closes another opens. The house was quietly sliding into decay and then I had some very good fortune.'

'Yes, I heard from the Archdeacon that you discovered some very valuable statues.'

'Indeed, and they fetched an acceptable price at auction, enough for me to have the necessary resources to pay for the restoration work on the house. And speaking of the Archdeacon, how are you getting on with him?'

'Very well.'

'Yes, he's a dear man,' said her ladyship. 'A little too cerebral for some but his heart is in the right place.'

'Yes, it is,' agreed Ashley.

'And are you settling in at St Christopher's?'

'Very much so.'

'And you are not finding Barton-in-the-Dale too sleepy a place?'

'No, it suits me very well.'

'Good. I must say,' said Lady Wadsworth after a pause, 'you have certainly made something of an impact in the short time you have been here.'

'I should like to think for the better,' her visitor replied.

Lady Wadsworth tilted her head and looked searchingly at her visitor.

Ah, thought Ashley, now we're getting to it – the point of the interview. Next would come the criticisms of the innovations she had been making at St Christopher's: introducing the modern hymns, the new order of service and the use of a contemporary Bible. Ashley felt obliged to say something. 'I appreciate that some of the changes I have made have not gone down too well with some of the parishioners, particularly the older ones, but—'

The butler arrived with a silver tray on which had been arranged an elegant silver coffeepot, two delicate china cups and saucers, and a silver milk jug, sugar bowl, tongs and spoons. On a large china plate was a selection of biscuits and a solid block of fruit cake.

'Ah, the coffee,' said Lady Wadsworth. 'Do you take sugar?'

'No, thank you,' replied Ashley.

'A biscuit, a piece of cake?'

'No, thank you.'

Watson poured the coffee, gave a slight bow and stood by the door. 'As I was saying,' continued Ashley, 'some of the changes I have introduced have not gone down too well with a few of my congregation.'

Lady Wadsworth sipped her coffee, before selecting a biscuit which she crunched noisily. 'Watson here says that I should move with the times,' she said. 'He thinks I live in the Dark Ages, don't you, Watson.'

'I believe that changes are inevitable, your ladyship,' he replied. 'Had electricity not been installed here I should still be lighting candles, and had the flushing toilet not been invented–'

'Thank you, Watson,' said Lady Wadsworth tersely. 'That will be all.'

When the butler had left she sighed. 'I know things have got to change but I do so like the traditional services and the King James Bible. But I have not invited you here to talk about such matters. I am minded to have a plaque placed in the church and wanted to ask how you'd feel about it. I thought a brass tablet in the nave or the chancel commemorating my brother, who was killed in the last war, would be fitting. I have mentioned on several occasions to the Archdeacon my desire to have such a memorial in St Christopher's but he has been so very busy and we have never got around to it.' She stood, brushed the crumbs from her skirt and walked to the fireplace, where she pointed to the coat-of-arms. 'I thought a plaque with the Wadsworth crest and some appropriate words would be in order. What do you think?'

'I certainly have no objection,' Ashley told her. 'If the Archdeacon has agreed I can't see that there will be a problem.' She was relieved that there had not been the anticipated confrontation about the changes she had made at the church. 'I wonder, however, if I might suggest an alternative?'

'An alternative?' repeated Lady Wadsworth, returning to her chair. 'Do tell.'

'A window,' replied Ashley. 'As you are aware, St Christopher's was badly damaged following the Reformation. The statues were smashed, the saints beheaded and the tombs vandalised. Sadly all the stained glass windows were destroyed. Most have been replaced over the years, but one small window in the transept has been boarded up. Perhaps you might consider dedicating a new stained glass window to the memory of your brother? It could be called the Wadsworth Memorial Window.'

Lady Wadsworth thought for a moment and then clapped her hands. 'I like it. I really like it. I think it is an excellent idea. A memorial window would be much more prominent than a brass plaque and much more colourful too.'

'And you could of course oversee the design,' said Ashley, 'to include the Wadsworth coat-of-arms and the dedication.'

When Ashley emerged from Limebeck House, Emmet O'Malley was staring at her bicycle. He was a tall, broad-shouldered young man with a mass of unruly black curls and a wide-boned weathered face.

Before Easter he had arrived at Elisabeth's cottage with his young daughter Roisin, asking if he might site his caravan in her paddock. Wearing a colourful kerchief around his neck and a silver earring, he looked like the archetypal gypsy one might see in a picture book. He explained that he was not a conventional traveller, a Romany or a tinker, it was just that he liked to be on the road, but finding those in the village friendly and seeing how well his daughter had settled at the village school, he decided to stay for a few weeks. When he was offered the job at the big house and the promise of a soon-to-be refurbished lodge, he had been persuaded to stay longer.

'Oh dear,' said Ashley as she joined him. 'It looks as if I've a long walk back to the village.' The front tyre on her bicycle was flat.

'Not at all,' said Emmet. 'I'll fix it in no time. Just needs a puncture repair kit and haven't I just the thing in my caravan. I'm Emmet O'Malley, by the way,' he told her, flashing a set of straight white teeth. 'I work for Lady Wadsworth, the odd-job man or as she calls me the general factotum.'

'I'm Ashley Underwood. I'm pleased you meet you, Mr O'Malley.'

'And I'm pleased to meet you too, Ashley Underwood,' he said, shaking her hand. 'Now why don't you go back inside and I'll let you know when I'm done. It won't take long.'

'It's such a nice day,' replied Ashley. 'I think I'll sit out here in the sunshine and admire the view.'

'And what a view it is,' said Emmet, looking at the expanse of countryside which stretched before them. The parkland with its backdrop of dark, wooded fells, rough moorland and hazy peaks was spectacular. 'They certainly knew where to build these great houses.'

'They did indeed,' agreed Ashley.

'I'll be back in a moment,' he said.

'So you've ridden up here on the old bike,' said Emmet when he had returned and started to remove the wheel of the bicycle.

'That's how I get around the village,' she told him. 'It keeps me pretty fit.'

'I can see that,' he said, winking. 'You look very fit to me.' A hint of playfulness entered his voice.

'You have a touch of the blarney, Mr O'Malley,' said Ashley, colouring a little.

'Ah well, that's the Irish in me,' he said. 'Do you know Ireland at all?'

'Yes, I spent a year in Galway before going to university,' she told him. 'It was there that I became a real fan of Irish literature and traditional music.'

'Did you now?' he said. 'And which folk group is your favourite? The Dubliners, the Chieftains?'

'I like all those but my favourite has to be De Dannan,' she said. 'I have all their music: *The Mist Covered Mountain, Star-Spangled Molly, A Jacket of Batteries.*'

'And I suppose if I told you that De Dannan is my favourite group too,' replied Emmet, 'you would not believe me. You would say it was a touch of the blarney.'

'I tend to believe what people say, Mr O'Malley,' said Ashley. 'It goes with the job.'

'And what job would that be?' he asked.

'I'm a priest,' she told him.

'Sure, you're not like any priest that I've ever met,' said Emmet.

'Church of England,' she told him. 'So you see, I accept what people tell me.'

'Sure that can be a dangerous thing to do,' he said. 'The world is full of storytellers and dissemblers.'

'Well, until they prove me wrong, I tend to trust people,' Ashley told him.

'The group's playing in Clayton next Saturday,' Emmet told her.

'Pardon?'

'De Dannan, they are playing in Clayton next Saturday.'

'Really? I didn't know.'

'I'm taking my daughter Roisin. She wants to be a musician when she grows up.'

'Roisin,' repeated Ashley. 'Is your daughter the little girl who goes to the village school?'

'The same,' he replied.

'I met her last week when I called in to take the assembly. She played the flute. She's a talented little player.'

'She's the apple of my eye is Roisin,' admitted Emmet, 'and she so loves it up here that she doesn't want to leave. She's the reason we are not moving on.' He breathed in and sighed. 'Sure 'tis like another world. Just look at the view.'

And on that bright, clear morning the handyman and the curate paused for a moment to take in the panorama which stretched before them. Beneath a vast, blank curve of blue there stretched the brilliant greens of the pastureland, rolling and billowing up to the richer, darker hues of the far-off fells. Fat, creamy sheep grazed lazily before the white-silvered limestone walls, rabbits cropped the grass at the edge of a nearby field and a fat pheasant strutted along the path bordering the estate. In the still, windless sky a wedge of birds moved slowly south, high above a trembling kestrel.

'It is rather special,' said Ashley.

'It is that,' agreed Emmet, with a flash of white teeth. 'But we can't be spending the whole day admiring the view, now can we?' He held the bicycle before him. 'Now then, all repaired so you can be on your way.'

'Thank you so much, Mr O'Malley,' said Ashley.

'Emmet.'

'Thank you, Emmet.'

'My pleasure, and perhaps I'll be seeing you at the De Dannan concert next week?'

'Perhaps,' she replied.

11

The junior children stood excitedly in a group outside the school. They were to spend a day exploring the village as part of their local history project, visiting the church, the mill dam, the former alms-houses and Limebeck House.

'Now I want you to pay a lot of attention to what we are to see today,' said Elisabeth.

'And to be on your very best behaviour,' added Mrs Robertshaw. She resisted the temptation when she said this to look at Robbie, who stood a little apart from the rest, grim-faced and with his hands stuffed in his pockets.

Over the last week the boy had been his usual moody self, producing little work, avoiding the other children and respond-ing to any questions asked of him in a short, offhand manner. Mercifully he had not had any angry outbursts or been insolent but Elisabeth still found him difficult and uncommunicative. She had been massively patient with the boy over the few weeks he had been at the school, avoiding confrontation and making few demands upon him. She hoped that in time and with support and encouragement he might settle down and start behaving like the other children. She didn't want to give up on the child, but sometimes in her cottage in the evenings when she was alone and pensive, she wondered if this was a losing battle.

Mrs Goldstein had seen the boy again and found him surly and unforthcoming. She had spoken to his parents and learnt Robbie was no different at home. Mr Banks she found obdurate and unsympathetic when she suggested Robbie be referred to a consultant paediatrician and neurologist. Despite his wife's entreaty, he dismissed it as what he called 'the boy's attention-seeking'.

In her report to Elisabeth the psychologist recommended that should there still be no improvement in the boy's attitude and behaviour over the next couple of weeks then it would be better for him to be educated in a referral unit, where there were smaller classes, greater individual support and specialist teachers. Elisabeth had spoken about this to Michael and was surprised and disappointed that he agreed with the psychologist.

'Look, Elisabeth,' he had told her, sighing, 'you can't win every battle. To be frank, I'm a little tired about hearing about Robbie and his problems. There are other children in the school to think about. He might be better in another school. It's not that I am uncaring or indifferent about the boy, but from what you have told me he has a disorder and needs professionals who know how to cope with children like this. From what you have said he's anti-social, doesn't do as he is told or get on with the other children and he can be aggressive. He'll probably be better in a smaller group where extra support can be offered.'

Following this conversation Elisabeth had not raised Robbie's name again with him, but she was determined to persevere with the boy for the time being.

Although her colleagues would no doubt have agreed with Mrs Goldstein and Michael, she had been strengthened in her resolve by the attitude of the other children in the school. She knew after many years in the job that young people are quick to feel aggrieved if one child is seen to be treated more favourably than others and allowed greater freedom. Her pupils, though, had been surprisingly understanding. They knew, of course, that here was a boy with a problem and didn't seem to resent the fact that he was treated rather differently. Perhaps they understood more than the adults what she was trying to do.

That morning at St Christopher's, Ashley welcomed the visitors at the door of the church and took them on a tour, pointing out the items of interest: the great golden lectern in the shape of an eagle with outstretched wings, the huge organ with the impressive pipes, the stained glass windows depicting the saints which had replaced the earlier medieval ones. The children were most interested in the various brass memorial plaques which lined the ancient stone walls, commemorating those who had died in the wars.

'This one,' Ashley told them, pointing to a small tablet, 'is to honour one of the village's most famous sons, Private George Hardy, who fought in the Anglo-Zulu war and was killed at the Battle of Isandlwana on 22 January 1879.'

''Ow did 'Ardy die?' asked Danny.

'I'm sorry?' replied the curate, looking puzzled.

''Ow did 'Ardy die?' repeated Danny.

'How did this particular soldier die?' translated Elisabeth, smiling.

'I see,' said Ashley, laughing. 'I'm not quite used to the Yorkshire accent just yet. Well, Danny, I imagine he was killed by a Zulu spear.'

'Actually it's called an assegai,' piped up Oscar. 'It was the traditional weapon used by the Zulus and the warriors had cow-hide shields as well, but I don't know the name for them. I shall look it up when I get home.'

'Thank you for that,' said Ashley kindly. 'We seem to have a little expert with us.' In the south transept she stopped at an elaborate raised tomb in pale grey stone. 'Now we come to the final resting place of Robert De Buslie,' she said.

'Is there a body under there?' asked Chardonnay, screwing up her face.

'The remains of one, yes,' the curate told her. 'This particular knight probably belonged to a very old and extremely rich family and when he died his wife or his children would have paid for this elaborate tomb to be erected over his grave, with the stone sculpture of him as he looked as a young man. Of course it is now very worn and worse for wear.'

'He's right big, isn't he,' remarked Chantelle. 'I bet if they dug him up and looked at his skellington he wouldn't be as big as that.'

'Actually he was,' said Ashley. 'I think this is a life-size effigy. He was about six foot seven inches tall. He must have been a rather frightening figure in all his armour.'

'When did he die?' asked Eddie Lake.

'He lived many, many years ago,' replied Ashley.

'He's medieval,' Oscar piped up again, running a hand across the figure and peering like an expert at the carved face though his large glasses. 'Probably the twelfth century.'

'That's right,' began Ashley, 'and—'

'He will have been a Crusader and fought in the Holy Land,' continued Oscar.

'You're a very knowledgeable young man,' the curate told him.

'And it was a quite common feature,' the boy carried on in a rather superior tone of voice, 'to have these effigies in old churches.'

'My goodness,' said Ashley, 'I think I ought to employ you to take visitors around St Christopher's. You know more than I do.'

Oscar smiled. 'Well, I do like history,' he told her. 'I'm interested in genealogy at the moment.'

'Why are his legs crossed?' asked Chantelle, 'and why is his head resting on his helmet? He looks as if he's having a kip.'

'Now that's interesting,' answered Oscar before the curate

could reply. 'Some people think that those knights with crossed legs died in their sleep, but this is not true. Most people think those with crossed legs died in battle.'

The children now faced Oscar, who was clearly the authority of the tombs of medieval knights.

'Is that his dog?' asked Chantelle, looking at the knight's feet where a stone hound lay curled up.

'No, it's a symbol of loyalty,' remarked Oscar. 'They sometimes had their feet resting on lions or other creatures.'

'I think I'd 'ave mi feet restin' on mi ferret,' said Danny, which made the children laugh.

'Somebody's knocked his hands off,' said Ernest Pocock.

'Yes, I'm afraid a great deal in the church has been destroyed over the years,' Ashley told him. 'All the lovely stained glass windows were smashed, the statues shattered and the tombs damaged.'

'Vandalism,' said Oscar, shaking his head like a grouchy old man bemoaning the behaviour of modern youth.

'Shall we move on?' said Ashley, smiling to herself. She had never met such a knowledgeable and precocious child.

As this exchange was taking place, Robbie had remained where he was beneath the brass plaque to Private Hardy. Seeing the lone figure, Elisabeth went to join him.

'He must have been a very brave young man,' she said quietly. 'He was only eighteen when he was killed. He hadn't had much of a life, had he? Imagine leaving the village and his family when the snow was covering the ground and going halfway across the world to die on some hot, dry, dusty battlefield in Africa.'

The boy didn't answer but was clearly listening. He continued to stare at the plaque.

'Would you like to come and join the others, Robbie?' asked Elisabeth.

The boy shook his head. 'I'd like to stop here for a bit,' he replied.

Elisabeth left him and joined the other children. The curate had stopped at an ornately carved wooden screen between the chancel and nave, at the centre of which was a large crucifix.

'Now we come to what is called the rood screen,' said Ashley. 'This separates the altar from the rest of the church. The original rood screen would have had statues of Our Lady and St John and would have been much larger and probably had bright paintings on it. It was destroyed, so this is a much later version. Now has anyone an idea why there should be a rood screen here?'

'Is it so that the vicar can get changed behind it without anyone watching?' suggested Chardonnay. 'I mean, it would be rude if people could see him.'

'Well, there is some truth in that. It did give the priest some privacy from the congregation, although I think he would have changed in the vestry. Rood actually means a large cross like the one above you rather than rude like, er . . .' She thought for a moment struggling to think of the most appropriate alternative.

'Vulgar?' suggested Oscar.

'Exactly,' said Ashley.

As the children filed out of the church Elisabeth approached Robbie again. He was still staring up at the plaque. She rested a hand on his shoulder. On past occasions when she had done this he had pulled away, resisting any physical contact, but that morning he let her hand remain there.

'This seems to have interested you,' she said.

The boy nodded and made no effort to move.

'Come along now, Robbie,' she said. 'We have to go.'

'That's my name,' muttered the boy. 'My real name.'

'Pardon?'

'Hardy is my dad's name,' he said.

'Oh,' said Elisabeth. 'I didn't know that.'

'Banks is *his* name.'

'His name?'

'My stepdad. I'm not called Banks, not really. They changed it when he came to live with us. He changed everything. My real name is Robin Hardy.'

'I see. Well, perhaps George Hardy was one of your distant relations.'

'It's a common enough name,' replied the boy.

Elisabeth, despite her inclinations to do so, decided that this was neither the time nor the place to quiz the child. 'Let's catch up with the others,' she said.

At the mill dam the children were told to move well away from the bank, for the water, black and thick as oil, looked deep and dangerous.

'I wouldn't like to come down here at night, miss,' said Chardonnay, shivering. 'My nan said there's a ghost which haunts this place. She saw it when she was a lass. It chased her through the woods.'

Elisabeth smiled. 'Well, that's a good reason for children not to come down here by themselves,' she said. 'We don't want anyone falling into the water.'

'My gran told me that when she was a girl they used to skate on the millpond in winter if it froze over,' said Chantelle. 'She told me once that a little girl called Florence fell through the ice and drowned. They tried to drag her out but she disappeared beneath the ice, screaming and shouting. My gran said they found the body later after the thaw. It was all cold and white and mangled and trapped underneath the waterwheel.'

'Happen she's the ghost, miss,' remarked Eddie Lake.

'An interesting tale,' said Elisabeth, 'but I think that the story of the ghost is just a story.'

'Don't you believe in ghosts, miss?' asked Chantelle.

'No, I don't,' replied Elisabeth. She quickly changed the subject, for she saw that some of the children were looking decidedly nervous. The sky had clouded over, hiding the sun, and a light wind rustled the leaves. The old waterwheel creaked ominously. 'Now, can anyone tell me what the purpose of this mill dam was?' she asked cheerfully.

Oscar raised a hand. 'A mill dam is constructed on a stream to create a millpond,' he said confidently. 'The water is dammed to work the big wheel and provide energy so that the miller can grind his corn.'

'Thank you, Oscar,' said Elisabeth. 'I don't think I could have explained it better myself.'

'The interesting thing about this particular mill dam,' continued the boy, 'is that—'

'Miss!' interrupted Chardonnay. 'Can Oscar shurrup? He's been rabbiting on all morning. I'm sick of hearing his voice.'

There were grunts of agreement from the other children.

'Now, now, Chardonnay,' reprimanded Elisabeth good-humouredly. 'Oscar has been very informative. However, it might be an idea to hear from someone else.'

'Ask Danny, miss,' said Chardonnay. 'He comes down here a lot, don't you Danny? He's dead good at anything to do with nature.'

The boy coloured up. 'No, you're all right,' he mumbled.

'Come along, Danny,' urged Elisabeth. 'Can you tell us something about the wildlife which lives near the mill dam?'

'Well, I don't know much about t'watter wheel an' t'mill,' said the boy, 'but I do know that it's a sooart o' place weer lots o' animals an' birds come, a sort o' sanctuary. If you're dead still an' wait an' watch, you'll sometimes see a weasel or a watter vole or a fat rat or a vixen and 'er cubs. Last week I saw a stoat. Mebbe you'll catch sight of a badger snuffling for food but they like to come out at night. Then there are all sooarts of birds – wrens and nuthatches, kingfishers and kestrels, robins and skylarks, an' all these different flowers an' plants and trees. It's just someweer special.' With all eyes upon him, Danny suddenly felt embarrassed. 'Well, that's about it really,' he mumbled.

'No, go on, Danny,' urged Chardonnay, who had a soft spot for the boy. 'It's really interesting, isn't it, miss?'

'Yes, it is,' agreed Elisabeth. 'I'm sure we would all like to know a bit more.'

The other children shouted in agreement.

'What's your favourite bird then, Danny?' asked Malcolm Stubbins.

'I don't really 'ave a favourite. I like t'robin 'cos 'e's cheeky an' comes dead close an' don't seem afraid like lots of t'birds. I like t'heron an' watchin' 'im fly wi' 'is long legs trailin' behind 'im or t'kestrel' ovverin' or t'swallows divin an' swoopin'.'

'But if you had to choose,' asked Eddie Lake, 'which one would it be?'

The boy thought for moment and sucked in his bottom lip. 'Well, I reckon it 'ad' 'ave to be t'short-eared owl. Usually owls come out at neet but this un 'e 'unts by daylight.'

'What's it look like?' asked Chantelle.

''E's mottled yellow and brown wi' reight big eyes like fog lamps. 'E likes t'heather moors, weer there's lots of voles an' mice an' rats to eat. 'E don't like shrews cos they've a nasty taste and 'e's not partial to moles eether. Sometimes if ya dead quiet and patient tha can catch sight of' im down 'ere. If ya 'ear this sort o' barkin' sound, well that'll be 'im.' Danny smiled. 'An' to impress t'female, 'e swoops down to t'ground clappin' 'is wings together.

'I suppose t'thing I like when I'm down t'woods is t'birdsong. Birds all sing a different tune, some sort o' trill an' t'others whistle, some screech an' some squawk. They're all different.'

'And which is your favourite birdsong?' asked Eddie.

'I reckon it'd 'ave to be t'skylark.'

'What bird don't you like, Danny?' asked Chantelle.

'I'm not keen on t'cuckoo,' he said. 'It's a big bird, a foot or more long an' slate grey in colour wi' a speckled white chest. T'hen cuckoo's lazy but clever. She comes in summer an' waits until all t'other birds 'ave built their nests an' laid their eggs. Then she lays *'er* eggs 'mongst 'em. T'cuckoo's egg is kept warm an' when it 'atches t'chick chucks out any other eggs from t' nest. 'E gets each one o' t'eggs across 'is back between 'is wings an' crawls backwards until t'egg rolls out o' t'nest. When 'e's got rid of 'em all, 'e lies down an' shuts 'is eyes an' pretends that 'e's been asleep all t'time. I once saw a meadow pipit perchin' on a post feedin' this massive babby cuckoo, stuffin' its gob wi' food. I reckon she were dead frit, too scared do owt else. Mi granddad used to say it's wickedest bird of all is t'cuckoo, for it's a jealous creature an' won't share t'love of t'mother bird wi' t'other chicks. 'E wants all her love.'

'And that's how we get the expression, "a cuckoo in the nest",' Mrs Robertshaw told the children, 'meaning a jealous stranger who comes into someone's home and crowds everyone else out.'

During the account Elisabeth was watching Robbie. He was staring intently at Danny, completely engrossed in what was being said. Perhaps he thinks there's a cuckoo in his nest, she thought, that he's being crowded out and that's a reason for his anger and resentment.

'Well, we had better be moving,' she said. 'We're expected at Limebeck House. Thank you, Danny, that was really interesting, but if you do come down here, children, you must be very careful, the water is deep and can be dangerous.'

'And if you're not careful,' added Chardonnay, 'you might end up under the waterwheel like Florence with your eyes popping out of your sockets and your body all mangled up and your hair all tangled and—'

'Thank you, Chardonnay,' said Elisabeth, 'I think we've heard enough about Florence.'

* * *

Emmet O'Malley stood at the top of the flight of worn stone steps in front of the great black door of Limebeck House waiting to welcome the visitors.

'Good morning,' he said cheerfully.

'Good morning,' chorused the children.

'This is Mr O'Malley,' Elisabeth told them, 'and he works here at Limebeck House. He's going to tell us something about the estate, so please listen carefully.'

'Now if you would all like to gather around, children,' said Emmet.

The children clustered around him, Chardonnay and Chantelle pushing their way to the front the better to secure the best places.

'Make way for the prop forwards,' muttered Malcolm Stubbins.

'That will do, Malcolm,' said Elisabeth, trying to conceal a smile.

'Limebeck House was built about two hundred and fifty years ago for Sir William Wadsworth,' Emmet told them. 'He was a very rich and important man and wanted a big house with lovely gardens and wonderful views, so he employed a famous architect called Joseph Charlesworth to design the house, the parkland and the gardens, which were used by the family for walking, riding and shooting. At one time a great number of people were employed here. There were butlers, valets, maids, chauffeurs, footmen, grooms, groundsmen, gardeners, gamekeepers, woodmen, carpenters and estate labourers. There was even a man to wind up the clocks and one to kill the moles. This way of life provided jobs for many local people, and sometimes they worked here for all their lives and never travelled far from the house.'

'How many people worked here at the same time?' asked Chantelle.

'I'm not that sure,' replied Emmet, 'but I should think in the region of fifty or sixty.'

'And how many work here now?' asked Eddie.

Emmet smiled. 'Well, there's the butler Mr Watson and myself, and Mrs Fish and her sister who come in every day to do the cooking and cleaning.'

'Just four!' exclaimed Malcolm.

'Just four,' Emmet told him. 'Now if you all turn around and look at the view for a moment, you will see a vast park bounded by woodland and once studded with ornamental trees, some of which still remain. That great cedar tree and the two huge elms you can see date back many centuries and were incorporated into the landscape when the house was built.'

'It's a bit neglected,' observed Oscar.

'It is,' agreed Emmet. He looked at the lawn, once neatly trimmed and level but now lumpy with molehills. To the sides, grass and thistles were knee-high.

'There was a lake with a little jetty and a summerhouse,' he continued, 'and—'

'Excuse me, Mr O'Malley,' said Oscar, waving his hand in the air like a daffodil in a strong wind, 'how big is this estate?'

'It used to be about four thousand acres. It's quite a bit less now but it's still a lot of land. Over the years much of it has been sold and some of the parkland is now used for growing crops.'

'It's rather sad,' remarked Mrs Robertshaw, 'that so much is overgrown and neglected.'

'It is,' agreed Emmet, 'but of course it's very expensive to maintain such a huge area. There are, however, plans to renovate the inside of the house, repair some of the outbuildings and the lodge and refurbish the workers' cottages. Eventually it is hoped that the gardens will be restored and maybe opened to the public.'

As Emmet continued with his commentary, Mrs Robertshaw nudged Elisabeth's arm. 'He's gone,' she whispered.

'Who has?'

'Robbie. I can't see him anywhere.'

Elisabeth scanned the children but there was no sign of the boy. She went in search of him.

The walled vegetable garden was built of mellow red brick and accessed through an arch. Inside it was a jungle of wild flowers and thistles, choking brambles and rank bushes which might once have been called shrubs. It was thick with twisting buddleia and sharp-stemmed briars, a crop of dandelions, frothy white cow parsley, clumps of tall stinging nettles and a mass of other weeds. The walls were swathed in thick ivy. There was an ornamental pond, choked with lush green vegetation which rose from water the colour of tea. Elisabeth saw Robbie sitting on an old bench, a sad and lonely little figure gazing sightlessly ahead of him. On his knee was a small wire-haired dog. The animal, sensing Elisabeth's approach, cocked its head but didn't move.

'He belongs to Lady Wadsworth,' said Elisabeth, moving closer. 'And he's called Gordon, because when she got him he reminded her of her grandfather, who had big sandy whiskers and the same bright little eyes.' Robbie didn't answer but continued to stroke the dog. 'Border Terrier,' she told him. 'He's good at ratting but he can be a little scamp. He seems to have taken to you.'

'The thing about animals,' said Robbie fiercely, not looking up, 'is that they don't get at you all the time like grown-ups do.' He lifted the dog gently from his knee, placed him on the ground and headed off to join the other children. The animal trotted after him.

As the children wandered off down the drive to go back to school, shepherded by Mrs Robertshaw, Elisabeth remained behind to thank Emmet.

'That was really interesting and very productive,' she told him. 'We will get a great deal of work out of this morning when we are back at school.'

'It was a pleasure,' he replied.

'You are very happy here, aren't you?'

'I am,' he said.

'So no plans to move?'

'No, not at the moment.'

'You could do with a bit of help getting the gardens into shape.'

'You're not wrong there,' he agreed. 'Lady Wadsworth has said that if I can find someone to give me a hand I should employ them.'

'Really?'

'But it'll be difficult to find a willing worker who doesn't mind a bit of hard labour, being outside in all weather and who is willing to work long hours for not much money.'

'Oh, I don't know,' she said, a thought entering her head.

Later that afternoon Elisabeth had an appointment with the Director of Education.

'I thought I'd touch base with you regarding the plans for the amalgamation,' said Ms Tricklebank. 'I believe that you have the meeting with the parents at Urebank next week?'

'Yes,' said Elisabeth. 'I have to admit I'm a little nervous about the reaction I might get.'

'I wouldn't worry. When I spoke there to explain the reorganisation of the education service the parents seemed quite relaxed about it. I think they accepted that the school would have to amalgamate otherwise it would have meant closure.'

'I guess you have had a report from Mr Nettles about the meeting we had here at County Hall with the staff of Urebank?' said Elisabeth.

'I have,' replied the Director of Education. 'He said it was a productive meeting and that everyone seemed reasonably happy.'

'Is that what he said?' asked Elisabeth.

'Did you not feel that?' asked Ms Tricklebank. 'I detect a note of doubt in your voice.'

'I think I must have been at another meeting if he said that it was productive. Mr Richardson and Mr Jolly were certainly not well pleased and I was far from happy at how things went.'

Ms Tricklebank sat up in her chair. 'You had better tell me more.'

'I was very disappointed,' said Elisabeth, 'that neither Mr Richardson nor his deputy head had any intention of being helpful or cooperative. Ms Tricklebank, I have to be honest with you, I think it is going to be impossible for me to work with two people who will be holding senior positions in the new set-up and who show no interest in collaborating.'

'One moment,' said the Director. She picked up the phone. 'Marlene,' she said, 'would you ask Mr Nettles to come and see me immediately?'

A moment later they heard scurrying footsteps down the corridor followed by a knock at the door.

'Come in,' called Ms Tricklebank.

Mr Nettles entered, an obsequious smile on his face. 'Oh, hello, Mrs Devine,' he said.

'Sit down, Mr Nettles,' said Ms Tricklebank. 'In your report about the meeting here at County Hall with the staff of Urebank and those from Barton you led me to understand that it had been a constructive meeting. I think the words you used were "productive" and "happy".'

'I felt it had gone pretty well,' he replied defensively.

'Mrs Devine does not share that view.'

The education officer flinched slightly, with a small twitch of the head. 'Oh,' he said.

'Mr Nettles,' said Elisabeth, 'the meeting was not at all productive or happy; it was frosty and ineffective. Anything I suggested, such as consultation on the development plan, was rebuffed. Mr Richardson is clearly unwilling to be a part of any planning and it was obvious to all present that he will be most dismissive of anything I wish to implement.'

'I think you are overreacting somewhat, Mrs Devine,' Mr Nettles said in a deeply patronising tone of voice, 'and I do think you are being a bit hard on Mr Richardson. I am sure that he will come around. You must understand he is very disappointed that he was not appointed to the post of head teacher.'

'So, now he takes his bat home?' asked Elisabeth.

He opened his mouth to speak but the Director held up her hand, cutting him off.

'Mr Nettles,' she said, 'it is imperative that the staff of the new school work together, and I look to you to make certain Mrs Devine has maximum support.'

'If you feel it necessary I shall have a word with Mr Richardson,' the education officer replied half-heartedly.

'Please do so,' said Ms Tricklebank.

After the meeting Elisabeth found the office of the Parks and Recreation Department in an annexe to the rear of County Hall. Behind a tidy desk sat a tall woman dressed in a prim blouse buttoned high at the neck, with a pair of thin-rimmed spectacles perched on the end of her nose.

'My name is Mrs Devine,' Elisabeth told her. 'I am head teacher at Barton-in-the-Dale village school and wonder if you can help me.'

'I'll try my best,' replied the woman.

'I want an address of a young man,' said Elisabeth. The woman raised an eyebrow. 'He used to work in the gardens here. He was on community service. He's about eighteen, thin build with a shaven head and silver rings and studs in his ears. He had a tattooed snake around his neck.'

'Oh yes, I remember him,' she said.

'Well, I would like to contact him.'

'I'm afraid I cannot give out details of employees,' the woman replied.

'Yes, I should have realised that,' said Elisabeth. 'The thing is, he was unemployed when I met him and very keen to get a job as a gardener. I may be able to put some work his way.'

'Well, I could ask this young man to get in touch with you if he is interested.'

'Oh, I think he will be interested,' said Elisabeth, taking a pen and a notebook from her handbag to write down her address.

12

'Well, if I can't talk to you about it, Michael, then who can I speak to?'

'I know, I know, Elisabeth, and I am not unsympathetic, but it's becoming quite an obsession with you.'

'That's unfair. You know that—'

'Let me finish, please,' he interrupted. 'You don't seem to talk about much else these days. You have to learn to turn off when you get back from school. It dominates your life, and this boy in particular. You can't keep on bringing your worries home. When I was at medical school a wise old consultant told us that to be a good doctor you must be more detached and leave your concerns at the gates of the hospital or you will worry yourself into the ground and be no good to anybody.'

Michael had in truth found this advice hard to follow. There had been occasions when after examining a patient or informing them of the results of some medical tests he could see that the condition was hopeless. At those times there had been a heavy feeling in the pit of his stomach. He had felt so despondent and ineffectual and had struggled to find the words to say. But what could he say to a young woman whose cancer was incurable, to the old ex-miner whose lungs were so choked with murderous dust that his life expectancy was short, to the father of the young footballer whose son had developed a muscle-wasting disease or to the mother of a bright little girl and tell her that her daughter would eventually lose her sight? As a GP he dealt on a daily basis with people's coughs and sneezes, bad backs and sprained ankles, boils and rashes, and saw his fair share of lead-swingers and hypochondriacs, but sometimes he saw a patient who was seriously ill, desperately looking for some hope, and it was then so very hard to leave his concerns at the surgery gate.

'I can't do that, Michael,' Elisabeth replied, breaking into his thoughts. 'It's not in my nature to just click a switch and turn off at four o' clock.'

'This Robbie has really got to you, hasn't he?' There was an edge to his voice.

'Yes, of course he has,' she replied. 'I've never known a child like this before, so desperately unhappy, moody, angry, never smiling. I think I understand a bit more why he behaves as he does. He started to open up when we went on the visit to the church. The circumstances at home don't appear all that good. His stepfather is a very controlling individual from what I can gather, and from what his wife says about him, he hasn't a good word to say about the boy.'

'You don't know that he's controlling,' Michael told her.

'What do you mean?'

'You've met the boy's stepfather once. How can you form a judgement based on one meeting?'

'From what I have inferred and what Robbie has let slip, and from what the psychologist told me,' Elisabeth told him.

Michael sighed. 'I really don't know what to say, but if it bothers you so much and you're losing sleep over it, then I suggest you get both parents into school again and try to sort it out.'

'We have a parents' consultation meeting next week,' Elisabeth told him. 'I will talk to them then, that is if they both come.'

'That's sorted that out then,' said Michael. He put his arm around her and gently kissed her cheek. 'I know how much this worries you,' he told her, 'and how dedicated you are, but darling, do try and switch off, for your own good. Now, could we let the matter drop and talk about something else?'

The school looked at its best for the first parents' consultation meeting of the new term. Mr Gribbon and Mrs Pugh stood at the end of the corridor, dressed in their new, matching grey nylon overalls, and surveyed the bright, welcoming and immaculate building with pride.

'Excellent work if I may say so, Bronwyn,' said the caretaker, jangling the great bunch of keys in his pocket. 'The school's never looked better.'

'Yes, I have to admit it's very tidy,' agreed the cleaner. She sniffed the air. Mr Gribbon had been very liberal with the aftershave, she thought.

'Course in the olden days when Miss Sowerbutts was head teacher here,' said the caretaker, 'it wasn't like this, you know. She didn't go in for all this window-dressing, as she called it. "It decorates the margins of the serious business of education," she used to say. Course things changed with the arrival of Mrs Devine.'

'I think the kiddies deserve a nice environment in which to work,' said Mrs Pugh.

'Aye, if they look after it,' said the caretaker, 'and don't carry on putting foreign objects down the toilets, dropping litter and scuffing my floors.'

'You want to see them down at Urebank,' remarked Mrs Pugh. 'You'd soon have something to complain about if you did, Mr Gribbon.'

'Maybe you're right,' he said. 'They're not too bad here, but it takes a fair bit of elbow grease to get it in the shape it's in now. It doesn't just happen by magic. When this amalgamation takes place next term I reckon I'll be getting extra staff, and of course I shall want you full-time.'

Mrs Pugh raised an eyebrow. 'Well, you know I'm willing,' she said.

'However did I manage before you came to work here?' the caretaker told her. He placed his hand on her arm and squeezed it gently.

As the two of them chatted on, Elisabeth toured the school. She was well pleased with what she saw. Paintwork was shining, floors had a clean and polished look, brass door handles sparkled and there was not a sign of graffiti or litter. The display boards, which stretched the full length of the corridor, were covered in line drawings, paintings, photographs and children's writing. Everything looked cheerful and orderly. There was a profusion of bright flowers to the front of the school, and at the rear there was an attractive and informal lawn area with ornamental trees, shrubs, a small pond, garden benches and picnic tables. A large sculpture, created by the children under the supervision of Mrs Atticus when she was on teaching practice at the school, had pride of place.

In the staff-room later, Elisabeth found Mrs Pugh and Mr Gribbon, shoulder to shoulder, cleaning the sink together and laughing.

'You two seem to be hard at it,' she remarked.

'I beg your pardon, Mrs Devine?' spluttered the caretaker, colour suffusing his face.

'Hard at work,' said Elisabeth.

'Oh, oh, yes,' Mr Gribbon replied, smiling.

'I've just been having a look around the school, doing a final check before the parents arrive.'

'I hope everything is satisfactory?' Mr Gribbon remarked, fishing for a compliment.

'More than satisfactory,' replied Elisabeth. 'You have both done a splendid job.'

'We try our best, Mrs Devine,' replied the caretaker, basking in the praise. 'I can't take all the credit. A lot of it is down to Mrs Pugh. I do hope you'll be able to make Bronwyn – Mrs

Pugh that is – a permanent feature down here when the schools merge.'

'I shall try my best, Mr Gribbon,' she told him for the umpteenth time.

'Well, I must get on. I have a tea urn to turn on,' he told her before making a hasty exit.

'He's a card, Mr Gribbon, isn't he?' said Mrs Pugh cheerfully when the caretaker had gone.

'Indeed he is,' said Elisabeth. 'Now you should be getting off home. It's nearly six o'clock.'

'Just finishing off here,' said the cleaner. As she gathered up the cleaning materials, she rattled on. 'I heard that you met my hubby again over at Forest View last Saturday.'

'I did, yes,' replied Elisabeth.

'My Owen is very taken with you. Nice lady she is, he told me. And he said that your son is making very good progress. Doing very nicely he is.'

'Yes, John is very happy at Forest View and is quite taken with your husband too,' Elisabeth told her. 'He seems to respond rather better to men than to women.'

'You're not wrong there, Mrs Devine. He was always more at home with the lads when he played rugby or when he's down at the pub talking to his pals about sport and politics than he was with me,' said the cleaner.

'I was speaking about John, Mrs Pugh,' said Elisabeth good-humouredly.

'Oh yes, of course you were. My hubby says he's a lovely lad, is your John.'

'He is,' said Elisabeth.

'So easy-going and gentle Owen says, and happy in his own world. It's a pity more children aren't like him.' Realising what she had said, she shook her head. 'I'm sorry, Mrs Devine, I didn't mean—'

'I know, Mrs Pugh,' replied Elisabeth.

'Well, I'll make a move,' said the cleaner. 'The kettle's boiled if you want a cup of tea.' With that she departed, humming to herself.

Elisabeth put a tea-bag in a mug and poked it with a spoon. She thought for a moment of John and Mrs Pugh's words. How she wished that her son could enjoy life to the full like most children, but the cleaner was right. Thankfully John was a quiet and even-tempered boy. As with many autistic people, he liked routine, disliked closed rooms and found it difficult to relate to others and to show emotion. Unlike some of the autistic children at Forest View, however, who could be unpredictable and sometimes violent, John seemed happy in his own private world. Elisabeth often wondered if John understood anything, but on the odd occasion when she mentioned a memory there would be a reaction – a slight turn of the head, a small change of expression, a rapid blink of an eye.

How different the Forest View parents' consultation evening had been from the ones she was used to in mainstream schools and the one she was anticipating that evening. There had been no discussion of how her son's reading was coming along or what his number work was like, no comments on his art work or sporting accomplishments. It mainly concerned the small improvements in his behaviour.

The door burst open and Mrs Robertshaw bustled in. 'The parents are arriving already,' she said, 'and it's not six o'clock yet.' She threw off her coat and joined Elisabeth at the sink. 'Is that a cup of tea on the go?' she asked, switching the kettle on again. 'When Miss Sowerbutts was here she made the parents wait outside. On one wet evening they were getting soaked to the skin but she wouldn't open the doors until six thirty. Then there was a mad rush to get first in the queue. "Make it short and sweet," she used to say. "Some of these parents never know when to shut up." I think this system of appointments is much better and it's a nice touch to provide some refreshments while they're waiting.' Elisabeth was staring at the floating tea-bag, still thinking of John. 'Are you all right, Elisabeth?'

'I'm fine, thank you, Elsie,' she said, snapping out of her reverie. 'Here, you have this mug of tea. I'm not that bothered. I shall go and see the first parent.'

'Oscar's mother and father are waiting in your room,' said Mrs Robertshaw. 'They asked to speak to you in particular before coming to see me. I don't know what it's about, but the boy's mother looks tired and worried, mind you she always does. I suppose coping with Oscar is enough to tire anyone out.'

In the classroom Elisabeth found an extremely thin and intense-looking woman dressed in a charcoal grey suit with narrow chalk stripes. Her large eyes had dark shadows under them and her greying hair was caught back untidily in a black ribbon. The man with her was tall and equally thin. He had a long, pale face, a large nose and thick black hair tied back in a ponytail. They certainly looked an odd couple.

'Hello,' said Elisabeth. 'You must be Oscar's mother and father.'

The woman came over and held out a bony hand. Her face was pale and anxious. 'It's very good of you to see us, Mrs Devine. We know you will be very busy this evening but we do need to have a word with you about Oscar.'

'Do sit down,' said Elisabeth indicating the two chairs by her desk. 'I should say at the outset that Oscar is a real little character, a pleasure to have in the school. Mrs Robertshaw will tell you when you see her that he sets the standard by which the other children in the class are judged. He's a mine of information, his work is of a very high quality and he has a sharp and insightful mind. In fact—'

'Mrs Devine,' interrupted the woman, 'it's not about his work that we wish to see you.' She looked at her husband as if expecting him to say something but he remained silent. 'It's about a . . . well, a rather delicate matter,' she continued. 'The thing is, Oscar has been asking questions.'

'Oh yes,' Elisabeth chuckled, 'he's a great one for asking questions.'

'Well, lately he's been asking rather difficult questions about where he comes from. I don't mean the facts of life. He worked those out at a very early age, having observed his gerbils. No, it's about tracing his family tree.'

'Ah,' said Elisabeth, 'I think I may know what this is about.'

'You do?' said the man suddenly.

'Oscar was reading a book in the library a few weeks ago,' Elisabeth told them. 'It was about genetics. He discovered that parents who both have blue eyes always have children who have blue eyes too. Of course his eyes are brown. He also asked if both parents have dark hair will the child have dark hair too.'

'And what did you tell him?' asked Oscar's mother.

'That I didn't know, which, to be honest I don't.'

'He's been quizzing us about the very same thing, hasn't he, Granville?'

'He has, yes,' said her husband.

'He said he thought he might be a throwback,' Elisabeth told her.

'A throwback?' exclaimed the woman.

'That in the distant past one of his ancestors must have had brown eyes and red hair.'

'I think it is impossible,' said the boy's mother miserably. She took a breath and bit her bottom lip. 'The thing is, Mrs Devine, my husband is not Oscar's real father – not his biological father that is.' Her husband held her hand and squeezed it. 'This is very difficult. When I was at university, I studied for some time in France. I was young and impressionable and met another student out there. I'm sure I don't need to fill in the details. I met Granville later and he—'

'You really don't need to explain this,' said Elisabeth, resting a hand on the woman's arm. 'These things happen. Now from what I gather, Oscar doesn't know this.'

'No, he doesn't.'

'This is a bit tricky,' said Elisabeth.

'Yes, it is,' agreed the woman. 'I have talked it over with my husband and we feel the time has now come to tell Oscar. We knew that one day it would come out. He's a very inquisitive child and nothing much gets past him.'

'We've always been open and honest with Oscar, Mrs Devine,' said the man, 'and answered his questions truthfully. On this occasion we felt he might cope with the truth better when he was older. We now think with hindsight we should have been candid with him earlier.'

'Oscar is a very strong-minded and happy little character,' said Elisabeth. 'He's self-reliant and sensible and very mature for his age. It will be a shock, I am sure, but I am certain that he will cope. In my experience children are surprisingly resilient.'

'I hope so,' said the woman. 'We intend to tell him this weekend. He might be in a bit of a state in school on Monday.'

'I will keep a very close eye on Oscar next week,' Elisabeth assured her.

'He respects you very much, Mrs Devine,' said the boy's mother. 'He admires you, as do my husband and I. You have transformed this school in the short time you have been here. You are so different from the previous head teacher. I would never have brought this matter up with Miss Sowerbutts. I know you will deal with the situation sensitively. Perhaps you will have a word with Oscar's teacher and let her know the situation? I would prefer that, rather than tell Mrs Robertshaw myself.'

'Of course,' said Elisabeth.

After seeing many of the parents of the children in her

class, Elisabeth felt gratified by all the positive comments she received. The children, so she was told, felt happy and secure in the school, the standard of their work had improved markedly and they enjoyed all the extra-curricular activities which were provided. Chantelle's mother said she had seen a real change for the better in her daughter over the last few months. 'She was such a moody madam,' announced the girl's mother, 'and never liked coming to school. It was a job getting her out of bed of a morning but now she's keen to get out of the house.' Chardonnay's father, a large, rather intimidating man with a shaven head and a selection of colourful tattoos on his arms, also spoke of his daughter's improved attitude to school. 'Now that her talent has been recognised,' he told Elisabeth proudly, 'our Chardonnay has it in her mind to become a singer, professional like.' Elisabeth told them that there were some excellent music colleges to which their daughter might apply after she had completed her secondary education but she would have to work hard and pass her exams to secure a place. The father laughed. 'Nay, nay, Mrs Devine,' he said, 'she don't want to be one of these opera singers. She has her sights set on being a pop star, or she could do the clubs. There's a lot of brass in that.'

'She's certainly a talented young lady,' said Elisabeth, 'and of course, you will be aware she's taking the lead part in the school production.'

'We were dead chuffed when we heard,' said the mother, 'but our Chardonnay, well, she still seems a bit worried. I mean she exhumes confidence most of the time and, as you well know, she has a lot to say for herself, but she wonders whether she is up to the part. She can handle the singing no problem and I reckon she can cope with the acting. So I really don't know what's up with her.'

'I think she'll make an excellent Dorothy,' Elisabeth

reassured her. 'I've already had a word with your daughter but I will speak to her again.'

The most pleased parent was Mrs Holgate. Her son Darren, a quiet, attentive boy, had been diagnosed as dyslexic. His self-esteem and his confidence had been low and, although he enjoyed writing, he had become frustrated at not being able to read and spell as well as his peers. Elisabeth, with the help of Mrs Goldstein, had planned a programme of extra help for him and his progress had been rapid.

'He's a different boy, Mrs Devine,' said Mrs Holgate. 'I would never have imagined in a hundred years him taking a lead in a school play. When he told me he had been asked to be the narrator in *The Wizard of Oz* I couldn't take it in.'

'Mrs Robertshaw says he's very good,' Elisabeth told her.

'You've worked miracles, Mrs Devine,' said the parent. 'I can't thank you enough for what you've done for my Darren.'

'Things seem to be going very well, judging by all the smiling faces,' Michael told her as he sat down by her desk a little later.

'What are you doing here?' Elisabeth whispered.

'I've come to find out how James and Danny are getting on,' he told her, smiling widely and reaching across to hold her hand. Elisabeth snatched her hand away. 'I'm sure you can't object to a concerned parent wanting to know how his sons are getting on at school.'

'Michael Stirling,' she said, 'you don't have an appointment and anyway I can tell you how James and Danny are getting on at school any time. Now will you please go away.'

'That's no way to speak to the man you love and whom you are to marry,' he said, still smiling.

'From what you've told me on so many occasions you are sick and tired of hearing me talk about school.' Elisabeth could feel the eyes on her of the few parents who still wished to see her. 'People are looking.'

'Let them look. I've as much right as any other parent to know how my children are getting on. Ouch!' he cried as he felt a kick under the desk.

'Please, Michael, will you go. I'll tell you all about the boys when I next see you, not that it will be something that you don't already know.'

'OK,' he said. 'May I see you for a drink afterwards?'

'Not tonight, Michael, I'm bushed.'

'Look, Elisabeth, I'm sorry I was sharp with you last week,' he said.

'That's fine,' she said, looking flustered. 'Now will you go?'

Eddie Lake's mother, a tall, elegant woman approaching middle age and dressed in a stylish pale green silk suit, gave an arch smile as she sat down. 'I should have thought you two see quite enough of each other without meeting in school, Mrs Devine,' she said.

'Excuse me?'

'You and your fiancé.'

'Dr Stirling was here, like all the other parents, to talk about his sons,' she replied rather stiffly. 'I don't discuss school after four o'clock,' she fibbed. 'Now, Eddie is doing very nicely.'

By eight o'clock and after a steady stream of parents, Elisabeth was tired but happy. Michael was right, things had gone well. Then Mrs Stubbins arrived. Malcolm's mother was a round, shapeless woman with bright frizzy dyed ginger hair, an impressive set of double chins and immense hips. She sat and became hugely wedged in the chair, which creaked ominously when she plonked herself down.

'Good evening, Mrs Stubbins,' said Elisabeth cheerfully.

'Hello, Mrs Devine,' replied the woman. Her mouth drooped downwards as if in perpetual hostility.

'Malcolm seems to have—' began Elisabeth.

'Can I just ask how long that Robbie is going to be at the

school?' interrupted Mrs Stubbins in an inimical tone of voice.

'And why do you wish to know that, Mrs Stubbins?' asked Elisabeth calmly but preparing herself for the confrontation which was likely to follow.

'Because he's a damned nuisance, that's why!'

Elisabeth could have reminded the woman that it wasn't that long ago that her own son had been a 'damned nuisance' and had been expelled from Urebank for his unacceptable behaviour, but she resisted and waited for the harangue which would inevitably follow. Over the years she had learnt, when dealing with antagonistic parents, not to enter into a confrontation. The simple technique of staring until the angry parent became silent was a powerful method of over-coming opposition.

'My Malcolm says the lad's got a screw loose,' continued Mrs Stubbins angrily. 'He's cheeky and answers back and none of the other kids like him, I know that for a fact. He does exactly what he wants and he gets away with it. And he's said some nasty things to my Malcolm, very nasty things.' The woman stopped, having run out of things to say.

'And Malcolm hit him,' said Elisabeth.

'What?'

'I said Malcolm hit him,' repeated Elisabeth.

'He never told me that.'

'You know, Mrs Stubbins, I always say to parents if you don't believe half of what your child says happens at school, I won't believe half of what they say happens at home. In my experience children are very selective in what they tell their parents and their teachers.'

'Well, he shouldn't have hit the lad,' said Mrs Stubbins in a lower and less antagonistic voice. She smoothed an eyebrow with a little finger and shuffled uncomfortably in her seat.

'No, he should not,' said Elisabeth, 'and Malcolm knows

that I do not tolerate violence. I will admit that in this case your son was provoked and that is why I decided to be lenient with him and, unless there was a repetition, I told him I would let the matter drop.'

'But that boy ought to be in a special school,' said the parent. 'There's no telling what the lad might do.'

'May I stop you there, Mrs Stubbins?' said Elisabeth. 'We are here to discuss Malcolm, not to talk about another pupil.'

'But if he interferes with my son's education,' continued the parent, 'I have a right as Malcolm's mother—'

'I have said I do not wish to discuss another pupil, Mrs Stubbins,' Elisabeth told her. 'As you can see, I do have another parent wishing to see me, so let us talk about Malcolm.'

Five minutes later Mrs Stubbins eased herself out of the chair and left the classroom, a stony expression on her round red face.

Mrs Banks, the last parent to see Elisabeth, looked in a nervous state as she sat down, twisting her wedding ring round and round on her finger. She lifted her thin bony face and swallowed nervously.

'Good evening, Mrs Devine,' she said.

'Good evening,' replied Elisabeth. 'I am sorry to have kept you waiting. Is your husband not with you?'

'No, no he isn't. Frank's on a job away from home at the moment.'

'I thought I might have the opportunity of seeing you both,' Elisabeth told her. 'There are a few things I wished to talk to you about.'

'I didn't know whether or not to come and see you, Mrs Devine,' said the woman. 'Frank thought it best if I didn't and told me not to come, but as he's away I thought—' She reached into her bag for a handkerchief, dabbed her eyes and blew her nose.

'Well, I'm glad you have come to see me,' said Elisabeth.

'There are things we need to discuss. Robbie wasn't at school today and—'

'I can't go on, Mrs Devine,' Mrs Banks suddenly butted in. 'I just can't. It's got too much for me. Robbie's got worse. He's become even more insolent and defiant and says the most awful, hurtful things. It came to a head last night. Frank has a short fuse and well, he and Robbie went at each other hammer and tongs. They had a terrible argument. I've not had a wink of sleep.'

'What was the argument about?' asked Elisabeth.

'It started as it always does with Robbie being his difficult self. When he came home after that visit you had to the church the other week he wouldn't eat his tea. Then he disappeared to his room not wanting to come down. When he finally did, he started going on and on about his real dad and how he hated his stepfather and that his name wasn't Banks at all but Hardy. He started again yesterday and Frank hit him. I know he shouldn't have, but he was provoked. He really was. Then Robbie ran out of the house and didn't get back until late. I didn't know where he'd been and he wouldn't tell me. Last night Frank gave me this ultimatum. He said it was either him or Robbie.'

'And what did he mean by that?' asked Elisabeth.

'That I had to choose between them.'

'I see.'

'I've been thinking about it all night, Mrs Devine. I'm at the end of my tether.' She closed her eyes momentarily and locked her hands together to still a small tremor. 'Anyway, this morning before he set off on his job, Frank told me again. He said that either Robbie goes or he does. He went off early this morning for a few days plastering in Huddersfield and he said that when he gets back he wants an answer.'

'And have you thought about what you might do?' asked Elisabeth.

Her mouth trembled and her eyes filled with tears. 'Robbie will have to go, Mrs Devine. I can't see an alternative. I shall have to put him in care. I can't see any other way. I've tried with him, I really have. I wouldn't be able to handle him on my own if Frank walked out on me. My last husband did that and I can't be doing with it again. I just couldn't manage by myself. We thought that if Robbie started afresh at a new school he might settle down and behave himself, but he's been as bad if not worse since he started here.'

'Actually Mrs Banks,' said Elisabeth, rather stung by the criticism, 'Robbie's behaviour has improved markedly. He's started to apply himself to his work, he doesn't have as many flare-ups and has become a little bit more amenable.'

'Well, not at home he hasn't,' said the boy's mother, shaking her head. 'And I heard every word that woman who saw you before me said about him. What she said is right, he does answer back and needs to be in a special school.'

'I gather Robbie doesn't see his father?'

'He doesn't and I don't want him to either. Went off with another woman, he did, when Robbie was a baby and he's made no effort to keep in contact.'

'So you've made up your mind about Robbie going into care?' asked Elisabeth.

'As I said,' replied Mrs Banks, 'I can't see as how I have any other option.' She blew her nose again and got up to go. 'Anyway, Robbie won't be in school tomorrow either. I've got a Miss Parsons from the Social Services coming round later in the morning to see me. She wants to discuss things and wants Robbie to be there.'

'Perhaps you ought to put off any decision until you have spoken to her,' Elisabeth suggested. 'I do know Miss Parsons and I have every confidence that—'

'No, my mind's made up,' Mrs Banks butted in.

'And what about Robbie?' asked Elisabeth.

'What about him?'

'Have you talked to him about what you intend to do?'

'No, I haven't. He'd just fly off the handle. Get into one of his tantrums. I shall wait until Miss Parsons calls round. Anyway, I just thought I ought to come and tell you. If he is put into care, I suppose he'll have to go to another school near to where they put him, or to one of these residential special schools or behavioural units where they know how to deal with boys like Robbie. You've tried your best but it's not worked. I'm sure you'll not be unhappy about him leaving, what with all the trouble he causes.'

'You are wrong, Mrs Banks,' Elisabeth told her, getting to her feet and keeping her voice steady to disguise her anger, 'I will not be at all happy to see Robbie leave Barton-in-the-Dale.'

On the way home Elisabeth came upon Mr Massey emerging from the Blacksmith's Arms.

'Mrs Devine,' he slurred. 'How lovely to see you.' He remained upright only with the greatest difficulty.

'Good evening, Mr Massey,' she replied.

'And what a lovely evening it is,' he said.

'It is indeed,' she agreed, walking off.

'And may I say how lovely you look this evening.'

Elisabeth laughed. 'Everything appears to be lovely tonight, Mr Massey,' she said. 'Now if you will excuse me, I really do have to get on home. I've had a particularly tiring day.'

'Before you scoot off, Mrs Devine, have you given any more thought to my offer?'

'You mean about the track by my cottage?'

'I do.'

'I have a lot on my mind, Mr Massey. I haven't given it much thought.'

'Well, I wish you would,' he said. 'I'm prepared to make a very generous offer. Ready cash. And I mean when you sell the place, I bet the person what buys your cottage will bite my hand off.'

'That may be the case. Now I really must go.'

'Perhaps I should have a word with Dr Stirling?'

'And why would you do that, Mr Massey? Dr Stirling does not own the cottage. I do.'

'Well, he's to be your better half soon enough and I reckon he'll have an opinion.'

'He might very well have an opinion,' said Elisabeth, 'but Wisteria Cottage belongs to me and I shall do with it what I see fit. Goodnight.'

Fred breathed out noisily as he saw Elisabeth walk briskly down the street. 'Modern bloody women,' he said, before tottering off to his bed.

13

On the following Monday morning Elisabeth waited nervously for the arrival of Oscar. He would need all her sensitivity and support today, she thought. She tried to imagine what it must be like to suddenly be told that the man you believed to be your father was not. It would be devastating. The boy would no doubt be in turmoil, his feelings topsy-turvy. He would be bewildered and deeply upset, and such a traumatic revelation could have dire consequences as he grew up. Perhaps Oscar would not be in school that morning, she told herself. Maybe he would be too confused and wounded to come out of his bedroom that day.

It was therefore with surprise and some relief that at just after eight o'clock Elisabeth saw the familiar figure of Oscar strolling down the path to the school, his briefcase swinging in his hand. He was always the first pupil to arrive, for his parents left the house for work early and usually dropped him off at the school gate. He would then make straight for the library and could be found there poring over some book or other.

Elisabeth found Oscar as expected in the library, a large atlas on his knee.

'Hello, Oscar,' she said, sitting next to him.

'Good morning, Mrs Devine,' he replied, sounding surprisingly happy.

'And what are you reading this morning?'

'Well, actually I'm researching,' he replied serious-faced. 'After our visit to the church and learning something about the Zulu war, I have become very interested in that period in history. I thought I'd look up a few of the places where there were various battles.'

'Oscar,' said Elisabeth, 'did your parents have a word with you over the weekend?' She was unsure whether or not the boy's parents had raised the matter of their son's lineage as they had told her they would, so she was deliberately guarded in what she said.

Oscar was shrewd enough to understand why Elisabeth should ask such a question. He closed the atlas and rested his small hands on the cover. 'I guess my parents spoke about my birth with you at last week's consultation evening?'

'Yes, they did mention it,' she replied.

'Well,' said Oscar, 'you will know what the conversation at the weekend was all about then. My interest in tracing my family tree and asking questions about eye and hair colour seems to have opened a can of worms.' He sounded very grown-up and matter-of-fact. 'It is impossible for parents who both have blue eyes to have a child with brown eyes, so it appears that my father is not in fact my real father. Well, of course he is my real father. I haven't known any other, but he is not what my mother calls my natural father.'

'I see,' said Elisabeth. 'And how do you feel about this?'

'How do I feel?' murmured the boy. 'I don't really know how I feel. It's come as quite a shock, of course.' He looked up at Elisabeth. 'But you see, Mrs Devine, I think I'm very lucky with my parents. Some children have a much more difficult time at home than I do and have to put up with a lot more. Danny, for example, doesn't have parents, James's mother was killed, Malcolm has never seen his father and Roisin's mother died. I've got the best parents in the world and I wouldn't change them for anything. They have always been there for me and wanted the best for me. They are different from lots of adults. They listen to what I have to say, they answer my questions and if they make a mistake they apologise. Of course when I get older I might want to find out a bit more about this natural father but at the moment I am really not that bothered.' He opened the atlas and pointed to a spot on the map. 'I've just found where the famous battle of Rorke's Drift took place,' he said. 'Would you like to see?'

There were tears in Elisabeth's eyes. 'Do you know something, Oscar,' she said, 'you are a remarkable young man.'

'And what are you looking so pleased with yourself about?' asked the school secretary. 'You're like the cat that got the cream.'

Mr Gribbon, standing at the office door, certainly appeared in a better frame of mind these days. There had been a time when he moaned interminably about his bad back and all the extra work he had to take on with the arrival of Mrs Devine. He now seemed a different man, whistling as he buffed his precious floors and walking down the corridor with a smile on his face and a spring in his step. His appearance had changed too. He had taken to wearing a white shirt and tie beneath a recently purchased, grey nylon overall which crackled when he walked. His approach could be predicted by the smell of a sickly sweet aftershave. This transformation in the caretaker was largely due to the good offices of Mrs Pugh, the part-time cleaner.

'To be honest, Mrs Scrimshaw, I am well pleased,' he replied. 'There were quite a number of very positive comments from parents last week at the consultation evening about the state of the school. "Never looked better," I was told, and Mrs Devine was very appreciative too.'

'I'm very happy to hear it,' replied Mrs Scrimshaw. 'I don't hear you complaining about that bad back of yours lately.'

'No, it's been fine, touch wood,' the caretaker replied. 'I do

have a few twinges now and again but I'm not one to bellyache.'
The secretary rolled her eyes skywards and sighed. 'Of course,
Mrs Pugh has insisted on doing quite a lot of the heavy work,'
he continued. 'She's been a boon, that woman. Nothing's too
much trouble for her and she's a whiz with a feather duster. I
just hope they can make her permanent down here when this
amalgamation takes place. She's not happy at Urebank.'

'Yes, well, I'm up to my eyes in the amalgamation at the
moment, what with all these papers to sort out,' said the school
secretary. 'Mrs Devine's speaking to the parents at Urebank
tonight and needs to give them details of the merger. I wouldn't
like to be in her shoes, facing that lot down there.'

'Bloody Nora!' exclaimed the caretaker. 'Pardon my French.
She's going down there, is she? It'll be like a Christian chucked
to the lions. From what Mrs Pugh tells me, that headmaster at
Urebank is a nasty piece of work. She says the deputy's not
much better. He's called Mr Jolly. That's a laugh for a start.
She says he's about as jolly as a satsuma.'

'A satsuma?' repeated the secretary, perplexed.

'You know, one of them big waves.'

'A tsunami,' said the secretary.

'Whatever. No, I wouldn't like to be in Mrs Devine's shoes,'
remarked the caretaker.

'Yes, I've heard she'll have a difficult job on her hands.' said
Mrs Scrimshaw. 'I certainly wouldn't want to work down
there.'

'Well,' said the caretaker, shaking his head ominously, 'you
might have to move down to the other premises come the
amalgamation.'

Mrs Scrimshaw stiffened and pursed her lips. 'Haven't you
got a floor to buff?' she asked.

The meeting at Urebank had been arranged by Mr Nettles to
acquaint parents of the changes which would be taking place

the following autumn term, when the two schools would combine. Elisabeth had already addressed the parents' meeting at Barton-in-the-Dale and what she had said had been well received. It was unlikely, she thought, that she could expect the same positive reception from the parents at the other school. At the village school in Barton she was on familiar ground, at Urebank she would be in enemy territory.

'Really, I can manage,' Elisabeth told Michael when he arrived at her cottage the evening of the meeting. 'There is really no need for you to come with me.'

'I want to,' he replied.

'I don't need anybody to hold my hand, you know.'

'But I like holding your hand.'

'I'm a big girl, Michael,' she told him, 'and can handle things myself.'

'I know,' he said. 'I just want to give you some moral support.'

'And there I was thinking you were sick and tired of me always talking about school,' she said.

'Yes, I'm sorry I said that,' he told her. 'I do know how committed you are to what you do, and I think my comments were unfair. I was rather short with you. Forgive me?' He gave her the look a small boy might give when caught with his hand in the biscuit jar.

'Of course,' she replied, smiling and kissing his cheek, 'and when we are married I will try not to be so tied up with school.'

'Is that a promise?'

'It is.'

'So, may I come?' asked Michael

'If you do, don't say anything because by rights you shouldn't be there. This is a meeting for parents only.'

He touched his forelock. 'Yes, miss,' he replied.

Michael guessed Elisabeth would need a deal of moral support that evening, for there would be a few at Urebank who would not be positively inclined about the changes and be unhappy with her as the new head teacher.

'How do I look?' asked Elisabeth. She had dressed for the occasion in a smart, pale grey suit, a pearl-coloured silk blouse, plain black stockings and grey patent leather shoes. She had tied back her hair into a neat little bun and she wore the minimum of make-up and no jewellery.

'I prefer you in those black lacy stockings and the red shoes with the silver heels,' Michael said. 'You know, the outfit you wore when you came to interview for the headship of the village school. You looked stunning.'

'I thought the red shoes with silver heels would be a bit over the top for this occasion,' she told him. 'I want to look efficient, professional and like I know what I'm doing.'

'Well, you are dressed for the part,' Michael reassured her, 'and I have little doubt that you will win them over.'

In the entrance hall at Urebank Junior and Infant School, Elisabeth found a harassed-looking Mr Nettles in earnest conversation with two men: Major C. J. Neville-Gravitas, Chairman of Governors of Barton-in-the-Dale, and Councillor Cyril Smout, Chairman of Governors at Urebank. The former was attired in a dark blue barathea blazer with brash gold buttons, pressed grey trousers, crisp white shirt and regimental tie knotted tightly under the chin and fixed with a small gold pin. In contrast, the other individual was a broad man with an exceptionally thick neck, vast florid face and small darting eyes. He wore a shapeless linen jacket through which his substantial stomach pushed out forcefully.

''Ere she comes,' announced the councillor loudly when he caught sight of Elisabeth. She was carrying a smart black briefcase and looked every inch the successful businesswoman.

'I'll see you later,' whispered Michael, squeezing Elisabeth's hand and then letting her go ahead of him. 'Good luck.' He disappeared around the side of the school.

'Good evening,' said Elisabeth, walking into the entrance and trying to sound cheerful and confident.

'And a very good evening to you, Elisabeth,' said the major in a hearty tone of voice. He stroked his bristly moustache. Fine-looking woman, he thought to himself.

'Mrs Devine,' said the education officer, assuming his most ingratiating smile.

'Good evening, Mr Nettles,' she said.

'We were—' he began.

'We was just sooartin out who should say what,' Councillor Smout explained, cutting him short. 'I mean, I know you will 'ave a lot to say for yourself, Mrs Devine, but somebody's got to do t'introductions. I'm 'appy to oblige and feel that since I am Chairman of Governors 'ere at Urebank it should fall to me to do it.'

'Then again,' said the major, 'as I am interim Chair of Governors in this new set-up I think that I should do the honours, if you follow my drift.'

'But I felt it would be best coming from me,' said Mr Nettles, 'as the representative of the Director of Education. We must be very careful to follow the correct procedures and practices.'

Elisabeth's heart sank. They were like spoilt children arguing over who had the biggest piece of cake. The meeting had not even started and there was squabbling already. She took a breath.

'The matter is easily resolved,' she said smiling but with a decisiveness in her voice. 'I suggest none of you do it. I am quite happy to introduce myself, and of course I can call upon you gentlemen should I need any advice or points for clarification. We really do not want this meeting to drag on for too long, do we?' Before they could register any objections to what she had suggested, Elisabeth moved on quickly. 'Is Mr Richardson here yet?' she asked.

''E's not comin',' the councillor told her.

'He rang me today and said he felt it would not be appropriate for him to attend,' explained Mr Nettles, looking rather sheepish.

'Really?' said Elisabeth. 'I should have thought the very opposite. As the head teacher of Urebank and the deputy head teacher designate of the new school it seems to me it is very appropriate for him to attend.'

''E's still smartin' at not gettin' t'job what you got,' the councillor told her.

'And is Mr Jolly not coming either?' Elisabeth asked.

'No, he felt that it would not be a good idea either,' said Mr Nettles, looking even more uncomfortable.

To be honest Elisabeth was not disappointed that the two people who she guessed would give her the greatest degree of trouble were not there that evening, but their absence did not bode well for the future. They were all supposed to work together in the newly formed school. 'Well, since we have a little time yet before the parents start arriving,' she said, 'I should like to have a look around the school – that is, if you have no objection, councillor.'

'No, no, none at all,' said Councillor Smout. 'You 'ave a gander.'

Elisabeth opened her briefcase and took out a wad of paper, which she passed to the education officer. 'I wonder, Mr Nettles,' she said pleasantly, 'if you would be so kind as to place one of these hand-outs on each chair. I have put something together to explain a few things to the parents.' With that she set off on a tour of the building.

In the brightest and tidiest classroom she discovered the infant teacher and her colleague. Maureen Hawthorn and Margaret Ryan, both dressed in remarkably similar brightly patterned cotton dresses which looked like converted curtains, were busy chattering over cups of tea. They both got to their feet when the new head teacher designate walked in.

'I hope I'm not disturbing you,' said Elisabeth.

'Oh no, Mrs Devine,' said Mrs Ryan.

'Not at all,' added her colleague.

'We were just having a natter.'

'And a cup of tea,' said Mrs Hawthorn.

'You have the classroom looking lovely,' Elisabeth told them, glancing at the colourful displays.

'Oh well,' said Mrs Ryan, 'I do think it's nice to provide a stimulating environment.'

'Particularly for the little ones,' added Mrs Hawthorn

'I do so agree,' said Elisabeth.

'We thought we'd stay for the meeting,' said Mrs Ryan.

'I hope you don't mind,' added Mrs Hawthorne.

'If you would prefer us not to come,' said the first teacher.

'Then we'll go,' said the other.

'I'm very pleased you have both decided to stay,' Elisabeth told them. 'I am sure the parents will appreciate you being present.'

The two women smiled in unison.

'We were . . . er . . . sorry about the meeting at County Hall,' said Mrs Ryan.

'Very sorry,' echoed her colleague.

'We thought Mr Richardson's behaviour was inexcusable.'

'Indeed, inexcusable,' echoed Mrs Hawthorne.

'Well, perhaps he'll come round,' said Elisabeth, with little conviction that he would.

'Perhaps you might care to look at some of the children's work?' asked Mrs Ryan.

'And see what we've been doing?' added her colleague.

'I'd like that very much,' replied Elisabeth.

At that moment Elisabeth knew that she could work with

these two teachers. They too knew that they could get on with her.

Elisabeth's stomach tightened and her heart began to thump in her chest. Before her in the school hall were row upon row of parents. Several, arms folded tightly over their chests, observed her with expressions of exaggerated disdain, some stared at her blankly and others scrutinised her with a mixture of curiosity and expectation. She took a deep breath and, with her hands clasped firmly in front of her, entered the fray.

'Good evening,' she said brightly.

There were a few mumbled responses.

'My name is Elisabeth Devine, at present head teacher of Barton-in-the-Dale village school and the head teacher designate of the newly established Barton-with-Urebank Primary School. I should like to welcome you to this meeting. I am delighted that so many of you have come along this evening. Firstly, I should like to introduce three of my colleagues. On the front row is County Councillor Smout, whom you all know.' She noticed a few exchanged looks and grimaces. 'Next to him is Major Neville-Gravitas, who is the interim Chair of Governors at the new school, and Mr Nettles, an education officer who will have a liaison role.'

The three aforementioned figures occupied the most prominent positions in the middle of the front row. Councillor Smout sat with his legs apart, his hands comfortably placed across his bulging stomach, his head tilted a little to the side and his eyes closed. He looked like a Toby jug. The major, who was slightly deaf, cupped an ear with a hand the better to hear and the education officer sat upright, a finger pressed over his lips. They resembled the three monkeys – see no evil, hear no evil, speak no evil.

'This evening,' continued Elisabeth, 'I wish to tell you about our plans and answer any questions you may wish to ask.

Quite a lot of information regarding the staffing, curriculum, timetable and transport is contained in the papers on your chair, which you can read at your leisure.' She paused to take in her audience. The faces had not changed. 'I have to be honest with you when I say I am a little nervous about how things will go. I have never been involved in the amalgamation of two schools before. Each of the schools has a distinct identity and different ways of working. I will need some support and understanding to get things right. By nature I am an optimistic person, however. There are many benefits in the coming together of Barton and Urebank: more space, extra resources, a better pupil-teacher ratio, a greater range of extra-curricular activities, to name but a few.'

She caught sight of Michael standing at the rear of the hall. He smiled and gave a thumbs-up sign. 'Now I should like to say a few words about what I believe.' She paused for effect and took another deep breath. 'I believe that all children ought to have the very best education we can give them. That is my vision and my commitment. Every child regardless of background or ability, race or religion is entitled to the very best. Children deserve enthusiastic, committed and hard-working teachers and a curriculum which is balanced, appropriate and challenging.' Her eyes were suddenly drawn to a tall, gaunt woman dressed in tight-fitting jeans and with long silver hoops in her ears who was giving her a look of barely suppressed animosity. 'My mother used the expression: "Fine words butter no parsnips." Maybe that is what some of you are thinking now. Well, I will say this. It is a fact that people will always doubt what you say but they will believe in what you do, so I ask you to judge me on what I do. My door is always open, so if you have any concerns about your child's education you can let me know and I promise you I shall work with you to resolve things. Now I will take questions.'

A round-faced little woman raised a hand. 'I would like to ask why things couldn't have stayed as they was?' Her tone was enquiring rather than reproachful.

'I think Councillor Smout, who is a member of the Education Committee which made the decision to amalgamate the schools, is better suited to answer that question than I,' replied Elisabeth.

Well played, thought Michael.

Reluctantly the councillor stood up, clearly displeased that he should have been unexpectedly called upon to deal with this potentially contentious issue. Annoyance shone in his eyes and a vein in his temple stood out and throbbed angrily. His face flushed crimson.

'Look,' he said, 'we've been through all this afore at t'last meeting we 'ad 'ere about t'merger.' His tone of voice was peevish and condescending. 'What I said then, I'll say again. We 'ave to make cuts in t'education budget, an' to do that we 'ave to either close some o' t'schools or join 'em up. That's t'top an' bottom of it.' He sat down.

'Are there any more questions?'

'Where is Mr Richardson tonight?' came a loud voice from the back of the hall.

'I'm afraid I can't answer that,' replied Elisabeth, 'but maybe Mr Nettles can?'

Brilliant, thought Michael.

The education officer hesitated for a moment and then got to his feet.

'Well, er, Mr Richardson is indisposed,' he said feebly.

'And what about Mr Jolly?' came the voice again, 'is he indisposed as well?'

'I believe so,' said Mr Nettles before resuming his seat.

There were chuckles and grunts from the audience.

'Another question?' asked Elisabeth. There was now a lightness in her voice.

The tall woman in the tight-fitting jeans and wearing the silver hoops stood up. She placed her hands on her hips.

Here it comes, thought Elisabeth, preparing herself for the onslaught.

'I have two kids here in the juniors,' said the woman, 'and neither of them is happy in this school.' Her voice was loud and strident. 'It don't surprise me one little bit that Mr Richardson and Mr Jolly aren't here, because you can never get hold of them and if you do manage to, they're about as much use as a pulled tooth.'

Elisabeth felt it proper to intervene at this point, for things were getting personal. 'I think perhaps we might—'

'Let me finish, Mrs Devine,' said the woman. 'I know for a fact that there are other parents who feel the same as what I do and the Chairman of our Governors sitting down the front knows it too.' Councillor Smout shifted uneasily in his chair. 'So I for one think joining up the schools is a good thing and what I say is bloody good luck to you.' She sat down to a ripple of applause.

'You were wonderful,' said Michael, as Elisabeth climbed into his car following the meeting.

'It wasn't that bad, was it?' she replied, flushed with success.

'It couldn't have gone better. The look on Councillor Smout's face must have been a picture when you knocked the ball into his court, and that Nettles man must have wished the floor would open and swallow him up when you whacked the ball his way. And what about the woman who stood up at the end? That was a turn-up for the books. I did say that you would win them over. You are quite a woman, Elisabeth Devine. Now I am taking you for a celebratory drink.'

The lounge of the Blacksmith's Arms was noisy and crowded but they managed to find a table in the corner.

'Champagne?' asked Michael.

'Pardon?'

'To celebrate your success this evening.'

'A white wine will be fine, thank you. A small one. We don't want to be too late. I told Mrs O'Connor we would be back before ten.'

Michael went to the bar to order the drinks.

Fred Massey, who never missed much, had seen the couple come into the pub. He finished his pint in one great gulp and then shuffled off his stool in the public bar and ambled over to the corner table.

'Evening, Mrs Devine,' he said, smiling and showing a set of discoloured tombstone teeth.

'Good evening, Mr Massey,' she replied.

'And how are you tonight?'

'I'm well, thank you.'

'Lovely weather we're having.'

'It is.'

'And have you given any further thought to my generous offer to buy that track of yours?'

'Yes, Mr Massey, I have.'

He sat down and leaned across the table, looking like a fox ready to pounce on its prey. 'And?' he asked eagerly.

'I've decided not to sell,' said Elisabeth.

'Not to sell!' he repeated.

'That's right.'

'Well, I think you're making the wrong decision. There'll be a tidy bit of cash up front.'

'Money's not everything, Mr Massey,' Elisabeth told the man who believed the very opposite.

'And as I've said before, the person what buys yon cottage will no doubt jump at the chance of making a bit of brass. You'll regret not selling it to me then.'

'And who says I'm going to sell the cottage, Mr Massey?' asked Elisabeth.

'You won't be wanting two properties once you move to Clumber Lodge, now will you?' he told her.

'I might.'

The old man rubbed the stubble on his chin. 'Well, I can't see the logic in that,' he said.

Michael returned with the drinks. 'Good evening, Mr Massey,' he said.

'Evening, doctor,' replied Fred, getting to his feet.

'And how are you keeping?'

'Fair to middling, doctor,' replied Fred. 'I was just trying to persuade Mrs Devine here to sell me that bit of track what runs by her cottage.'

'Yes, Elisabeth told me you were interested in buying it.'

'She won't have none of it,' grumbled Fred. 'Without that track they can't build on my field, and if they can't build I'll be depriving all these people who are looking for somewhere to live. Perhaps you can make her see sense.'

'Mr Massey,' said Michael, 'I think you have known Mrs Devine for long enough by now to appreciate that she is a woman of singular qualities, one of which is a steely determination. Once she has made up her mind about something, nothing will shift her.'

'Yes, well—' said Fred, scowling, and leaving the sentence unfinished he returned to the bar.

'I'm glad I made my mind up about you,' said Elisabeth, reaching over and taking Michael's hand.

'So am I,' he replied.

14

Ashley was staring up at the dark brown damp patch and flaking paint on the church roof when she caught sight of a small boy. He was sitting by the sepulchre of the medieval knight, watching her keenly. Bright sunshine shone through the stained glass window above the tomb and enveloped him in rainbow colours.

'Hello,' she said brightly, walking over to him.

'I'm not doing anything,' he replied mulishly, folding his arms and hunching his shoulders. 'I'm just sitting here.'

'That's all right,' she said.

'And I'm not going to nick anything either, if that's what you think.' There was anger in his voice.

'I didn't think that,' said Ashley calmly.

'I bet you did.'

Ashley laughed. 'No, I really didn't.'

'Grown-ups always think I'm up to no good.'

'Well, I'm a grown-up and I don't think you're up to no good.'

'I bet you do,' he mumbled.

'No, I don't. Shouldn't you be out in the sunshine on such a lovely summer day?'

He stood up. 'Do you want me to go?'

'No. I like people to visit the church, particularly young people.'

'Yes, well, I'll go if that's what you want,' said the boy.

'Wouldn't you prefer to be out playing with your friends?'

'I don't have any bloody friends,' he said in a matter-of-fact voice. He sat down.

'You shouldn't swear, you know.'

'Why?'

'Well, I for one don't like to hear it.'

'You're like all adults, telling kids what to do and what to say. I can bloody swear if I want to.'

'Well, don't do it in church, there's a good boy.'

He lifted his eyes to hers and gave a twisted smile. 'I'm not a good boy.'

'What's your name?'

'Why do you want to know?'

'If I'm talking to someone I like to know their name, but you needn't tell me if you don't want to.'

After a little hesitation he said, 'Robbie. Robbie Hardy.'

'Well, mine's Ashley.' She sat next to him. 'Have you been to the church before?'

'When we came with the school. You showed us round.'

'I thought I recognised you.'

'It's quiet in here and there are no people. That's what I like. You can sit here on a bench and nobody bothers you.' The light shining through the stained glass gave a livid tinge to the boy's face. 'Most of the time anyway,' he added meaningfully.

Ashley smiled. What a fractious child he is, she thought.

'Do you want me to go?' she asked.

'Suit yourself,' Robbie replied.

'When I was your age I used to go into the local church,' Ashley told him, her tone light and seamless. 'I went by myself and would sit beneath the great arched roof, between tall stone pillars, and see the sun shining through the stained glass window and casting rainbows on the floor. It was quite magical.'

'It's only the sun shining through glass,' said the boy. 'Nothing magical about that.'

'I thought it was,' she said wistfully.

They sat there for a moment without speaking.

Ashley sensed that this was a troubled child, as lonely and unhappy as she had been when she was his age. She too had been an angry child, suspicious of adults. All she seemed to recall as a small girl at home were the arguments and smouldering silences. After her parents' acrimonious divorce she had gone to live with her mother, who had become bitter and resentful, constantly complaining about the man who had deserted her for another woman and forced her out of the large house to live in a poky little flat. Ashley had had to leave the attic bedroom she so loved, her friends and her school. There was nothing in the flat except grumbles and recriminations, no saving moments of laughter or shared pleasure. Nothing she did seemed to please her mother. It was if she resented her very presence. She had felt miserable and lonely, believing that neither parent really loved her. She tried to love her mother but it didn't work; she couldn't love her father, for she never saw him. And so she learnt to hide her feelings, conceal her thoughts.

It took a long time for her to learn to love. She found the visits to the local church and the sympathetic vicar a great comfort, and then she met a teacher who really seemed to understand. She was introduced to the world of literature, her escape. And then she found the Bible. It told her that if she was not loved on earth there was a God in heaven who loved her unconditionally. She learnt to love the gentle, forgiving, benign figure who stared down from the cross above the altar. And it was this that drew her to the ministry.

Of course she received no encouragement from her mother when Ashley told her she saw a life for herself in the Church.

'But then you have never listened to any advice I had to give,' she told her daughter. 'You were a wilful child, always wanting your own way like your father. I don't know what good you imagine you will do becoming a vicar.' Over the last few years she had visited her mother each month. The old lady, still living in the same small flat, remained her angry and aggrieved self and Ashley would always leave feeling despondent.

'Do you live in the village?' she asked Robbie after a while.

'You ask a lot of questions, don't you?'

'I've been told I'm a nosy person,' said Ashley.

'I live at a children's home, if you must know. My mum didn't want me.'

Ashley was taken aback by the boy's bluntness but decided not to probe. She now understood the brooding resentment and anger of a child who felt he had been abandoned.

'You know, I felt like that when I was your age,' she said.

Robbie looked up and fixed her with his bright green eyes. 'You don't know nothing about how I feel,' he told her.

'I think I do.'

'How could you?'

'I didn't have a very happy childhood. My father left when I was little and I lived with my mother. I had the feeling she really didn't want me. It's a terrible feeling, isn't it, to feel you're not wanted.'

'Yes,' replied the boy quietly.

'I liked to get out of the flat where we lived to be on my own. I used to sit in the church where no one would bother me, just like you.' It had been a long time since she had spoken so openly about her own childhood. Perhaps she was telling this hurt and lonely little boy because he, more than most, could really understand what she had felt like when she was his age. 'I was such a sulky girl, angry with people. I felt cheated when I saw all the happy children at school.'

'I feel like that,' he said, and began staring at the floor.

Ashley lay a hand on his arm. 'But you know, Robbie,' she

said, 'I made up my mind I was going to be happy and to find pleasure in small things like the colours from a stained glass window with the sun shining through. I decided to make the best of what I had. You see, there is no one in the world who has everything and everyone has their share of unhappiness. I realised that there is not much hope of being happy when you hold on to those hurt feelings and thoughts.'

Robbie got up. 'I've got to go,' he said.

'Well, I hope you'll come back,' she said.

He shrugged before walking away and into the shadows.

After pouring herself a large glass of extra dry sherry, Miss Sowerbutts stood by the window in the small tidy sitting-room of her cottage. She looked out over her neat conventional little garden, the square of immaculate lawn and the straight-stemmed flowers standing like ranks of soldiers in the narrow borders. She seethed at the thought of a monstrous housing estate rising up on the field beyond, ruining her view and invading her privacy. She imagined all those featureless egg-box houses in shiny red brick, no doubt with balconies and large picture windows overlooking her garden, and was filled with rage. And it was not only her view that would be spoilt. There would be the commotion from the traffic, loud neigh-bours and no doubt hordes of noisy children and barking dogs. She took a sip of the sherry.

The cat wove silently between her legs, lifting its long tail and purring.

'Stop that!' snapped Miss Sowerbutts. 'Stop it at once! You've already been fed. I really don't know what has got into you lately, Tabitha.'

The cat loped off and settled in the sunshine in front of the window, where it stretched out on its back, its front paws hanging limply from its chest and its silky stomach exposed to the warmth.

'And don't think you can settle down there,' its owner told it. She nudged it with her foot. The cat arched its back and hissed.

'And you can stop that as well. You can go into your basket until you learn to behave yourself.' She shooed the creature from the room.

Having consigned the cat to the kitchen, Miss Sowerbutts returned to the window and drained the glass she was holding. She couldn't bear the thought of all those houses. Then there was the antagonistic attitude of that Devine woman, who refused to give a straight answer to a perfectly reasonable question about the track down the side of her cottage.

Of course she had not liked the woman from the start, in her fancy red shoes and black stockings, spouting all that educational jargon and gobbledegook. Miss Sowerbutts still felt a deep resentment that the governors of the village school had not 'deemed it appropriate', as the Chairman had told her, that she should be involved in the appointment of her successor. It was no wonder that education was in such a dire state with head teachers like her. Insufferable woman. The Devine woman would sell the track out of spite, of course, and no doubt gain great pleasure to think that a great sprawling housing estate would be built smack bang behind the cottage. She had no need to worry, thought Miss Sowerbutts bitterly, getting married to the local GP and then sitting pretty in Clumber Lodge. It didn't take her long to get those long red nails of hers into Dr Stirling, and him getting married again when his wife was still warm in the grave. Well, this estate was just not going to happen, Miss Sowerbutts determined. She poured herself another generous glass of sherry and took a gulp.

The doorbell rang.

Miss Sowerbutts secreted the sherry and the bottle behind a table lamp, straightened the creases in her shapeless tweed skirt and went to answer the door. At the sight of her visitor she felt her chest tighten and she gave a small gasp. Then, recovering her composure, she assumed her usual prim and straight-backed attitude.

'You!' she said, startled. Her voice trembled a little. 'My goodness.'

'Hello, Hilda,' said the man, a large fleshy-faced individual with thinning grey hair and pale blue eyes. He held out his hand in a vague gesture but she ignored it and stood stiff and erect, staring.

'Might I come in?' he asked gingerly.

'Yes,' she replied, pressing her thin lips together. 'You had better. Go through into the sitting-room.'

The visitor took off his shoes and left them in the hall. Miss Sowerbutts noticed there was a small hole in the heel of one of his socks. He was quick to see the pristine state of the cottage, the immaculate lace curtains, the highly polished furniture and, in particular, the pale carpet. Her visitor went ahead of Miss Sowerbutts into the sitting-room with its rose-coloured curtains, small sofa and matching chairs. The magnolia walls were bare save for a painting of a leaping ballerina in a rose pink tutu. The room was oppressively tidy. There was the cloying smell of lavender air freshener and just the hint of sherry.

'It's been a long time, Hilda,' he said, smiling.

'Forty years,' she told him in a dry, precise voice, looking away to avoid meeting his eyes.

'That long?' He walked to the window and stared out at the panorama. 'Lovely view,' he said.

'For the present,' she replied. 'A local farmer has it in mind to build houses on that field. He will do it over my dead body.' There was real anger in her voice.

'You sound very determined.'

'Oh, I am!' she exclaimed. 'I intend to fight it all the way. I shall get up a petition. It's unconscionable that the odious little man should completely ruin my view.'

'You don't sound like the Hilda Sowerbutts I knew,' said the man.

'Meaning?'

'Oh, you know, you were never a very forceful person as a student, quite reserved in fact, not that confident in your own abilities.'

'I'm sure I don't know what you mean.'

'What did our tutor at college say about you?'

'I can't remember. It was a long time ago.'

'Old Dr Trollope said you would be a great teacher if you believed more in yourself.'

'Well, I don't recall,' she replied dismissively. 'Anyway, people do change.'

'Yes, they do indeed,' he agreed.

'You had better sit down,' she told him.

As her visitor sat he caught sight of the glass and the decanter of sherry half-hidden behind the table lamp and smiled to himself. He remembered how, unlike everyone else in their year at college, she had never touched a drop of alcohol. There had certainly been a change in the shy, abstemious, fresh-faced young woman he had once known. He looked over at the thin figure with the heavily lined face and drooping mouth. She perched unsmiling on the edge of the sofa.

'So what brings you here after so long?' she asked. 'I'm sure it's not to admire the view from my cottage.'

'It's about your letter,' he told her.

'Letter? I don't recall having written to you.'

'You wrote to St John's with your views on the present situation in education. I'm the Vice Principal at the college and your letter landed on my desk.'

'You are the Vice Principal?' she said, sounding surprised.

'I am, yes.' Then he added tactfully, 'I deal with letters such as yours.'

'I see.'

'And when I saw the name on the letter I knew it must be the Hilda Sowerbutts I was at college with and I thought I would come and see you personally.' He failed to mention that he had an appointment at the village school that afternoon.

'Well, there was really no need to trouble yourself,' she replied pertly.

'It's no trouble,' he replied, raising a smile. 'I thought it might be nice to see you again.'

'Catch up on old times,' she remarked. She laughed unsmilingly.

'I gather from your letter that you were the head teacher here at the village school?'

'Yes, I was. I retired last year and as I said in the letter I have become increasingly dismayed at the state of education, with all these trendy methods, modern approaches and flash-in-the-pan initiatives which are promoted by inspectors and advisers and, I shouldn't wonder, by college lecturers. I am heartily sick and tired of hearing about these syndromes and conditions which children are now labelled with. If a child can't spell they say he's dyslexic, if he misbehaves he's got some sort of disorder, if he won't concentrate then he's got some fancy-named condition. All stuff and nonsense in my view.'

'Yes, you made it very clear in your letter what you think,' he said, looking at the floor.

'And I have to say,' she continued, 'the colleges and university departments of education must accept their share of the blame. When we were at college we were taught very differently. I don't know how Dr Trollope would view all these changes.'

What a sad, rather embittered woman she appeared to have

become, thought her visitor, sitting there so stiff and self-righteous. Perhaps beneath that plain, sallow and remote woman there was something of the girl he once knew. Perhaps she was not a person without feeling, and circumstances in her life had pushed her in that direction, to a life of loneliness and regret.

'I hope that at St John's,' he said, looking up, 'we prepare the students well for life in the classroom and teach them the necessary skills. Perhaps you might care to pay us a visit. I'd be delighted to show you around and reassure you that we are not promoting "trendy methods, modern approaches and flash-in-the-pan initiatives".'

'I think not,' she replied.

He changed the subject, not wishing to debate the matter of modern education with her further. It was unlikely, he thought, that his words would have any effect. 'You never married, Hilda?'

'No.'

'I was married,' he said. 'Kathleen died last year.' He smiled ruefully.

'I'm sorry,' she said.

'We were looking forward to my retirement next term. It wasn't to be.'

'Have you family?' she asked.

'Sadly no,' he said. 'We thought of adopting but decided against it.'

'It's a big step.'

'It is.'

They sat in an embarrassed silence for a moment, each thinking of what to say next.

'Well, if you will forgive me,' said Miss Sowerbutts, rising from her chair to indicate that it was time for her visitor to leave, 'I have to take my cat to the vet's this morning. She's been behaving very strangely of late.'

'Yes, yes, of course,' he said getting to his feet. 'It was good to see you again, Hilda. Well, goodbye, and if you do wish to take me up on the offer of a tour around St John's, you know where to find me.'

Miss Sowerbutts held out her hand for a perfunctory shake. 'Goodbye, Patrick,' she said.

She watched him for a moment as he fastened his shoes. He breathed heavily when he bent. As he walked down the path she continued to stare before slowly closing the door and returning to the sitting-room. She looked across her garden at the panorama. It seemed an enormously long time since she had walked across the fields with Patrick during that summer vacation from college. They had strolled to the church whose grey stone tower she could now see in the distance rising between the trees. He had taken her hand in his and she had shuddered with the thrill of it. And how he talked. He had told her it was the Irish in him, how Oscar Wilde had once remarked, 'If only one could teach the English how to talk and the Irish how to listen.' He had told her how he loved the sounds and smells of the countryside, the twittering swallows, the call of a distant curlew, the raucous cawing of the rooks, the hedgerows choked with dog rose, the crunching of the dry grass underfoot and the munching, glassy-eyed cows. She recalled it all. He was determined to get a post in a country school away from the smoke and noise of city life. They had walked hand-in-hand and stopped at the rank buddleia by the churchyard, its drooping purple blossoms crowded with tortoiseshell, peacock and cabbage white butterflies. 'My little sister calls them "flutterbyes",' he had told her, laughing. She remembered it well. She had never felt as free or as happy.

Of course she knew from the start that her parents would never approve of Patrick – a council house boy, Irish, Catholic, coarse Liverpudlian accent. 'You can do a great deal better than him,' her father had told her. 'I didn't send you to a top private school and give you every advantage to throw yourself away on the first man who takes an interest, and certainly not someone like that.' She had looked at him standing by the fireplace, holding forth as was his wont, and could not remember a time when she hadn't disliked her father. He was a bad-tempered, bullying, oppressive man and nothing she did pleased him. 'Teaching!' he had snorted when she told him she wanted to go to college. 'Those that can, do, those who can't, teach,' he had said, laughing at his own wisecrack. It was made clear that it was her brother Henry whom he preferred, the only son, who would take over the business. Her mother had said nothing. She was quiet and compliant and did what her husband ordered. When Patrick had left after a particularly unpleasant dinner at which he had been cross-examined unmercifully and made to feel gauche and uncomfortable, she recalled her brother's remark that, 'He can't even hold his knife and fork properly.' Her father had laughed. 'Bog Irish,' her brother had continued disparagingly. She had seen very little of Henry over the years and then he had died – a heart attack on the golf course.

When she left college there had been a change in Miss Sowerbutts. She vowed she would not follow the path of her mother, to become a wife whose husband could order her about. She would not be dominated by a man.

She saw little of her brother's son. David had invited her down to Surrey for Christmas the previous year but she found it onerous. She did not enjoy having to spend the day with him and that fussy little wife of his, eating overcooked turkey, watching inane television programmes and having to endure the noisy children, who received far too many presents for her liking and ate far too much.

Miss Sowerbutts felt her eyes pricking with tears and her hands trembled. Patrick's visit had upset her. It brought back painful memories, a time she had wanted to forget. How had she been described earlier, she thought – 'reserved', 'under-confident'. She had not been strong enough to confront her parents when she had told them she was in love, that she wanted to marry Patrick, and they had expressed their strong disapproval. There had been arguments and threats and she had been worn down until she finally submitted. She had been weak. She should have fought for him, she had told herself so many times in the years that followed, but back then, as with every matter which arose in that dark, misera-ble, humourless house, she had given in. When her father had forbidden her to see Patrick again, she had seen the life she had dreamed of fading away. She had felt like a parched and weary traveller reaching an oasis with shady palm trees and cool water only to see, as she reached out, the mirage vanish before her. She took a deep breath. Over the years she had learnt to be strong though, not to rely on anybody, to be dominated by anyone. She now fought back the tears and reached for the sherry.

The vet's small waiting-room was crowded. There was a motley group of animal lovers nursing various sick animals and birds or cradling boxes or baskets containing their treas-ured pets. Miss Sowerbutts, carrying a wicker cat basket containing a mewling Tabitha, looked around for somewhere to sit and sighed irritably when she saw that there was no seat available.

'Let that old lady sit down, Chelsea,' a fat woman with dyed blonde hair and pale, heavily freckled skin told an equally fat and freckled girl who was nursing a docile-looking flop-eared rabbit.

The girl groaned and pulled a face. 'Do I have to, mam?'

'Yes, you do,' barked the woman, 'so shift yourself and let that old lady have a seat.'

Miss Sowerbutts winced at hearing herself described as

'that old lady'. She took the proffered seat, placing the cat basket on her lap.

'He's busy today,' the woman said.

Miss Sowerbutts looked ahead unseeingly. 'So it appears,' she replied.

'Mind you, it will be worse tomorrow,' continued the woman. 'Saturdays are always hectic.'

'What you got in the basket, missis?' asked the girl.

'A cat.'

'I don't like cats. My rabbit's got the runs,' said the girl.

'Shouldn't you be at school?' asked Miss Sowerbutts.

'I've got the runs as well,' replied the girl.

'Really,' replied Miss Sowerbutts, glancing at her watch and considering whether or not to come back another time. Why didn't vets let you make appointments like the doctor or the dentist, she thought.

'I reckon it's all the greens she's been feeding it,' the woman said.

'What?'

'Chelsea's rabbit,' the woman explained. 'It's got diarrhoea something chronic.'

Miss Sowerbutts ignored her.

The door opened and a barrel-bodied figure strode into the room carrying a bulldog. He was a broad individual with an exceptionally thick neck, the flabby folds of which overlapped the top of his collar, and a vast pallid face. Everyone turned to look at the dog. Like its owner it too was barrel-bodied. It had pinky-white jowls and pale unfriendly eyes. A set of vicious-looking teeth like tank traps projected from its lower jaw. The creature was breathing noisily and dribbling.

'Morning all,' said the man jovially as he looked around for a seat. The dog made a deep rumbling noise like a distant train. People shifted uncomfortably on their chairs and held their pets that bit more tightly.

A woman clutching a whimpering white toy poodle got up and scurried for the door, followed by a man with a squawking macaw in a cage and a boy with a gerbil in a box.

The man found a chair opposite Miss Sowerbutts. The dog rested its fat, round head on his knees and gave another deep throaty growl.

'She's off colour,' announced the man to no one in particular. 'She's very susceptible at this time of year, like a lot of English bulldogs. Asthmatic, you see. It's the pollen. Gets up her nose something terrible.' The dog rumbled as if in agreement. 'Born of noble stock is Trixie, with a pedigree as long as the Queen's.' He patted the fat head. 'Gentle as a lamb she is most of the time. She'd let anyone walk straight into the house and she wouldn't make a sound. Course, they'd not get out again.' He chuckled. 'Teeth like clamps. One snap of them jaws and she'd not let go. Locks on, you see. You could hit her over the head with a sledge hammer and she'd still hang on.' The dog blinked lazily, lifted its fat, round face from between the man's legs, yawned massively and displayed the fearsome set of teeth. It then fixed the flop-eared rabbit with its small pale eyes.

'Come along, Chelsea,' said the woman with the dyed hair. 'We'll come back another time.'

'It's the wolfish ancestry,' the man explained to Miss Sowerbutts when the mother and daughter had gone. 'It's over ten thousand years, you know, since dogs were first domesticated. Did you know that?'

'No, I didn't,' she replied indifferently.

'But they still retain their wild instincts,' said the man. 'Course, over the years many of their wild traits have been modified but all dogs still have that basic urge to kill. Even the most endearing of puppies is quite capable of savagery.'

'I am really not interested,' said Miss Sowerbutts coldly.

'Pardon me,' said the man.

The dog sniffed the air, cocked its fat head to one side, stared intently at the basket on Miss Sowerbutts's lap and growled.

She fixed the dog with a basilisk glare. The animal withdrew its head quickly and whimpered. It had met its match.

The vet, a young man with a wide friendly face, held the cat and gently stroked its head.

'A most beautiful creature,' he said.

Miss Sowerbutts permitted herself a small smile. 'She's a Lilac Point Siamese,' she told him.

'Well, she looks very healthy to me,' said the vet. 'What seems to be the problem?'

'She's just not herself. She was a very even-tempered, quite undemanding cat but of late she constantly meows, rubs up against my legs and seeks attention all the time.'

'I see. Has her routine changed at all?' he asked.

'Yes, it has,' Miss Sowerbutts replied. 'I had occasion to go into hospital and Tabitha was looked after while I was away. I did explain to the person who had charge of her that she has a special diet of lightly boiled fish and fat-free chicken and that she should never under any circumstances be let out of the house. The person who looked after her no doubt spoilt her, fed her on all sorts of unsuitable food and I have an idea she was let out to roam the garden.'

The vet nodded and placed the cat back in the basket. 'I think I know the problem,' he said. 'This is not a medical condition, it is a psychological one.'

'Psychological,' repeated Miss Sowerbutts.

'Yes, it is an eating disorder, probably stress-related. You see this constant attention-seeking and change in its behaviour pattern is most likely due to an obsession with food. There was a fascinating article about this very thing in the *Journal of Veterinary Behaviour*. Interestingly, the authors of this report

studied a Siamese cat very much like your own. I have an idea
it was called Otto. It would jump on its owner as she prepared
the meals, roam around the house irritably and try to eat from
the tin as well as stealing food from another cat. Now with this
condition—'

Miss Sowerbutts, who had remained uncharacteristically
silent throughout this lecture, suddenly held up a hand. 'One
moment,' she said. 'Condition? Disorder? Syndrome? I don't
believe what I am hearing. Not content with labelling children
with these ridiculous descriptions,' she continued angrily,
'people are now labelling animals with them.' She scooped up
the cat and the basket. 'I bid you good day.'

When she arrived back at her cottage, in a particularly bad
mood, Miss Sowerbutts put the cat in the kitchen and poured
herself another reviving glass of sherry. She then decided on a
plan of action to stop the proposed housing development. She
had already written to various people complaining: officials at
the town hall planning office, the Leader of the Council, her
local councillor, her Member of Parliament, the Chairman of
English Heritage and the National Parks' Commissioner. The
few replies she had received she considered to be very unhelpful and typically evasive. Now she would organise a petition.

The following afternoon, armed with a clip-board and
sheets of paper, her first port of call was Miss Brakespeare's
house.

'Oh,' cried her former colleague, when she opened the front
door to find Miss Sowerbutts standing on the step.

'Good afternoon, Miriam,' said her visitor. 'May I come in?'
Without waiting for an answer she strode into the hall. 'There
is something I need your help with.'

Miss Brakespeare gave an inward sigh. 'You had better go
through, but I was about to head out. I have a choir practice
this afternoon and George and I—'

'I won't keep you long,' said Miss Sowerbutts, walking ahead and into the sitting-room.

There she found Mrs Brakespeare sitting in her usual chair by the window.

'You know Mother of course,' said Miss Brakespeare. She raised her voice. 'It's Miss Sowerbutts, Mother.'

'I do have eyes, Miriam,' replied Mrs Brakespeare, 'and there might be a lot wrong with me, but I'm not deaf so you don't need to shout.'

'Good morning,' said Miss Sowerbutts, and sat straight-backed on the settee clutching her clip-board. 'I need you to sign this petition,' she told her former colleague.

'A petition?' repeated Miss Brakespeare.

'That's right. To stop the development of the housing estate in the village, the one that that dreadful Mr Massey has it in mind to have built. And perhaps you would append your name too, Mrs Brakespeare.'

'Oh no,' replied the old lady. 'I don't put my signature to anything and certainly not to any petition.'

'It's to stop the houses being built,' explained Miss Sowerbutts.

'I heard you the first time. I don't care what it's for,' the old lady told her. 'As I've just said, I'm not signing anything.'

'Well, perhaps you will sign, Miriam,' said Miss Sowerbutts irritably. 'You can be the very first.' She held up the clip-board. 'Just print your name and address on the top line and then sign it.'

'I do like to discuss things with George,' said Miss Brakespeare.

'I don't see the necessity of consulting Mr Tomlinson,' replied Miss Sowerbutts.

'She discusses everything with him,' said Mrs Brakespeare, pulling a face. 'She used to discuss things with me. She's getting married to him, you know. He's the man who plays the organ at the Methodist Chapel. I don't know why at her time of life she wants to get married and I've told her so, not that she listens to me.'

'Mother, would you not discuss me as if I'm not here,' said her daughter.

'And when they're married,' said the old lady, ignoring her daughter's protest, 'we're all moving to a bungalow in Scarborough, so the building of houses in the village won't affect us.'

'It might not affect you, Mrs Brakespeare,' said Miss Sowerbutts shrilly, 'but it will certainly affect me.'

'Well, that's your problem and not ours,' said the old lady peevishly.

'I see,' said Miss Sowerbutts, rising to her feet. 'So much for community solidarity. I have to say I did not anticipate such an indifferent response. I shall ask again, Miriam, will you sign the petition?'

'As I said,' replied Miss Brakespeare, 'I would need to talk things over with George.' Two red spots had appeared on her cheeks.

'Well, I am extremely disappointed with your attitude. I expected more help from you than this. When I think of all the unstinting support I gave you when you were my deputy head teacher—'

'Support!' interrupted Mrs Brakespeare with a hollow laugh. 'The other way round, more like. Miriam was always at your beck and call when she worked with you at the village school. Do this and do that! She never had a minute's peace. From what she told me you were stuck in your room all day.'

'I beg your pardon!' exclaimed Miss Sowerbutts.

'Mother, please—' began Miss Brakespeare.

'Don't Mother me, Miriam. Let's be right, Miss Sowerbutts, you took advantage of my daughter's good nature. If she had a bit more gumption she would have told you years ago. You're not the head teacher of the school now, so you can't go badgering and bullying her as you used to do.'

'Badgering and bullying?' repeated Miss Sowerbutts, enraged.

'Mother, really—' began her daughter again.

'No, Miriam, let's be right, it has to be said,' announced the old lady, braving the visitor's icy stare. 'You put on my daughter, Miss Sowerbutts, and you well know it. And if I were not so ladylike I'd tell you where to stick that petition of yours. Now, I am waiting for my tea.'

15

'You did your level best,' said Miss Parsons. 'Nobody could have dealt with Robbie as well as you.' Elisabeth and the social worker were sitting in the staff-room one Monday lunchtime.

'I wish I could have done more,' replied Elisabeth. 'I really felt I was getting somewhere with Robbie. His behaviour didn't improve massively – he could still be uncooperative and rude – but it was getting better. So what will happen to him now?'

'He's in care at the moment and then I am hoping he can be fostered. There is a wonderful couple who live this side of Clayton who have fostered more children than I can count and know how to deal with the most difficult and disturbed children. I'm taking Robbie over to meet them tomorrow.'

'I just cannot get my head around the attitude of the boy's mother,' said Elisabeth, 'abandoning him like that.'

'Don't be too hard on Mrs Banks,' said the social worker. 'She really was at the end of her tether.'

'Parents should be there for their children – through good times and bad,' said Elisabeth.

'She'd had enough of Robbie's tantrums and disruptive behaviour,' said Miss Parsons, 'and she was faced with a decision no mother should have to face. Her marriage was on the line. She had to make a choice. You might not agree with it, but sometimes it's best for a parent who can't cope to have some respite and put the child in care for the time being. And more importantly it is sometimes best for the child. Maybe when Robbie gets older he'll be able to go home.'

'And how is he coping?' asked Elisabeth.

'Remarkably well, all things considered,' said the social worker. 'In fact I think in some ways he is glad to leave. You know what always amazes me about children is their ability to cope, their strength and resilience. Sometimes they survive the most appalling situations and manage to get through them.'

'But get damaged in the process,' remarked Elisabeth.

'Not always. I've known people who have been neglected or abused as children and they have got though it and turned out to be well-adjusted, happy adults and caring parents, determined that their own children will not have to go through what they have been through.'

'Well, I hope things work out for Robbie,' said Elisabeth, 'I really do.'

Mrs Scrimshaw appeared at the door. 'I'm sorry to disturb you, Mrs Devine, but there's a youth wishing to speak to you. Mr Gribbon is keeping an eye on him.'

Elisabeth found the young man with the shaven head and coloured tattoo in the entrance. Mr Gribbon, jangling his keys like a gaoler, was watching him like a starving man might gaze at a feast.

'This lad here said you wanted to see him, Mrs Devine,' the caretaker declared.

'That's right, Mr Gribbon. Would you like to follow me?' she told the boy, 'and we can have a talk.'

'Yes, miss,' replied the boy.

'Shall I come with you, Mrs Devine?' asked Mr Gribbon.

'No, thank you,' replied Elisabeth. 'And what are you called?' she asked the youth as they walked down the corridor.

'Jason, miss.'

'I'm Mrs Devine and the head teacher here at the village school.'

'We met at County Hall, miss,' said the boy.

'That's right, and I complimented you on the state of the gardens. Do you know why I have asked you to come and see me?'

'I was told it was something about a job, miss,' replied the boy.

'Yes, that's right. I may have found you some work if you are interested. I have had a word with Mr O'Malley, who manages the estate at Limebeck House, and he is looking for someone to help with the gardens there.'

The boy's eyes lit up. 'As a gardener?'

'It will be hard work – trimming hedges, weeding, pruning, cutting grass, planting flowers and probably more besides. It is a big estate and there is much to do. Might you be interested?'

'You bet!' exclaimed the boy.

'You will have to get there very early—'

'I can get the first bus from Clayton.'

'You will have to work all hours, take orders, be trustworthy and not get into any trouble.'

'I can do all that, miss,' said the boy excitedly.

'Well, if you go up and see Mr O'Malley tomorrow morning he'll speak to you. Limebeck House is the big stone house just outside the village. If you take the Marfleet road you can't miss it.'

'Thanks, miss,' said the boy. 'Thanks for taking a chance with me. I won't let you down.'

Mrs Sloughthwaite, the fount of all village information, folded her dimpled arms under her substantial bosom.

'Would you like skimmed or semi-skimmed, Reverend,' she asked, 'or are you partial to some of this evacuated kind?'

'You mean evaporated,' said Mrs Pocock, who had called into the shop to glean the latest bit of gossip. 'Personally I can't stand the taste of it.'

'The semi-skimmed will be fine, thank you, Mrs Sloughthwaite,' said the Archdeacon.

'And have all the weddings been sorted out?' asked the shopkeeper, reaching for the milk. 'Won't be long now before young Bianca ties the knot and then there's Mrs Fish's other granddaughter and Mrs Devine and Dr Stirling's nuptials.'

'I believe so,' replied the Archdeacon. 'Reverend Underwood has everything under control. She will be conducting the ceremonies.'

'It's a rum do though,' remarked Mrs Pocock.

'What is?' asked the shopkeeper.

'Bianca having the baby and then getting married. In my day it was the other way round.'

'Times have changed,' said Mrs Sloughthwaite. 'I don't like to miss a wedding.'

Mrs Sloughthwaite didn't like to miss anything that occurred in Barton-in-the-Dale. She had closed the village store especially to attend the last one. 'I always think a summer wedding is providential to a winter one. When Joyce Fish's first granddaughter got wed she must have been frozen to death in that low-cut dress, and as I said to Mrs Lloyd at the time, the bridesmaids were blue with cold, shivering down the aisle. You could have grated a lemon on their goose bumps.'

The Archdeacon gave a weak smile. 'Yes, I believe you have mentioned that to me before. Might I have a packet of rich tea biscuits please?'

'What about a Venetian chocolate selection box? They're much nicer.'

'Thank you, no. I must watch my weight,' said the Archdeacon.

'Get away with you, Mr Atticus,' said Mrs Sloughthwaite, 'I've seen more fat on a butcher's pencil.'

'*Avoirdupois* and all that,' said the cleric, patting his stomach.

'And all what?' enquired Mrs Sloughthwaite.

'His paunch,' Mrs Pocock told her. 'My husband's got one. All that ale he sups. It's French for a beer belly.'

The Archdeacon winced.

'I didn't know you were fluid in French?' said the shopkeeper.

'There are lots of things you don't know about me,' replied Mrs Pocock.

'You're right there,' agreed Mrs Sloughthwaite, stretching to get the biscuits from a top shelf.

'And may I have a small jar of decaffeinated coffee, please?' requested the Archdeacon. 'My wife prefers it to the normal kind.'

'And is Mrs Atticus still liking it at the village school?' asked the shopkeeper. She assumed the thoughtful, conciliatory tone of one who wished to draw out confidences.

'She's not there at the moment,' the Archdeacon told her. 'Marcia has completed her teaching practice.'

'I hear from Miss Brakespeare that Mrs Devine had a visit from some big-wig at the college to find out how she was getting along.'

'Yes,' the cleric told her. 'The Vice Principal called in to see her.' My goodness, he thought, news travels like wildfire in the village.

'Evidently he was very impressed with Mrs Atticus.'

'Indeed. He was most satisfied.' He failed to mention that his wife had been asked to apply for the art coordinator's post at Clayton Juniors. 'How much do I owe you for the—'

Mrs Sloughthwaite was not to be diverted from extracting

as much information as possible. 'So she's fully qualificated now, then?'

'I'm sorry?' said the Archdeacon.

'Mrs Atticus. She's a proper teacher now?'

'Yes, indeed. She has completed her training and will receive her Certificate in Education towards the beginning of July.'

'And then she'll be looking for a job?' She continued doggedly to fish for information which she could relay later to her customers.

'I imagine so.'

'Maybe she can stay at the village school,' said Mrs Sloughthwaite. 'They'll be looking for new staff when the amalgamation takes place, won't they?' She reached for the coffee, then straightened up, stretched herself and rubbed her back.

'I really couldn't say,' replied the Archdeacon. 'How much is that?' he asked, opening a small leather purse, keen to extricate himself from the inquisition.

'She'll no doubt get a very good testimonical from Mrs Devine.'

'A what?' asked the cleric.

'Character reference when she applies for jobs. I should imagine Mrs Devine is well pleased with her.'

'Yes, indeed, Mrs Devine is most satisfied.'

'And I guess you can pull a few strings, Reverend, in finding her a position,' added Mrs Pocock, 'you being well-in with the powers that be.'

'No, no!' retorted the Archdeacon, affronted. 'I am not in favour of any kind of nepotism.'

'Neither am I,' agreed the shopkeeper, ignorant as to the meaning of the word.

The Venerable Atticus passed a five pound note across the counter. 'Perhaps you might put any change which is forthcoming in the charity tin,' he said, keen to be away.

The shopkeeper was not one to give up. 'So where is she thinking of teaching then?' she asked.

'I really couldn't say,' replied the Archdeacon hastily. 'It's very early days. Well, I must rush.'

The door opened and Miss Sowerbutts made an entrance. She was wearing a shapeless brown coat, bullet-proof stockings, heavy brogues and a knitted hat resembling a tea cosy, attire totally unsuitable for the mild weather. She was clutching a clip-board and a rolled-up poster. A battered old canvas bag hung from her arm.

Mr Atticus sighed inwardly and arranged his face into a forced smile. There was little chance now of him getting away. She was sure to want something or other.

'Well, I'm off,' said Mrs Pocock. Like everyone else in the village she disliked Miss Sowerbutts and didn't give her the time of day.

'One moment,' said Miss Sowerbutts, keen to get the woman's signature on her petition. 'I would like you to . . .'

'Can't stop,' replied Mrs Pocock, rushing out of the door.

'Good afternoon, Miss Sowerbutts,' said the Archdeacon, looking at the hard, humourless face before him.

'Good afternoon, Mr Atticus,' she replied stiffly. Her face was as tight as a mask.

'It's a lovely bright day, isn't it?' he said. 'It makes one glad to be alive.'

She scowled, tensing with displeasure. 'I am not likely to be full of the joys of spring, Mr Atticus,' she opined, 'with the prospect of a housing estate at the back of my cottage.'

'No, no, I guess not,' he said, not wishing to pursue this line of conversation.

'Grasping, that's what Fred Massey is,' she said angrily. 'Always out to make money by fair means or foul, just like his father. I remember Silas Massey. He was a disagreeable, avaricious old man and his son is a pea out of the same greedy pod.

Show him a heap and he'd be on top of it. He hadn't two pennies to rub together and the family was as poor as dormice due to his drinking. Then with all his wheeling and dealing he became rich overnight.'

'"Whether a man be rich or poor,"' said the Archdeacon, tiring of the constant complaints and grumbles, '"if he has a good heart towards the Lord, he shall at all times rejoice with a cheerful countenance."'

'I beg your pardon?' asked Miss Sowerbutts. There was an expression of distaste on her far from cheerful countenance.

'Ecclesiasticus, chapter 26,' replied the cleric.

She gave him a glacial stare. 'Spare me the homily, Mr Atticus. And as for a cheerful countenance . . .' She broke off.

'How is that lovely cat of yours?' asked the Archdeacon, keen to draw her away from the topic of the housing estate.

'She's not been the same since I was in hospital and she went to stay at Clumber Lodge with Dr Stirling. The house-keeper spoilt her and gave her the wrong food. I specifically said that she has a special diet of fish and chicken.'

'It was good of Dr Stirling and Mrs O'Connor to look after it,' observed Mrs Sloughthwaite, adjusting her nylon overall and smoothing the creases over her hips. 'I certainly wouldn't want a cat around the place shedding hairs and deprecating on the carpet.'

'She does not shed hairs and is perfectly house-trained,' said Miss Sowerbutts sharply.

Mr Atticus, seeing his chance of escape, made for the door. 'Well, must run,' he said, and scooping up his purchases swiftly departed.

'One moment, Mr Atticus,' Miss Sowerbutts shouted after him. 'I would like you to sign—'

But he had gone.

'What can I get you?' asked the shopkeeper in a chilly tone

of voice. There existed a mutual antagonism between her and Miss Sowerbutts, and neither women wasted time with pleasantries.

'I don't wish to purchase anything,' said Miss Sowerbutts. 'I would like you to put this petition in a prominent place and display this poster in your window.' She placed the clip-board and the poster on the counter. 'I am collecting signatures in order to stop the proposed housing development in the field at the back of my cottage. I shall leave them here.'

'I don't think so,' said Mrs Sloughthwaite, drawing in her double chins.

'I beg your pardon?'

'I don't hold with partitions and such.' To be honest the shopkeeper was not at all keen on the proposed housing development, feeling it would spoil the character of the village, but she was not inclined to give any support to this woman, whom she found objectionable and who rarely patronised her store. 'And I don't put posters up either,' she added.

Miss Sowerbutts fixed Mrs Sloughthwaite with a penetrating stare. 'I notice you have a poster in the window advertising the forthcoming organ recital at the church.'

'That's different,' said Mrs Sloughthwaite. Her voice was cool and contained. 'I'm in favour of organ music and have no objection to the houses being built.'

'Well, I shall have words with your superior at the General Post Office,' Miss Sowerbutts said in an imperious tone of voice.

'You can have words with whoever you like,' the shopkeeper told her, clasping her hands beneath her substantial bosom, 'but what happens in my store is up to me.'

Miss Sowerbutts snatched up the clip-board and the poster and left, banging the door noisily behind her. She strode angrily down the high street on her way to coerce the shopkeepers into displaying her posters and putting a copy of a petition on their counters.

Bianca, on her lunch break from the Rumbling Tum café, was walking self-importantly arm-in-arm with Clarence on their way to the Blacksmith's Arms to see Fred Massey. Miss Sowerbutts, her eyes angry and imperious, caught sight of them and marched across the road to confront them.

'You can tell that uncle of yours,' she told Clarence crossly, 'that I shall fight him all the way. If he thinks he can build at the rear of my cottage he can think again.'

'I . . . I . . . I've n . . . n . . . not—' began Clarence, trying to find the words. Since he had been a pupil at the village school when Miss Sowerbutts had been head teacher, he had been intimidated by this fearsome woman who now blocked his way.

'He don't work for his uncle any more,' said Bianca boldly. 'So you can tell him yourself.'

'Listen to me, young lady—' began Miss Sowerbutts.

'I don't have to,' the girl answered back petulantly. 'You're not the head teacher telling kids what to do any more. Come along, Clarence, we have an appointment.'

They left Miss Sowerbutts open-mouthed and seething on the pavement.

'And let me do all the talking,' said Bianca as they walked towards the pub.

'Yes, but—' he started.

'I know your Uncle Fred,' she said. 'If I leave it to you, he'll have you back working for him in no time at all and for next to nothing. He's a mean old devil, as tight as a tick's arse, and I'm not having you being his dogsbody any more.'

'I know that, but—'

'You've me and the baby to think of now,' she butted in, 'and we need the money. He's got to pay you a proper wage and we want to live in one of them small cottages he owns, done up and rent free.'

'He'll never agree to that!' exclaimed Clarence, shaking his head.

'Yes, he will. From what I've heard in the café he's desperate for some help, so we'll play it casual like. We don't want him to think that you're dead keen to come back and work for him.'

'I am though,' said Clarence sadly. 'I hate it in the factory. I'm sick of the smell of bread and it's dead hot and noisy and I keep burning myself on the ovens and I don't like the blokes I have to work with and the foreman's always at me.'

'I know, but we won't tell your Uncle Fred any of that,' said Bianca.

'My uncle Fred won't go along with what you're asking.'

'Oh yes he will, if we play our cards right.'

Barton-in-the-Dale had two public houses: the Mucky Duck and the Blacksmith's Arms. The former, once called the Dog and Duck, was the haunt of the 'off-comed-'uns' and the younger folk in the village. It was a bright, garish and noisy place, with thumping music, games machines, karaoke nights, happy hours and pub quizzes. It was avoided by the locals, who frequented the Blacksmith's Arms, a dark and run-down pub which hadn't changed in years.

The interior was dim and reeked of beer and wood smoke. Despite the mildness of the weather a fire crackled in the inglenook fireplace. It was the landlord's boast that the fire had been kept burning in the grate for over a century.

At the public bar Fred Massey was nursing his pint of bitter and holding forth about the planned housing development on his field. 'I'll tell you this,' he was telling the landlord, 'if Mrs high-and-mighty Devine doesn't play ball and sell me that bit of land down the side of her cottage, then I shall have to go with plan C.'

'Oh yes,' said the publican, 'and what's plan C then?'

'That's for me to know,' Fred told him tapping his nose.

Clarence and Bianca came in and sat at a small sticky-topped table by the window.

'It's a dump in here,' whispered Bianca. 'We'll stop as long as it takes to make your Uncle Fred come round and then we'll go to the Mucky Duck and celebrate.'

There had been quite a transformation in the young woman since she had become a mother and moved into the council flat with Clarence. She had lost weight, took greater care with her appearance, had become far more self-confident and had got herself a job at the café in the village. She had been to see Ashley to arrange the baby's christening and her wedding and the curate had been surprised at the single-mindedness of this young woman, who people in the village said was clumsy and dim-witted. Mrs Sloughthwaite, always the observant one, had remarked to a customer over the counter on the change in the girl. 'That lass is not as daft as she seems,' she had pronounced.

'I'll go and have a word with my Uncle Fred,' said Clarence, getting to his feet.

'No, not yet,' said Bianca, taking his arm and pulling him back into the chair. 'Sit down. He'll come over when he sees us.'

'Suppose he doesn't?'

'He will.'

'That nephew of yours has just walked in,' the landlord told Fred.

'Oh yes?' he replied, trying to sound unconcerned.

'Aren't you going to have a word with him then?'

'Aye, happen I am,' said Fred, 'when I feel like it.'

'Well, he's not making a move to come and see you,' said the landlord.

After a while Fred eased himself off the stool and ambled over to the corner table.

'Hello, Clarence,' he said.

'Hello, Uncle Fred,' replied Clarence.

'And how are you getting on at the bread factory?'

'Oh, he's doing really well,' answered Bianca. 'He gets paid well and the hours are regular, not like when he worked for you.'

He ignored the slight and faced his nephew. 'And you like it in Clayton then, do you?' Fred asked him.

'We like it very much,' Bianca said pertly. 'I told you that when you came into the café. Don't you remember? I said that we're very happy there.'

'I bet you miss being outdoors though, don't you, Clarence?' asked Fred.

'Well, the thing is—' his nephew started.

'What, miss all the early mornings, them cold winds and snow and rain,' interrupted Bianca, 'when he could be inside in the warm? You must be joking.'

'My nephew does have a tongue in his head,' Fred told her irritably. 'He's not a ventriloquist's dummy. He can answer for himself, you know.'

'Go on then, Clarence,' said Bianca, prodding him with an elbow, 'tell your Uncle Fred how happy we are in Clayton.'

'We're happy in Clayton,' he repeated unconvincingly.

'Well, you know that if you was to change your mind,' said Fred, 'there's always a job back on the farm with me. No hard feelings.'

'I was thinking—' began Clarence.

'I hear you're finding it difficult to get anyone to help you on the farm, Mr Massey,' said Bianca nonchalantly.

'I don't know who's told you that!' snapped Fred.

'People what come in the café.'

'Well, they're wrong!' he cried angrily. 'I've got folk queuing up to work for me.'

'Not what I've heard,' Bianca replied calmly.

'Well, you've heard wrong,' said Fred. 'But if Clarence

wants to come and work for me again, as I've said, there'll be no hard feelings, water under the bridge. I won't hold it against him that he up and left me. After all, blood is thicker than water.' He looked at his nephew expectantly but Clarence remained silent with a hang-dog expression on his face. 'What about it then, Clarence, do you want to come back and work for me again?' asked Fred.

'If the conditions are right,' Bianca said, 'he'll consider it.'

'Conditions?' snorted Fred. 'He'll consider it?'

'Come along, Clarence,' said Bianca, rising from her chair. 'Let's go to the Mucky Duck. It's like a funeral parlour in here.'

'Hang on! Hang on!' exclaimed Fred, speaking again to Bianca. 'Don't be in such a hurry. I'll tell you what I'll do. I'll increase his wages.'

'And match what he gets at the bread factory?' asked Bianca.

'Aye, I reckon I could,' Fred said begrudgingly.

'And what about one of your cottages for us to live in?'

'You can come and stay at the farmhouse with me.'

'I don't know about that,' said Bianca.

'Go on,' urged Clarence.

'If we do,' said Bianca, 'it'll be rent free and don't expect me to do the cooking and cleaning.' Her childishly round face was rigid with determination.

'By the heck, lass, you're not backwards in coming forwards, are you?' said Fred.

'Well?' she asked, folding her arms. 'Are we agreed?'

'You drive a hard bargain and no mistake.'

'Well?'

'All right then,' said Fred.

Bianca smiled. 'That's settled. Do you want to get the drinks in then, Uncle Fred?' she said. 'Mine's a dry white wine – large one.'

* * *

'You made it then,' said Emmet, looking genuinely pleased to see her.

Ashley smiled. 'I did.'

'Roisin spotted you,' he said, smiling and showing a set of perfect white teeth. 'She saw you down at the front tapping away and swaying with the music. The great thing about Irish traditional music is that you can't stop yourself being carried away with the rhythm. It makes you want to get up and dance. Joyous it is, full of life, pulsing with melody.'

'You're quite the poet, Mr O'Malley,' said Ashley. 'Hello, Roisin.'

'Hello,' replied the girl.

What a pretty child she is, thought Ashley, looking at the girl's large wide-set eyes the colour of polished jade and the long rust-coloured hair, curly and shining. 'And did you enjoy the concert?'

'Oh yes, it was really good,' Roisin replied. 'I wish I could play like that. I play the flute you know.'

'Yes, I heard you when I came into your school,' Ashley told her. 'You were excellent. If you keep practising you will be every bit as good as the musicians we have just been hearing.'

'And my daddy plays the fiddle.'

'Not very well,' added Emmet.

The girl slipped her hand in his, shook her head and sighed noisily. 'He always says he's not very good, but he is,' she said. 'He's good at lots of things, my daddy. He can paint and make models and sing and knows all about animals and birds and flowers and—'

'Whoa!' interrupted her father, 'that's enough.'

'A man of many talents,' said Ashley.

'You're in mufti tonight,' Emmet said, moving the conversation away from himself. The fact that he hadn't taken his eyes off Ashley since coming out of the theatre had not escaped his young daughter's notice.

'Mufti?'

'You know – civilian clothes.'

Ashley laughed. 'I don't always wear my cassock and collar, you know. Actually it sometimes puts people off.'

'You look nice,' said Roisin. She nudged her father. 'Doesn't she look nice, Daddy?'

'She does,' agreed her father. 'She looks very nice.'

'Thank you,' said Ashley, 'and so do you.'

'He scrubs up well, doesn't he?' said the child with a cheeky grin.

Ashley looked at the girl's father, at the wide tanned face framed in a mass of shiny black curls. And such eyes! Irish eyes. Long-lashed, as bright as blue glass. 'Yes, he does,' she said, colouring a little.

'It's a lovely evening,' said Emmet, sensing her embarrassment and looking up at the sky.

'It is,' Ashley agreed.

They stood there for a moment as the theatre crowd petered out, each of them searching for something to say.

'Daddy said he would show me the river,' said Roisin. 'There are swans.'

'I wonder—' Emmet began. He was about to continue but stopped himself.

'You could come too,' said Roisin to Ashley.

'You might like to join us for a drink,' said Emmet. 'We could sit out by the river. I know a nice pub. But then it might not be quite the done thing – a vicar drinking in a pub.'

'Nonsense!' laughed Ashley. 'Priests have been known to drink.'

'Tell me about it,' said Emmet. 'My old priest in Galway, Father Mike, could drink anyone under the table.'

'I don't think I could manage that,' said Ashley.

'Well, it would only be the one,' said Emmet. 'I don't want to be too long. I let Roisin stay up a bit later at the weekends, but not too late.'

'Will you come?' asked the girl.

'I should love to join you,' Ashley replied.

'You would?' asked Emmet.

'Yes, I would,' she said.

It was such a treat for Ashley on that mild summer evening to be away from church matters, to have a respite from talking theology with the Archdeacon or education with his wife, to leave weddings and funerals and christenings and parish visits behind for a short while and to talk about Ireland and music and poetry.

Emmet had got the drinks and they had found a table overlooking the river. Roisin, who stood a little away from them, was watching the swans as they glided on the water.

'She's a lovely little girl,' said Ashley.

'Ah, she is that,' said her father proudly. He thought for a moment. 'Her mother died. In childbirth. There were complications.'

Ashley nodded. 'I'm sorry.'

'It was a bad time for me,' he said quietly, looking at his shoes. 'A bad time.'

'What was your wife's name?'

'She was called Rowena.' He failed to mention that he had not been married.

'The beautiful Saxon heroine in *Ivanhoe*.'

'That's right.'

'It's not an Irish name.'

'No, it's not but she always thought of herself as Irish. Her parents are from an Anglo-Irish family, members of the once ruling elite who owned most of the land in Ireland at one time. Her father is Sir Eustace Urquhart. Families like Rowena's are really English in terms of politics and culture and interests and in the past didn't really mix with the locals. They kept very much to themselves.' He smiled. 'The playwright Brendan Behan famously defined an Anglo-Irishman as "a Protestant with a horse".' His face suddenly lit up. 'But Rowena was different, a free spirit, her own woman. She was so full of life and pretty strong-minded as well. She found life in the big house by the lake cloying and claustrophobic and she kicked against that sort of privileged existence, all the social events, the hunting and shooting and big dinners. She rebelled against the restrictions and narrow self-interest of her class. When she met me at a folk festival her parents disowned her. Sorry, I'm going on. I must be boring you stiff.'

'Not at all,' replied Ashley. She was fascinated and wanted to ask more about this intriguing man who on the surface appeared so carefree and happy with life, but did not feel it was her place to enquire directly. There was much more to Emmet O'Malley than met the eye. Still waters run deep, she thought, looking at the river.

'I've not talked to anybody like this for a long time,' he said.

'I'm trained to be a good listener,' said Ashley, smiling. Looking into the long-lashed blue eyes she reflected that she had rarely met a man who touched her emotions so quickly.

'And what about *your* family?' he asked.

'Not much to tell,' she replied evasively. 'Pretty ordinary really.' She looked at her watch. 'Gosh, look at the time.'

'Yes,' he said rubbing his hands, 'we should be making tracks.' He turned and shouted to his daughter. 'Come along now, Roisin, we must be going.'

The little girl ran up and sat on her father's knee, wrapped her arms around his neck and pecked him on the cheek.

'I must go too,' said Ashley. 'I'm going to miss the last bus if I don't hurry.'

'You can come back with us, can't she, Daddy?' said Roisin. 'We've come in the old Land Rover.'

'Well, yes,' said Emmet. 'It'll be a bit of a squash, I'm afraid, because there are no back seats, but you are very welcome.'

So the Reverend Dr Underwood and Lady Wadsworth's

handyman-cum-gardener sat in the front of the old rattling Land Rover with Roisin, smiling like a Cheshire cat, sandwiched between them. As the vehicle shuddered to a halt outside the rectory, Ashley saw the twitching of a curtain.

'We are being observed,' she whispered. 'I feel like a naughty schoolgirl.'

'Oh dear,' said Emmet, 'I hope I haven't got you into trouble, gallivanting around the country with a man of dubious reputation.'

'I'm a grown woman,' laughed Ashley. 'And anyway, who said you have a dubious reputation?'

'Perhaps I'll tell you all about myself another time,' he said, with a mischievous glint in his blue eyes, 'and you can tell me all about yourself.'

'Another time then,' said Ashley. 'Goodnight, Roisin. Goodnight, Emmet.'

He watched her walk up the path. 'A free spirit,' he whispered to himself.

16

The Venerable Atticus surveyed his breakfast and smiled indulgently. There was an egg fried to his liking, two rashers of crispy smoked bacon, some wild mushrooms, a slice of black pudding, a tomato and a square of lightly toasted brown wholemeal bread. He said a silent prayer in thanksgiving. Prior to the arrival of his curate, a time when his wife did the cooking at the rectory, his usual Sunday morning repast had consisted of a bowl of cornflakes or an insipid-looking, under-cooked poached egg dumped on a square of burnt toast. He would miss this when he moved to Clayton.

'You spoil him, you know, Ashley,' remarked Mrs Atticus, taking a sip of her camomile tea. 'He's bursting out of his cassock these days, getting increasingly portly around the middle.'

'They say that there is nothing like a hearty breakfast to start the day,' she replied.

'But his consumption of all this fatty food,' said Mrs Atticus, 'will make him obese in no time at all. He'll end up like the bishop.'

'Perhaps I should look for some healthy-eating recipes for him,' said Ashley.

'Would you mind not talking about me as if I were not present,' said the Archdeacon, reaching across the table for the marmalade jar. 'And I might add that today, being the Sabbath, I shall be very busy and therefore in need of sustenance.'

'I too shall be very busy, Charles,' retorted his wife.

'Of course, of course, my dear,' replied her husband before spearing a mushroom.

'I have the designs for the stage set for *The Wizard of Oz* to complete,' she told the curate. 'Mrs Devine has asked me to take charge. I have quite enough on, if truth be told, but I really couldn't say no since she's been so very good encouraging me to train as a teacher and having me on practice at the village school.'

'You have done so well, Marcia,' said Ashley. 'Charles tells me you are to be awarded a distinction in your certificate.'

'I have to admit I do feel quite pleased with myself,' Mrs Atticus replied. 'Anyway, enough about me. Did you enjoy the concert last night?'

'Yes, very much.'

'I heard a car. Did you get a lift back?'

'I did. I was intending to get the last bus but Mr O'Malley very kindly offered to take me, since he was coming back to Barton.'

'Oh, he was at the concert, was he?' asked Mrs Atticus, feigning ignorance. She had seen the Land Rover pull up outside the front gate of the rectory and had recognised the driver.

'Yes, with his daughter.'

'She's a bright little button, is Roisin,' said Mrs Atticus, taking a sip of her tea. 'When I was on teaching practice at the school she displayed quite an aptitude for art and she plays the flute beautifully.'

'Yes,' agreed the curate.

'And she's a very polite and interested child. He has brought her up well.'

'She's delightful,' agreed Ashley.

'Charles!' exclaimed Mrs Atticus suddenly. 'There is far too much butter on that toast. Restrain yourself. I shall have to put you on some of that low-fat spread if you persist in over-indulging.' She turned her attention back to Ashley. 'So you and Mr O'Malley are aficionados . . . of Irish folk music, that is?'

'Yes, we are.'

'My dear,' interposed the Archdeacon, 'you are probing.'

'I am doing nothing of the sort. I am merely making conversation. Of course you are too busy with your sustenance, as you call it, to contribute anything which might be of interest.'

The Archdeacon sighed.

She addressed Ashley again. 'I have to say, I find Mr O'Malley rather intriguing. He's something of a mystery, isn't he? He arrives in the village looking like a gypsy with a child and no wife to be seen and living in a caravan. I guess he has an interesting past.' She paused for Ashley to volunteer information but when none was forthcoming she continued. 'Perhaps he's running away from something.'

'I wouldn't know,' said Ashley, keeping what little she did know of the man to herself.

'And how are things going with your fund-raising activities?' asked the Archdeacon, keen to change the subject.

'Very well,' the curate told him. 'Planning for the summer fête is going well, the Mothers' Union are arranging a bring-and-buy sale, and, as you know, Mr Tomlinson has agreed to give an organ recital next month. I thought perhaps we might have cheese and wine afterwards.'

'In the church?' asked the Archdeacon, raising an eyebrow.

'Well, yes,' replied Ashley. She could see that this idea was not going down well.

'Some might take exception to that,' he said.

'Oh, for goodness' sake Charles,' said his wife testily. 'It's not going to be a drunken orgy! People won't be dancing naked down the aisle. How can anyone object to a chunk of Cheddar and a glass of Sauvignon Blanc? We are not Methodists, you know.'

'It's just that over-indulgence in alcohol has been at the root of so much crime and marital disharmony—' began her husband.

'Like over-indulgence in butter?' Mrs Atticus asked, taking charge of the butter dish.

'Hardly the same,' replied the Archdeacon. 'There is so much alcohol abuse these days that—'

'Take no notice of Charles, Ashley,' interrupted Mrs Atticus. 'He's something of a stuffy old thing at times.'

'Marcia, if I might be allowed to finish,' said the Archdeacon, irked at being cut off mid-sentence, 'I am not at all adverse to a glass of sherry now and again, but to witness the young people in Clayton on Saturday night who have had too much to drink is like gazing at a scene from a Bosch painting. I just think that bringing alcohol into the church might give the wrong impression.'

'I have to say, Charles,' said his wife, 'that since you have become Archdeacon you do tend to get on your high horse about things and have become increasingly puritanical of late.'

The Archdeacon decided not to respond. It would be fruitless, for he never won an argument with his wife. The words in Ecclesiasticus came to mind. Was it chapter 25, he thought, where it said something about a silent and loving woman being a gift of the Lord? He recalled it now. And didn't it continue: 'As the climbing of the sandy way is to the feet of the aged, so is a wife full of words to a quiet man'? He stood up to go. 'If you will excuse me—' he began.

'Isn't there something you need to have a word with Ashley about?' asked Mrs Atticus, breaking into his reverie.

'I'm sorry?'

'You know – about what the bishop said to you yesterday.'

'Ah, yes,' said the Archdeacon. 'Perhaps this is a propitious moment for me to acquaint you with some news, Ashley.'

'This sounds ominous,' said the curate.

'I had better sit down,' the Archdeacon told her. He placed his hands on the table with priestly precision. 'The thing is—' he began.

The previous day the Venerable Atticus had been summoned to the bishop's palace. His lordship, a round, jolly looking individual with abundant grey crinkly hair and kindly eyes, had indicated a seat in front of his desk. He had steepled his chubby fingers and smiled widely.

'I trust there is nothing amiss, my lord,' the Archdeacon had asked nervously.

'No, no, Charles, quite the reverse. In the short time you have been Archdeacon, I have heard most favourable comments from all those with whom you have come into contact, and I myself have been most pleased with your work.'

'I am gratified to hear that, my lord.'

'I said at the outset,' the bishop continued, 'that I felt there was none more suitable than yourself for this demanding position within the Church, that you would be the oil to help things run smoothly, the very glue to hold together the parishes in the diocese. Your advice and wisdom on a host of matters spiritual, legal and practical has been invaluable.' The bishop coughed and clasped his hands before him on the desk. 'We did, however, discuss on your appointment the question of your eventual move to Clayton, did we not?'

'Ah, yes, we did,' the Archdeacon agreed.

'And, as you quite rightly observed, an archdeacon, on his appointment, is under normal circumstances obliged to leave the church where he is the vicar. You will no doubt recall that I did consent to you remaining at Barton-in-the-Dale because your predecessor, the Venerable Dr Bentley, was not a well man and was getting on in years. I mentioned he had become increasingly anxious of late about moving from the archdeaconry premises here at Cathedral House, where he has lived for many years and has amassed a most extensive library. I did feel it would be unchristian of me at that time to request that he vacate his present residence for you and your wife to move in.'

'I do recall that,' the Archdeacon said, wondering why the bishop should have felt it necessary to repeat what he already knew.

'Well, Dr Bentley has now found most suitable accommodation. He has donated his extensive library to the university and moved to live near his sister in Tewksbury. The archdeacon's house is now free.'

The Venerable Atticus took a small breath as if he was about to speak, but he didn't say anything and then looked down at his hands.

'I would therefore,' the bishop continued, 'like you and your wife to move to Clayton as soon as is convenient.'

Archdeacon Atticus looked for a moment through the great sash window and on to the cathedral precincts. A move here was something Marcia had originally desired, that is until she had begun her training at the village school. However, were his wife to be appointed to the position at Clayton Junior School, the move would prove most opportune.

'I shall of course abide by your decision, my lord,' the Archdeacon said at last, thinking of the best way to raise the matter with his curate.

'Some news?' enquired Ashley now, as she poured another cup of coffee.

'Indeed,' replied the Archdeacon, 'some news. Something of a curate's egg.'

'Not bad news, I hope,' said Ashley.

'Not in one sense, but maybe in another.'

'Do get to the point, Charles,' said Mrs Atticus, irritated. 'You do tend to ramble on.'

'I had occasion yesterday to have an interview with the bishop,' said the Archdeacon.

'He is keen for Charles to move to Clayton,' said Mrs Atticus with ruthless directness.

'My dear,' said her husband in a rather weary tone of voice, 'please allow me to explain. As you are no doubt aware, Ashley, it is most unusual, indeed unprecedented in this diocese, for an archdeacon to remain in the parish where he was a vicar. You see—'

'I am sure Ashley is very aware of this, Charles,' said Mrs Atticus. 'The thing is, we have to move. Now, since I started training as a teacher and was based at the village school, which was most convenient, there was no possibility of me countenancing any move. The travelling from Clayton, particularly in the winter months, and the unpredictable transport would have been far too much for me to cope with.' The Archdeacon was tempted to reproach his wife for rambling on, as she had done with him, but he resisted. 'I was hoping there might be a post at the village school,' Mrs Atticus continued, 'but then an opportunity arose which I felt I could not ignore. My college tutor informed me that there is an opening for an art coordinator at Clayton Juniors, which is just up my street. He has every confidence that I will be appointed. Obviously I do not wish to count my chickens, but with a distinction in my Certificate in Education and with an excellent reference from Mrs Devine, I feel confident that I am in with a good chance. The head teacher and Chairman of Governors at Clayton Juniors sound very keen on an application and I gather there have been very few other people interested in the position.'

'Well, I wish you the very best, Marcia,' said Ashley, looking genuinely pleased. 'You deserve it after all the hard work you have put in, and they would be foolish not to appoint you as the art coordinator.'

'If I might interpose at this juncture,' said the Archdeacon. 'You will appreciate, Ashley, that it will mean the appointment of a new vicar of Barton, and the bishop has in mind a Reverend Algernon Sparshott, at present a curate at Marfleet.'

'Who has four children,' added Mrs Atticus, raising an eyebrow. 'How the poor man manages to provide for them on a curate's pittance I do not know.'

'So I will need to find somewhere else to live,' said Ashley, pre-empting the Archdeacon's next point.

'I'm afraid so.'

'I quite understand that,' she said. 'When I was offered the post of curate I imagined that I would be lodging or renting somewhere in the village. You both have been most generous in allowing me to stay with you for so long and I have been very happy here. I shall start looking at once.'

'You are most understanding,' said the Archdeacon.

'And you will come and visit us when we move to Clayton,' added his wife.

Miss Brakespeare dabbed the perfume on her wrists and behind her ears, then, stretching her mouth, looked in the mirror and applied some cherry-coloured lipstick. With the arrival of Elisabeth Devine and then meeting George Tomlinson, the chapel organist, she had undergone a new lease of life and a transformation in her appearance. She now took considerable trouble over the way she looked.

'You're always prinking and preening yourself these days, Miriam,' said her mother, watching from her chair by the window. 'The time you spend looking at yourself in the mirror.'

Her daughter ignored her and patted her newly permed hair.

'Off gallivanting again, I suppose.'

'If singing in the choir at the chapel on Sunday is gallivanting,' replied her daughter, 'then yes, I am.'

'It's not as if you have much of a voice,' said her mother disparagingly.

'Well, George seems to think I have,' retorted her daughter. 'After the service I'm staying on to go through the pieces for the charity concert he's giving at the church.'

'Huh. I can't see he'll get many turning out to hear a lot of dreary church music.'

'You might be surprised, Mother,' said Miss Brakespeare. 'George has quite a following.'

'You're never away from that George Tomlinson these days,' said her mother. 'It's as if you two are joined at the hip.'

'Please do not refer to him as "that George Tomlinson", in that tone of voice,' chided her daughter. 'He is my fiancé and when we are married I shall see a whole lot more of him.' She patted her tinted hair and added, 'And so will you for that matter.'

Miss Brakespeare had lived with and looked after her mother since she had started teaching some thirty-five years before. Life with this irascible and cheerless woman had always been uneasy and strained. Mrs Brakespeare was a meticulously selfish woman who thought of nothing but her own comfort and well-being and constantly complained about her many debilitating ailments. She ritually contradicted her daughter and never missed an opportunity to make critical remarks about everyone and anything.

'I can't say as how I like that dress you're wearing,' she said now, with a painful expression on her face.

'I guessed you wouldn't,' Miss Brakespeare replied nonchalantly.

'It's a very unbecoming shade of green and it's all ruffled and rucked.'

'That's the fashion,' she was told.

'Well, I don't like it.'

'You are not wearing it,' said her daughter.

'You look like a cabbage,' said her mother. 'I've told you

before you don't suit that shade with your colouring. It's too loud.'

'And since when have you been a fashion expert?' asked her daughter.

'You're too long in the tooth to be wearing an outfit like that. "Mutton dressed as lamb", as my grandmother would say.'

Miss Brakespeare turned to face her mother. 'Do you know, you have a singular talent for making a person feel thoroughly uncomfortable and depressed. I can't recall the last time you had a nice word or gave a compliment. Father used to say, "If you can't say something nice about someone, then don't say it."'

She looked at the photograph in the silver frame on the mantelpiece. It was of a young soldier, slim and smiling in his army uniform. Miss Brakespeare remembered the quiet, gentle-natured man who had died when she was a girl. She picked up the music for the choir practice and, sitting opposite her mother, leafed through the papers humming the tune.

'Oh, he never had a bad word to say about anybody, your father,' said Mrs Brakespeare disparagingly. 'Too easy-going for his own good, that was his trouble. You take after your father in that. He was never assertive or ambitious. Stayed as a lance corporal in the army all through the war and what did his commanding officer write on his discharge papers? "Of sound character as far as I know." Shows you how much of an impression he must have made. The times I tried to get him to go for promotion when he worked at the Post Office. He could have been a manager if he had had a bit more gumption. People put on his good nature. They took advantage of him – as they do with you. Are you listening to me, Miriam?'

'I have heard all this countless times, Mother,' she replied. 'It becomes rather tiresome after a while.'

'You have a very sharp tongue,' said the older woman.

Three words came to Miss Brakespeare's mind – 'pan', 'kettle' and 'black'. 'George will be here in a moment,' she reminded her mother. 'We are going to call in and see Miss Sowerbutts before chapel.'

'Whatever for?' exclaimed Mrs Brakespeare.

'I felt sorry for her when she called,' replied her daughter. 'You were very offhand with her. I've had a word with George and we've decided to sign her petition.'

'Dreadful woman,' scoffed Mrs Brakespeare. 'She put upon you for years.'

'Please don't go into that again, Mother. I'm weary of you telling me.'

'Well, it's true and it's exactly what I was saying earlier about people taking advantage of your good nature.'

The doorbell rang.

'That will be George now,' said Miss Brakespeare, jumping to her feet.

'It's George this and George that, these days,' mumbled the old woman to herself. 'I'm sick of hearing his name.'

'Hello, Miriam,' said the visitor brightly as he walked into the hall. He pecked her on the cheek. 'You look lovely and summery. That colour really suits you.'

George Tomlinson was an angular man with a chinless face and a large aristocratic nose. He was dressed in a light cotton suit and a panama hat.

'You look very dapper too, George,' replied Miss Brakespeare. 'Quite the man-about-town.'

'Give me strength,' muttered Mrs Brakespeare, eavesdropping on their conversation.

'Go through into the lounge, George,' Miss Brakespeare told him. 'I won't be a minute. I've just got to put Mother's lunch in the oven.'

'Good afternoon, Mrs Brakespeare,' said George, walking into the room.

'Afternoon,' replied the old lady. She leaned back in her chair, her eyes fixed upon the visitor.

'How are you feeling?' he asked.

'Not well at all,' she replied. 'Not that anyone's interested,' she added peevishly.

'I hope you might come to the recital I'm giving at St Christopher's?' he said.

Mrs Brakespeare gave a small twisted smile. 'I don't think so,' she replied. 'I can't be doing with sitting for long on one of those hard wooden pews. I do like organ music,' she continued pointedly, 'but not the sort *you* play.'

'And what sort of organ music do you like?' he asked.

'The sort you can tap your feet to,' she told him. 'Tunes from the shows, like *Oklahoma* and *The Sound of Music*. The kind Reginald Dixon used to play in the Tower Ballroom in Blackpool or Max Jaffa at the Scarborough Spa. I don't like all that Bach and Handel. Too many fancy notes for my liking and it seems to go on for ever.'

George Tomlinson was a quiet, gentle-natured man, very much like Miss Brakespeare's father in temperament. Perhaps that was why she had fallen for him. His wife had died two years before, and in his grief his great consolation had been playing the organ at the chapel. He would spend hours in the semi-darkness immersed in the thundering sound. Elisabeth, hearing of his musical talent, had asked him to come into the village school and teach the pupils singing at lunchtimes. He had started a choir, which had flourished. It had been a new lease of life for him. It was at the village school that he had seen more and more of Miss Brakespeare and an attachment had been formed. On his visits to the Brakespeares' house George soon got the measure of the old lady's selfishness. He observed her censorious nature, witnessed the nit-picking and the constant complaints about ill-health; he had seen too often the wearisome demands she made upon her daughter. If she was going to live with them, he told himself, she would have to change.

'Mrs Brakespeare,' he said now, sitting opposite her and crossing his thin legs. 'I am glad I have this opportunity of having a quiet word with you alone.'

'Oh yes?' replied the old woman, looking at him suspiciously.

'As you know, when Miriam and I go to live in Scarborough, we would like you to come and live with us.'

'Yes, you've told me,' she replied.

'But there are certain things which have to be made clear.'

'What things?'

'Certain ground rules,' he told her.

A shadow of displeasure crossed Mrs Brakespeare's face. 'Ground rules?' she repeated. 'What do you mean by ground rules?'

'Conditions.'

'Conditions?' repeated the old lady.

'Old people should not expect, as a matter of right, that their children should give up their lives for them, and I have to tell you frankly that you have expected that of Miriam.'

'I beg your pardon?' exclaimed Mrs Brakespeare, shooting up in her chair.

'I want to get a few things straight from the outset,' he said. 'Then we can avoid any problems which could arise later on.' His manner remained perfectly composed. 'Miriam has been a model daughter. She has devoted her life to caring for you, cooking, cleaning, washing, arranging holidays and umpteen other things and she has done it willingly. Now she is to become my wife and if you come and live with us—'

'If!' interrupted Mrs Brakespeare.

'If you come and live with us,' said George, ignoring the interruption, 'I would expect you to be better-tempered and begin to appreciate what she does for you. I am quite happy

that you should come and live with us in Scarborough but I
will not have you constantly complaining about my wife and
finding fault with her.'

'Well, I've never heard the like, talking to me like that,' said
Mrs Brakespeare. She began to sob and, taking a small lace
handkerchief from her sleeve, blew her nose loudly.

'It had to be said, Mrs Brakespeare,' George told her,
unmoved by the histrionics. 'So perhaps you might bear this
in mind.'

'I'm lost for words,' said the old lady panting. 'I shall have
to take my tablets. I'm coming over all peculiar.'

George passed her a small brown bottle which was on an
occasional table to the side of the chair. Mrs Brakespeare
posted three coloured pills in her mouth, swallowed, and then
continued to cry. 'That it should come to this,' she wept theatrically, dabbing her eyes with the small lace handkerchief and
blowing her nose again.

'I am sorry if what I have said has upset you,' said George,
'but I think it is best to lay one's cards on the table from the
beginning. The last thing I would want is for you to go into a
care home, but should the arrangement of living with us not
work out, then we might have to consider it.'

'Care home!' moaned the old lady.

'All set,' trilled Miss Brakespeare, bustling into the room.
'Have you two been having a nice chat?' she asked, smiling.

Miss Sowerbutts did not answer the door of her cottage when
Miss Brakespeare knocked.

'It's not likely that she's gone out this morning,' said her
former colleague. 'She's not a church-goer and she likes to do
the crossword in the paper on Sunday.'

George, shading his eyes, peered through the window. 'I
think we had better go in, Miriam,' he said.

Fortunately the door was unlocked. They found Miss

Sowerbutts slumped in her chair, her eyes rolling and a dribble coming from the corner of her mouth.

'I'll call an ambulance,' said George.

Ashley was on her way to the village following Morning Service when she caught sight of a tall, fair, very good-looking man staring up at the church spire.

'May I help you?' she asked.

'No, not really,' he replied, brushing back a strand of blond hair. 'I was just looking at the church. When you've been away from this country for a time, you forget how beautiful England really is and how you've taken for granted all the amazing countryside and these magnificent old buildings.'

'Yes, we are very lucky,' she told him. 'Are you staying in the village or here on a visit?'

The man looked at the stunning young woman with the soft golden hair and dazzling blue eyes. 'I'm sorry?' he muttered, unable to take his eyes from her.

'I said are you staying in Barton or here on a visit?' Ashley asked him again.

'Oh, right. Yes, I'm staying here for a couple of weeks – at Wisteria Cottage. In fact, I had better get back. I said I'd cook the Sunday lunch.'

'You're staying with Mrs Devine?'

'That's right.'

'She's a wonderful head teacher.'

'Yes, I'm sure she is.'

'I'll walk with you if I may,' said Ashley. 'I'm going that way.'

'I'd like that,' said the man.

An ambulance sped past with all lights flashing and the strident siren sounding.

'It always gives me the jitters hearing the sound of an ambulance,' Ashley said briskly. 'I can't help but think of the poor soul inside.' She smiled. 'I always say a prayer for the person on their way to hospital.'

The man touched his leg. He had experienced more than his fair share of hospital visits of late. 'I'm Giles Ardingly, by the way,' he said, extending a hand.

'Ashley Underwood,' she replied. 'I'm pleased to meet you.'

'And I take it from the clerical garb you are wearing, that you are the vicar?'

'Goodness no!' she cried. 'I'm just the curate. Do I look old enough to be the vicar?'

'No, no, of course not, it's just . . . Oh dear . . . I had better stop before I dig a deeper hole.'

Ashley laughed. 'We had better make a move if you are to get the Sunday roast in the oven.'

They set off walking. The man moved with a pronounced limp. At the lych-gate he stopped, breathed in and looked down the village high street at the pale stone cottages with orange pantile roofs, squares of velvety lawns and neatly tended borders which displayed a profusion of vivid flowers. He stared at the ancient walls of greenish white limestone, the great trees flourishing in their finest summer greenery, and old stone troughs bursting with petunias, primulas and geraniums. He thought of the arid land from which he had just returned, the burning heat, the dust and the flies and the deaths. He covered his eyes for a moment.

'Are you all right?' asked Ashley.

'Oh yes,' he sighed. 'It's just so good to be home. It's so green, so peaceful.'

They resumed their walk, passing the Blacksmith's Arms and the village store and post office, the greengrocer's and butcher's, the hardware shop and the Rumbling Tum café, until they came to the ornate monument built in honour of the second Viscount Wadsworth. Giles paused and looked up at the large dull-bronze statue of the former local squire.

The Viscount, attired in military uniform, stood on a large plinth, one hand on his hip, the other holding the hilt of a sword. He stared ahead self-importantly. His legs were apart and his chin jutted out as if to say to the world: 'Now then, look at me. I am somebody to be reckoned with.' The statue was so enormously vulgar that it was obvious the second Viscount had been a man with a pathological desire to be in the public eye and to be remembered. The effect of coming face-to-face with the imposing figure was rather diminished at this particular moment, however, for perched on the monumental head was a fat pigeon pecking at a piece of bread in its claw.

'I wonder if the chap up there ever saw any action,' said Giles thoughtfully.

'Probably not,' said Ashley.

'No, probably not,' repeated the man under his breath.

'Well, this is where I leave you,' said Ashley.

'Perhaps I will see you around,' replied Giles. 'As I said, I'm staying in the village for a while.'

'Well, you can see quite a lot of me today if you are interested,' she replied.

'Really?'

'I'm taking all the services at St Christopher's. You might like to come along to one of them.'

'Ah, I see,' said the man laughing. 'I thought for a moment you were being a bit forward, particularly for a priest.'

'So shall I see you at Evensong?' she asked.

'I'm afraid I'm not much of a church-goer,' he replied.

'Ah well,' said Ashley, smiling, 'it was a nice try.'

She watched the man slowly limp away. He turned and waved.

Ashley called in at the village store for her Sunday paper.

'Hello, Reverend Underwood,' said the shopkeeper. 'I see you're in your canonicals today.'

'I don the dog collar on Sundays, Mrs Sloughthwaite,' replied Ashley, smiling. 'I must admit I prefer to wear the civvies during the week. I don't think the Archdeacon quite approves, but he hasn't said anything.'

'Well, it's a lovely day,' said the shopkeeper.

'Yes, Mrs Sloughthwaite, it is,' replied Ashley. 'It makes you glad to be alive on a day like this and to get such a nice cheerful welcome from you.'

'Service with servility, that's my motto,' said Mrs Sloughthwaite.

'I do hope this lovely weather will last,' said the curate.

'Let's hope it keeps fine for the weddings,' observed Mrs Sloughthwaite. 'I think there must be something in the water. I've never heard of so many weddings in the village: first the Fish girl, then Bianca and Clarence, and then Mrs Devine and Dr Stirling. And who would have thought that Miss Brakespeare would be tying the knot at her time of life? Mind you, funerals and weddings are all par for the corpse for you, aren't they?'

'We ought to be out in the sunshine rather than inside on a day like this,' said Ashley.

'Oh, some of us have got to make a living, Dr Underwood, and Sunday is one of my busiest days,' the shopkeeper observed. 'And to be honest I don't mind. Work is my solstice as they say. Now what can I get you?'

'May I have my Sunday paper,' said the curate, 'and a copy of the local paper as well, please? I'm on the lookout for a flat or a small cottage to rent.'

'You're moving out of the rectory then?'

'Yes, I'm afraid I have to. Archdeacon Atticus and his wife will be moving to live in Clayton within the month and a new vicar will be installed. He has a large family so they will need all the rooms. Ideally I would like a place of my own, but I may have to settle for bed and breakfast somewhere.'

'I might be able to help you there,' said Mrs Sloughthwaite. 'Now that one granddaughter's gone and another's getting married and will soon be leaving too, Mrs Fish will have a room. Shall I have a word with her?'

'I'll see if I can find somewhere to rent first,' said Ashley. 'So if you do hear of anything—'

'You'll be the first to know. By the way, did you see the ambulance?'

'I did.'

'I wonder who was being whisked off to hospital? You'll soon find out, of course, what with you being the chaplette at the Royal Infirmary.'

'Chaplain,' Ashley told her.

'Beg pardon?'

Ashley felt it would be fruitless to explain. 'I'm not on duty today,' she said. 'It's Father Daly's turn.'

'He's a nice old priest,' remarked the shopkeeper, 'but my goodness, he could do with a new hassock. I've seen better clothes on Fred Massey and that's saying something.'

'He's a very unworldly man,' Ashley told her.

'Who, Fred Massey?'

'Father Daly,' said Ashley.

'I was going to say,' chuckled the shopkeeper. 'You can't get worldlier than Fred Massey. Can I get you anything else?'

'Mrs Atticus asked if I could get some low-fat margarine,' said Ashley. 'She is trying to wean the Archdeacon off butter.'

'Yes, he has put on a fair bit of weight,' replied Mrs Sloughthwaite with a smile on her plump face. 'It's all that nice food you've been giving him.' She reached for a tub of low-fat spread. 'This monogludinous sodomite margarine is what you want.'

Ashley smiled, and reached into her handbag for her purse.

'So did you manage to help that young man?' asked Mrs

Sloughthwaite. Ashley looked baffled. 'The young man you were talking to. I couldn't help but notice.'

'Oh, we were just chatting. He's staying in the village at Wisteria Cottage.'

'Is he now,' murmured the shopkeeper, wondering why a good-looking young man like that would be staying with Mrs Devine.

17

Miss Brakespeare stood on the step at Clumber Lodge, a Siamese cat twisting in her arms.

'I'm sorry to disturb you, Mrs O'Connor,' she said, 'but I was wondering if you might look after Miss Sowerbutts's cat again. I'd take it myself, but my mother is allergic to animals. They bring on her asthma and she comes out in a rash.'

'Don't tell me Miss Sowerbutts is in hospital again?' said the housekeeper, shaking her head.

'I'm afraid she is,' replied Miss Brakespeare.

'You had better come in,' said Mrs O'Connor. 'Dr Stirling has taken James for his piano lesson, so there's just me and Danny at home. Put the cat in the sitting-room. I can't have it meandering around my legs in the kitchen. It's a terrible nuisance so it is.'

The two women sat at the kitchen table.

'So what happened this time?' asked Mrs O'Connor.

'Miss Sowerbutts has had a stroke,' Miss Brakespeare told her. 'George – Mr Tomlinson that is – went with me to visit her before chapel. She wanted me to sign this petition about the housing estate planned on the field at the back of her cottage. She called round to see me last week to get Mother and me to sign it but I said I would have to discuss it with George. We tend to talk things over before we decide on anything. Anyway, Mother refused to sign it and in fact was quite snappy with Miss Sowerbutts. Having considered it, George felt that I should sign it. He's very environmentally conscious and—'

'But what about Miss Sowerbutts?' interrupted the house-keeper, keen to stop the woman's rambling.

'Oh yes, well, we called at her cottage but no one answered the door. George looked through the window and saw Miss Sowerbutts slumped in her chair. Fortunately the cottage door wasn't locked so we went in. We thought at first she was dead. She looked in a dreadful state, grey in the face and slumped back in her chair. Then her eyes moved and she tried to speak. George, who has first aid training, thought he might give her mouth-to-mouth resuscitation but then thought better of it. He phoned for an ambulance and Miss Sowerbutts was rushed to the Royal Infirmary at Clayton.'

'She's certainly been in the wars, so she has,' declared Mrs O'Connor. 'First, she goes full length at the supermarket on a wet floor by the frozen pizzas and breaks her arm and bruises her legs, then she trips over the cat and falls down the stairs and gets concussion and another broken bone, and now she's had a stroke.'

'George thinks that the concussion and the stress have brought this on,' said Miss Brakespeare. 'We're going in to the hospital now to see how she is.'

'Well, I hope she pulls through,' said Mrs O'Connor. 'A stroke at her time of life is a terrible thing, so it is. I can't say I take to the woman, but all the same I shall say a prayer to St Jude. He's the saint of hopeless cases.'

When the visitor had gone, Danny appeared at the kitchen door.

'Who was that, Mrs O'Connor?' he asked.

'Miss Brakespeare. She came around with that wretched cat. It's in the sitting-room out of harm's way. Don't let it out. I don't want it in the kitchen mooching about and getting under my feet. Miss Sowerbutts has been taken to hospital again, so we are lumbered with it.'

'What 'appened?'

'She's had some sort of stroke,' Mrs O'Connor told him. 'Evidently she's in a bad way. I can't say as how I like the woman, but I wouldn't wish that on my worst enemy.'

'Will she be all right?' asked Danny.

'It's doubtful. By the sound of it, I can't see as how she'll recover. As my Grandmother Mullarkey used to say: "There is a remedy for everything but death." Anyway, what are you up to today?'

'I've got a bit o' work to do, Mrs O'Connor,' Danny told the housekeeper. 'I want to tidy up mi granddad's grave an' plant a few flowers and then I said I'd fettle Mrs Devine's garden.'

'Yes, well, I've got to be off,' said Mrs O'Connor. 'There's a cottage pie in the oven for your dinner. I'd better feed that creature before I go.'

'It's supposed to 'ave a special diet,' Danny told her, 'fish or chicken.'

'It will get what it's given, so it will,' she said.

Later that day Ashley was walking up the path to the rectory when she caught sight of a small figure planting some flowers on a grave.

'Hello, Danny,' she said.

''Ello, miss,' replied the boy, rubbing the earth off his hands and standing up.

'You come here quite often, don't you?' she said. 'I've seen how well you look after your grandfather's grave.'

'Aye, I do come regular, miss.' He pointed to the plants. 'I'm purrin in some marigolds and geraniums and cyclamens. Mrs Siddall at t'greengrocer's let me 'ave 'em cheap. They'll make a nice display.'

'You miss your grandfather, don't you, Danny?'

'I do,' replied the boy. 'We used to do a lot of things together. Mi granddad could turn 'is 'and to owt: build drystone walls, repair roofs, set traps, tickle a trout, skin a rabbit, pluck a pheasant. There weren't much 'e couldn't do. 'E used to show me 'ow to do it. Aye, we did lots o' things together, mi granddad an' me. I could talk to him about owt. 'E never shouted at me and he never 'it me. I can't remember 'im losin' 'is temper. 'E were more of a friend really.' The boy sighed. 'Aye, I do miss 'im.'

'He sounds a very special person,' said Ashley. 'I wish I had met him.'

''Course I'm 'appy enough wi' Dr Stirlin',' said Danny. 'Don't get me wrong. It were really good of 'im to look after me, but it's not t'same as livin' wi' mi granddad, if tha sees what I mean.'

'I do.'

'Did you have a special granddad, miss?' asked the boy.

'No, not like yours, Danny,' she said. 'I never knew my father's parents and my other grandfather was rather fierce and bad-tempered. I'm afraid he didn't have much time for me. He believed that children should be seen but not heard.' She thought for a moment of the tall, gaunt old man, brusque and overbearing, with the stern expression. Like his daughter, he had rarely had a good word to say about her. 'Well, I must get on, Danny. It's been nice talking to you.'

When the curate had disappeared around the side of the rectory, a small figure moved out from behind a tree where he had been keeping out of sight. It was Robbie. He stood at the lych-gate.

''Ey up!' shouted Danny when he caught sight of him. Robbie approached, his hands punched deeply into the bottoms of his pockets.

'What did *she* want?' asked Robbie.

'Nowt, she were just talkin'. She's dead nice.'

'And dead nosy.'

Danny shook his head. 'Thy 'asn't got a good word to say about anybody thee, 'as tha?'

Robbie shrugged.

'Any road, weer 'ave you been all week?'

'What?'

'Tha's not been at school.'

'I don't suppose anyone's missed me,' said the boy sullenly.

'No, not really,' said Danny bluntly. 'We all thought tha'd been hexpelled.'

'Well, I haven't.' He watched Danny for a moment. 'I've been put into care.'

Danny placed his hands on his hips. 'Crikey!' he exclaimed.

'I'm going to be fostered,' Robbie told him.

'But you 'ave a mum and dad, don't you?'

'I have a mum but not a dad, not a real one anyway. I told you, he's my stepdad and I hate him.'

'Where are you now then?'

'I'm in a children's home in Clayton.'

'What's it like?' asked Danny.

'It's OK. I go to live with this couple tomorrow.'

'That's tough.'

'No, it's not,' replied the boy. 'I'm glad to be going. It can't be worse than at home. I hated it there. I'm glad I'm not there any more.' He kicked at a weed.

'Will you 'ave to move school?' asked Danny.

'No.'

'Well, that's good, in't it?'

Robbie shrugged.

'What are your foster parents like?'

'They're OK. She talks a lot, he hardly says anything. They live on a farm.'

'Crikey, you're lucky!' cried Danny. 'I'd love to live on a farm.'

'*You're* being fostered, aren't you?' asked Robbie.

'Aye, I am,' said Danny. 'After mi granddad died, Dr Stirling looked after me and now 'e's going to adopt me. I did spend a

bit o' time wi' mi grandma but we didn't get on. She was glad
to be rid of me.'

'My mum and stepdad are glad to get rid of me,' said
Robbie.

'Well, 'appen you'll be better off wi' foster parents. Course
thas'll 'ave to behave thissen. You can be a pain in t'bum at
times. Pass us that trowel, will you,' said Danny.

'What are you doing?' asked the boy as he passed Danny
the implement.

'What does it look as if I'm doin'? I'm purrin' some beddin'
plants on my granddad's grave.'

'What for?'

'Tha does ask some daft questions. It's to mek it look nice.'

'Can't see the point,' said Robbie. He watched for a moment.
'Are you going down to the mill dam?'

'No, I'm off to Missis Devine's cottage after I'm finished
'ere, to do a bit o' work in 'er garden. Tha can come wi' me if
tha wants. She won't mind.'

'I could do,' said Robbie.

'But if tha does, you 'ave to behave thissen an' not be rude
to 'er.'

'You like her, don't you?' asked Robbie.

'Aye, I do. She were really good when mi granddad died.
An' she's a brilliant head teacher. Not all adults are like yer
stepdad, tha knows. An' I'll tell thee summat else, she's been
dead patient wi' thee. Tha'd 'ave found 'eadteacher at Clayton's
not like Missis Devine, I'll tell thee that. I were theer for a bit
and I din't like it.'

Robbie scratched his head as if considering what he had
heard.

At Wisteria Cottage Elisabeth came out to meet them.

'Hello, you two,' she said. She was surprised to see Robbie
there but made no comment.

'Hello, miss,' replied Danny. 'I thowt I'd fettle yer garden today.'

'I see you've got an assistant, Danny,' said Elisabeth.

'Is it all right if Robbie helps me, miss?'

'Of course it is,' she said. 'There's quite a bit of weeding to do, I'm afraid, and the lawn wants a good mow.'

'No problem,' said Danny. 'I'll fetch t'mower in a minute.'

'The rabbits have been at my plants again,' said Elisabeth.

'Aye, they're right devils. I shall 'ave to bring Ferdy round to sooart 'em out.'

Robbie was about to follow as Danny walked off to get the mower but Elisabeth touched his arm. 'Could I have a word, Robbie?' she said. On the Friday Robbie and his foster carers had been to see her and she had been asked if the boy could remain at the village school, something to which she had agreed.

The boy stopped and regarded her suspiciously. 'What?' he asked guardedly.

'I am sorry that things didn't work out for you at home.'

'I'm better where I am,' he muttered.

'And you are being fostered tomorrow.'

'Yes, I am.'

'Mr and Mrs Ross sound like a really nice couple. I have to admit that you have not been an easy boy, Robbie, but maybe you've had a lot to put up with. I do hope you will be happy with your foster carers and try to get on with them and that you settle back in at school.'

The boy nodded and then looked up. 'Thanks, miss,' he murmured.

'Pardon?'

'Thanks for letting me stay at your school.'

Danny arrived back pushing the mower. 'Hey up, miss, there's a strange man in your kitchen.'

'Ah, my very special visitor,' Elisabeth told the boys. 'When you've finished you can come and meet him.'

★ ★ ★

Father Daly was a tall, imposing man with a Roman-nosed face and short, carefully combed silver hair. He wore a rather shabby-looking, ill-fitting cassock, threadbare at the cuffs and along the collar, and great scuffed black boots. His eyes, dark and penetrating, nestled in a net of wrinkles and the long, generous mouth seemed to be permanently smiling.

'Bridget,' he said at the end of the evening Mass. 'I was hoping to catch you.'

'Hello, Father,' said Mrs O'Connor.

'Could you spare a minute to come into the presbytery? I would like to have a word with you about something.'

The sitting-room in the priest's house was like an exotic junk shop – a mass of clutter and colour. Every surface seemed to be covered in something: plaster statues of saints painted in garish colours, carved African figures in dark polished wood, stacks of books and piles of papers, glasses and crockery, boxes and tins, brass candlesticks, rosary beads, a chess board with ivory pieces, dusty potted plants, a violin with no strings and all manner of other objects. It was like the set for a film version of *The Old Curiosity Shop*.

'It's a tad untidy,' apologised Father Daly. 'Move those papers off the chair, Bridget, and sit down.'

'It wants a good sorting-out in here, so it does, Father,' observed Mrs O'Connor, glancing around the chaotic room. 'What you need is a housekeeper.'

'Well, that is exactly what I was wishing to talk to you about,' said the priest. 'I gather that Mrs Devine is to be married to Dr Stirling very soon.'

'She is, and they make a lovely couple, so they do,' replied Mrs O'Connor.

'I was wondering,' said the priest, 'will you be continuing to act as housekeeper at Clumber Lodge after they are married?'

'I don't expect I will,' replied Mrs O'Connor. 'Two women in a kitchen spell trouble, as my Grandmother Mullarkey used to say. Mrs Stirling might want a bit of help with the cleaning and cooking now and again but I probably won't be spending a lot of time there in future.'

'Might you then be available to do a bit of cleaning and cooking here for me?' asked the priest.

'I'm sure I could manage that, Father,' she replied.

'I'm afraid I couldn't pay you a lot.'

'Don't worry your head about that,' said Mrs O'Connor.

'Well, that's settled then,' said the priest, looking very pleased. 'There was another favour I would ask of you. You will be aware that I am chaplain at Clayton Royal Infirmary. I called in earlier today and there is a patient there who has been admitted this morning. The poor woman has had a massive stroke and can't move or speak and is in this coma-tose state. I was wondering if you might visit her. She is in a very bad way and has not had a visitor. It would help her recovery – and pray God she does recover – if people could talk to her, stimulate her mind a little and keep her company for a short while.'

'What's the patient's name?' asked Mrs O'Connor.

'Miss Sowerbutts,' Father Daly told her. 'She was formerly the head teacher at the village school. You may perhaps have come across her.'

'Oh yes, Father Daly, I've come across Miss Sowerbutts,' said Mrs O'Connor, pouting. 'Everyone in Barton has come across Miss Sowerbutts.'

'So will you visit her, Bridget?' asked the priest.

'If you want me to, Father,' replied the housekeeper. 'I'll call in tomorrow morning.'

The following day Mrs Sloughthwaite, installed behind her counter and propping her impressive cleavage on the top, was giving Mrs Pocock a full-blown account of Miss Sowerbutts's hospitalisation. Mrs O'Connor had called in that morning on her way to the hospital 'on her mission of mercy', as she called it, and relayed the news which the shop-keeper was now embellishing with gusto. By lunchtime all the village would know.

'I gather she's not long for this world,' said Mrs Sloughthwaite with alarming directness. 'Massive stroke it was and left her parasitic from what the doctor told Father Daly who told Mrs O'Connor who told me. There's very little hope for her.' She sighed theatrically and then added, 'As my mother used to say, "The only certainty in life is death."'

'Probably the stress caused by Fred Massey and his build-ing plans what brought it on,' observed the customer.

'You might be right,' said Mrs Sloughthwaite. 'I won't be visiting her in hospital, though. It would be hypercritical of me if I did, since I never liked the woman. She'll be sadly missed – but not by me.'

'She's not dead yet,' said Mrs Pocock.

'No, but by the sound of it her days are numbered. From what Mrs O'Connor said, Miss Brakespeare found her hardly breathing when she called. George Tomlinson was with her and has first aid training him being a scoutmaster and he was about to give her mouth-to-mouth rustication when she opened her eyes.'

'My husband's mother had a stroke,' said Mrs Pocock, 'and she didn't linger long before she gave up the ghost.'

'It makes you think though, doesn't it?' said the shopkeeper.

'What does?'

'How you can be fit and well one minute and dead the next.'

'It does,' agreed her customer, nodding absently. 'You never know what's around the corner. Anyway, changing the subject, who's in line for Miss Sowerbutts's money, do you think?'

'She's got a nephew who lives down south,' Mrs

Sloughthwaite told her. Hardly sees anything of him from what I gather but you can bet he'll be up here sharpish like a rat up a drainpipe, sniffing around. You know what they say – "Where there's a will there's a relative."'

'She'll not be badly off,' declared the customer.

'No,' agreed the shopkeeper. 'Her family owned the mill until her brother squandered all the money, and of course she's taught for all those years and must have put a bit away. I reckon she has nice fat pension. And as for spending, she's as tight as a miser's purse.'

'I don't mean to be unkind,' said Mrs Pocock, raising a sardonic eyebrow, 'but it's a fact that there'll be few in the village who will miss her and I guess Mrs Devine won't be shedding many tears after all the trouble she's caused her.'

'Speaking of Mrs Devine—' began the shopkeeper. She stopped what she was saying when the shop bell rang. Like a pantomime villain, Fred Massey made his entrance. He strode towards the counter, smelling of stale beer and wood smoke.

'Give us twenty of them tipped,' he said glumly, thrusting out his obstinate jaw and pointing to the display of cigarettes behind the counter.

Mrs Sloughthwaite folded her arms across her chest and adopted a face as blank as a figurehead on the front of a ship. 'And the magic word?' she asked, sounding like a teacher speaking to a naughty child.

'What?'

'There is such a word as "please", you know,' she told him.

'Look, give us the fags,' chuntered Fred, and then added, 'if you please. I'm not in the mood for small talk.'

The shopkeeper reached for the packet of cigarettes. Fred poured out the contents of a battered wallet on the counter.

'Fagin's hoard,' observed the shopkeeper.

Fred counted out the exact money and pushed it in the shopkeeper's direction.

'How are your building plans going?' asked Mrs Pocock provocatively.

Fred turned and acknowledged her with an almost imperceptible nod of the head.

'Don't you talk to me about building plans,' he growled. He ran a hand through his greasy hair and wrinkled his forehead into a frown. 'Old Ma Sowerbutts has got up a petition to try and stop me. That hatchet-faced harridan's been going around all the shops in the village with her posters and her bloody big clip-board browbeating and bullying people into signing up. And she's been writing letters all over the show.'

'Well, she won't be doing that now, will she?' said Mrs Pocock, smiling tightly.

'How come?' asked Fred.

'Because she's stretched out on a hospital bed like a landed fish on a slab, that's why,' said the shopkeeper.

'What's up with her then?' asked Fred.

'She's had a stroke,' Mrs Pocock told him.

'Most likely caused by the stress you've put her though,' said Mrs Sloughthwaite, with practised aplomb.

'What I've put her through!' spluttered Fred. 'I've not done nothing. Never mind about the stress I've put her through, what about the stress she's put me through?'

'She's very good at getting damages,' added Mrs Pocock. 'I mean, she got a good hand-out from the supermarket when she slipped and broke her arm. No doubt, if she recovers, she'll be getting in touch with one of those compensation lawyers.'

'She can do what she wants,' chuntered Fred, with the air of a condemned man who has begun to accept his fate. 'I've got enough on my plate at the moment what with Clarence and that interfering girlfriend of his moving in with me. She's another one, is that Bianca, who's as hard as a tack and twice as sharp. Took over the farmhouse she has, laiking about all day and spending my money like water. Now she wants me to shell out for when they get wed. And that baby of hers never stops crying. I've not had a wink of sleep since they came to live with me.' He stretched his throat from his collar and scratched it. 'Then there's that Irish gypsy up at Limebeck House doing all the jobs I should be doing by rights and I've heard he's set somebody on to help him, some tattooed youth. Taking bread out of my mouth, that's what it is. I used to do all the work in the village until that O'Malley man came along. And that young Danny Stainthorpe is still fettling the church-yard which I should be doing.'

'You're not a happy man, are you, Fred?' asked Mrs Sloughthwaite with a mischievous gleam in her eye.

'No, I'm bloody not,' said Fred in a tense, indignant voice.

'If you carry on like that you'll end up in the next bed to Miss Sowerbutts with a stroke yourself. Take a leaf out of my book and learn to weather life's vicissitudes with good humour.'

Fred opened his mouth and closed it again. Then, stuffing the packet of cigarettes and the wallet in his pocket, he left the store, banging the door behind him.

'I hear that he's been pestering Mrs Devine to sell that track down the side of her cottage, but she won't,' said Mrs Pocock. 'That's put a stop to his plans.'

'That reminds me,' said Mrs Sloughthwaite, lowering her voice as if she were being overheard. 'I've another piece of news regarding Mrs Devine. She's got a man staying with her. What do you think to that? According to Mrs Lloyd there was a red sports car parked outside Wisteria Cottage on Saturday night and it was still there this morning.'

'You don't say,' said Mrs Pocock.

'And she saw him at the kitchen window in a dressing gown – some fancy silk get-up. Now there's a thing.'

'Nora Lloyd must have telescopic eyes to see in at the back window of Wisteria Cottage,' said Mrs Pocock.

'She walks her dog,' Mrs Sloughthwaite told her, 'and goes by the track down the side. She couldn't help but notice. There he was as large as life and twice as natural, making himself a cup of tea. And she saw him on the Sunday afternoon sitting in the garden with Mrs Devine and they were thick as thieves, laughing and chattering as if there was no tomorrow.'

'You don't think there's something going on, do you?' asked Mrs Pocock.

'I hope not. I mean, she's getting married in a month. She's hardly likely to be playing fast and loose at this stage, now is she?'

'She might be having second thoughts about getting wed,' said Mrs Pocock. 'Stranger things have happened. Maybe she's getting cold feet. What did he look like, this man? Did Mrs Lloyd tell you?'

'I saw him myself talking to the curate on the high street yesterday. I only got a glimpse of him of course, but he was about six foot, slim, aged thirty-five or thereabouts with long-ish blond hair curling around his ears and he had a limp. He was dressed very smartly in one of those waxed jackets with corrugated collars and cavalry twill trousers. He looked like a well-to-do farmer.'

Mrs Sloughthwaite had sharpened her powers of observation over many years of noting people's appearance, way of speaking and mannerisms. She missed nothing and was adept at extracting information. It was as if, through abundant practice, she could see people's thoughts in their eyes and their secrets written on their faces. It wouldn't be long before she discovered everything there was to know about the mystery man staying at Wisteria Cottage.

The object of the shopkeeper's conversation had arrived at Wisteria Cottage on the previous Saturday night after a long and tiring journey. He found the key under the plant pot in the porch, let himself into the cottage, had a shower, made himself a sandwich, helped himself to a stiff drink and was about to retire when there was a knock on the door.

On the doorstep stood Michael Stirling. He had seen the light on in the cottage as he made his way home after evening surgery and knew that Elisabeth was away on a weekend course and would not be back until the following day. He decided to investigate.

'Good evening,' he said with a wary look in his eyes.

'Oh, hello,' said Giles brightly. He appeared as if he had made himself very much at home, in a dressing gown and clutching a glass of whisky. 'May I help you?'

'I saw the light on in the cottage,' said Michael.

'Oh, yes.'

'Who exactly are you?' asked Michael.

'Now I might ask you the same question,' retorted Giles.

'My name is Michael Stirling. And you?'

'Ah, the good doctor. Come in, come in. I'm Elisabeth's brother, Giles.'

Michael heaved a sigh. 'Giles,' he said. 'I thought she had burglars.'

'Don't stand there on the doorstep, come on in,' he repeated. 'I have a bit of leave and thought I'd surprise her.'

'Well, you certainly surprised me,' admitted Michael, stepping into the cottage.

'It's good to meet you at long last,' said Giles.

'And you,' replied Michael.

'When is my sister due back?'

'Early tomorrow afternoon,' Michael told him. 'She's speaking on some sort of a management course today and staying over in York this evening. Look, I won't stop. I can see you're ready for bed. I just wanted to check that—'

'No, no, you mustn't go. Elisabeth would never forgive me

if I didn't offer you a drink. Anyway, we need to get to know each other. We'll soon be brothers-in-law. Whisky all right?'

'That's fine,' said Michael. 'Just a very small one. I have to drive Mrs O'Connor, my housekeeper, home. She's looking after the boys tonight.'

Giles limped to the sideboard and winced as he poured the drink. Michael could see that Elisabeth's brother was in some pain.

'Elisabeth mentioned you have a son and that you want to adopt, young Danny, isn't it?' he said, handing Michael a glass.

'That's right.'

'Two adolescent boys! Sooner you than me. I remember what I was like at their age, a real tearaway.'

'They're very well-behaved,' Michael told him, 'and Elisabeth is very good with them.' He watched Giles massaging his calf. 'Your leg, are you having trouble with it?'

'Just a bit.'

'Would you like me to have a look?'

'No, no, just stiffening of the joints.'

'Why not call into the surgery?'

'Maybe I will,' said Giles dismissively.

An hour later the two men were still talking, their topic of conversation understandably being Elisabeth.

'She's had a rough time of it over the past few years,' explained Giles. 'The death of our parents hit her hard, then having to cope with a disabled son and a feckless husband running off with another woman and, having screwed up his life, appearing six years later wanting her back just when she was getting things back together.'

'I know,' said Michael, looking down at his glass. 'We have both had a difficult time these last few years.'

'Of course, I'm sorry. She told me about your wife's accident.'

'The thing is,' said Michael, looking up, 'I love your sister. I never thought I would love anyone again after my wife died but I do really love Elisabeth. We intend to put the past behind us. I want you to know that I will do my level best to make her happy and to be a good husband and that—'

'Look, Michael,' interrupted Giles, 'I'm not Elisabeth's father. You're not asking for her hand in marriage. I know the sort of man you are. She's told me all about you and I'm delighted for you both.'

'That's good to hear.'

'I think you and I are going to get on,' said Giles, holding up his glass. 'Down the hatch.'

The following morning Elisabeth's brother was up early, and looking out over the garden from the kitchen window he had caught sight of an elderly woman with a small dog peering over the gate to the cottage. He waved but she pretended not to have noticed him and hurried off. Mrs Lloyd would later relate what she had seen to Mrs Sloughthwaite. That morning, it being a bright and cloudless day, he had walked into the village and it was then that he had met Ashley, a woman he was determined to see more of.

18

'I can't see why they shouldn't leave us alone,' complained Mr Gribbon. 'Now we've got VIPs visiting the place.' He'd button-holed the school secretary on her way to the office at the start of the school week.

'It's because we are very successful that they are coming,' she informed him, walking past.

'That's as may be, Mrs Scrimshaw,' he grumbled, following her to the school office, 'but it'll mean a lot more hard graft making the place spick and span.' He jangled his keys irritably. 'You know what a stickler Mrs Devine is for having every-thing right.'

'Oh, I'm sure that you and the matchless Mrs Pugh will be able to manage,' she told him, arriving at her office. She hung up her coat, sat at the desk, placed her spectacles on the end of her nose and turned on the computer.

'I see you've got the hang of that machine then,' the care-taker remarked.

'Yes, it's very straightforward when you know how,' replied Mrs Scrimshaw, tapping the keyboard.

'I only have her part-time, you know,' said Mr Gribbon, leaning on the frame of the door. 'There's only so much she can do.'

'Pardon?'

'Mrs Pugh. I've only got her part-time.'

'I'm sure you will both manage,' she said, beginning to type.

'And what about that little juvenile delinquent?'

'Who?'

'That Robbie.'

'What about him?'

'Well, I thought we'd got rid of him when he went into care but now he's coming back.

Suppose he kicks off when them VIPs are looking round? He's like a ticking time bomb, that kid. He could explode any minute. You'll never guess what he said to Mrs Pugh when she told him to take his hands out of his pockets.'

'I'm not really interested,' replied Mrs Scrimshaw.

'I don't know why Mrs Devine is having him back.'

The secretary stopped typing and removed her glasses. 'Because that's the way she is. Have you learnt nothing about Mrs Devine since she's been the head teacher here? She doesn't write children off. The boy has been a lot better behaved lately. He's had a pretty hard time of it, apparently. From what I've heard, the child just needs some affection and security in his life.'

'Oh, I'd give him some security all right,' said the caretaker. 'I'd lock the little devil up.'

'You will have to excuse me,' said the school secretary, weary of listening to his whinging. 'I have a lot to get on with.'

On the Friday Elisabeth had received a letter from the Director of Education informing her that the newly appointed Minister of State for Education, Sir Maurice Carisbrooke, would be visiting the county and wished to see a range of schools which demonstrated good practice. Ms Tricklebank asked if it would be possible for him to call in at Barton-in-the-Dale, accompanied by Mr Steel, the District HMI.

'It's a real feather in our cap,' Elisabeth told her staff at the Monday morning meeting, but the teachers stared as if she had announced that in five minutes' time they would be taken out and shot.

'I shall go to pieces, I know I will,' stammered Miss Brakespeare.

'No, you won't, Miriam,' Elisabeth reassured her. 'You'll be fine.'

'Of course you will,' agreed Mrs Robertshaw. 'You'll know a great deal more about education than some jumped-up politician. This man will probably have never set foot in a classroom or taught a child and will, no doubt, be the product of some posh public school.'

'That may be so,' said Elisabeth, 'but people like Sir Maurice wield a great deal of power and make the decisions in education which affect us all.'

'Will they be watching us teach?' asked Miss Wilson nervously.

'I should imagine they will be calling in to the classrooms,' replied Elisabeth, 'but I'm sure they won't stay long.'

'And I suppose they'll be asking us questions, quizzing us about what we do,' remarked Mrs Robertshaw.

'If they do, I have every confidence that you will cope with it admirably, Elsie.'

'Oh, I don't doubt I shall cope,' replied her colleague bullishly, 'and I shall have a few well-chosen words if he asks my opinion about the present state of education. I shall tell him straight about the ridiculous amount of paperwork we have to deal with and the pressures we teachers have to face.'

'I wouldn't get his back up, Elsie,' said Miss Brakespeare. 'You never know what he might do.'

'It's not the Gestapo, Miriam,' she retorted. 'I'm not going to be locked up and tortured for expressing my views. I assume the point of this visit is some sort of fact-finding exercise, and that being the case he needs to know what we at the chalk-face feel. I will be perfectly honest with him if he asks what I think but shall, of course, be my usual diplomatic self.'

Elisabeth smiled and exchanged a look with her deputy

head teacher. 'Now the classrooms and the children's work want to look their best, and we need to impress upon the pupils just how important this visit is. I have asked Mrs Atticus to come into school next Friday morning when the visit will take place. She will look after my class so I can be on hand. I shall ask a couple of the older children from my class to take the visitors on a tour of the school.'

'Is that wise?' asked Mrs Robertshaw.

'I think so,' replied Elisabeth. 'They will get a much better feel for the place and what we do by talking to the children rather than myself.'

'It's a bit risky,' said the teacher. 'You never know what they will say.'

'All good things, I should imagine,' replied Elisabeth.

'Perhaps you should ask Malcolm Stubbins to stay at home on the day of the visit,' suggested Miss Brakespeare. 'He's very unpredictable in what he says and Ernest Pocock can be a pain as well.'

'No,' replied Elisabeth, 'our visitors will take us as they find us.'

'It's just a mercy that Robbie Banks isn't with us any more,' said Mrs Robertshaw. 'I can just imagine how he would react to all these visitors, answering back and having one of his outbursts.'

'Well, regarding Robbie,' said Elisabeth, 'he will be returning to the school this morning.'

'What!' cried Mrs Robertshaw. 'I thought he'd gone into care in Clayton.'

'He's being fostered at the moment,' Elisabeth told her. 'I had a call from his social worker and she's placed him with a rather unconventional couple. I saw them on Friday after school and I took to them immediately. They clearly like children and are very experienced at looking after mixed-up and troublesome ones. They live at Treetop Farm, this side of Clayton.'

'Well, they will have their work cut out with that young man,' remarked Mrs Robertshaw.

'Maybe,' said Elisabeth. 'Anyway, Robbie and his foster carers are keen that he should stay at Barton.'

'Robbie wants to stay here?' asked Miss Brakespeare.

'He does, yes,' Elisabeth told her.

'Then we must be doing something right,' said the deputy head teacher. 'Let's hope he returns in a better frame of mind.'

'Oh, Elisabeth, you do make problems for yourself,' said Mrs Robertshaw. 'That boy needs specialist help. I really don't think I can deal with him.'

'I am not expecting you to,' replied Elisabeth. 'He will remain with me until the end of term and then at the start of the new school year in September he will be in the top juniors anyway so will still be in my class.'

'It's not just that,' said her colleague. 'It's the effect he has on all the other children.'

'Elsie, I think you have known me long enough to be aware of my philosophy. I am not prepared to give up on a child.'

'There's only so much one can do with that sort —' started the teacher.

'All children deserve the best we can offer,' Elisabeth told her, 'and that includes the difficult, demanding and the ill-favoured.'

'And the repellent,' added Mrs Robertshaw.

'Yes, even the repellent, not that I like that particular term,' said Elisabeth, annoyed at the teacher's reaction. 'I know the child – and he is a child after all – is a handful but I gather he has had to put up with a great deal at home. He's a sad, angry, confused little boy. I think with this fresh start his behaviour might improve. We've seen signs of that already. Surely it's a positive thing that he wants to come back here? I really do believe that with some compassion and reassurance we will see a greater change in Robbie's conduct.' Mrs Robertshaw opened her mouth to respond but Elisabeth cut her off. 'Now, if there is nothing else . . .'

In the corridor Elisabeth found the caretaker waiting for her.

'There's the clergywoman in the entrance, Mrs Devine,' he said, 'wanting a quick word.'

'Who?'

'That young woman who's taken over from the vicar at St Christopher's.'

'Oh, the curate. I wonder, Mr Gribbon, could you show her down to my classroom please? Tell her I'll be there presently.'

Ashley sat before the teacher's desk. 'I'm sorry to come unannounced,' she said when Elisabeth entered the room, 'but I was hoping to catch you before school starts. I won't keep you long.'

'I'm always pleased to see you,' said Elisabeth, sitting down. 'Now what can I do for you?'

'I've had a visitor to the church, a boy called Robbie,' Ashley told her.

'At the church?' said Elisabeth, taken aback. 'That does surprise me.'

'He came in by himself. He says he likes the peace and quiet and to get away from people. He seems quite a mixed-up little boy. He doesn't seem to have any friends and is such a sad and lonely child.'

'He is,' agreed Elisabeth.

'What's he like at school?'

'A bit of a handful,' replied Elisabeth.

'Could you tell me a little about his background?'

'Well, until recently he's lived with his mother and his stepfather, but things at home have clearly been very stressful. Robbie doesn't get on at all with his stepfather, who seems to find fault with the boy at every turn. He's quite a controlling sort of man. Robbie reacts. He's badly behaved and disobedient and has a real temper. I'm afraid his parents have found themselves unable to cope with his bad behaviour and put him into care. He's now being fostered. Robbie is a very angry and difficult child. Everybody – Michael, the educational psychologist, the teachers here at the school – thinks he might be better off in a special school for children with behavioural problems, but I am loath to give up on the boy.'

'Don't,' said Ashley.

'I won't,' Elisabeth told her. 'Robbie will be back at school today. You know, you are the one person who seems to agree that he should stay here. Why do you say that?'

'Because I see something of myself in him.'

'In Robbie?'

'You might not think it, but when I was his age I was a handful and went through a difficult time. I always felt that my parents didn't really want me. It's a terrible feeling that you don't belong and perhaps never could. You know, children can accept almost anything if they feel loved and have a secure home. My childhood wasn't like that. I was lonely and resentful and angry with the world and became wilful and stubborn.'

'That is hard to believe,' said Elisabeth.

'Oh, it's true. A child should expect love from a parent, unconditional love, but I didn't receive it. My father left and I have never seen him since. Living with my mother there was no reassurance, no praise, no real affection and no acceptance. It wears you down. It gives you no hope for the future. I determined after a while not to feel sad or lonely or inadequate and got angry instead, and I became badly behaved and disobedient, a bit of a handful as you might say. I think Robbie might be going through what I went through. Then someone took an interest in me, put up with my moods, listened to what I had to say, accepted me for who I was, encouraged me and gave me some belief in myself and I got things together. Robbie needs someone like that. Robbie needs someone like you. That's all I wanted to say.' She got up to go. 'I can hear the children arriving. I can see myself out.' Before Elisabeth could stop her she was out of the door and down the corridor.

Robbie arrived early that Monday morning. He made his way to his classroom, where Elisabeth found him sitting at his desk, flicking through a book.

'Hello, Robbie,' she said.

'Hi,' he replied, looking up and closing the book.

'Could we try "miss" this time, do you think?' she said.

He nodded. 'Yes, miss,' he replied under his breath.

'May I see what you are reading?' she asked cheerfully.

He passed the book across the desk.

'A book about dogs,' said Elisabeth, examining the cover. 'Lady Wadsworth's dog seemed to have taken a shine to you when we visited Limebeck House, didn't he?'

The boy nodded again. 'Animals don't order you about,' he said quietly. 'They don't tell you what to do. They don't get at you all the time. That's why I like them.'

'Is there a dog at the house where you're being fostered?' she asked.

'Three,' the boy told her. 'They're Border Collies – Tom, Dick and Harry.'

'Three dogs!'

'It's a farm. Treetop Farm.'

'And how are you settling in there?'

'OK.'

'Your foster carers seem very nice people,' she said.

'Yes, they're all right,' he said before adding, 'miss.'

'I'm pleased to see you back, Robbie, and I hope you will settle in here too.'

Elisabeth had seen Robbie and his foster carers on the previous Friday. Mrs Ross was larger-than-life: a round, red-faced, jolly woman with long grey hair gathered up untidily in a tortoiseshell comb and large friendly eyes behind enormous coloured frames. She wore a scarlet cardigan and bright tartan skirt, a rope of large, blue glass beads around her neck and long silver dangly earrings. Her husband, a burly man with a thick head of woolly hair and copious white whiskers which gave him the appearance of a benevolent sleepy old lion, wore a great smile. Robbie sat between them. His face had been expressionless.

'Now, Mrs Devine,' said Mrs Ross, 'as you know, next week Robbie here is coming to live with us up at Treetop Farm. When we met each other at the care home we had a little chat and Robbie told me that he wishes to stay at this school. Me and Hamish, my hubby, have no objection to that.' She had the sort of voice which could penetrate bricks and mortar. 'I hope that you're willing to have him back? Moving schools would be another disruption in his life, something he could do without, so I hope he can stay. Hamish will drop him off in the morning and make sure that he gets here on time and Robbie can get the bus home.'

'Of course Robbie can come back,' replied Elisabeth.

'Well, that's settled then,' said the woman.

'Not quite. If you do come back to Barton, Robbie,' said Elisabeth, addressing the boy, 'I expect that you will be better behaved and make an effort with your work.'

'You can be sure of that, Mrs Devine,' said the foster carer. 'As I said, we've had a little chat and he knows how things stand. He's a bright lad, bit quiet at the moment but he'll soon settle in.'

'Did you hear what I said, Robbie?' asked Elisabeth.

The boy nodded.

'He's getting on well with the beasts,' said Mr Ross.

'The beasts?' Elisabeth looked mystified.

'The animals, Mrs Devine. The dogs took to the lad straight away. Couldn't keep them away from him.'

'There was one other thing,' said Mrs Ross. 'When he comes back he would like to be called Robbie Hardy. Hardy is his dad's name.'

'That's fine,' said Elisabeth.

'And he would like to stay in your class.'

'All right.' Elisabeth smiled, hearing the woman lay down the requirements. 'I had already decided that anyway. Robbie can start back next Monday. Anything else?'

'I don't think so,' Mrs Ross said. 'Have you anything to say, Robbie?'

The boy shook his head. He then looked Elisabeth in the eye. 'Thanks,' he said.

'Good lad,' said Mr Ross, patting the boy on the back.

After morning assembly on the Monday Elisabeth spoke to two of the pupils in her class.

'Are we in trouble, miss?' asked Chardonnay.

'No, you are not in trouble,' she was told.

'Why have you asked to see us, miss?' persisted the girl.

'Chardonnay,' said Elisabeth, 'I am just about to tell you.'

'Sorry, miss.'

'This coming Friday,' she said, 'we have two very important visitors. I would like you both, who are in the top class and responsible young people, to take them around the school and into the classrooms, show them the library and answer any questions they might ask.'

'Who are they, miss?' asked Chardonnay. 'I hope it's that dishy footballer again.'

'I'm afraid it is not the dishy footballer,' Elisabeth told her. 'There will be Sir Maurice Carisbrooke, the Minister of Education, and Mr Steel.'

'That school inspector with the squeaky shoes?'

'Yes, you have met Mr Steel before. I would like you and Edward to look after them. Now it is important that these important visitors leave with a good impression of the school. Don't be afraid of telling them what it is like here, what you do in class and all about the various activities in which you take part.'

'Don't you worry, miss,' said Chardonnay. 'I'll put them right.'

Little Eddie Lake rolled his eyes and shook his head.

'I am sure you will, Chardonnay,' said Elisabeth.

At morning break Miss Brakespeare broke the news to her colleagues about the former head teacher.

'A bit of sad news,' she said. 'Miss Sowerbutts is seriously ill in hospital. She's suffered a massive stroke. I know that some people do not get on with her and find her rather trying at times, but she has taught in the village school and been head teacher here all her career. I am sure you would all want to wish her a speedy recovery, although from what I gather there is little hope of that.'

'Yes indeed, Miriam,' said Elisabeth. 'We will say a prayer for her in assembly tomorrow morning and send her some flowers and a get-well card from the school.'

Miss Brakespeare thought of Miss Sowerbutts, white and immobile in the hospital bed. She would be unable to appreciate the flowers or read the card.

At the same time as Miss Brakespeare was informing her colleagues of Miss Sowerbutts's stroke, the topic of her conversation was in a single room at the hospital. With a face as white as plaster and a body as stiff as a corpse, the patient lay staring at the ceiling. She looked a sorry sight: old and thin and desolate. On seeing Mrs O'Connor, who leaned over the bed, she tried to speak. All she could manage was a stifled gurgling sound.

'Hello, Miss Sowerbutts,' said the visitor, raising her voice and speaking with deliberation. 'I heard you were in hospital and thought I'd pop in and see how you are.'

The patient made a guttural noise; it was clear that she wanted to call out but the words would not come.

'I was sorry to hear about your troubles, so I was,' said Mrs O'Connor. 'I've got some holy water.' She held up a small plastic bottle. 'It's from Lourdes. Mrs Mullane brought it back when she visited the grotto last year. It has miraculous powers. I'm going to sprinkle some on you and dab your face with it.'

The patient looked aghast but was unable to resist. As Mrs O'Connor applied the water a man appeared at the door. He was a plain-looking individual with a broad, pallid face creased on the forehead and around the eyes, a large, hawkish and high-bridged nose and wisps of sandy hair on an otherwise bald head.

'What exactly are you doing?' he asked.

'Saints alive!' gasped Mrs O'Connor. 'You made me jump.'

'I asked you what you were doing?' asked the man again.

'I'm putting some holy water on the patient,' she explained. 'It's from the grotto at Lourdes and has miraculous powers.'

'It will take a great deal more than holy water to cure her,' said the man.

'Oh, I know that, doctor,' said Mrs O'Connor, 'but miracles sometimes do happen.'

'I am not a doctor,' he said. 'I am Miss Sowerbutts's nephew.'

'Oh!'

'I assume you are Miss Brakespeare, who contacted me about my aunt's illness?'

'No, I'm Mrs O'Connor. I'm a friend – well, more of an acquaintance really.'

'Do you know Miss Brakespeare?' asked the man.

'I do.'

'And where she lives?'

'She's got a bungalow down Northgate.'

'You know the number?'

Mrs O'Connor resented the man's brusque manner. He sounded like a barrister cross-examining a witness. 'She lives at number sixty-six but she'll not be in now. She teaches at the school all day. She'll be free at lunchtime.'

'I need to see Miss Brakespeare before I return home,' said the nephew. I shall have to put my aunt's affairs in order, he was thinking, see her solicitor, get the power of attorney. Clearly, by the looks of her, his aunt was not long for this world.

He leaned over the bed. 'It's David, Aunt Hilda,' he said. 'I came up as soon as I heard.' His aunt gurgled. The nephew turned to Mrs O'Connor. 'Do you know how long she's been like this?'

'It happened yesterday morning.'

'She looks in a very bad way.'

'I gather it was a severe stroke.'

'Well, I had better go and see what the doctor has to say,' he said, heading for the door. Then, with ruthless directness, he added, 'Though I really don't think there is much one can do for my aunt. It's very sad.'

Mrs O'Connor resumed her ministrations. 'He can say what he likes,' she said out loud, 'but where there's life, there's always hope.' She resisted uttering one of her grandmother's other aphorisms: 'Hope for the best but expect the worst.'

She took Miss Sowerbutts's hand in hers and started to chant a prayer.

'O Lord, support her all the day long of this, her
    troubled life,
Until the shades lengthen and the evening comes,

And the busy world is hushed, the fever of life is over,
    and her work done.
Then Lord, in Thy mercy, grant her safe lodging, a holy
    rest, and peace at last.'

After Mrs O'Connor had set off for home and the nephew
had gone in search of Miss Brakespeare, the ward sister, on
her rounds, to her amazement found the patient sitting up in
bed. With her dark, darting eyes and sharp beak of a nose,
Miss Sowerbutts looked like a hungry blackbird out for the
early worm.

'Is there the possibility of a cup of tea?' she asked.

'Good gracious,' said the sister, 'you're . . .' She struggled
for the word. 'You've recovered! How are you feeling?'

'I'm feeling a whole lot better,' Miss Sowerbutts told her,
'and I could enjoy a cup of tea – very strong, with a splash of
milk and no sugar.'

'I'll get the doctor,' said the sister.

'And the cup of tea!' the patient shouted after her.

Two doctors, several medical students and Mr Greenwood,
the neurologist, gathered around Miss Sowerbutts's bed later
that morning.

'Strokes and migraines share certain symptoms,' explained
the specialist. He was a tall man, immaculately dressed in a
dark brown suit, canary yellow waistcoat and forest green
bow tie. He sported a fancy silver chain and fob. Grey pebble-
like eyes were magnified behind rimless spectacles. His long
pewter-coloured hair was thick and heavy. 'This similarity in
the symptoms,' he continued, 'may lead someone with a
migraine to fear they are having a stroke. This patient has not
had a stroke, she has had an acute migraine.' He turned to a
nervous-looking young man. 'What is a migraine, Mr Ash?'

'It's a severe type of headache,' replied the student.

'Its cause?'

'Spasms of the arteries leading into the head.'

'And what is a stroke, Miss Birkinshaw?' he asked, peering at her.

A rather intense-looking young woman with her hair scraped back savagely on her scalp and large pale eyes moved towards the bed and pointed to Miss Sowerbutts's head. 'A stroke is an interruption of blood to the brain which kills the cells in the immediate area and affects those in the surrounding areas. The most common type of stroke is the ischaemic stroke, which is caused by an embolism blocking a blood vessel to the brain.'

'Good, good,' said the specialist, indicating Miss Sowerbutts with a vague gesture of the hand. 'This patient has had a severe migraine which has caused no damage either in the short term or the long term.'

'Thank goodness for that,' remarked Miss Sowerbutts. 'I thought that—'

The specialist held up a thin hand as if stopping traffic. 'One moment,' he said sharply. He did not like his examination of the students to be interrupted by the patient. He turned to face the would-be doctors. 'A stroke, on the other hand, does result in brain damage and that varies from mild to disabling and in severe cases can cause a coma or death.' The specialist looked at a doctor over his steel-rimmed spectacles. 'With careful examination, it is possible to tell the difference between a migraine and stroke at the very outset. This patient,' he continued, 'experienced what are known as focal neurological symptoms, manifested in numbness, tingling, speech impairment and muscle weakness on one side of the body. These symptoms usually disappear within an hour or two; however, in this case they have persisted rather longer.'

'Might I ask what caused this?' enquired Miss Sowerbutts.

Mr Greenwood pinched the bridge of his nose. 'Overactivity of the brain cells,' he explained. 'It is caused by the slow spreading of hyperactive nerve activity across the brain surface. In layman's language you have an over-active brain.'

Miss Sowerbutts seemed delighted with the reason. 'An over-active brain,' she repeated. 'Well, well, well.'

Later that day Miss Sowerbutts, having been discharged from the hospital, took a taxi home. She was quite light-headed and in uncharacteristic good humour, feeling a sense of contentment quite unfamiliar in her recent life. Completely out of character, for she was always very careful with her money, she gave the taxi driver a generous tip. It was good to be back at her cottage after such an ordeal. She'd had some time to think about things as she lay in her hospital bed. Perhaps it was time, she thought, to count her blessings. Coming face-to-face with her own mortality had been salutary. She felt as she imagined someone sentenced to death might feel on hearing of a reprieve.

On the doorstep she fumbled in her handbag for her keys. The small pocket where she always kept them was empty. She sighed in exasperation. It was then that she noticed that the door was ajar. Clearly Miss Brakespeare had taken her keys and forgotten to lock the house, she thought. Miss Sowerbutts entered, to be greeted by a sight which made her gasp. On the small table in the hall were her treasured possessions in a jumble: her grandfather's gold pocket watch and chain and the photograph of him in the silver frame which had pride of place on the mantelpiece, her small Japanese ivory figures, which she kept on a small shelf, her porcelain ornaments from the display cabinet and the jewellery box from her dressing table. Beneath, in a cardboard box, were her cut glass decanter and glasses, the table lamp and antique miniatures. The painting of the leaping ballerina in the rose pink tutu was leaning against the wall next to the Windsor chair. Her two Persian rugs had been rolled up. There was a burglar in the house, she thought, preparing to make a getaway with the spoils. Or maybe he would be coming back for them later. Over my dead body, she said to herself and, reaching for the telephone, dialled 999.

'Police,' she said in an undertone when someone answered her call. 'I wish to report a burglary.'

She froze at the sound of footsteps on the landing and, gripping the telephone in her hand, waited for the intruder to show himself.

A figure appeared at the top of the stairs.

'Aunt Hilda!' exclaimed her nephew. He looked stunned, like a man who had been hit on the head.

'David?' she cried. 'Is that you?'

'Yes, it's me, Aunt Hilda.'

'I'm sorry to have bothered you,' she said down the phone. 'I've made a mistake.' She replaced the receiver.

Her nephew hurried down the stairs and planted a kiss on her cheek. 'It's so good to see you up and about!' he gushed. 'I was very worried about you.'

'Really?' She raised an eyebrow.

'You've made a remarkable recovery.' He smiled in a vapid way.

'Haven't I just,' she replied, smiling wryly.

'It's amazing.'

'I really don't think there is much one can do for my aunt,' said Miss Sowerbutts, giving her nephew a level stare.

'I'm sorry?'

'That is what you said, David, when you made your flying visit to the hospital, remember? "I really don't think there is much one can do for my aunt." I may have been comatose but I was not deaf.'

A muscle in her nephew's cheek jumped. 'Well, I honestly did think—' The sentence petered out feebly.

'That it would not be long before I was dead,' she said bluntly.

He swallowed nervously. 'Of course not, Aunt Hilda!' he protested.

'It was thought that I had suffered a stroke,' she told him, 'but it was a severe migraine. As you can see, I am fully recovered.'

'I'm delighted to see you fit and well.'

She gave a weak little smile. 'And how did you get in?'

'I got the keys from that friend of yours – Miss Brakespeare,' he told her. 'I called in at the school at lunchtime.'

'How very resourceful of you,' she said, with more than a hint of sarcasm in her reply. She rescued the decanter and a glass from the cardboard box. 'I think I could enjoy a sherry,' she said, walking into the sitting-room and casting a critical eye around. It looked as if it had been rifled for anything of value.

'I see you've been very busy in here,' she said.

'You're probably wondering why I have—'

'Stripped the place?' she said, completing the sentence. She poured herself a large sherry and took a sip. She was quite enjoying this exchange.

'The thing is, Aunt Hilda,' said her nephew, his face flushed with embarrassment, 'I thought you would be in hospital for some time and it occurred to me that an empty cottage is an open invitation to thieves. I thought I would take your valuables for safe-keeping.'

'How very solicitous of you, David,' said his aunt, looking at him as if he were an object of mild curiosity.

'I thought it best to be on the safe side,' he told her defensively.

'And you have certainly wasted no time.' It was a sweetly damning reply. 'You barely said a sentence to me before you were out of the hospital door.' Her nephew looked uncomfortable and shuffled from one foot to the other.

'The thing is, the doctor . . .' he began.

'Well, now that I am back there is no need to take my valuables for safe-keeping.' She emphasised the last few words. 'Perhaps you wouldn't mind putting all the items back where they belong.'

'Of course.'

She noticed her bureau was open and papers were scattered on the top. 'And did you find what you were looking for in there?' she asked.

'I was intending to make sure that all your affairs were put in order,' he told her.

'You are very much like your father, you know, David,' she told him, looking at the chinless face and large nose. 'You are like him to look at and you share the same disposition.' She did not mean it as a compliment and he was aware of that. She finished the sherry in one gulp. 'Now I am going to have a rest. I have had a long and dispiriting day. I guess you need to be getting off home – after, that is, you have replaced all my things.'

'Is there anything else I can do, Aunt Hilda?' he asked feebly.

'No, David,' she replied, 'I think you have done quite enough.'

In the Blacksmith's Arms, Major Neville-Gravitas was giving the landlord the benefit of his opinion about the state of the British Army when Elisabeth, her brother and Michael Stirling entered. Perched on his lonely stool at the other end of the bar was a disgruntled-looking Fred Massey, nursing his pint of bitter.

'Ah, good evening Mrs Devine,' said the major, swivelling around on his bar stool when he heard the door open.

'Good evening, Major Gravitas,' she replied.

'I see you have two escorts tonight,' he said.

'This is my brother Giles,' she explained. 'He's staying with me for a couple of weeks.'

'Very pleased to meet you,' said the major.

'Likewise,' said Giles, shaking the outstretched hand.

'I'm Chairman of the Governing Body at the village school, for my sins,' said Major Gravitas. He turned to Elisabeth. 'I trust you are well prepared for the visit of the minister?'

'Yes, as prepared as we will ever be,' she told him.

'It is good to know that we are held in such high esteem,' said the major. 'Of course we are very proud of the village school. It has become quite a showpiece in the county.'

'No thanks to you,' came a voice from the end of the bar.

Elisabeth turned to see a hunched and brooding figure on a stool. 'Good evening, Mr Massey,' she said.

'Evening, Mrs Devine,' he grunted. 'Not changed your mind about selling me that bit of land?'

'I'm afraid not.'

'Pity,' he mumbled. 'You could make yourself a bob or two if you did.'

'Money's not everything, Mr Massey,' Elisabeth told him. 'You know what they say – money can't buy you happiness.'

'That's as may be,' he retorted, 'but what use is happiness, if it can't buy you money?'

'Let me get the drinks,' said Michael, laughing.

'That's very decent of you, Dr Stirling,' said the major. 'Chin-chin,' he said, before draining the glass he had before him and getting ready for another. 'Mine's a malt.'

'The major here was telling me about the British Army,' said the landlord, as he got the drinks. 'He was saying it's not like the army he knew.'

'Really?' said Giles, 'and what conclusions have you come to, major?'

'Well, I was saying that the armed forces are not what they used to be. I'm afraid that like so many other things in the world today, standards have dropped.'

'In what way?' asked Giles, sounding nettled.

'Now don't get me wrong,' said the major, 'we still have one of the finest fighting forces in the world, but it's not like when I was a serving officer. I had to go through rigorous training.'

'To supervise the soup in the canteen,' observed Fred Massey.

'Behave yourself, Fred,' said the landlord, 'otherwise you can be on your bike.'

'I was asking in what way standards have dropped?' asked Giles.

'For a start,' said the major, 'we didn't have all the equipment they have now and all these sophisticated weapons and body armour. I'm not saying it's not still a dangerous job, but soldiers these days have a much easier time of it.'

'Perhaps you should tell that to the soldiers on the front line,' said Giles. The annoyance in his voice could be heard clearly. 'I am sure they would have something to say about that. Or perhaps you might care to share your views with the parents of those young men and women who have lost their lives.'

'Oh, it's hazardous, there's no doubt about that,' said the major, oblivious of the offence he seemed to be causing, 'but there's not the same element of risk there used to be, if you follow my drift.'

Giles bristled and felt his throat contact. 'No, I'm afraid I don't follow your drift at all.' The major made a half-hearted effort to interrupt but Giles, who was now red in the face, talked over him, audible to the entire room including Fred Massey, who was clearly enjoying the altercation. 'It's still a dirty, dangerous, risky and sometimes thankless line of work,' he said, 'and it leaves soldiers maimed and scarred and some of those scars you cannot see. What you have just said is a load of bloody nonsense.'

'I . . . I was only saying—' started the major indignantly.

'You know, Major Gravitas,' said Giles angrily, 'you really

ought to get your facts right before you start airing such stupid views in public. And it's particularly galling to hear them from someone who served in the British Army.'

'That's telling him,' chuckled Fred, before finishing his pint and sliding off the bar stool. 'And on that note I shall bid you all a good night.'

'Let's sit down,' said Elisabeth, taking Giles's arm. She could see this was developing into a full-scale war of words.

'Stupid bloody man,' said Giles, taking a seat. 'Not the same element of risk, my foot. He wants to be out there in the thick of it.'

'Forget it,' said Michael, resting a hand on Giles's shoulder, 'he's just an old man who lives in the past and likes the sound of his own voice. He really meant no harm. They were just empty words.'

'I want to go,' said Giles, suddenly jumping to his feet. He limped to the door. Elisabeth shrugged and followed.

'I'll stay and pay for the drinks,' Michael told her, 'and catch up with you later.'

When Elisabeth and her brother had gone, Michael sat next to the major at the bar. 'Perhaps I should explain why he went off at the deep end like that,' he said.

'Most rude,' said the major. 'I was merely expressing an opinion, and after all I was in the British Army for twenty years so I do know something about the military.'

'Yes, so does he,' said Michael.

'I didn't mean to denigrate our troops,' said the old soldier sheepishly.

'Elisabeth's brother is in the British army,' Dr Stirling told him. 'He is a major like yourself and has seen some pretty fierce action recently in the Middle East.'

'Good God, I didn't know!' exclaimed the major.

'He doesn't talk much about it. He was wounded trying to save the lives of some of his men, pulling them out from under a vehicle whilst under heavy fire. He's seen more than his fair share of injury and death. He was awarded the Military Cross for conspicuous bravery.'

The major looked crestfallen. 'Had I known I wouldn't have, well you know . . .' The sentence petered out.

'I know you wouldn't, major,' said Michael. 'Sometimes we all say things which we later regret.'

'I do tend to shoot my mouth off at times,' said Major Gravitas, looking distressed. 'I must apologise to him.'

'Leave it for the moment,' said Michael.

The landlord, who had been privy to this conversation, passed a double whisky across the bar for the major. 'You have this on the house, major,' he said. 'You look as if you need it.'

19

Sir Maurice Carisbooke was thin and stiff as a broom handle. He had short-cropped, neatly parted, iron grey hair, eyes like blue china marbles behind thick, black-framed glasses and a wide, generous mouth. Dressed in a finely cut, pinstriped grey suit with matching waistcoat and an expensive silk tie, the newly appointed Minister of Education resembled a prosperous barrister.

He was accompanied on the morning of his visit by Mr Steel HMI. Elisabeth came to meet her visitors as they made their way down the path.

'My dear Mrs Devine,' gushed the minister in electioneering mode, smiling widely and extending a hand, 'I am delighted to meet you. Mr Steel here has told me many things about your school, which I am most interested to see. It is very good of you to allow us to visit.'

Elisabeth was tempted to reply that she was not really in a position to refuse a government minister entry to the school, but she smiled, shook his hand and replied, 'It's a pleasure.'

Sir Maurice was the consummate politician: charming, good-humoured, engaging, shrewd and, of course, ambitious and calculating. He knew the value of making people feel important, remembering their names, putting them at their ease, asking after their families. He also knew the importance of saying the right things to those who might advance his career, and he made a determined effort to keep in with those who could be useful. Already, as the recently appointed

Minister of Education, he was gaining a reputation as a man who got on with people, liked to visit schools, talk to teachers and listen to their concerns.

In the entrance two smartly dressed pupils were waiting. The boy shuffled nervously from one foot to the other and bit his lower lip. Wide-eyed and anxious, he looked like a frightened rabbit caught in the headlights' glare. In contrast the pupil next to him, a large girl with huge bunches of mousy brown hair which stuck out like giant earmuffs, displayed no sign of nerves; she stood beaming, showing a mouthful of shining braces, and with her arms folded over her chest. As the visitors entered the building she curtseyed.

'I thought you might like a couple of the children to show you around first, Sir Maurice,' said Elisabeth. 'They will give you an honest picture of Barton-in-the-Dale and answer any questions you might care to ask. Then we can perhaps meet at afternoon break in the staff-room.'

'An excellent idea,' replied the minister.

'If you would like to follow me,' announced Chardonnay. 'We'll start with the infants.'

Sir Maurice, his hands clasped behind his back, followed the pupils down the corridor with Mr Steel close at his heels.

'May I see what you are writing?' the minister asked a small round-faced child in one of the infants' classrooms.

The boy slid his exercise book across the table and surveyed the visitor with some suspicion.

'Are you the important visitor Mrs Devine told us abaat in assembly?' asked the child.

'I am.'

'The Monster of Education?'

'Something like that,' replied Sir Maurice. 'So what are you writing about?'

'I'm writin' abaat our farm,' he said.

'And where is your farm?' he was asked.

'Up tops.'

'And what animals do you have on your farm?'

'Tups, yows, gimmers, porkers, beasts and fowls,' the boy told him.

'I see,' replied Sir Maurice, having no idea what the child had just told him.

The minister examined the boy's book, which was full of large, spidery, largely illegible writing. 'What is this word?' he asked.

'Can't yer read?' asked the infant.

'I'm not quite sure about this word.'

'Ayammer,' said the child.

'And what is "ayammer"?' asked the minister. 'Is it a sort of sheep?'

'Nay, it's summat tha knocks nails in wi',' said the boy.

'And this word "anaksor"?'

'Summat tha cut things up wi'.' The boy shook his head. 'Tha dunt know much abaat tools, does tha mister?'

Sir Maurice, who had not picked up a hammer or a hack-saw in his life, admitted that he did not. He smiled wanly and turned to another pupil, a small girl who was chanting from a list of words on a 'Phonics Word Sheet'.

'I'm practising my reading,' said the girl when she was asked what she was doing. She continued to chant. 'There are fat cats and flat cats, furry cats and purry cats, small cats and tall cats, hairy cats and . . .' She stopped suddenly and tried to spell out a difficult word. 'S-c-a-r-y. What does this say?' she asked.

'Scary', the minister told her.

'It doesn't sound like that when you spell it out.'

'No, it doesn't.'

The child pointed to the title on the worksheet. 'Can you tell me something?' she asked.

'I'll try,' said Sir Maurice.

'Can you tell me why "phonics" isn't spelled the way it sounds – f-o-n-i-c-s?'

'I'm afraid I can't,' replied the minister.

The boy who had been questioned earlier leaned across the table and whispered in the girl's ear. 'No good you askin' 'im, Charlotte. 'E knows nowt abaat owt.'

In a corner of the classroom sat a bright-eyed little boy. A green candle of mucus emerged from one crusty nostril. He was splashing paint on to a large piece of sugar paper.

'Hullo,' said Sir Maurice. 'May I ask what you are doing?'

'Painting!' came the blunt reply. He looked at the visitor as if he were stupid.

'It looks very good.'

'Aye, well,' the boy told him, 'Mrs Atticus who runs the art cub says I'm a dab hand with a paintbrush.'

The minister scrutinised the child's work. It depicted a large happy-looking man with long hair and a bushy beard. He was wearing a sort of multi-coloured smock and was holding what looked like a large knobbly stone.

'Who is this?' asked Sir Maurice pointing to the figure.

'Jesus.'

'And what is he holding?'

'His tortoise.'

'Now I never knew Jesus had a tortoise,' said the minister, smiling.

'Did you not?' said the child.

'No.'

''E knows nowt abaat owt, Harry,' remarked the child on the next table.

'When we say the "Our Father" in assembly,' explained the young artist, 'it's always mentioned.'

'The tortoise?'

'Aye.'

The minister recited 'The Lord's Prayer' in his head; he was mystified.

'Tell me,' he said at last, 'where does it mention the tortoise?'

'Miss says: "We will now say the prayer of Jesus' tortoise."'

'The prayer Jesus taught us,' said the minister, laughing.

'That's right,' said the child. 'Jesus' tortoise.'

In the lower juniors the minister was given a lesson on sheep by another farmer's child. He had asked the boy what he was interested in outside school and was subjected to a lecture on the different varieties of sheep on the farm where the boy lived.

'We 'ave Swaledales which are up on t'fells and moorland,' the boy told the visitor. 'They're a very bold, 'ardy sheep an' are partial to t'climate up theer. They're a long-bodied breed and t'wool meks champion rugs. Mi dad's now well into Wensleydale Longwools not to be confused wi' yer Leicester Longwools. Yer see, what sets yer Wensleydale breed apart from t'other long-wool sheep is its blue-grey face and curly fleece. On our farm we 'ave Wensleydale tups for crossing wi' 'ill breeds like yer Swaledales. Now my Uncle Jack 'e swears by mules.'

'Rather than sheep?' remarked the minister.

'Eh?'

'Your uncle prefers to keep mules rather than sheep?'

'I don't know what yer on abaat.' The child shook his head.

'Asses,' said Sir Maurice.

'Eh?'

'He keeps donkeys rather than sheep.'

'Nay,' said the boy laughing, 'yer mule *is* a sheep. It's cross-bred from a Swaledale yow out of a Bluefaced Leicester jock but it can include sheep bred from a Scottish Blackface yow.'

'I'm afraid you've lost me,' admitted Sir Maurice.

The boy gave him a pitying look like an expert might give an ignoramus. 'Aye, I could see yer weren't tekkin much in,' said the child, nodding sagely.

'Well, I had better see what the other children are doing,' said the minister.

'Mi uncle also keeps hoggs,' said the boy.

'Ah, pigs.'

'Eh?'

'Your uncle keeps pigs.'

'No he doesn't.'

'You said he did.'

'Yer hogg is a young male sheep not for breeding,' the boy told him. 'Most male lambs are castrated at birth. You tie a rubber band round its penis and it shrivels up.' The boy produced a rubber band and wound it around his index finger to demonstrate.

'How very interesting,' muttered Sir Maurice. 'So, I guess you would like to be a sheep farmer when you leave school?' asked the minister.

'Not flippin' likely!' exclaimed the boy. 'There's no money in it. I wants to be a butcher.'

By the window sat a flaxen-haired, angelic-faced girl of about eight with wide innocent eyes and a complexion a model would die for. She was engrossed in her reading.

'That looks a very interesting book,' said the minister, smiling.

The child looked up with a most serious expression on her small face. 'Mrs Devine says we should not speak to strangers,' she told him with a child's honest abruptness.

'And she is quite right, but I know Mrs Devine and she has invited me into your school, so I'm not really a stranger.'

'Are you a friend of hers then?'

'Yes,' he replied. 'I suppose I am.'

'Mrs Devine says that children have to be very careful about talking to people they don't know and not to take sweets from them or go for a ride with them in their car.'

'That is very good advice,' said the minister. 'And tell me

what you would do if someone did offer you sweets or asked you to get in his car?'

The girl thought for a moment. 'I'd kick him in the nuts,' she replied.

The Minister of Education decided to move on.

Between visiting the classrooms Chardonnay kept up a running commentary, telling Sir Maurice everything she considered he might wish to know about the school – how well-behaved and hard-working the pupils were, about the extra-curricular activities, the excellent teaching and the exceptional test results, and there was much praise for Mrs Devine.

'I don't think the school could have found a better advocate,' the minister remarked in an aside to Mr Steel.

'Course it wasn't always like this, you know,' said Chardonnay.

'Really?'

'It was only when Mrs Devine started here as the head teacher that things changed.'

'I take it you weren't altogether happy before?' volunteered the minister.

'No, I wasn't,' said Chardonnay, before adding casually, 'The other head teacher was a right old bag.'

At morning break, as Chardonnay escorted the important visitors to the staff-room, they passed the library. Oscar, as usual, was engrossed in a book.

'That looks interesting,' observed Sir Maurice.

Oscar's head came up sharply like a hound on hearing a hunting horn. 'I'm sorry,' he said. 'Did you say something?'

'I said that looks interesting – your book.'

'It is,' agreed Oscar. 'It's very interesting. It's a novel called *Kim*.'

'May I look?' asked the minister. He was passed the book. 'Rudyard Kipling,' he said, reading the front cover. 'I recall reading this novel when I was a young boy.'

'It's quite difficult in places,' Oscar told him, 'what with all these Indian words, and there's an awful lot of detailed description. Maybe yours was a simplified version. Sometimes difficult novels are abridged.'

'To be honest I can't recall,' said the minister. 'I do remember it was a rattling good adventure story.'

'Mmm,' murmured Oscar. 'Perhaps it was the simplified version after all. This is not really an adventure story.'

'And are you enjoying the novel?' he was asked.

'Oh yes, I quite like it.'

'And what do you like about it?'

'I like the descriptions of India, the customs and superstitions, and I like the character of Kim.'

'And what is it about him that you particularly admire?' asked the minister.

Oscar thought for a moment and rubbed his chin. Then he cleared his throat. 'Well, he's clever, mischievous, a trickster and a storyteller and of course he's a spy. I think he would be a really interesting person to meet. Would you agree?'

'I couldn't have put it better myself, young man,' said the Minster of Education, amused by this strange, bright and articulate boy.

'So, have you had a nice time in our school?' asked Chardonnay when she arrived with the VIPs at the staff-room at afternoon break.

'Very much, thank you,' replied the minister, 'and you have been a most excellent escort.'

'We aim to please,' said the girl, repeating a well-used phrase of her mother's. Then before departing she gave another curtsey and added, 'Well, goodbye, Maurice.'

'Goodbye, Chardonnay,' replied the Minister of Education affably.

★ ★ ★

When the important visitors had departed at the end of the school day, Elisabeth called a staff meeting to discuss how things had gone. She invited Mrs Scrimshaw, Mr Gribbon and Mrs Pugh to join the teachers.

'I think things went pretty well,' she said.

'I should say very well indeed,' said Mrs Robertshaw. 'I have to admit I was not looking forward to some minister scrutinising what I was doing, but Sir Maurice was a very agreeable man and he was most interested in my views on the present state of education. It was a good opportunity for me to tell him about the unremitting amount of paperwork we teachers have to deal with and the constant government interference.'

'I hope you didn't upset him,' said Miss Brakespeare.

'Fiddlesticks!' exclaimed her colleague. 'Some of these politicians need to be told what's what, that's all. Anyway, as I've said, he was most interested in my point of view. Indeed he asked me to write down a few of my observations and send them to him.'

'He seemed quite pleased with what we were doing in the infants,' said Miss Wilson, 'and, unlike some adults, he was very much at home with the children, talking to them, listening to them read and asking questions.'

'He appeared fascinated in what we were studying,' said Mrs Atticus, 'and surprised at the children's knowledge of British history. Evidently, as he told me, it is not taught very much in schools these days.'

'And he was most complimentary about the state of the premises, wasn't he, Mrs Pugh?' said the caretaker smugly.

'He was, Mr Gribbon,' she said. 'Very complimentary.'

'And he said some nice things to me too,' said Mrs Scrimshaw, not wishing to be left out of the accolades.

'Before he left Sir Maurice asked me to thank you all,' said Elisabeth, 'and to say how very much he had enjoyed the visit and how impressed he was with the work we are doing.'

She failed to mention that before leaving Mr Steel had taken her aside and suggested she might consider applying for a school inspector's position which would be coming vacant soon.

'I gather from Ms Tricklebank that plans for the amalgamation of the two schools are not going that smoothly,' he had told her. 'This might be an ideal opportunity for you to put this behind you and move on. It's worth thinking about.'

When her colleagues had gone Elisabeth tidied her desk, collected her marking and then, as usual, she walked around the silent school, turned off a few lights and closed doors. Before heading for home she sat in the staff-room and reflected on the day. The visitors had been fulsome in their praise and had seen the school at its best. 'This is one of our outstanding schools,' Mr Steel had informed the minister at the start of the day. Before leaving, Sir Maurice himself had commented on the purposeful atmosphere, the happy and confident children, the excellent standards and the dedicated teachers. Elisabeth wondered if all this would change with the amalgamation. Would all that she had achieved in the short time she had been at the school be undermined by Mr Richardson and Mr Jolly, who appeared unwilling to accept the situation and work with her? Mr Steel's words rang in her head: 'This might be an ideal opportunity for you to put this behind you and move on.' Perhaps she should think about it after all.

'Still here, Mrs Devine?' said the caretaker, poking his head around the staff-room door.

'I'm just going, Mr Gribbon,' she told him.

'No news yet about making Mrs Pugh permanent here at Barton?'

'No news,' Elisabeth replied. 'Once the teachers' positions have been filled then the ancillary staff will be appointed. I shall do my level best to make sure we have Mrs Pugh here full-time.'

'I appreciate that, Mrs Devine,' said the caretaker. 'She'll be glad to leave Urebank, that's for sure. She doesn't get on with the headmaster down there and his deputy's not much better. They don't treat her like what you do. She speaks very highly of you, Mrs Devine.'

'That's good to hear,' said Elisabeth.

'She says you could cut the atmosphere down there with a knife,' continued the caretaker. 'All the headmaster and his sidekick do is moan and groan and complain. I tell you, Mrs Devine, it'll not be easy working with them two.'

'No, I guess not,' said Elisabeth. That has put the damper on the day, she thought. 'Well, I must be off,' she told the caretaker, not wishing to hear any more bad news.

Her heart sank when she saw Miss Hilda Sowerbutts waiting at the gate. She took a deep breath and prepared herself for another altercation with the woman.

'Good afternoon, Mrs Devine,' said her nemesis. 'Might I have a word with you?'

'Good afternoon, Miss Sowerbutts,' replied Elisabeth, approaching the stiff-backed figure. 'I am pleased to see you have made a good recovery. It must have been a very worrying time for you.'

'Traumatic, would be the word I should use,' Miss Sowerbutts told her, 'but as it turned out it was all a bit of a storm in a teacup really. Everyone thought I was on my last legs. Stuff and nonsense of course. It was a migraine and not a stroke as they thought.'

'Yes, I heard from Miss Brakespeare,' said Elisabeth. 'Now, you wished to have a word with me?'

Miss Sowerbutts coughed. 'Firstly, I should like to thank you for the flowers and the get-well card. They were much appreciated.'

'It was the least we could do,' said Elisabeth, rather taken aback by an expression of gratitude from someone who had been her antagonist since she had taken over as head teacher.

'Some people have been very kind,' continued Miss Sowerbutts. She paused as if considering what to say next.

'Was there something else?' asked Elisabeth.

'I won't take up much more of your time, Mrs Devine,' she said. 'I just wanted to thank you for not agreeing to sell the track down the side of your cottage to Mr Massey. It seems that now there is no means of access to the field at the back of my cottage, his plan to build houses there has been scuppered, for the moment at least. Of course, when you sell the cottage I don't doubt that the new owners will accommodate him and sell the land, but I shall meet that hurdle if it arises. We live in a mercenary world, Mrs Devine. I should imagine that those who purchase your cottage will jump at the chance of making some quick money.'

'I don't intend to sell the cottage,' Elisabeth told her.

'Not sell the cottage!' exclaimed Miss Sowerbutts.

'No, I mean to keep it.'

'But I assumed you would be moving into Clumber Lodge when you marry Dr Stirling.'

'Yes, that is my plan,' replied Elisabeth, 'but I have spent a great deal of time and money getting Wisteria Cottage exactly as I want it. It is my intention to rent it. Reverend Underwood has to leave the rectory when the new vicar takes over at St Christopher's. She has agreed to move into Wisteria Cottage, which suits us both very well.'

'I must say, Mrs Devine, that is the most wonderful piece of news,' said Miss Sowerbutts, hardly able to contain her excitement. 'I cannot tell you how delighted I am to hear it.'

'I thought the matter over,' Elisabeth told her, 'and I came to the conclusion that a housing estate built on that site would be out of keeping with the rest of the village.'

'I concur with that,' replied the former head teacher. It was the first occasion she had agreed with her successor.

'Well, it's been a long day,' said Elisabeth, 'so if there is nothing else?'

'Of course, of course,' replied Miss Sowerbutts. 'I won't detain you further. I shall bid you good afternoon.'

As the comical figure in the shapeless brown coat and knitted hat strode off clutching the battered old canvas bag she always carried, Elisabeth wondered for a moment whether the woman's brush with death might have changed her for the better.

After school Danny called in to Wisteria Cottage. Elisabeth had asked him to plant some flowers and shrubs – the varieties which would discourage the rabbits and were recommended by the young gardener she had met at County Hall. Giles sat on the grass in the garden in the shade of the heavy horse-chestnut tree, its leaves fanning out like fingers and casting shadows across the lawn. His legs were stretched out before him.

'Hello,' said Danny.

'Well, if it isn't young Danny Stainthorpe,' replied Giles.

'Aye, that's me.'

'Come over here and sit down for a minute.'

'I've got things to do,' Danny told him. 'There are all these plants Mrs Devine wants purrin in.'

'They can wait,' said Giles. 'It's about time we got to know each other, don't you think?'

Danny sat next to him, his back resting against the great curved trunk of the tree.

'Now,' said Giles, 'it looks as if I'm going to be your uncle.'

'Mi uncle!'

'When my sister gets married, I guess that's what I'll be.'

'Mi uncle,' said Danny, wide-eyed. 'I've never 'ad an uncle.'

'So how do you feel about that?'

'Champion!' exclaimed the boy.

'Now my sister has told me all about you, young Danny,' said Giles.

'Oh 'eck. I 'ope it's nowt bad.'

'Quite the reverse. She says you're a good lad, you do as you're told and are something of an expert when it comes to animals and plants.'

'I reckon I do know a bit,' said the boy, smiling. 'I've 'eard all abaat thee an' all.'

'Nowt bad I 'ope?' said Giles, smiling and mimicking the boy's accent.

'Tha in t'army aren't tha?' said Danny.

'I am.'

'An' an 'ero,' said the boy.

'A hero,' repeated Giles. 'Is that what they say?'

'Everybody says thy are. Tha's gorra medal for bravery.'

'Yes,' said Giles quietly, 'I have a medal for bravery.'

'Mi granddad got a medal for bravery,' said Danny. 'I've got it at home. 'E was at Dunkirk and rescued lots of men. 'E din't talk about it much.'

'You must be very proud of him,' said Giles.

'I am that.'

They sat in silence for a while.

'What does it feel like to be really brave and not to be frit of owt, to fight people what are trying to kill you an' not be afraid?'

'We are all afraid at some time, Danny,' Giles told him. 'I'm no exception. It's what you do with that fear that counts. I suppose that you never know what you will do until you are faced with danger.' He massaged the muscles on his injured leg.

Giles brushed the hair out of his eyes and looked up through the branches of the tree to the empty sky. A hero with a medal for bravery, he thought. He hadn't felt brave when he was out there in the scorching heat, in a dry and dusty and barren land, wondering what was behind the next corner, who might be up on a roof with a gun, what might be buried underfoot. He had been afraid then. Fear had been his constant companion. He tried to recall the times when he had not felt afraid. At first he had yearned to see action. He'd been trained for it, primed for it, but he had no knowledge of what lay ahead, had not been prepared for the heat and the flies and the smells, to see men blown to pieces by land mines, others losing limbs, being blinded, the sight of splinters of bone, burnt faces and the blood. He shivered at the thought. Before returning home on leave he had held in his arms a young soldier, mortally wounded by a sniper, and heard him murmur his mother's name before he died. Giles put his hand over his eyes, covering his face.

'Are you all right?' asked Danny.

Giles gave the stock answer. 'Yes, I'm fine.' There was a tremble in his voice. He rubbed his eyes. 'Hay fever,' he lied. 'Always makes my eyes water.'

Danny rested a hand on Giles's arm. He knew this was not hay fever. 'Yeah, it gets me like that sometimes.'

For a while the boy and the man said nothing. They sat under the tree with their eyes closed. It was an uneasy silence.

After a while Danny reached into his pocket and took his ferret out of his coat. 'This is Ferdy,' he said. 'Most people don't take to him.'

'Ah, a ferret,' said Giles. 'May I hold him?'

'Really?'

'Yes, really.'

'Tha'are fust person who's wanted to 'old mi ferret,' said Danny, passing over the creature. 'Most people are dead scared of 'im. Just put yer 'and ' under 'is belly but don't squeeze 'im, otherwise 'e'll fasten on wi' 'is teeth and you'll know abaat it. Put yer thumb under 'is leg an' point it towards 'is back and then yer can stroke 'im wi' yer other 'and.'

Giles did as he was instructed.

'Yer 'andling 'im ' reight well,' said the boy.

'And do you know what the mascot is for the Yorkshire Regiment, Danny?' asked Giles.

'It's not a ferret, is it?'

'It is.'

'Well, I'll go to t'bottom of our stairs,' laughed Danny, using a favourite expression of his grandfather's.

When she arrived back at her cottage Elisabeth was greeted by the rich aroma of cooking meat and herbs.

'I've made dinner,' Giles shouted when he heard the door. He had put on a brave face again, dispelling the earlier thoughts that haunted his dreams and appearing the happy, devil-may-care character he presented to the world.

'I never realised you were such a good cook,' she said, coming into the kitchen.

Her brother, wearing a brightly flowered apron, was taking a casserole out of the oven. 'There are many things you don't know about me, sister of mine,' he said.

'Smells delicious,' said Elisabeth. 'I thought we might pop down to the Blacksmith's Arms later. I could ask Michael to join us.'

'Do you think the landlord will let me in after my outburst?' Giles asked.

'Don't be silly, of course he will,' she replied. 'Major Gravitas sometimes says things without thinking. I'm sure he regrets what he said. So, what about it? I feel in the mood for a bit of a celebration.'

'I take it the mandarin from London was suitably impressed with what he saw today.'

'Yes, he was. It went really well.'

'I never doubted it,' said her brother. He stopped what he was doing and put his arm around his sister. 'You know, I'm really happy for you, Lizzie,' he said. 'You've had a bloody rotten time these last couple of years, what with Simon leaving, coping with John on your own and starting a new life here. I'm really proud of you. You're a real trouper.'

'Thanks, Giles,' she said, her eyes beginning to fill up. 'And you know how very proud I am of you. It must have been ghastly out there. You've never really told me what it was like. You've not told me what happened.'

'I don't want to talk about it, sis,' he replied. 'I was just doing what I was trained to do. I was lucky. Some weren't.'

'But I would really like to know.'

'Please don't press me,' he said lightly. 'Now, come on, I'm going to open a bottle of wine to celebrate your successful day.'

'Actually,' said Elisabeth, 'I have been asked to apply for a school inspector's job.'

'Really?'

'There's a post coming up soon and the HMI who visited the school today thinks I should put in an application.'

'That's great. And will you?'

'Of course I'm flattered to have been asked, but I don't think so.'

'What's stopping you?' asked her brother. 'It's a step up and I think you would be really good at it.'

'Giles, I am getting married in a few weeks,' she told him. 'I've only been head teacher here for a year and the last thing I want is a new job.'

'You ought to talk it over with Michael.'

'Perhaps I should,' she said, 'but for the moment I'm not thinking about it. Now you do remember that Ashley Underwood is calling round later to talk about renting the cottage?'

'How could I forget,' said her brother smiling. 'We could perhaps ask her to stay for something to eat. What do you think?'

'A nice idea,' said Elisabeth. 'I'll give her a ring.'

Elisabeth lifted the lid on the casserole dish. 'I hope you've not overdone the garlic,' she said, sniffing.

'That was delicious,' said Ashley, placing her knife and fork together carefully. She had called round later as promised and sorted out with Elisabeth the rental of the cottage, and had readily accepted the invitation to stay for dinner.

'I usually do the cooking at the rectory but it's my night off,' she explained. She tried to visualise the Archdeacon's expression when he saw what his wife served up that evening. Ashley had seen a sad-looking salad in the fridge with two slices of pale ham edged in fat, a wilting lettuce leaf and half a rubbery hard-boiled egg covered in glutinous mayonnaise.

'I'm afraid there's no dessert,' said Giles. 'I've not yet mastered the culinary skill of making puddings.'

'Then you must come round for dinner at the rectory one evening and try some of mine,' said the curate. 'Perhaps I can give you a few tips. Show you a thing or two.'

'I'd enjoy that,' replied Giles. Was she flirting with him? he thought. 'We're going for a drink later at the Blacksmith's Arms, if you would care to join us,' he said chancing his arm.

'That's kind of you, but I have a hospital visit later this evening. Anyway, I don't think the Archdeacon would altogether approve of my frequenting a public house.' She wondered how he would have reacted if she had told him she had been drinking by the river with Emmet. 'He is a dear man but he does have very strong views when it comes to drink. I wasn't able to persuade him to allow me to serve a glass of wine to those coming to the concert in St Christopher's next week.'

'Now you don't appear to me,' said Giles, leaning across the table and giving one of his winning smiles, 'the sort of woman who bothers about what other people think. You sound to me as independent and strong-minded as my sister here.'

'Perhaps you would like to come to the concert,' said Ashley, colouring a little. 'Mr Tomlinson of the Methodist Chapel is giving an organ recital to raise money for the roof repair.'

'I should be delighted to come,' replied Giles. 'I just love organ music.' He winked at his sister.

20

'You can say what you like,' Mrs O'Connor told the proprietor of the village store and the most regular customer. 'It was nothing short of a miracle.'

''Course it wasn't,' huffed Mrs Pocock. 'The doctor just made a stupid mistake, that's all.'

'Well, I don't suppose anyone has ever made a clever mistake,' observed Mrs Sloughthwaite. 'It's always tickled me that phrase, a stupid mistake.'

Mrs Pocock screwed up her face. 'What I'm saying is that at first they thought Miss Sowerbutts had had a stroke and it turned out to be nothing more than a bad headache.'

'All I know,' said Mrs O'Connor, 'is that she was at death's door one minute and up and about the next.'

'As to her being at death's door,' observed the shopkeeper, 'there's many a one who would have helped her through it, I can tell you. There wouldn't have been many mourners at *her* funeral, I can tell you that.'

'She was at death's door,' repeated Mrs O'Connor, 'and made a miraculous recovery after a generous sprinkling with my Lourdes holy water. One minute she was flat out in a hospital bed and the next thing she's walking around as large as life. As I said to Father Daly, he ought to get on the line to the Vatican and have it recorded.'

'Well, I don't believe it,' said Mrs Pocock.

'And what's more, her brush with the Grim Reaper has made her a changed woman, so it has,' Mrs O'Connor informed her listeners. 'Miss Sowerbutts is a different person.'

'In what way?' asked Mrs Pocock.

'She's a lot more agreeable, so she is.'

'I'd like to see that,' said the shopkeeper. 'In my book a leopard doesn't change its stripes.'

'When she came round to collect that cat of hers – and I'll tell you I was glad to see the back of the wretched creature – she brought me a box of chocolates for looking after it and I've never seen her smile as much.'

'She did what?' exclaimed Mrs Pocock.

'And,' added Mrs O'Connor, 'she was as pleasant as could be, thanking me for going to visit her in hospital and for my kind words and prayers at her bedside.'

'It must have addled her brain,' said Mrs Pocock disparagingly.

'Or it's the result of the drugs she's been given,' added the shopkeeper. 'It's completely out of character for her to do anything like that.'

'I'm telling you she's a changed woman, so she is,' said Mrs O'Connor.

'I'll believe it when I see it,' said the shopkeeper, unconvinced. 'She's always been a crabby, crotchety, cantankerous old woman and as welcome in my store as an ulcerated tooth.'

At that very moment the doorbell tinkled and Miss Sowerbutts made her entrance. She was dressed in a light linen coat and carrying a new handbag. She had dispensed with the tea cosy and wore a straw hat with a ribbon around it.

The three women stared open-mouthed.

'Good morning,' said Miss Sowerbutts brightly.

'Good morning,' muttered the three women in unison.

'It's a lovely day, don't you think,' she remarked and without waiting for a reply placed a piece of paper on the counter.

'I wonder if you might make up this order, Mrs Sloughthwaite,' she said. 'As you are probably aware, I have been in hospital. Coming home I find that my pantry, like the old lady who lived in a shoe, is bare.'

The shopkeeper was lost for words. Miss Sowerbutts rarely patronised her store, and when she did she invariably complained later about the quality of what she had bought.

'I shall call in for it later in the day if that is convenient,' said Miss Sowerbutts, 'and settle up with you then if that is acceptable.'

'Yes, of course,' mumbled Mrs Sloughthwaite, catching sight of the smug expression on Mrs O'Connor's face.

'And do you have any more tickets for the organ recital in the church this evening?' she asked.

'I do,' replied Mrs Sloughthwaite.

Miss Sowerbutts took her purse from her handbag and placed a ten pound note on the counter. 'I would like two, please,' she said.

'Two?' asked the shopkeeper, sounding taken aback. 'You would like *two* tickets?'

'That's right.'

Mrs Sloughthwaite reached behind the till and passed the tickets over the counter.

Miss Sowerbutts scooped the tickets up with a flourish and posted them in her bag. 'Many thanks,' she said, smiling. 'I shall wish you all a good day.' And with that, she strode to the door.

'A miracle, so it is,' said Mrs O'Connor when Miss Sowerbutts had gone. 'What did I say? A miracle.'

'I was hoping I might bump into you,' said Emmet, leaning out of the window of his Land Rover. 'There's something I've been meaning to talk to you about.' He had been driving down the high street and caught sight of a bicycle he recognised propped up outside the village store and he had decided to stop. Working for most of the time at Limebeck House, there wasn't much of an opportunity for a chance meeting with the young curate, to whom he had taken quite a shine. He had waited until she emerged from the village store.

'I am in a bit of a rush,' Ashley told him. 'I have to take my bicycle back to the rectory and then get the bus into Clayton. I need to be at the hospital this morning and I'm running a bit late. Was it important?'

'You are not unwell, I hope?' he asked.

'No, no, I'm one of the chaplains there,' she told him. 'I visit the patients a couple times a week. So, was it something important?

'Pardon?'

'That you wanted to talk to me about.'

He tried to think of a reason for waylaying her but nothing came to mind. 'Not really. But—'

'You see, if I don't get a move on,' she told him, 'I shall miss the next bus and there isn't another one for an hour.'

'I'll run you there,' said Emmet suddenly.

'Pardon?'

'I'll run you to the hospital. It's on my way.'

'Are you going into Clayton?' she asked.

I am now, he told himself. 'Yes, I have a few errands to run for Lady Wadsworth.'

'Oh well,' she said. 'If it's no trouble, it would be a big help. I've been running around like a scalded cat this morning.'

'Have you time for a coffee?' he asked, chancing his arm.

She glanced again at her watch. 'Well, if you are running me into Clayton, I think I have,' she replied, 'but what about my bicycle?'

'We can put that in the back of the Land Rover,' he told her, 'and I'll drop it off at the rectory later.'

Mrs Sloughthwaite, standing with her arms folded at the door of her store, observed the two chatting away and then heading off in the direction of the Rumbling Tum café. 'Well, well, well,' she said out loud. 'Who would have thought it?'

They sat at the table by the window. Emmet thought Ashley looked particularly pretty that morning, with the sun shining on her soft golden hair. He stared at her for a moment, at the strikingly smooth skin, deep-set blue eyes, the high cheek-bones, small nose and curve of her lips.

'Just a coffee for me, please,' Ashley told the waitress, a smartly dressed young woman with short, neatly cut hair that was a bright magenta colour.

Bianca pointed to the menu. 'We've got cappuccino, espresso, latte, macchiato, decaffeinated, mocha, Turkish black or flat white.'

'Just an ordinary coffee will be fine,' said Ashley.

'And the same for me,' said Emmet.

'She's trying to go a bit continental,' confided the waitress in a hushed voice.

'I'm sorry?'

'The owner. She's bought this machine and trying to go a bit up-market, but nobody asks for these fancy coffees.'

'It's Bianca, isn't it?' asked Ashley, suddenly recognising the speaker.

'Yes,' replied the girl.

'I christened your baby, didn't I?'

'And you're going to marry me and my boyfriend,' the girl told her.

'I'm sorry, I didn't recognise you,' said Ashley.

'I've had a make-over,' said the girl, smiling. 'I've been on a diet and had my hair done different.'

'Well, the colour suits you,' said Ashley. 'And how is your little one?'

'Oh, Brandon, he's doing really well,' Bianca told her,

becoming animated at the mention of her baby. 'We live up at Tanfield Farm now with Clarence's Uncle Fred. He's a pain in the ar . . .' – she checked herself – 'neck most of the time, Uncle Fred that is, not my Clarence, but it's working out all right and we're managing to put a bit of money by.'

'And have all the arrangements been made for the wedding?' asked Ashley.

'I've got my dress,' Bianca told her, 'and we've booked the reception in the Blacksmith's Arms and all the invitations have gone out. I've just got to get the flowers for the church, but everything's so expensive. I think we'll make do with a few roses.'

'Something's just occurred to me,' said Ashley. 'You know Mrs Devine and Dr Stirling are getting married about the same time as you?'

'Yes, I heard.'

'Well, their wedding is a couple of days before yours. How would you feel about me asking Mrs Devine if she might consider leaving the flowers they are having in the church? It would save you having to get fresh ones and it would cut down the cost. Of course you may want your own and—'

'No, no!' interrupted the girl. 'That's fine.'

'Well, I'll have a word with Mrs Devine. I'm sure she'll be agreeable.'

'Thanks ever so,' said Bianca, beaming. 'I'll get your coffees.'

'She's a bonny girl,' said Emmet, 'but I'm not sure about the hair.'

'She looks completely different,' said Ashley. 'When I first met her she was a large, rather ungainly young woman with lank hair and she didn't really bother with her appearance. Since she's met that boyfriend of hers and had the baby she's been a different person.'

'That's what love does for you,' replied Emmet, looking into her pale blue eyes. He had taken greater care with his own appearance of late.

'Anyway, what is it you wanted to speak to me about?' she asked.

Emmet tried to think but his mind went blank. 'It was – do you know I can't remember now.'

'Well, it can't have been that important,' she said as the coffees arrived. She took a sip. 'It's just nice to sit down for a moment. I've been up to my eyes organising the organ recital at the church for this evening and— '

'Oh, I know,' said Emmet, suddenly having a flash of inspiration. 'It was to see if you needed any help with the recital.'

'Most things have been arranged, but you could lend a hand this afternoon if you're free, moving some of the pews and setting up the table for the drinks, that sort of thing?'

'Consider it done,' he said.

'Thank you, that's really kind of you,' Ashley replied.

They talked for a while about the renovations to Limebeck House, how Roisin was getting on at school, Ashley's move to Wisteria Cottage when it became vacant, and the new vicar who would be arriving soon. 'Now I think I had better be making tracks,' said Ashley.

Emmet pointed through the café window at his old Land Rover parked outside. 'Your carriage awaits,' he said.

Coming out of the hospital later that morning, Ashley noticed a sports car she recognised in the car park and the man getting into it.

'Hello!' she shouted.

The man turned and waved and then came to join her. 'Ah, the Reverend Underwood,' said Giles.

'Ashley, please,' she replied. 'Have you been at the hospital?'

''Fraid so,' he replied patting his leg. 'It's been playing up lately. My future brother-in-law, the good Dr Stirling, insisted I let them take a look.'

'Rugby accident, was it?' she asked.

'No, no, nothing like that,' he told her, deciding not to mention that it was the result of the wound he had received when he was on active service. Clearly his reputation as a hero had not fully circulated the village. Giles thought Ashley looked particularly attractive that day. She had the deepest of blue eyes and the fairest complexion and a soft mass of golden hair. The Reverend Underwood was one of the most strikingly beautiful women he had ever seen.

'Have I got something on my face?' she asked.

'Pardon?'

'You're staring.'

'Oh, I'm sorry. I was just wondering if you would like a lift. I am going back to Barton.'

'Thank you,' she replied. 'That would be really helpful. I have quite a bit to do getting the church ready for the organ recital this evening.'

'Need any help?' he asked. 'I'm at a loose end and should be happy to lend a hand.'

'Just a bit of lifting, but I think I can manage.'

'Oh, I'm a dab hand at lifting,' he replied.

'But your leg—' she began.

'Nothing wrong with the old arms,' he told her. 'I'll call round to the church this afternoon.'

'Well, if you're sure.'

Later that day Mrs Sloughthwaite stood at the window of her store – her usual place when not behind the counter – and observed the curate climbing out of the red sports car and saying goodbye to Mrs Stirling's brother. 'Well, well, well,' she said out loud. 'It gets more interesting.'

Ashley was busy arranging the flowers on the altar that afternoon when the two men arrived together at St Christopher's.

'My knights in shining armour,' she said, coming down the aisle to greet them. 'Have you two met?'

'No,' they both replied.

'Giles, this is Emmet,' she said, 'Emmet – Giles.'

The two men shook hands. Both seemed rather put out that another man had arrived to help.

'I'd like the pews in the Lady Chapel to be turned around to face the organ,' said Ashley brightly, 'and then if you could set up the two trestle tables near the font at the back for the refreshments that would be a great help. I'm making a Pineapple and Orange Cooler for this evening. The Archdeacon doesn't quite approve of the serving of wine in the church so it will have to be a non-alcoholic drink, I'm afraid. It sounds unlikely, but according to the recipe it tastes really quite good, not like pineapple and orange at all but more like cider. It should be very refreshing on such a lovely summer evening, don't you think? Anyway, I must go and see Mrs Siddall at the greengrocer's. She has very kindly donated the fruit, which needs collecting.'

'I'll come and help you,' said the two men in unison.

'There's really no need,' said Ashley, 'but one of you might collect the glasses from the Blacksmith's Arms. The landlord is lending them with no charge. Isn't that kind? Thank you so much for helping out,' she added. 'I'll see you this evening.'

Both men looked crestfallen as they watched the woman of their dreams sweep out of the church.

That evening Ashley stood in the porch of St Christopher's to welcome the members of the audience. She was looking especially pleased, for the evening was a sell-out; it appeared that most of the village was supporting the event. On one side of her stood Emmet, dressed in a smart jacket, white shirt and, unusually for him, a tie. On her other side stood Giles, looking very dashing in a light linen suit, his lilac-coloured shirt loosened at the neck. There was a floppy silk handkerchief in his breast pocket.

'Like two bookends,' remarked Mrs Pocock as she made her way down to the front of the church with her friends.

Mrs Sloughthwaite smiled to herself. She would be divulging the juicy piece of gossip about the young curate and her two admirers when she had a captive audience in her store. This was not the right time, she thought.

Before her companions could stop her, Mrs O'Connor sat on the front pew next to Mrs Brakespeare. Neither Mrs Sloughthwaite nor Mrs Pocock was eager to be seated next to the poker-faced and miserable old hypochondriac, but they had little choice.

'I've been dragooned into this,' Mrs Brakespeare complained to the shopkeeper.

'Dragooned?' repeated Mrs Sloughthwaite.

'Bullied and browbeaten, harangued and harassed by my daughter, that's what! A lot of hoity-toity organ music is not my idea of a good night out, I can tell you.'

'Well, it's all in a good cause,' remarked Mrs Pocock with a self-satisfied look on her face.

'I was all for staying at home,' continued Mrs Brakespeare.

I wish you had, thought the shopkeeper, preparing herself for a blow-by-blow account of the woman's ailments.

'I told my Miriam,' grumbled Mrs Brakespeare, 'I said I can't sit for long on one of those hard wooden pews what with my arthritis and curvature of the spine, and I can't stand for long with my varicose veins. Then there's my lumbago.'

'Could I get you a drink?' asked Mrs O'Connor.

'I'd like a nice strong cup of tea, not that wishy-washy fruit concoction they're serving,' whinged Mrs Brakespeare.

'Well, I think I'll get myself one, so I will,' said Mrs O'Connor.

'Get us one while you're about it, will you,' said Mrs Sloughthwaite.

'And one for me,' added Mrs Pocock.

Ashley had taken the great punch bowl into the church earlier that afternoon. Mrs Atticus had arrived and had been asked to sample the contents.

'It's very bland,' she had remarked, screwing up her face.

'It is rather,' Ashley had agreed. 'I'm afraid I didn't read the recipe correctly. I was in such a rush to get everything done. It said the liquid has to be left in a warm room for three to four days until it bubbles and ferments.'

'We will soon fix that,' Mrs Atticus had told her, striding off. She had returned a few moments' later with two bottles of white wine, a bottle of sweet sherry and half a bottle of vodka.

'This will liven things up a bit,' she had announced and proceeded to pour the contents of the bottles into the large bowl.

'But the Archdeacon—' Ashley had begun.

'What Charles doesn't see . . .' Mrs Atticus had told her, winking.

'Actually it doesn't taste all that bad,' remarked Mrs Pocock now. She had been given a glass of the Pineapple and Orange Cooler, which she downed in quick time. 'It's got quite a kick to it.' She licked her lips. 'I think I might enjoy a top-up. Anybody else?'

'Yes, please,' replied her friends, who had both drained their glasses.

'I might as well try a glass,' said Mrs Brakespeare, 'since there's nothing else on offer.'

Miss Brakespeare arrived a moment later with a drink for her mother. 'Oh, I see you've got one,' she said, turning to go.

'I'd like another!' snapped Mrs Brakespeare, gulping down the contents of her glass and reaching for the drink.

Mrs Sloughthwaite looked around the church to make a mental note of who was there. She caught sight of Dr Stirling and Mrs Devine in earnest conversation, a scowling Fred Massey with Bianca and Clarence, Major Neville-Gravitas boring one of the vergers, the teachers, secretary and the care-taker from the school and various pupils, and then her eyes rested on a couple sitting near the back. 'Well I never,' she murmured. She nudged Mrs Pocock. 'Don't turn round, but look who's sitting behind you,' she said.

Mrs Pocock twisted her body around. 'Who?' she asked.

'At the back!' hissed the shopkeeper. 'By that old stone tomb. It's Miss Sowerbutts and she's with a man!'

Sitting straight-backed and dressed in a bright summer frock was the woman in question. Next to her was a large fleshy-faced individual with thinning grey hair.

'Who is he?' asked Mrs Pocock.

'I've no idea,' replied the shopkeeper, but she determined to soon find out.

Presently Lady Wadsworth made her grand entrance, accompanied by the Archdeacon. She had dressed for the occasion in her brightest summer ensemble – a shapeless multi-coloured cotton tent of a dress, a huge red hat with a feather and spotless white gloves. She was liberally bedecked in an assortment of heavy, expensive-looking jewellery. The mask of brown powder which covered her face made her look like someone who had just returned from a Mediterranean cruise. With the wave of bright russet-coloured hair and the lipstick as thick and red as congealed blood, she looked wonderfully impressive and every inch the Lady of the Manor.

'Mutton dressed as lamb,' observed Mrs Pocock disparagingly.

'It is heart-warming to see so many in St Christopher's,' announced the Archdeacon to the audience when the noise in the church subsided. He stood before the altar with the guest of honour at his side. 'I should like to thank you all for support-ing this very worthy cause. Without further ado, it gives me great pleasure to ask Lady Wadsworth, who has kindly graced us with her presence this evening, to say a few words of introduction.'

The lady of the manor surveyed the audience with haughty grandeur. 'The Wadsworths have lived in Barton-in-the-Dale for centuries,' she said in a loud voice full of aristocratic confidence. She was, of course, being a little economical with the truth, for it was only in the mid-eighteenth century that her forebear, Sir William Wadsworth, had moved near the village and built Limebeck House. 'In all that time this beautiful and ancient church has been very dear to my family and has been at the very centre of village life. Sadly it needs the roof repairing and the heating replaced, which of course costs a deal of money.'

'She ought to shell out some of hers,' whispered Mrs Pocock to her neighbour. 'She's not short of a bob or two, not after she sold them statues.'

'This evening,' continued Lady Wadsworth, 'we have the first of a number of fund-raising ventures to which I give my whole-hearted support. I do entreat you all to do the same. I shall now pass you back to the Archdeacon, who will introduce our talented performer.'

There was a ripple of applause as she took her seat to the side of the altar.

'She makes the Queen sound common, so she does,' observed Mrs O'Connor.

'Many of you will know our recitalist,' said the Archdeacon. 'Tonight he will be delighting us on the organ with a selection of his favourite pieces. Please put your hands together and welcome Mr George Tomlinson.'

Having played a number of classical melodies by Bach, Haydn, Fauré and Holst, interrupted only by the occasional hiccupping from the front pew, the organist then performed a medley of popular tunes, finishing with songs from the musicals.

Following the performance, as people drifted away, the Archdeacon approached Ashley accompanied by a tall clerical individual with straight colourless hair and large pale eyes set wide apart.

'Ashley, my dear,' he said. 'Many congratulations. I think we can count this evening as a resounding success. Very well done. Now,' he turned to his fellow clergyman, 'may I introduce the Reverend Algernon Sparshott. As you know, he has been appointed as the new vicar here at Barton.'

The man nodded and gave a slight smile. There was an expression of extreme sanctity on his narrow bony face. He looked at the curate ponderingly.

'I'm pleased to meet you,' said Ashley amiably. 'I am sure you will be very happy here. It's a warm community and we have quite a loyal congregation.'

'Please excuse me,' said the Archdeacon. 'I must go and thank Mr Tomlinson. I shall leave Reverend Sparshott in your capable hands, Ashley.' He swept away.

'Tell me, Dr Underwood,' asked the Reverend Sparshott, 'how many of these *events*' – he stressed the word – 'have you planned?'

'It's early days yet,' she replied, 'but I have a history lecture and a flower arranging demonstration organised, and the head teacher at the village school is to put on a concert where the children will perform.'

'I trust you will not be envisioning a bingo session in the church,' he said. Solemn eyes gazed at her in the rather unnerving way of young children.

'Of course not,' she replied, stung by the man's comment. It was clear from his tone of voice and the unsmiling expression on his pale face that he was not being flippant.

'And did you enjoy the evening?' she asked.

'To be frank,' he said stiffly, 'I did feel that the inclusion of the more modern and popular music was inappropriate.' He sounded priggish. 'I may appear old-fashioned but I do feel a church should be a place of worship, prayer and contemplation and not a centre of light entertainment.'

'So are you not in favour of the various fund-raising activities?' she asked. It was a rhetorical question, for she could quite easily predict his answer, but she asked it all the same.

'I am not opposed to church activities *per se*,' he replied with bumptious self-confidence, 'but to be frank, I feel that lectures and school concerts and flower arranging demonstrations are best undertaken in a community centre or village hall and not in the House of God.'

Ashley allowed the statement to resonate for a moment while she thought of how to respond. 'I see,' she said at last looking at him levelly. 'Perhaps we might discuss this when you are in post?'

'Perhaps,' he replied in a dry precise voice.

She could feel her cheeks burn. The man gave every indication that he disliked her for some reason. She couldn't understand why. It couldn't be personal, for he had only just met her. Was it because he felt intimidated by having a curate with superior academic qualifications to his own – an Oxford scholar with a doctorate in divinity – or was it because he was not in favour of women priests? Maybe there was also a hint of jealousy. He had seen how well she related to people and how popular she was in the community. Perhaps he felt she needed to be put in her place from the outset, that she should be in no doubt that he was the vicar and it was he who made the decisions.

'On another matter, Reverend Underwood,' he continued loftily, 'I am anxious to move into the rectory as soon as possible. Has the Archdeacon given you any indication when he intends to relocate to Clayton?'

'No, he hasn't,' she replied.

'No intimation at all?'

'None,' she told him. 'Perhaps you should ask him.' Ashley

felt anger rising in her but decided not to say anything and to take her leave. 'If you will excuse me, I too would like to thank Mr Tomlinson for giving up his time so generously to help raise funds for the church. It was particularly kind of him since he is not a member of this congregation, being a Methodist.' She walked away, simmering.

The Archdeacon returned to join the new vicar. He was accompanied by his wife, Elisabeth and Michael.

'You and Ashley seemed to be getting on very well, Reverend Sparshott,' he said. 'May I introduce you to my wife Marcia, Mrs Devine, the head teacher of the village school and Dr Stirling our local GP?'

The clergyman nodded and acknowledged them with a restrained smile.

'I hear you have four children,' said Elisabeth.

'I do,' he replied.

'And what are they called?' she asked.

'Rufus and Reuben, Ruth and Rebekah. I have two sets of twins.'

'I can assure you that they will be very happy here at the village school,' said the Archdeacon.

'I have already arranged for my children to attend St Paul's Preparatory School in Ruston,' he was told.

The Archdeacon and his wife exchanged glances.

'The school in the village has an excellent reputation,' said Michael. 'It's received an outstanding report from the inspector. Indeed, the Minister of Education himself has commended it most highly.'

'That is as may be, Dr Stirling,' replied the new vicar, 'but I feel my children will be better catered for at St Paul's.'

'Tell me, Reverend Sparshott,' said Mrs Atticus, giving him one of her vengeful looks, 'how can you conclude that your children will be better catered for at St Paul's without visiting the village school to compare it?'

'To be frank,' he replied, 'I am of the considered opinion that the small independent school tends to be more traditional, has better discipline and more of a work ethic than the state school.'

'My goodness,' said Mrs Atticus, sounding piqued, 'for a clergyman you seem remarkably knowledgeable about education.'

The sarcasm was lost on the cleric. 'I should like to think so,' he replied.

'You might like to visit the village school sometime anyway, Reverend Sparshott,' said Elisabeth pleasantly, 'and see how well-behaved and hard-working the pupils are.'

'I cannot see the point of paying for a child's education,' said Mrs Atticus before the clergyman could reply, 'when you have a first-rate school on your doorstep.'

'I do the best that I feel is appropriate for my children, Mrs Atticus,' said the Reverend Sparshott abruptly. 'It is of course up to me as the parent where my children are educated.'

'Yes, but—' she began.

The clergyman held up a hand as if to give a blessing and smiled thinly. 'Mrs Atticus,' he said, 'forgive me, but I am disinclined to discuss further my children's education with you.'

She flinched irritably, but before she could respond he turned his pale clerical face to the Archdeacon, who was feeling most uncomfortable. He is not the sort of man I warm to, thought the Venerable Atticus, who had a sharp ear for pretentiousness. In this he was not alone, for those near to him were of the same opinion. 'I was hoping to move into the rectory in the next few weeks,' the new vicar said. 'I believe that Dr Underwood has made arrangements to find alternative accommodation?'

'Yes,' said the Archdeacon looking displeased. 'She will be renting a cottage in the village.'

'So when will *you* be vacating—' he started.

'Vacating!' repeated Mrs Atticus, doing her best to contain her indignation. There was a stern, pinched look on her face.

'The rectory,' said the new vicar completing the sentence. 'When will you be vacating the rectory?' There was the ominous hint of a smile.

'We shall be vacating the rectory all in good time, Reverend Sparshott,' the Archdeacon told him, with uncharacteristic sharpness in his voice.

'Thank you so much for inviting me,' said the Vice Principal of St John's College.

'I recall how you used to like organ music,' said Miss Sowerbutts, 'and I felt you might enjoy it. I know I was a little rude and inhospitable when you visited. It came as quite a shock seeing you after all those years and I was going through a bad patch: so many things on my mind, so much to think about.'

'Of course, of course, I quite understand,' he replied. 'I am so pleased the situation regarding the building of the houses has been resolved and, more importantly, that you are fully recovered after your ordeal.'

'A great weight has been lifted,' she said. 'I am afraid that I misjudged a certain person.' She glanced in the direction of Elisabeth.

'Well, I'm pleased you got in touch.'

'And I'm glad you were able to come this evening.'

'It must have been quite a dreadful experience collapsing and being rushed to hospital.'

'It was,' she agreed. 'Quite dreadful.'

'I'm delighted that you are now fit and well and back to your old self.'

'No, Patrick,' she said, 'I am not back to my old self. I had this wake-up call, you see. When I was in that hospital bed and thought that it was the end, I had time to think, to go over things which had happened in my life, and I came to realise how lucky I have been, that I really didn't appreciate all that I had. It was a strange experience, almost life-changing.'

'Occasionally in life,' he said, 'we all need a wake-up call, and when we get to our age I think we tend to put more things in perspective. I've come to the conclusion that the little things in life are sometimes more important than the big things, if that makes any sense.'

'It makes a lot of sense,' she replied.

'Well, now that we have made contact again after all these years, perhaps you might let me return the favour and invite you to come to a concert at the college and maybe have a bite to eat afterwards? You might be interested to see how things have changed at St John's.'

'I should like that very much, Patrick,' she replied. 'Very much indeed.'

'What did I say?' Mrs Sloughthwaite asked her friends as they stood before her counter the following morning.

'What did you say?' asked Mrs Pocock.

'I said that there must be something in the water, what with all these assassignations,' the shopkeeper told her. 'First Mrs Devine getting married and then Miss Brakespeare and George Tomlinson tying the knot. Then Clarence and Bianca. It won't be long before Joyce Fish's other granddaughter walks down the aisle and I shouldn't wonder if the young curate won't be far behind, what with the young men buzzing around her like wasps in a jam dish.'

'And who would have thought Miss Sowerbutts of all people would find herself a man?' said Mrs Pocock.

'I should imagine hers is a purely plutonic relationship,' said the shopkeeper. 'I mean, she's a bit long in the tooth for romance. I can't imagine anyone in their right minds wanting to spend the rest of their life with her.'

'Well, you never know,' said Mrs Pocock. 'There's nowt as queer as folk, as they say. I shouldn't be at all surprised if she finds herself at the altar before too long.'

Mrs O'Connor sighed. 'It just goes to show, so it does,' she remarked.

'What does?' asked the shopkeeper.

'That there's hope for us yet, Mrs Sloughthwaite.'

21

'I think you are being a trifle unkind to describe him as odious, my dear,' said the Archdeacon. He crunched noisily on a triangle of dry toast. His wife had removed the butter dish and the marmalade jar from the breakfast table and had vetoed anything fried. It was the morning after the recital.

'Not at all, Charles,' disagreed Mrs Atticus forcefully. 'If anything it's an understatement. I found the man quite repellent. Don't you agree, Ashley?'

'I didn't find the Reverend Sparshott very approachable,' replied the curate.

All three were feeling downcast, for the meeting with the new vicar the day before had put a damper on an otherwise very successful and good-humoured evening.

'I have to own that I found the Reverend Sparshott something of a cold fish,' remarked the Archdeacon.

'Cold fish!' exclaimed his wife. 'He's a dour, self-important and humourless man. He has just set foot in the church and he asks when we will be vacating the rectory. Vacate it, indeed! It made us sound like squatters. I pity you, Ashley, having to work with him. It will be intolerable for you. And I take great exception at being interrupted so rudely. I couldn't believe what he said about education – that independent schools have better discipline and more of a work ethic than state schools. On what, pray, does he base that sweeping statement? What does he know about education? And, I may add . . .'

As the denunciation continued, the Archdeacon, as was his

habit when he was subjected to one of Marcia's tirades, ceased to listen. On these occasions he often thought of some apposite words from the Bible. Psalm 14 came to his mind at that moment. How he wished his dear wife might sometimes heed the wise words: 'Set a guard on my mouth, O Lord, Keep watch over the door of my lips.'

'Have you nothing to say, Charles?' asked his wife, breaking into his thoughts.

'Pardon, my dear?'

'About the conduct of the new vicar.'

The Archdeacon shrugged. 'What can I say, Marcia?' he asked. 'The Reverend Sparshott was not, it has to be admitted, one of the most congenial of men but perhaps we are a little premature in judging him. I grant you he did give a somewhat unfortunate first impression, but I am sure that he is, at heart, a dedicated and zealous priest and may well turn out to be a very good vicar. I think one should reserve one's judgement and see how he fares.'

'Oh, Charles, really,' said his wife in an exasperated tone. 'You always manage to look for the good in people, don't you? Might there be an occasion, once in a while, when you are not so very favourably disposed to your fellow man?'

It was true that the Archdeacon always looked for the good in others, tried to be fair and see the other person's point of view. He was not by nature a judgemental man. He was inclined to remind his wife of the words in the Wisdom of Solomon, to 'beware of murmuring which is unprofitable and to refrain your tongue from backbiting', but he merely remarked, 'I'm a priest, my dear. I think that is what priests are supposed to do – to look for the good in others.'

'I really would like to believe what you say, Charles,' said Ashley sadly, 'but I don't feel I could work with him. I think I shall have to apply for another living.'

'No, no, Ashley, you must not do that!' cried the Archdeacon.

'I thought things through last night and have very much decided,' she told him.

'I do urge you to consider things carefully, Ashley,' said the Archdeacon. 'We should give the Reverend Sparshott a chance. Let us not condemn the man prematurely. It would be a great loss to the village and indeed to the church were you to leave. You have been like a breath of fresh air, and have made such a valuable contribution in the short time you have been with us.'

'Huh!' huffed Mrs Atticus. 'This is a fine kettle of fish when the first thing the new vicar does is push out the curate like a cuckoo in a nest.'

'Reverend Sparshott has not pushed anyone out, my dear,' her husband told her.

'As good as,' replied his wife. 'Well, if you want my opinion, Ashley, the sooner you find somewhere else the better. Of course my husband will give you a glowing reference, so there should be no problem there.' She then turned her attention to the Archdeacon and pursed her lips. 'It is a pity, though, Charles, that you don't feel inclined to exert your power as the Archdeacon and prevail upon the Reverend Sparshott to move somewhere else – preferably to the other side of the world. "When do you expect to vacate the rectory" indeed! It has quite put me off my breakfast.'

Mrs Scrimshaw was staring at the pile of papers on her desk when Mr Gribbon poked his head around the office door.

'So did you see who I saw at the concert at St Christopher's?' he asked, smirking.

'If you mean Miss Sowerbutts,' replied the secretary without looking up, 'yes, I did.'

'All dressed up like a dog's dinner she was,' said the caretaker. 'One minute she's nearly pushing up the daisies and the next she's as large as life and looking fitter than a butcher's dog. She's a tough old bird, I'll give her that.' The secretary did not respond but started to search under the papers. 'Who was it with her? Do you know?'

'Pardon?'

'The bloke she was with. Do you think it was her brother?'

'No, he's dead,' said Mrs Scrimshaw with an impatient twitch of the head. 'I had a box of paperclips somewhere,' she said. She began rootling in her desk drawer.

'Must be her fancy man, then.'

'Hardly.'

'You wouldn't credit it, would you, at her time of life?' Mr Gribbon chuckled. 'There's life in the old dog yet, as they say. Mind you, he wasn't anything to write home about.'

'Have you managed to fix the dripping tap in the boys' toilet yet?' she asked in an insistent tone of voice. 'You've been asked to do it I don't know how many times.'

'I've got to get a washer,' he told her. 'By the way, you haven't seen Mrs Pugh this morning, have you? She should be here by now.'

'No, I haven't,' she said. 'I'm sure I put a box of paperclips in this drawer.'

'She's never late,' said the caretaker looking at his watch. 'I hope she's all right.'

'Who?'

'Mrs Pugh. She does tend to overdo things. I'm always telling her to slow down.'

'Mr Gribbon,' said the secretary in an offhand tone of voice, 'I have a great deal to do this morning so could you please let me get on with it? There's this meeting after school today with the teachers from Urebank and I have to prepare these papers and collate them all, that's if I can find the wretched paperclips.'

'So we'll finally be meeting Mr Richardson,' said the caretaker, remaining where he was. 'From what Mrs Pugh tells me, he's a nasty piece of work and his dippy deputy is not much better.'

'You have told me all this before,' said the secretary. 'Now if you wouldn't mind—'

'If you ask me, I can't see this amalgamation working,' he said. 'Our lot will never get on with their lot and having two head teachers will be no joke, I can tell you. When two people ride a horse, one must take the back seat and I can't see it will be Mr Richardson doing that, from what I've heard about him.'

Oscar appeared at the door.

'Hello, Mrs Scrimshaw,' he said brightly.

'Hello, Oscar,' she replied.

'Hello, Mr Gribbon,' said the boy.

The caretaker grunted. 'And what do you want?' he asked.

'I want a word with Mrs Scrimshaw, actually,' said the boy, 'but now you are here I can kill two birds with one stone. That tap is still dripping in the boys' toilet.'

'Yes, I know.'

'I did mention it to you last week when you were talking to Mrs Pugh in your store-room.'

'I know you did!' the caretaker exclaimed, his face becoming flushed.

'I knocked on the door several times but you didn't answer,' said Oscar. 'I knew you were in there because I could hear noises. That's why I shouted through the keyhole.'

'I was busy. Now go on, clear off!'

'The tap probably needs a new washer,' said the boy.

'I am aware of that!' snapped Mr Gribbon.

'You see, you wouldn't think it, but a dripping tap wastes a great deal of water,' continued the boy blithely, undaunted by the caretaker's aggressive tone. 'I was reading about it in a book on conservation. Over time, millions of gallons of water could be lost from dripping taps.'

'Look, why don't you go back to your lesson?' asked the caretaker angrily.

'I've been sent to see Mrs Scrimshaw,' the boy replied.

'Well, see her then and sling your hook,' barked the caretaker.

'What is it, Oscar?' asked the secretary.

'Mrs Robertshaw asked me to return this box of paperclips which she borrowed.'

The secretary looked heavenwards. 'Give me strength,' she muttered.

Mr Gribbon and Oscar had not been gone above five minutes when the door of the office burst open and standing before Mrs Scrimshaw was a figure straight out of a gangster movie – a broad, muscular man with a bald, bullet-shaped head, thick neck and hands like spades. His nose was crooked and a red and a vicious-looking scar decorated his forehead.

'My God!' exclaimed Mrs Scrimshaw, scattering the papers and showering paperclips over the floor.

'Where is he?' growled the man.

The secretary picked up a ruler and held it before her like a weapon. 'W . . . w . . . who?' she asked in a frail voice.

'That Casanova of a caretaker, that weaselly womaniser, that lecherous wolf in sheep's clothing. Gibbon – him who's been playing fast and loose with my wife.'

'Are you Mr Pugh?' asked the secretary weakly.

'I am indeed,' replied the man. 'Owen Pugh, and I want to see that bare-faced philanderer to tell him to keep his wandering hands off my Bronwyn.'

Mrs Scrimshaw swallowed and tried to compose herself. Then she adopted the secretarial tone of voice she used with parents. 'If you would care to wait in the entrance,' she replied, 'I shall try and locate Mr Gribbon.'

She squeezed past the glowering figure and, still clutching the ruler, scurried off down the corridor.

Elisabeth was explaining a tricky arithmetical problem when the secretary appeared at the classroom door, madly gesticulating behind the glass.

'Get on with your work for a moment, please,' she told her class.

'There's Mr Pugh in the entrance and he's gunning for Mr Gribbon,' the secretary blurted out when Elisabeth joined her in the corridor. 'He thinks something's been going on between Mr Gribbon and his wife. He frightened the life out of me. He looks as if he could commit murder.'

'Go and find Mr Gribbon, please,' Elisabeth told Mrs Scrimshaw calmly, 'and tell him to make himself scarce.' She then hurried off down the corridor to the school entrance, to find an enraged Mr Pugh pacing up and down like a caged beast.

'Mr Pugh,' said Elisabeth pleasantly. 'Whatever seems to be the problem?'

'Oh, Mrs Devine.' He calmed down at the sight of her. 'It's your caretaker I've come to see.'

'Well, let's go into the staff-room and talk about it,' she replied.

'There's nothing to talk about,' he replied. 'That man wants locking up. He's a danger to women. He's been trying it on with my wife and I am not having it.'

'I'm sure there has been some sort of misunderstanding, Mr Pugh. Mr Gribbon doesn't strike me as the kind of man to try it on, as you put it.'

'There's been no misunderstanding, Mrs Devine. It all came out last night. That Gibbon man can't keep his hands to himself, making suggestions, brushing against Bronwyn when she's wiping the surfaces and touching her when she's buffing the floors. He's got hands like the tentacles of an octopus. She'll not be coming back to this school so long as that sex maniac is here.'

Elisabeth tried to conceal a smile. The last phrase, she thought, that one could imagine using to describe Mr Gribbon was 'sex maniac'.

'Well, unfortunately Mr Gribbon is indisposed today,' she lied. 'It's his bad back. It's always playing up.'

'I'll give him more than a bad back if I get hold of him,' said Mr Pugh.

'But I shall have a word with Mr Gribbon when he returns and sort out this matter.'

'You do that, Mrs Devine, and tell him to keep his roving hands off my Bronwyn.'

'And I think under the circumstances it might be better, as you say, if your wife did not return to work here, for the time being at any rate. After the amalgamation I shall recommend she be based at the other site down at Urebank, and she will have no further contact with Mr Gribbon. She has been an exemplary cleaner and I should be very pleased to furnish her with an excellent reference.'

'And this Gibbon man?'

'As I said, I shall have a word with him but please, Mr Pugh, leave this with me to deal with – and I should be very grateful if you would not come into school in such a manner in future. You quite frightened the secretary, you know.'

'I'm sorry about that, Mrs Devine,' he said, pacified. 'I know I have a bit of temper and I didn't mean to fly off the handle and frighten her, but if get my hands on that man he'll know about it.'

Elisabeth deftly changed the subject. 'I spoke to Mr Williams last week,' she said. 'He tells me John is making significant progress, gaining more confidence and enjoying his visits out of school. I hope that one day he might come and stay with me.'

The man's face mellowed. 'He's doing very nicely,' Mr Pugh told her. 'He likes his little trips. We took some of the youngsters to the park last week.' He smiled. 'Always the same, is John – easy-going, no trouble. Look, Mrs Devine, I'm sorry about this morning. I lost it. It was just that—'

'Let's put it behind us,' she told him. 'And thank you for all you are doing for my son. I really do appreciate it.'

When she had seen Mr Pugh off the premises, Elisabeth went in search of the caretaker. She caught sight of him creeping around the side of the school.

'A word, Mr Gribbon,' she said when she finally tracked him down in the store-room.

'Oh, Mrs Devine,' he said, looking shamefaced. 'I was just off to sort out a dripping tap in the boys' toilets.'

'It can wait,' she said. 'Could I see you at lunchtime, please? I think there is something we need to talk about.'

'Yes, yes, of course,' he said diffidently.

'In the staff-room then, where we will not be disturbed?'

'Look, Mrs Devine, if it's about this morning—' he began.

'It is, but we can discuss it better in private.'

'Now,' Elisabeth said as they sat facing each other in the staff-room later that morning, 'what have you to say about our unexpected visitor?'

'Well, not much,' replied Mr Gribbon, blustering. 'The man was off his rocker, coming into school like that.'

'So he had no call to behave as he did?' she asked.

'No, Mrs Devine, he hadn't.' The caretaker looked uncomfortable and shifted uneasily in the chair.

'And there is no truth in what Mr Pugh claims, that there is something going on between you and his wife?'

'Nothing to cause him to go off at the deep end like that,' replied the caretaker. 'Me and Bronwyn – Mrs Pugh, that is – we just get along well together. We sort of click.'

'Click?'

'We just like each other. She's a very approachable woman. We're friends, nothing more.'

'Mrs Pugh seems to think differently – from what she has told her husband she seems to say that you have been making some unwelcome approaches.'

'I was just being friendly and nothing more.'

'Mr Pugh thinks that you were rather too friendly, by all accounts,' said Elisabeth.

'I may have been a bit over-affectionate at times, Mrs Devine,' said the caretaker, stretching his neck and scratching his chin, 'but that's as far as it went. There was no hanky-panky, I can assure you of that.'

'Let us hope that Mrs Pugh does not lodge a formal complaint for sexual harassment.'

The colour drained from the caretaker's face. 'She wouldn't do that, would she?'

'Indeed she could,' Elisabeth told him, 'which would be unfortunate not only for you but also for the reputation of the school.'

'Oh dear,' sighed the caretaker.

'Now, I don't think it will come to that. I managed to calm Mr Pugh down and have agreed that his wife will no longer work here. After the amalgamation I am hopeful that she will be found a post at the other site. I trust this will be the end of the matter. It was fortunate that the Minister of Education and the school inspector were not in school when Mr Pugh decided to pay us a visit. Goodness knows what they would have thought.'

'So Mrs Pugh will not be coming back?' said the caretaker sadly.

'No, she will not,' said Elisabeth.

'I see. So will I get another part-time cleaner?' he asked,

'Please don't push your luck, Mr Gribbon,' said Elisabeth.

At lunchtimes Elisabeth took the opportunity of sitting with the children in the dining hall. It gave her the opportunity to get to know the pupils better, and she learnt a whole lot more about them in such a social and informal setting than she did in the classrooms.

'May I join you, Oscar?' she asked, sitting next to the boy.

'Of course, Mrs Devine,' he replied, pulling out the chair next to him for Elisabeth to sit down.

'Thank you,' she said. 'And how are things?'

'Oh, pretty good at the moment. I've got my grade five on the pianoforte.'

'Well done. That's a real achievement.'

'And I'm learning the flute.'

'This has nothing to do with Roisin by any chance, has it?' she asked, smiling.

'Maybe a little bit,' replied the boy.

'And Mrs Robertshaw tells me you make a wonderful wizard in the school play?'

'It's not a big part,' Oscar told her. 'There are very few lines to learn and he only comes in at the very end of the play, but I'm enjoying it. Thankfully I don't have to sing. I think I'm being typecast, you know.'

'Why is that?' asked Elisabeth.

'I suppose it's because I'm clever and know a lot of things,' the boy replied. To Oscar this wasn't a boast; he was merely stating a fact. 'If you will excuse me, Mrs Devine, I have to finish my lunch. It's getting cold and I have chess club this lunchtime.'

Elisabeth watched him for a moment. The boy was a precise eater, cutting up the meat carefully into squares and posting it into his mouth. When he had finished he placed his knife and fork neatly together, took out a handkerchief and dabbed the corners of his mouth.

'You have very good table manners,' remarked Elisabeth.

'My father says that "manners maketh the man",' he told her. '"When you are eating, always sit up in your chair, don't speak with your mouth full and never put your elbows on the table." That's what he says. I do sometimes put my elbows on the table and then he says that "all joints will be carved". He's only joking, of course.'

Oscar stood and picked up his plate to go.

'How are things at home?' asked Elisabeth.

'Oh, they're fine.' The boy thought for moment and placed his plate down on the table. He was perceptive enough to know what she was hinting at. 'I suppose you're wondering how I'm feeling after finding out about my father.'

'I'm just concerned whether you are all right,' she said.

Oscar sat down again. 'Well, Mrs Devine, my father and I have had a long talk about things. He told me that my mother was very brave bringing me up by herself. She was only young when she had me you see – a student. He told me that there were some in her family who thought she should have me adopted. Having a baby, they said, would interfere with her studies and her career, but she wouldn't give me up. My father said it would have been easier in a way for her if she had have done. Anyway, she couldn't be persuaded. It's quite a brave thing to do, isn't it?'

'It is,' agreed Elisabeth. 'It's a very brave thing to do.'

What never ceased to surprise her was how some children, like Oscar, coped so well with adversity. When faced with divorcing parents, serious illness, the death of a loved one, being placed in care, they could show an amazing resilience. Others, sadly, found it hard to deal with the pain they felt. It was these children more than any, she knew, who needed sensitive handling, support and affection.

Elisabeth joined Robbie, who was sitting by himself poking the chips on his plate. There had been some improvement in the boy's behaviour since his return to the school. He was no longer as angry and defiant and subject to outbursts of temper, but he remained sulky and aloof and, despite her efforts, was unwilling to take part in any of the school activities or to make any effort to find friends. Danny seemed the only pupil the boy appeared to have any time for. Robbie did the minimum amount of work in class and never volunteered an answer, but Elisabeth could see he was bright and she felt for the moment she would not press him.

'How are you liking Treetop Farm?' she asked now, sitting next to him.

'OK, miss,' he replied.

'And Mr and Mrs Ross? How are you getting on with them?'

'All right,' he answered. He stared down firmly at his plate.

'And have you seen your mother?' asked Elisabeth.

The boy looked up and eyed her with vague suspicion. 'No, and I don't want to see her,' he mumbled.

'Try not to judge her too harshly, Robbie. It must have been a very difficult decision she had to make.'

'You mean to choose between me and him?' There was a flash of the former rebelliousness and resentment, emotions which she knew could arise so quickly in the child.

'It's not quite as simple as that,' she said gently.

'It is to me,' said the boy. 'Anyway, I'm glad to be where I am.'

'You know, if you need to talk to me about anything . . .' she said, leaving the sentence unfinished.

The boy nodded.

'Now,' she said more brightly. 'I want to ask you to do something for me, Robbie.'

He peered at her with guarded curiosity but remained silent.

'You know that we are putting on *The Wizard of Oz* at the end of term?'

He nodded.

'Well, there's something I think you can help me with.'

'I can't act and I can't sing,' he told her, with some of his old truculence.

'I don't want you to act or to sing,' Elisabeth told him. 'We need someone to look after Toto, he's Dorothy's little dog. Mrs Robertshaw was going to have a toy dog, but Lady Wadsworth's Border Terrier seems so right for the part that she thought she'd risk having him on stage. The thing is, someone needs to look after him, make sure he behaves himself. Could you help out, do you think?'

'Why me?' he asked.

'Because when we visited Limebeck House Gordon liked you. He does not take to everyone, but he has taken to you. You are good with animals and I think you're the best person to look after him.'

He looked her straight in the eye with that sort of unsettling stare of his. 'I suppose you think I owe it to you because you took me back,' he said.

'No, Robbie, not at all. If you don't want to do it, then you don't have to. I shall ask someone else.'

'I'll think about it . . . miss,' he said.

'There's a rehearsal tomorrow after school, if you are interested. It will be Gordon's first appearance on stage. I really would be grateful if you could do this for me.'

The boy nodded but didn't reply.

The following day Robbie stood in the school entrance with the Border Terrier rubbing its small hairy body against his legs. He bent and tickled the bristly head. There were grunts of contentment from the dog.

'Now, young man,' said Emmet, 'you're going to take good care of Gordon, aren't you?'

'Yes.'

'He's a rather temperamental little dog. Do you know what that means?'

'Yes,' replied Robbie. 'It means he can be difficult.'

'Indeed,' said Emmet. 'Usually he's quite a good-natured and well-behaved beast, but sometimes he has his moments. He once bit the postman.' The dog raised its head. 'Did you know he was a rescue dog?'

'No.'

'Well, he was,' said Emmet. 'I believe he was an unwanted Christmas present. He was ill-treated and the owner threw him in the river in a sack. Lady Wadsworth's given him a good home but he's suspicious of people. He's very particular about who he likes and who he doesn't. He seems to sense those who like him.' The dog cocked its head and looked at Emmet as if understanding what was being said. 'He seems to have taken a shine to you, so he should keep out of mischief and do as he is told. Should he get a bit restless you can give him one of his little treats.' Emmet passed the boy a small plastic bag. 'I'll collect him at five o'clock.'

'You don't need to bother,' Robbie told him. 'Mr Ross said he'll run me back to Limebeck House with Gordon after the rehearsal.'

'Mr Ross at Treetop Farm?'

'Yes. I'm being fostered by him and Mrs Ross,' said Robbie. 'He collects me from school sometimes.'

Emmet knew about the boy from what his daughter had said of him, how difficult, moody and rude he could be and how he kept himself to himself. 'I'll save Mr Ross the trouble,' said Emmet. 'I'll be coming for Roisin anyway and then I could run you back home.'

'If you say so,' said the boy.

'I'll give Mr Ross a ring then, shall I?'

'You can if you want.'

'Well, take good care of Gordon, won't you.'

Robbie bent down and stroked the dog. 'Course I will,' he said.

During the rehearsal Robbie sat at the side of the stage. He never took his eyes off the dog. Gordon behaved perfectly, following Chardonnay around, sitting when commanded and seemingly taking an interest in the action.

When the children were packing up to go home, the dog trotted up to Robbie, jumped up on his knee and rested its head on the boy's lap. He patted its head gently.

Malcolm Stubbins approached.

'What's the mutt's name?' he asked.

'Gordon.'

'It's a funny-looking mongrel.'

'Not as funny-looking as you,' retorted Robbie.

'Just watch it, you,' said Malcolm, leaning forward and pushing his face close to Robbie's. 'You know what happened to you the last time you cheeked me off.'

'I'm dead scared,' said Robbie, pulling a face.

The dog, sensing hostility, raised its head, pricked up its ears and gave a low grumbling growl. It then showed a set of sharp teeth.

Malcolm backed away.

'It's all right, Gordon,' said Robbie, stroking the dog's head.

'Well, will you look at that,' said Mrs Robertshaw, nodding in the boy's direction. Elisabeth had called in to see how the rehearsal had gone and they stood watching from the back of the hall.

'What's Robbie been like?' she asked.

'He's been no trouble, thank goodness,' said the teacher, 'but he still seems to communicate in grunts. He's such a sullen and perverse child. His foster carers deserve a medal taking him on.'

'How is he getting on with the other children in the play?'

'He's not. They keep away from him and he makes no effort to be friendly. Danny is the only one he has any time for.'

Elisabeth watched Robbie petting the dog and talking to it. She saw one of his rare smiles.

'He's like a different boy right now, Elsie,' she said.

'He is with dogs,' replied the teacher. 'Pity it doesn't extend to humans.'

'Give him time,' said Elisabeth.

Mr Gribbon, who had kept a very low profile since Mr Pugh's visit, appeared at the door looking sheepish.

'I hope we haven't made too much mess,' Mrs Robertshaw shouted to him.

'Oh, don't worry about that,' he replied in an obsequious tone of voice. 'It's what I'm here for.' He was keen to get back in Elisabeth's good books after the Mr Pugh incident, so he wanted it to appear that nothing was any trouble for him. 'I fixed the tap, by the way, Mrs Devine,' he said.

Before leaving he cast a quick critical glance at the floor and noted the few scuff marks. He wondered if the dog was well-trained; he didn't fancy finding puddles when they had gone. He sighed inwardly. There would be no Mrs Pugh now, he thought, to wield his buffer.

Robbie sat in the back of the Land Rover with the dog on his knee. He looked out of the window and maintained a sullen silence despite Emmet's efforts to engage him in conversation.

'So, Gordon behaved himself, did he?' asked Emmet.

'He was really good,' answered Roisin when she realised Robbie was not going to reply.

'And how did you get on?'

'I think the witch is the best part,' said his daughter. 'I get to be really horrible and I have to cackle and stamp my feet. Mrs Robertshaw says that I will have a green face and long nails and wear a long black wig and a pointed hat. She said to ask you if you would make me a broomstick.'

'I think I could manage that,' replied her father. 'Didn't you want a part then, Robbie?'

'No,' replied the boy.

'Danny Stainthorpe is really good as the scarecrow who hasn't got a brain,' said Roisin. 'He makes everybody laugh and so does Eddie – he's the tin man who doesn't have a heart. When Malcolm – he's the cowardly lion – growls, so does Gordon, doesn't he, Robbie?'

'Yes,' the boy replied.

'So how do you like it at Treetop Farm?' asked Emmet.

'Are we nearly there yet?' asked Robbie.

'Nearly there,' replied Emmet, giving up on trying to get the boy to communicate.

22

Mr Nettles arrived as the bell sounded for the end of the school day. He looked flustered as he hurried up the path, clutching a set of folders.

Elisabeth was at the gate talking to a group of parents.

'Good afternoon, Mrs Devine,' he said, rudely interrupting the conversation. He was sweating and out of breath.

'Good afternoon,' replied Elisabeth in a peremptory tone. She was ruffled at having been cut off mid-sentence.

'I take it the staff from Urebank have not yet arrived?' he asked.

'No, not yet,' she replied curtly. 'If you would like to go into the staff-room I will be with you shortly.' She turned back to the parents. 'So as I was saying . . .'

When she arrived at the staff-room she found Mrs Robertshaw, in one of her belligerent moods, cornering the education officer by the sink and reproaching him as a teacher might a naughty child. She was stabbing the air with a finger.

'I just don't think the word is at all appropriate, that's all,' she was saying in a strident voice. 'You may be right that many people use it, but that does not mean it is acceptable. They are children, Mr Nettles, not "kids". Kids are young goats.'

'I take your point,' he replied feebly, his bottom pushed up against the sink. 'However, I would point out that the word is used quite widely and—'

'It doesn't make it correct,' she butted in. 'Children are children and not young animals.'

Miss Wilson, who was sitting in the corner marking books, looked at Elisabeth, raised an eyebrow and sighed. They were both used to their colleague airing her strong views on certain topics.

'I was just saying to Mr Nettles,' said Mrs Robertshaw, 'that it really annoys me to hear children referred to as "kids".'

'Yes, I could hear you from the corridor, Elsie,' said Elisabeth. 'I am sure Mr Nettles feels suitably chastened. Now, shall we have a cup of tea?'

Mr Jolly and the two infant teachers from Urebank arrived a few moments later. After being greeted by Elisabeth, the two women, wearing tight little smiles of apprehension, hurried to the chairs next to Miss Wilson, where they exchanged a few words. Mr Jolly, with a scarily blank expression, sat opposite them with an austere countenance and clutching his hands before him as if in handcuffs.

'Is Mr Richardson delayed?' asked the education officer.

'He will not be joining us,' replied Mr Jolly. 'He is indisposed.'

'Again?' muttered Mrs Robertshaw.

'He felt unwell towards the end of the day,' said the deputy head teacher of Urebank School to no one in particular.

Another snub, thought Elisabeth. It was going to be impossible to work with such a stumbling block. 'Well, I am sorry he has not been able to join us,' she said, the lightness in her voice concealing her anger.

'And when do you think we might have the pleasure of his company?' asked Mrs Robertshaw pointedly.

'I couldn't say,' replied Mr Jolly, tight-lipped.

'There seems little point in continuing without him,' said Elisabeth. 'The idea of this meeting was to discuss the development plan for the new school which I have prepared and to talk about the arrangements for the merger. I suggest we postpone the meeting until Mr Richardson is able to join us.'

'When he is disposed to do so,' added Mrs Robertshaw pointedly.

'I think that is a very sensible suggestion,' agreed Mr Nettles, collecting his folders together.

'However,' said Elisabeth, 'I think this is a good opportunity for our colleagues at Urebank to look around the school. Perhaps, Mrs Hawthorn and Mrs Ryan, you might like to see what we do in the infants here and get to know Miss Wilson, with whom you will be working.'

'We'd like that very much, Mrs Devine,' said Mrs Hawthorn.

'Very much indeed,' echoed her colleague.

They departed with Miss Wilson.

'Might I ask,' said Mr Jolly, getting to his feet, 'if my request to remain at the Urebank site has been considered? It was said at the last meeting, if my memory serves me right, that my concerns about moving down to Barton would be discussed at a later date.'

'If you wish to teach the juniors,' replied Elisabeth, 'then I am afraid you will have to be based here, that is unless you wish to teach the infants on the Urebank site.'

'So it has all been decided, has it?' he asked in that strange querulous voice. 'I will have to move down to Barton? Well, I have to say that I am very disappointed. If I do have to work on this site, then I trust that some financial provision will be made for the extra travelling I should have to do,' he said.

'If you are appointed,' Elisabeth told him.

He looked shocked. 'How do you mean, *if* I am appointed? I assume that I will be offered the position without having to apply,' he said.

'As I understand it,' Elisabeth told him, 'this being a senior post, you will have to go through the same process that Mr Richardson and myself did when the appointment of the head teacher of the merged schools arose.'

'But I thought—' he began.

'Mr Nettles might like to explain the procedure for the appointment of staff,' said Elisabeth, turning in the direction of the education officer.

'Oh, well . . . yes . . . I could . . .' stuttered Mr Nettles. He cleared his throat like a nervous messenger bringing bad news and, placing the folders down on the table, put his hands together beneath his chin as if in prayer. 'The thing is, Mr Jolly, initially you will be called for interview for the post of assistant head teacher to be based here at Barton. With Miss Brakespeare retiring, you will in the first instance be the only candidate for the position.'

'That's what I understood,' he said, sounding relieved.

'You will be interviewed,' said Mr Nettles, 'but in the event that you are unsuccessful—'

'Unsuccessful?' Mr Jolly burst out indignantly. 'Aren't I to be offered the post?'

'Then the position will be advertised,' continued the education officer. 'Of course, should you fail to be appointed, the local authority will very generously guarantee you a job with your salary protected and you will be redeployed to another school if you do not wish to remain here as a classroom teacher.'

Mr Jolly sat down, too astonished to speak.

Miss Sowerbutts was in her front garden when she caught sight of Danny halfway down the high street. He was clutching his ferret to his chest and whistling to himself when he heard a shrill voice behind him.

'Daniel Stainthorpe!' He recognised the strident voice of the feared and disliked former head teacher of the village school, for he had heard it many times before. It never failed to fill him with apprehension. The boy froze in his tracks.

'Daniel Stainthorpe!' came the voice again. 'Did you not hear me? I want a word with you.'

He popped the ferret into his pocket, crossed the road and stood hesitantly outside the cottage gate. 'Yes, Miss Sowerbutts?' he said.

'Come through,' she ordered. 'I want to show you my back garden.'

Danny followed Miss Sowerbutts down the path, wondering what she was going to complain about now.

She stood before her lawn. It looked like velvet: close cropped, bright green and lush. A profusion of flowers crowded the borders – geraniums, delphiniums, foxgloves, hollyhocks, sweet williams and poppies.

'Well?' she said, waving a hand in front of her.

'Pardon, miss?' said Danny, not knowing what he was expected to say.

'My lawn. What have you to say about that?'

'It looks all reight to me miss,' said Danny.

'Looks all right! Looks *all right*!' She gave a small laugh. 'It's quite magnificent! It's the finest lawn in the village, that's what it is. Since you got rid of those ghastly little black rascals, it's been better than it has ever been.'

'Black rascals, miss?' He was mystified about what she was referring to.

'The moles,' she said. 'They have gone and not returned.'

Danny didn't know what to say. He was keen to get away, for he could feel the ferret struggling in his coat pocket.

'My garden is my pride and joy, you know,' she said.

'It looks champion, miss,' said Danny. He had never seen the former head teacher so animated and good-humoured.

'It does, doesn't it, and take a look at my view,' she said quietly, as if speaking to herself, 'vast, unspoilt, uninterrupted, and so it shall remain.'

'Aye, tha's got a grand view all reight,' said the boy. 'Well, I'd best be off, miss.'

'Wait there,' said Miss Sowerbutts.

'But miss—' Danny began.

'Stay where you are!' she ordered. She went into her cottage and a moment later she emerged clutching a crisp five pound note.

'This is for you,' she said.

'No, Miss Sowerbutts,' said Danny shaking his head. 'I din't get rid of yer moles for brass.'

'Take it,' she commanded, thrusting the note into the boy's hand.

'Well, if tha sure,' said Danny. 'Thank you very much, miss.'

She noticed a movement in the boy's jacket pocket. 'Whatever have you got in there?' she asked.

Danny dug into his coat and produced a lithe, sandy-coloured, pointed-faced creature with small bright black eyes. 'It's Ferdy, mi pet ferret,' he told her.

Miss Sowerbutts recoiled as if some invisible force had grabbed her by the shoulders and dragged her back.

'Would you like to hold him, miss?' asked Danny, grinning.

Elisabeth snuggled up to Michael on the sofa at Clumber Lodge. It was a warm summer evening and with the windows open, the room was full of the scents of the garden and the sound of sparrows chattering in the trees.

'Happy?' he asked.

'Very.'

He smiled tenderly. 'Not long now and you will be Mrs Stirling. It's a big step. Are you sure you want to take me on? I'm quite a handful, you know.'

'I know,' she said, kissing his cheek and holding him tighter.

They sat there in contented silence.

'Danny's done a great job with the garden,' said Michael. 'It was like a jungle before he started on it.'

'He's a good lad. Never happier than when he is outdoors,' she said.

'I hope the boys will settle in at the new school next term,' Michael said. 'Clayton Comprehensive is a big place, very different from a small village school. You always worry that they might get in with a bad lot or be bullied.'

'They'll be fine,' she told him. She failed to mention that the recent inspection of the school had not been that good and that in her dealings with the headmaster she had found the man rather aloof.

'Yes, I'm sure you're right,' he said, yawning and closing his eyes. He stretched his legs out in front of him.

'Michael,' said Elisabeth after a while.

'Mm,' he murmured sleepily.

'I've been asked to apply for a job.'

He sat up. 'What job?'

Elisabeth sat up herself. 'Do you remember I told you about the visit of the Minister of Education?'

'Yes.'

'Well, the HMI, Mr Steel, who was with him mentioned to me that there was a post coming up for a school inspector in his district and he thought I might be interested.'

'A school inspector?'

'That's right. I'm flattered that he should think I'm capable.'

'You're capable all right. You can probably show this Mr Steel a thing or two.'

'It would be based at the Clayton office and I could work from home for some of the time. Do you think I should go for it?'

'You sound quite keen to me,' he said. 'But I thought you were happy at the village school?'

'I am happy, but with this amalgamation everything will change and I can see all sorts of problems arising.'

'Oh dear, not that again,' he sighed.

'I'm sorry to go on about it, but it's been on my mind more lately.'

'I'm afraid it's never been out of your mind,' said Michael. 'You worry too much.'

'It's going to be impossible for me to work with Mr Richardson.'

Michael sighed.

'It's all very well you sighing, Michael,' she said, irritated by his lack of sympathy, 'but you would soon complain if you had to work with another doctor who frustrates you every step of the way and undermines what you do. Mr Richardson won't attend planning meetings, hardly speaks to me when we do meet, and on the phone yesterday he was rude and dismissive. He is making no effort whatsoever to try and make things work.'

'Look, Elisabeth,' said Michael in a voice solicitous but firm, 'you have faced all sorts of setbacks and uphill battles since you started at the school and you've overcome them. You are talented, committed and, what's more, pretty formidable when you want to be, and you have a passion for education. You also have a rare skill for getting people to see your way of thinking. I should know. You convinced this stubborn-headed man you are going to marry to get James some specialist help. I'm sure you are fretting unnecessarily. It's just so out of character for you to walk away from a problem. You'll win this difficult man over, I'm sure of it.'

'I really think achieving that is beyond me,' she said.

'I seem to remember,' Michael said, 'that we have had something like this conversation before when I suggested you give up the job. You told me then that you really love what you do and wouldn't want to do anything else. You said you felt you made a real difference in the lives of the children, and that's true, you do make a difference. You made a difference with Danny and James and all the children in the school, and I reckon it won't be long before that Robbie will sort himself out with your help.'

'It's not the children, Michael,' said Elisabeth.

'You also told me that teaching is the most rewarding job in the world.'

'It is.'

'Becoming a school inspector would mean leaving all that behind. Is that what you really want?'

There was a knock and then a head appeared around the door. 'Is it all right for me to come in?' asked James.

'Yes, of course,' said his father.

'I'm not sort of, you know, disturbing anything?' he said, self-consciously.

'No, you're not disturbing anything,' said his father. 'Where's Danny?'

'Feeding his ferret,' James told him. 'I wanted to talk to you about the wedding. There's something on my mind.'

Elisabeth leaned forward expectantly. The boy had said very little about his father getting married again. She'd thought he was happy about it, but for a moment, as she saw the boy's anxious expression, she had the awful feeling that he wasn't.

'What about the wedding?' asked Michael.

'Well, I'm a bit worried,' said the boy.

'You had better come over here and sit down and tell us about it.'

James came and sat between them on the sofa.

'So,' said the boy's father, putting his arm around his shoulder, 'what's on your mind?'

'You said you would like me to be your best man.'

'I did.'

'The thing is, Mrs O'Connor says the best man has to make a speech.'

Elisabeth sighed with relief.

'He usually does,' said Michael, 'but if you feel unhappy about it then you don't have to.'

'I want to,' replied James. 'It's just that I'm not sure what I'm supposed to say.'

'Lots of nice things about your father,' said Elisabeth.

The boy smiled. 'That might be quite difficult,' he said with a cheeky grin on his face.

'I could help you with it if you like,' she said.

'Would you? That would be great,' said James. 'The other thing Mrs O'Connor said is that I will have to wear a kilt.'

'A kilt!' cried his father, laughing. 'Whatever gave her that idea?'

'She said that because you are Scottish you would be wearing a kilt and that I would have to wear one as well.'

'Mrs O'Connor seems to know a great deal more about my wedding than I do,' said Michael. 'Forget about the kilts.'

'Well, I'm glad about that,' said James.

The boy stood up and began to leave the room but stopped at the door and looked back at Elisabeth. 'I'm really glad you are marrying my father,' he said. 'It'll be great to have a mum again.'

Michael put his arm around Elisabeth and gave her a squeeze and a kiss on the cheek. 'Go for the job if you really want to,' he whispered.

It was the evening of the performance of *The Wizard of Oz*. The children were in unusually high spirits, chattering excitedly and laughing loudly, teasing each other, going over their lines, donning their costumes and having their make-up applied by Mrs Scrimshaw. Miss Wilson, who looked amazingly calm and in control, was giving the infants (the Munchkins, the bees and the Winged Monkeys) their final instructions. Mrs Robertshaw, in contrast, was vainly trying to organise the pupils who were taking the lead parts and was becoming increasingly fraught.

Elisabeth discovered Chardonnay in her classroom, sitting by herself mouthing the words she would be saying on the stage. She was dressed in a blue and white gingham dress and the bunches she usually wore in her hair had been converted into short plaits which stuck out at odd angles. She had generously rouged cheeks, startling blue eye-shadow and cherry-red lips. The school secretary had certainly gone to town on the make-up, thought Elisabeth.

'Are you all right, Chardonnay?' she asked.

'Yes miss. I'm just a bit nervous like.'

'You'll be fine.'

'I hope so.'

'Remember when you sang at the Christmas concert? Everyone said how very good you were.'

'I only had to sing then, miss, not say all these words. I might not remember them. What if I forget?'

'I shall be at the side of the stage with the script,' said Elisabeth, 'so if you do forget your lines, I can help you out. Now, I've got something for you.' She went to her desk and took out of the drawer a pair of red shoes with silver heels. 'I wonder if these might fit you?' she asked.

'For me, miss!' exclaimed the girl.

'Well, Dorothy has to have a pair of magic red slippers, doesn't she?'

'I've got these red pumps,' said the girl pointing to her feet, 'but those shoes are much nicer.'

'Try them on,' said Elisabeth.

Chardonnay did as she was told. 'They fit perfect, miss,' she said.

'Those are the shoes I wore when I came for the interview for the head teacher's post here at Barton. I think they brought me good luck. I think they might do the same thing for you tonight.'

'They're lovely, miss,' said the girl, stroking the soft leather. 'I'll take real good care of them.' She stood up and gave Elisabeth a hug. 'Thanks ever so, miss,' she said. Then she began to cry.

'Hey, hey, what's this?' said Elisabeth. 'You'll spoil your make-up.'

'I'm just happy, miss, that's all,' said the girl, 'and I don't want to leave to go to the big school next term.'

'Once you are there you'll soon forget about us,' Elisabeth told her.

'I won't, miss,' said Chardonnay. 'I'll never forget about you.'

Mr Gribbon, wearing his suit for the occasion, a brown shiny affair with wide lapels, appeared at the door with an apologetic cringe. 'Sorry to disturb you, Mrs Devine,' he said in an ingratiating tone of voice, 'but people are arriving. I thought you should know.' After the incident over Mrs Pugh, the caretaker had become almost reverential when he spoke to Elisabeth, constantly currying favour with her in the hope that the blot on his record might be overlooked when the post of caretaker arose with the amalgamation.

'Thank you, Mr Gribbon,' she replied. 'I'll be there in a moment. Good luck, Chardonnay,' she said before leaving the room.

Outside the hall Mrs Sloughthwaite, accompanied by her two friends, was in no hurry to take her seat. She had cornered Elisabeth's brother and was subjecting him to one of her cross-examinations. Giles smiled politely but his mind was clearly on something else. He kept craning his neck and glancing towards the entrance as if waiting for the arrival of someone.

'So you are to give Mrs Devine away then, Major Ardingly?' asked Mrs Sloughthwaite.

'I'm sorry?'

The shopkeeper raised her voice and spoke slowly and clearly as if to a small child. 'Your sister. You'll be walking her down the aisle I hear.'

'Yes indeed.'

'I take it your father can't make the wedding then?'

'No,' said Giles.

'That's a shame.'

'He's dead.'

'Oh, I am sorry,' said the shopkeeper, adopting her most sympathetic voice.

'Yes, 'fraid so. Both our parents are dead.'

'Gracious me, how very sad.'

'Yes, very,' said Giles.

'And you're not married yourself then, Major Ardingly?' she probed.

'No, no,' said Giles. 'I need to find the right woman.'

'Oh, I'm sure the right one will come along,' said Mrs Sloughthwaite. 'And will they be having a honeymoon?'

'I'm sorry?'

'Your sister and Dr Stirling. Will they be having a honeymoon?'

'Yes, of course.'

'Somewhere nice?' she probed.

'Pardon?'

'Are they going anywhere nice for their honeymoon?'

Giles, getting increasing wearied by the grilling, bent closer to his inquisitor. 'Can you keep a secret?' he whispered.

'I'm the very soul of indiscretion,' said Mrs Sloughthwaite in a muted voice.

He smiled. 'So can I. Keep a secret, that is.' He put a finger to his lips. 'It's hush-hush, my dear lady.'

Elisabeth, who was not privy to this exchange, came over. 'Don't you believe a word he says, Mrs Sloughthwaite,' she said, smiling. 'He's a great romancer, my brother.' She slipped a hand through his arm.

He hasn't said anything of note, thought the shopkeeper to herself, but she smiled back.

'Evening, Mrs Devine,' she said. 'I always come early to get a good seat.' Despite what she said she remained where she was. 'I don't like to miss anything.'

Never a truer word spoken, thought Elisabeth. There was little in the village that the shopkeeper missed.

'I was just asking your brother—' Mrs Sloughthwaite began with the persistence of a moth around a flame, when Mrs Pocock butted in.

'I was telling Mrs O'Connor that my Ernest has painted all the scenery,' she announced. 'Stage sets they're called in dramatic circles.'

'He has, and he did an excellent job,' Elisabeth told her.

'He's very artified is my Ernest,' said the proud mother. 'Takes after his grandfather. He was a painter.'

'And decorator,' added Mrs Sloughthwaite, peeved at being interrupted. 'Anyway, as I was asking—' she began again, making another stab at gleaning the information, but this time it was Mrs O'Connor who cut in.

'Dr Stirling asked me to tell you that he'll be along later, Mrs Devine,' she said. 'He's been called out on an emergency. You will have to get used to this when you are married, so you will.'

'I suppose so,' replied Elisabeth. She looked at her brother. 'Giles, why don't you find yourself a seat?'

'I'll just hang about for a minute, sis,' he said, looking around to see if he could spot Ashley.

'I was just asking your brother, Mrs Devine—' began Mrs Sloughthwaite in one last attempt.

'Please excuse me,' said Elisabeth, 'I can see Archdeacon and Mrs Atticus arriving.'

Mrs Sloughthwaite heaved a sigh. 'Come on you two,' she said to her companions, 'we might as well go in.'

'Please Marcia, don't start again,' the Archdeacon was saying. 'You are like the proverbial dog with a bone.'

'I'm merely saying that something needs to be done about him,' said his wife. 'I am never wrong on first impressions and I am sure I am not mistaken in this case. Reverend Sparshott will be an unmitigated disaster. Now, were my father still bishop he would have sorted this out in no time.' She saw Elisabeth and came over. 'What did you make of the new vicar?' she asked.

Behind her the Archdeacon sighed, pulled a face and shook his head dolefully.

'He seems a man of strong views which he is not afraid of expressing,' Elisabeth replied tactfully.

'High-handed, impolite and full of his own importance, that's what I think,' she said. 'I've told Charles that something needs to be done about him. The bishop must be told and must get him removed.'

'Shall we go in?' said her husband, and ignoring his wife's protests he took her arm and guided her into the hall.

Major Neville-Gravitas arrived with Ashley, whom he had met on the way up the path.

He approached Giles charily. 'Major Ardingly,' he began, brushing a hand over his bristled moustache, 'I just want to apologise for my tactless remarks the other evening in the Blacksmith's Arms. I was quite out of order and had I known—

'Don't trouble yourself,' replied Giles. He held out his hand. 'No hard feelings.'

'That's very decent of you,' replied the old soldier.

Before Giles could invite Ashley to sit with him, she was

whisked away by the major to the reserved seats on the front row.

Elisabeth saw something then which she could never have envisaged in a million years. Her eyes widened with surprise. Miss Sowerbutts, accompanied by the man who had been with her on the evening of the organ recital, entered the building. She looked a different woman. Her hair had been permed and she wore a smart suit in light green cotton. The former head teacher looked around her with an expression of mild curiosity. Elisabeth took a deep unsteady breath. A conversation, she knew, was likely to be tricky, with each of them tiptoeing around each other. She went to welcome her.

'Good evening, Miss Sowerbutts,' she said. 'I'm pleased to see you.'

'Good evening, Mrs Devine,' the former head teacher replied with a small twist of the mouth. 'May I introduce Mr Patrick Nolan, the Vice Principal of St John's College?' She betrayed a certain smugness in her voice at being seen in the company of such a distinguished person.

'Mrs Devine,' said the man, 'I'm delighted to meet you again.'

'You've met?' asked Miss Sowerbutts.

'One of the St John's students, Marcia Atticus, was on placement here for her teacher-training,' he told her. 'I called in to observe some of her lessons and excellent they were too. Mrs Atticus is a very capable woman and will make a first-rate teacher. She has received a distinction, you know, in her certificate and has just secured the post of art coordinator at Clayton Juniors. Quite a feather in her cap for someone who has recently qualified.'

'Yes, I have just heard,' said Elisabeth. 'I had hoped that she might get a position here.'

'Hilda and I were at St John's together,' explained Mr Nolan. 'We've just made contact again after many years.'

'We must not keep Mrs Devine, Patrick,' said Miss Sowerbutts. Gone was the usual acrimony in her voice when she had spoken to Elisabeth in the past. She sounded almost friendly. 'I'm sure she has many other people to see.'

'Do go down to the front,' Elisabeth told her. 'There is a row reserved for special guests.'

'No, no,' replied Miss Sowerbutts, 'we'll slip in at the back.'

'I insist,' said Elisabeth. 'As the former head teacher of the school you are of course a special guest.'

'Thank you,' she said with a nod of the head and led the way into the hall.

Five minutes before the performance was to begin, Lady Wadsworth made her grand entrance. She always timed her appearance so she would be the very last to arrive and cause heads to turn. She was accompanied by her lugubrious-looking butler, carrying a silk cushion, and Emmet, with her dog.

'My dear,' said the lady of the manor, extending a queenly hand to Elisabeth. 'Wonderful to be here.'

She was dressed in a scarlet skirt and black jacket, the latter decorated ostentatiously with colourful embroidery and silver sequins. As Mrs Sloughthwaite was later moved to comment, she looked like an ageing country and western singer.

Emmet disappeared to take the dog backstage and Elisabeth escorted Lady Wadsworth to her seat in the middle of the front row.

Mr Tomlinson, with Miss Brakespeare at his side, took his place at the piano.

The performance was about to begin.

Mrs Robertshaw strode to the front, looking red in the face and flustered. 'We've got a problem,' she whispered in Elisabeth's ear. 'Could I see you backstage?'

When they were well out of anyone's hearing in the school entrance, she explained. 'Robbie's not turned up.'

'Oh dear, what can have happened?' said Elisabeth.

'Mr O'Malley has agreed to sit with the dog. I just hope he remembers when it's supposed to be on stage.'

'Well, I'm sure he will be fine and I will be there to prompt him. Don't worry, Elsie, it's only a minor hiccup. It could be a lot worse. It's not as if we are waiting for a lead part to arrive.'

'It's so typical of the boy,' said Mrs Robertshaw crossly. She screwed up her face as if tasting something sour. 'I know you wanted to try and involve him in things, to feel a part of the school, and I commend you for that, but I did have my reservations about asking him to look after the dog. He's not reliable. He's unpredictable. I just wonder if he's done this deliberately.'

'No, Elsie,' replied Elisabeth, 'I don't believe that.'

'You really need to accept,' continued her colleague, 'that this is one pupil you are not going to get through to.'

'I don't accept that,' said Elisabeth forcefully, 'and I am not giving up on him. I never have given up on any child and I am not going to start now. I think enough adults have given up on Robbie in the past. I see something in the child and he is a child after all. You may find this difficult to believe but I actually like Robbie. Now I think we should get the show on the road.'

When Mrs Robertshaw had gone, a small figure appeared from where he had been standing out of sight, listening to the conversation. 'The car wouldn't start,' said Robbie. 'That's why I'm late.' He looked as if he was on the verge of tears.

'I thought it must be something like that,' replied Elisabeth casually. 'Well, come along then, Gordon's champing at the bit.'

The hubbub in the hall suddenly subsided when the lights dimmed. Elisabeth took her place out of sight at the side of the stage with the prompt book. Next to her sat Robbie with the wiry-haired terrier on his knee.

'Are you all right, Robbie?' Elisabeth asked.

'Yes, miss,' he replied.

'Nervous?'

'A bit.'

The hall lights dimmed. On to the bare stage with its plain grey curtain backdrop walked Darren, a moon-faced boy with a shock of curly black hair and a face as freckled as a hen's egg.

'I am your narrator for the evening,' he announced, with a slight tremor in his voice and his gullet rising and falling like a frog's. He coughed theatrically. 'Dorothy is a young orphaned girl who lives on a farm in the dark, dry and dreary country-side in America.'

Chardonnay appeared.

'She has a little hairy dog called Toto,' said Darren.

'Go on, Gordon,' urged Robbie, putting the dog on the floor. The terrier trotted dutifully on to the stage and sat next to Chardonnay. There was a loud 'Aaaahhhh!' from the audience.

'One day,' continued Darren, 'the farmhouse, with Dorothy and Toto inside, is swept up in a cyclone and dropped in Munchkin Country, ruled by the evil Wicked Witch of the East.'

The grey curtains were pulled back to reveal a brightly painted set with great red and yellow flowers, a startling blue stream, purple hills and in the distance a grey stone castle. A road of yellow brick curled into the distance.

'My Ernest did that,' Mrs Pocock whispered to Mrs Sloughthwaite.

Chantelle appeared on the stage cackling. The audience booed.

'The house falls on the witch and squashes her as flat as a pancake,' said Darren.

Chantelle staggered offstage screaming.

Darren, now in his stride, sounded more confident. 'The

good Witch of the North comes with the Munchkins to greet Dorothy and they give her the witch's magic red shoes.'

The stage filled with small chattering children dressed in a variety of bizarre coloured costumes. They clustered around a girl with corkscrew curls and with a silver crown on her head.

Darren continued. 'For Dorothy to get back home, the good Witch of the North tells her that she will have to travel down the road made of yellow bricks to the Emerald City and ask the Wizard of Oz to help her. On her way Dorothy meets a scarecrow.'

Danny entered, wearing a pair of baggy corduroy pants stuffed with straw, a floppy felt hat and an old threadbare jacket.

'I didn't know Fred Massey was in this play,' remarked Mrs Sloughthwaite in an undertone to Mrs Pocock.

'The scarecrow tells Dorothy he wants a brain,' said Darren.

'And why do you want a brain?' asked Chardonnay.

''Cos it's such an uncomfortable feelin' to know you thy are a fool,' Danny told her. 'If thy only 'ave brains in your 'ead you would be as good a man as any of 'em an' a better man than some of 'em. Brains are t'only things worth 'avin' in t'world, no matter whether you're a scarecrow or a man.'

'Well, how come you can talk if you haven't got a brain in your head?' asked Chardonnay

'I dunno,' replied Danny, 'but some people wi'out brains do an awful lot o' talkin'.'

Mrs Sloughthwaite glanced in the direction of the major. 'That's true enough,' she muttered.

'Dorothy then meets the Tin Woodman, who tells her he wants a heart,' said the narrator.

Eddie appeared walking stiffly in thick silver cardboard as if wearing exceedingly tight underwear. On his feet were silver trainers which lit up and flashed when he walked and on his head was a large colander.

'And why do you want a heart?' asked Chardonnay.

'You people with hearts,' replied Eddie, 'have something to guide you and need never do wrong, but I have no heart, and so I must be very careful. It is a terrible thing to feel the loss of my heart. While I was in love I was the happiest man on earth but no one can love who has not a heart. Brains are not the best things in the world. I once had a brain, and a heart also, so having tried them both, I should much rather have a heart.'

'Then Dorothy meets the fainthearted lion who wants to have courage,' said Darren.

Malcolm sprung on to the stage growling fiercely, but then began to whimper and bite his tail.

'He tells Dorothy he is a scaredy-cat and the thing he would like to have most in the world is courage.'

'And why do you want courage?' asked Chardonnay.

'It is my great sorrow to be afraid and it makes my life very unhappy,' said Malcolm, 'for whenever there is danger, my heart begins to beat fast.'

'Dorothy asks them to come with her to see the Wizard of Oz,' said Darren. 'So off they set along the road of yellow bricks for the Emerald City.'

Both Elisabeth and Robbie listened intently offstage to the words, for they meant much to both of them. For Elisabeth these three fanciful characters exemplified the qualities of intelligence, caring and courage which as a teacher she felt all young people should possess. She knew that some children like the Scarecrow, the Tin Woodman and the Lion were held back by their self-doubt and lack of confidence. For Robbie too, a lonely, insecure child who felt he had been abandoned, the words seemed to have a particular resonance. And when the play drew to a close and Oscar came on stage as the Wizard, it was as if he were speaking just to them.

'The Wizard tells the four travellers that they should believe in themselves,' said the narrator. 'To the Scarecrow he says—'

'A baby has brains, but it doesn't know much. Experience is the only thing that brings knowledge, and the longer you are on earth the more experience you are sure to get.'

'To the Tin Woodman he says—'

'A heart is not judged by how much you love but by how much you are loved by others.'

'To the fainthearted lion he says—'

'There is no living thing that is not afraid when it faces danger. The true courage is in facing danger when you are afraid, and that kind of courage you have in plenty.'

'And to Dorothy he says—'

'No matter how dreary and grey our homes are, we people of flesh and blood would rather live there than in any other country, be it ever so beautiful. There is no place like home.' The cast all gathered on stage and Chardonnay, in a clear, high, perfectly pitched voice sang 'Somewhere over the rainbow, way up high . . .'

And with her eyes blurred with tears, Elisabeth looked at the small hunched figure who sat beside her. Robbie tilted back his head to look at her, his own eyes wet with tears. His small mouth began to tremble and he brushed his cheeks with the back of his hand. Suddenly the tears came welling up in his eyes, spilling over. Then he began to sob, great heaving sobs. Elisabeth put her arm around him and he rested his head on her shoulder.

23

It was the day of the wedding, a bright, cloudless sunny day. Elisabeth stood with her brother in the garden at Wisteria Cottage ready for the horse and trap which would take them to St Christopher's. She looked stunning in a full-length ivory-coloured chiffon dress with a circlet of small white roses in her hair.

'You look beautiful, sis,' said Giles, bending to kiss her cheek.

'And you look very handsome, brother,' she replied.

Giles looked dashing in full military uniform. 'I hope I don't trip over this wretched sword,' he told her.

'You look more nervous than I feel,' said Elisabeth.

'Dad would have been so proud of you,' said Giles, 'and Mum wouldn't have stopped crying. I'm so pleased that things have turned out so well, Lizzie. Michael is a fine fellow and I know you'll be very happy.'

'I do too. I love him very much, you know.'

'I can see that,' said her brother. 'And I can tell he loves you very much too. That's all that matters in the world, isn't it? So, are you ready?'

'I've been ready since six this morning,' she replied.

It seemed as if the whole of Barton-in-the-Dale had turned out for the wedding. When they arrived at St Christopher's, Elisabeth and her brother saw that the path from the lych-gate to the great oak door of the church was lined with children from the village school.

Elisabeth climbed down from the carriage and took a deep breath.

The children cheered and waved and called out greetings as she and Giles walked up the path.

Danny, a great grin on his face, appeared and handed her a bouquet of white roses. She bent and kissed him.

'You look crackin',' he said.

Given the sign to start, Mr Tomlinson began to play 'The Arrival of the Queen of Sheba' by Handel with great gusto. The congregation stood. Elisabeth, on her brother's arm, walked slowly down the aisle of the ancient church towards the altar, where Michael and James, in grey morning suits, were waiting nervously and Ashley was standing to greet her. The whole of the congregation turned to watch her progress. And as the bride looked around at all the smiling faces – the major, looking every inch the retired army officer in his blue blazer with brash gold buttons, Mrs O'Connor in vivid green and Mrs Sloughthwaite sporting a strange feathered affair on her head which she called her 'fornicator', Bianca and Clarence, Archdeacon and Mrs Atticus, Miss Brakespeare dabbing away a tear with a handkerchief, Mrs Robertshaw and Miss Wilson, Mrs Goldstein and Miss Parsons and many parents and villagers – she saw amongst them a small twig of a boy with shiny chestnut brown hair standing by the great grey stone tomb of the medieval knight. As the sun streamed through the stained glass window it lit up the boy's pale freckled face, and he gave a small but distinct smile. Elisabeth met Robbie's gaze and she knew then for certain what she had always felt in her heart. And despite this being her very special day, she could not help thinking at that moment of the job she so loved. A school inspector's job was not for her. She could not leave the little village school.

ACKNOWLEDGEMENTS

I would like to thank all at Hodder for their unflagging support and encouragement, particularly my editor, Francesca Best, for her sharp eye and quiet wisdom and my publicist, Kerry Hood, for her wonderful efficiency and cheerful good humour.

Special thanks must go to Christine, my wife, for reading my manuscript, steering me in the right direction and for her unwavering support.

How it all began – the first charming instalment in the *Little Village School* series

GERVASE PHINN

The Little Village School

She was wearing red shoes! With silver heels!

Elisabeth Devine causes quite a stir on her arrival in the village. No one can understand why the head of a big inner city school would want to come to sleepy little Barton-in-the-Dale, to a primary with more problems than school dinners.

And that's not even counting the challenges the mysterious Elisabeth herself will face: a bitter former head teacher, a grumpy caretaker and a duplicitous chair of governors, to name but a few.

Then there's the gossip. After all, a woman who would wear red shoes to an interview is obviously capable of anything . . .

Out now in paperback and ebook

HODDER

Book Two in the *Little Village School* series

GERVASE PHINN

Trouble at the Little Village School

Elisabeth Devine certainly rocked the boat when she arrived in Barton-in-the-Dale to take over as head teacher of the little primary school. Now it's a new term, and after winning over the wary locals, she can finally settle in to her role. Or so she thinks . . .

For the school is hit by a brand-new bombshell: it's to be merged with its arch rival, and Elisabeth has to fight for the headship with Urebank's ruthless and calculating headmaster.

But add in some gossip and a helping of scandal, not to mention various newcomers bringing good things and bad to Barton, and that's not the only trouble that's brewing in the village.

Out now in paperback and ebook

HODDER

We love a happy ending. But, almost more
than that, we love the promise of a new beginning.

Join us at www.hodder.co.uk, or follow us on Twitter
@hodderbooks, and be part of a community of escapists
who enjoy nothing more than curling up with a good book.

Whether you want to find out more about this book,
or a particular author, watch trailers and interviews, have
the chance to win early limited editions, or simply browse
our expert readers' selection of the very best books,
we think you'll find what you're looking for.

And if you don't, that's the place to tell us what's missing.

We love what we do, and we'd love you to be part of it.

www.hodder.co.uk

 @hodderbooks

 HodderBooks

 HodderBooks